EMPIRE OF THE
MOGHUL

TRAITORS IN THE
SHADOWS

EMPIRE OF THE
MOGHUL

TRAITORS IN THE
SHADOWS

AN HISTORICAL NOVEL

ALEX
RUTHERFORD

headline
review

First published in Great Britain in 2015
by HEADLINE REVIEW
An imprint of HEADLINE PUBLISHING GROUP

1

Cataloguing in Publication Data is available from the British Library

ISBN 978 1 4722 0589 6 (Hardback)
ISBN 978 1 4722 0590 2 (Trade paperback)

Typeset in Bembo Std by Palimpsest Book Production Ltd, Falkirk, Stirlingshire

Printed and bound in Great Britain by Clays Ltd, St Ives plc

Headline's policy is to use papers that are natural, renewable and recyclable products and made from wood grown in well-managed forests and other controlled sources. The logging and manufacturing processes are expected to conform to the environmental regulations of the country of origin.

SKETCH MAP OF
Aurangzeb's World

PERSIA

AFGHANISTAN

Samarkand

R. Oxus

Balkh

Ferghana

Herat

R. Helmand

Kandahar

Ghazni

Kabul

R. Kabul

HINDU KUSH

HIMALAYAS

KASHMIR

Srinagar

R. Chenab

R. Ravi

R. Jhelum

R. Indus

Lahore

R. Sutlej

R. Indus

BALUCHISTAN

SIND

PUNJAB

R. Jumna

Delhi

Mathura

Fatehpur Sikri

Ajmer

Jodhpur
(Marwar)

RAJASTHAN

Amber
(Jaipur)

Udaipur
(Mewar)

GUJARAT

Cambay

Agra

Samugarh

R. Ganges

Gwalior

R. Chambal

MALWA

Mandu

Surat

Ahmednagar

Bijapur

DECCAN

Aurangabad

R. Tapti

Asirgarh

Burhanpur

R. Narmada

Allahabad

Varanasi

R. Ganges

Patna

BIHAR

Gaur

Hooghly

BENGAL

Golconda

'The art of reigning is so delicate that a king must be jealous of his own shadow'

Advice of the Emperor Aurangzeb

Chapter 1

The Tiger's Claws

'The great Bijapuri general Afzal Khan asked Shivaji for a truce so they could meet to agree terms for the Bijapuris to cease the conflict,' the bearded Maratha commander told his companion as they rode side by side through the Deccan hills to a council of war. 'Shivaji agreed to the truce and to the meeting but put no trust in Afzal Khan and so prepared carefully. He selected a clearing in some dense jungle beneath his hilltop fortress as the place to talk. Understanding Afzal Khan's vanity, he had a sumptuous silk-hung pavilion erected at its centre. He then had two pathways cut through the jungle to the clearing, one from his own fort and one from the direction of Afzal Khan's camp. He wrote to his enemy that only such a magnificent setting could live up to a momentous meeting between two such great leaders and invited Afzal Khan to arrive first to enjoy the splendours. He did all this so he would know by which route Afzal Khan would come and to give himself an unobstructed view from the hilltop of his enemy's approach before he himself set out.

'Not content with this, he sent fifty foot soldiers to conceal themselves in the jungle around the clearing, my men and I among them. He had us tie leafy branches to ourselves and our equipment to hide us better. As the time agreed for the meeting drew near, Shivaji – watching from the fort's high battlements – saw Afzal Khan approaching with about a hundred men. Quickly he sent a messenger – the Brahmin Gopinath – to remind Afzal Khan they'd agreed each would bring only one armed bodyguard and to suggest he leave the rest of his troops by a rock about a mile along the track which he had, as he put it, fortuitously marked earlier with a red cross.

'The Bijapuri general duly left his men at the rock and travelled the remaining distance to the pavilion in a palanquin with a single bodyguard. I was hidden in the long grass near the path with my men, all of us trying to remain still – no easy task, I can assure you, with the heat and the flies and mosquitoes buzzing around us. Our orders were to show ourselves only if Afzal Khan attempted some trick. As he passed, carried by four bearers in his gilded palanquin, he didn't seem to be wearing any armour – just a baggy cream robe held together by a jewelled belt. I recognised the muscular shaven-headed bodyguard walking behind him. I had good reason to – it was Sayyid Banda, a bald-headed giant of a man, whose blade left this scar you can still see across the bridge of my nose during our last battle. When the small procession reached the pavilion, about a hundred yards from where I was hiding, the bearers gently lowered the palanquin and withdrew down the track where they squatted on the ground. Afzal Khan motioned Sayyid Banda to enter the pavilion. He did so and a moment or two later reappeared. Apparently satisfied that all was as it should be, he signalled to Afzal Khan, who stepped from the palanquin and himself went inside.

'Next I heard a blast of trumpets from the fort on the hill. Shivaji approached on foot a few minutes later. He too was wearing simple garments, in his case of blue cotton. Like Afzal Khan, he'd brought just one bodyguard. When Shivaji was a few paces from the pavilion Afzal Khan appeared in the doorway. They made an ill-assorted pair – Afzal Khan broad, stocky and hairy as a bear, our leader small and wiry. Shivaji bowed as he neared the general, who stepped towards him with a broad smile on his face and spread his arms as if to embrace him. Then I caught the flash of metal. Afzal Khan had had a dagger concealed in his wide sleeve, and now struck for Shivaji's heart. But you know how quick and agile Shivaji can be. He swayed back. The slashing blade cut only his blue robe. As my men and I jumped to our feet and rushed forward, drawing our weapons, he hurled himself on Afzal Khan, who screamed and fell forward, blood crimsoning his pale clothes.'

'So it's true – Shivaji did use the *wagnuck*, the tiger's claws?'

'Yes. He'd concealed it in his right hand and its sharp steel did its work. While Shivaji and his bodyguard turned on Sayyid Banda, the bearers – brave men, I must say – ran forward and bundled the general into his palanquin and started back down the path, leaving a trail of blood behind them. I shouted to my men to seize the bearers while I dragged Afzal Khan from the palanquin. He was barely conscious, so it was an easy matter for me to finish him off with a sword thrust into his ample belly. Then I ran towards Shivaji, thinking to help him by avenging myself against Sayyid Banda, but the swordsman was already on his knees, dying. His hand clutched at his throat ripped open by the tiger's claws and his lifeblood was pumping on to the red Deccan earth.'

The commander stopped speaking, almost breathless, as if he had been reliving the fight once more.

'I never tire of that story,' his companion said a few moments later. 'But why do you think Shivaji's summoned us here today? Is he planning a new campaign?'

'We'll soon find out.'

The two men approached Shivaji's command tent and dismounted in the purpling dusk. Together they entered the tent to find the Maratha leader already in full flow, eyes afire with zeal and passion as he denounced the Moghul emperor Aurangzeb as an alien invader of the Marathas' homeland who had no respect for their faith. 'He calls us "mountain rats" but he's the vermin. To satisfy his lust for power he exterminated his own brothers and has imprisoned his father these past years to usurp the throne – vile crimes even by the tenets of his own religion. Rats or not, we've already bitten his hand and will do so again and again till we rid ourselves of him.'

With his men fired almost to frenzy by his oratory and dramatic gestures, Shivaji revealed his plan. 'We will go north and west, travelling by night and in small groups to draw as little attention to ourselves as possible. Then we will unite to seize and plunder the Moghuls' rich trading port of Surat. My spies tell me that in his foolishness and pride Aurangzeb leaves it but weakly defended, believing none dare attack. He will soon learn better, humbled before his people and our own. Now go and prepare for war, booty and everlasting glory!' His commanders bellowed their support.

'Let Aurangzeb's throat beware the tiger's claws,' one of the two late-coming officers said to the other as they departed.

• ◆ •

'This is the moment. Let the Moghuls pay in blood for their crimes and conquests. Remind them Hindustan is ours not theirs!' Shivaji kicked his heels into the flanks of his black stallion. The animal burst from the shelter of some brush out on to the soft tangerine sands of the beach as Shivaji charged at the head of his five hundred men towards the low mud walls surrounding Surat. His month-long journey west had been swift and for the most part undetected. Any Moghul commanders who had heard reports of the small bands in which they had travelled had dismissed them as mere roving groups of *dacoits* before resuming their lives of comfort. Soon they and their kind would learn their error.

Extending his sword before him, Shivaji bent to the already sweat-scummed neck of his horse as it leapt the first of the defences – a wall no more than three feet high. Behind it, a bearded Moghul soldier tried to raise his arm to protect himself but Shivaji's sword cut into it, severing it just above the wrist. Shivaji was beyond the man before he could strike again and his second blow caught a Moghul officer across his mouth, smashing his teeth and dropping his jaw, slack and bloody, on to his chest. The few other Moghul troops manning the outer defences were already running back towards the inner city walls, some abandoning their weapons as they fled. Then Shivaji heard a ragged series of cracks – musket shots. The purple-turbaned Maratha at his side slid slowly from his saddle, clawing at his chest, and was trampled beneath the hooves of those behind. Nearby a horse crumpled to the sandy ground, throwing its rider as it fell. Two or three other Marathas started to drop back, either themselves or their mounts wounded, but the rest galloped resolutely on.

Looking up at Surat, Shivaji saw a group of Moghul musketmen silhouetted on the flat roof of a two- or three-storey building just behind the closed south gates of the city. They were pushing their ramrods into the barrels of their muskets, preparing to fire again. 'Make for the gates before they can reload,' he shouted, turning his horse in that direction with his left hand while slashing with the sword in his right at the back of another fleeing Moghul soldier. Soon he and several of his men were at the gates. He was half hoping that those inside would open them just a little to admit any of their fleeing comrades who made it that far, but no. The defenders were hard-hearted and sensible enough to abandon their fellows to their fate rather than give him a chance to force an entry.

Shivaji thought quickly. How then were he and his men to get into the city?

Leap from horseback on to the walls? No. At about twelve feet they were too high. Form some kind of human ladder? No. Too risky, and it would take too long. Then he saw a small cannon barrel lying rusty and abandoned in the shadow of the mud wall. 'Grab that cannon barrel – we can use it as a battering ram,' he shouted as he leapt from his saddle and ran towards it, followed by several of his bodyguards. One of them fell but was quickly up again; a trip not a musket ball must have been the cause. Soon

Shivaji and eight of his men, all sweating profusely beneath their breastplates, had lifted the barrel and were in front of the gates.

'Shouldn't we hit at that small door in the left gate which they must use at night?' one of his men suggested.

'Good idea. Aim for the hinges,' Shivaji replied. 'All together at the count of three.' Gasping with the effort, they swung the heavy barrel back and using all their force crashed it into the door hinge. No effect. 'Again!' This time some of the wood splintered but the door remained firmly in position. 'Harder!' The third blow knocked the door from its hinges. One of his bodyguard – a short but powerfully built youth – was first through, followed by Shivaji himself and then by twenty or so more of his men. Bending low, they rushed towards the building from which the Moghuls had been shooting, just as one of the Moghuls fired again. The short young man sprawled into the dust, hit in the leg. One of the Marathas too had a loaded musket and coolly paused to take deliberate aim. A green-tunicked Moghul musketeer twisted and pitched from the roof, arms and legs flailing, to crash headfirst to the earth, shattering his skull and spilling his brains. The rest appeared to be trying to flee by jumping or lowering themselves to the ground but the Marathas were on them at once, thrusting and stabbing, and none got away.

As Shivaji and his men paused to take breath, one of his scouts ran up. 'The Moghuls are abandoning the city, sire. A large well-armed group fled on horseback through a north gate with what looked like several officers at their head. Others are rowing out to Moghul ships in the harbour which are already raising sail.'

'Cowards all! Start searching for their treasures – products of the taxes Aurangzeb pitilessly piles on us all . . . And be sure not to harm the common townspeople. They suffer as much at Moghul hands as we do. But look methodically. Our oppressors will have concealed their treasure vaults well.'

Shivaji himself led a small group towards the warehouses fronting the harbour, taking care to keep close to the walls of buildings in case the Moghuls' flight was a pretence and other troops remained in ambush on the rooftops. But all was quiet as he reached the sea, sparkling beneath the morning sun, and turned along the normally thronging but now deserted wharves. Some large bales of bright yellow cloth lay where dock labourers had dropped them as they fled. Two discarded barrels had spilled much of their contents of pepper into the dust. There was no sound beyond the lapping of the water and the occasional cries of the seabirds pecking at fish on abandoned stalls fringing the quay.

Quietly, Shivaji and his men approached a high brick wall surrounding several large sandstone buildings. Suddenly a musket ball whistled past his ear and others raised puffs of dust around his feet. One Maratha fell, clutching at his bleeding calf. 'Take cover where you can,' Shivaji yelled. The firing was coming from the brick-walled compound. Shivaji guessed from his spies' reports that it must house the European traders – an assumption confirmed when a pale face peered cautiously from an open casement in a higher storey of one of the buildings. A second man appeared at the window, holding a musket which he fired quickly before ducking back down. Despite his apparent haste another Maratha collapsed, the shoulder of his white tunic reddening. One of his comrades rushed forward, seized him beneath the arms and dragged him into the shelter of one of the cloth bales.

Shivaji thought for a moment. There was at least fifty feet of open ground around the compound's high walls. His men would not lack the courage to cross it, but some would undoubtedly fall. Why waste their lives? 'Pull back, but surround the compound and make sure no one gets in or out. We will search for the Moghul treasuries and decide what to do with these foreigners later.'

An hour or two passed, but despite discovering some silver coin in the old citadel Shivaji knew they had not found the main stocks of valuables that must exist. He was standing in the shade of two large palm trees puzzling where they might be hidden when a grizzled officer approached him. 'Sire, one of my men insists that when he stamped his feet on the sandstone paving around the edge of that water tank over there it sounded hollow in one place. He thinks there may be a vault beneath it. When I threw a stone into the water in the tank it didn't seem as deep as I would expect. He could be right.'

'Well then. Lift those pavings.'

The Marathas were quickly at work, levering up the flagstones with anything they could find. In less than ten minutes their efforts had uncovered steep steps leading down beneath the tank. A locked metal grille barred the way. A musketeer poured powder from his powder horn on to the lock, ignited it and stood back. A flash and a bang and the grille opened. Beyond through the smoke and gloom Shivaji saw some large iron-bound chests. 'Prise those open,' he shouted. His men rushed to obey and soon they had raised the heavy lids, revealing a mass of gold and silver coin.

A smiling Shivaji was still examining the contents of the largest of the chests, letting the coins run through his fingers, when another of his officers – a stout man he had left in charge of the cordon around the European compound – ran up. 'Sire, the Europeans are . . .' he said, gasping for breath.

'The Europeans are what?'

'They are offering to ransom themselves and their property.'

'Go on.'

After taking another gulp of air the man continued. 'One of the merchants – a white-haired man with a forked beard – came to a window, his hands in the air. He shouted in our language that he wished to talk to whoever was in charge. I came out into the open and told him I was. He said simply that the merchants would give us many *lakhs* in coin if we agreed to leave them and their compound untouched. I told him you were the only person who could decide but I would inform you at once.'

Shivaji paused to think. The Europeans were well armed. To overcome them by force would incur casualties and take time. Time during which the Moghuls might return, perhaps reinforced. The ransom offered was large, and when added to the contents of the chests around him would sate his men's hunger for plunder as well as finance his campaigns against Hindustan's oppressors for a considerable time. What's more, why should he make an enemy of these foreigners, whose own relations with the Moghuls were not, he had heard, that good? Their support – and in particular the modern weapons they could supply – might prove useful in his future struggles to free his homeland.

'Tell them I accept their offer.'

• ◆ •

Screeching crows searched for roosts as dusk began to fall on the Red Fort in Delhi and the Emperor Aurangzeb walked from his private apartments through the lines of his bowing courtiers and commanders to his open-sided Hall of Public Audience. He looked neither left nor right as he mounted the marble dais and seated himself on his father's golden, jewel-encrusted peacock throne. He presented an imposing if austere figure, tall and slim in plain cream robes, his long elegant fingers resting lightly on the throne's glittering arms. His beard, frosted with grey, was neatly trimmed. The unsmiling dark eyes above his hawk nose were fixed on the yellow silk clad person of the Governor of Surat, whom two guards were leading towards him. When he was twelve feet from the dais the governor threw himself full length to the ground.

'Rise. I do not require such extravagant and ostentatious shows of submission.' Aurangzeb's voice was quiet and emotionless. 'What I do require, however, is an explanation of your actions at Surat. How could you allow the upstart Shivaji and his hill bandits to loot the city?'

'Majesty, I did not have a big enough garrison. The Marathas came in their thousands. They took us by surprise. They were fanatics, careless of their own lives. Surat's defences have not been fully repaired since . . . since the . . . events just before you came to the throne . . .'

'How many men did you have, in fact?'

'No more than six hundred and fifty.'

'And cannon?'

'Ten, but small and of old design.'

'Why didn't you post outlying sentries on horseback to warn of any approaching danger?'

'I posted sentries . . . but not mounted. And I realise now not enough, Majesty.'

Aurangzeb held the governor with his silent gaze.

'Majesty, all I could do was to order the citizens to take their most precious possessions and flee for their lives into the countryside,' the governor stammered.

'As you did yourself?'

'Yes.' The governor hung his head.

'Leaving Surat to be plundered for four days?'

The governor nodded, his throat suddenly too dry to speak. The man's unease and fear were all too obvious. His face was running with sweat, staining the neck of his yellow silk tunic.

'How did the Europeans succeed in safeguarding their property when you could not protect mine?'

The governor's eyes were flickering from side to side in panic and he was twisting his hands together. 'Majesty, they had a small area to defend. I had a whole town.' He gulped for breath. 'The foreigners had new weapons . . . my men were too few . . . They feared the Marathas . . .'

Clearly the governor hadn't realised how much he already knew, Aurangzeb thought to himself – or the strength of his network of spies, or the grasp of detail on which he prided himself. 'But what about the three thousand troops who according to your previous report should have been garrisoning the town?' Aurangzeb produced a piece of paper. 'My treasurer has given me your receipt for the annual allowance you are paid for their maintenance from my imperial treasury. Isn't that your seal and signature?'

The governor, now shaking uncontrollably, dropped to his knees before Aurangzeb. He could not answer.

Knowing the man had appropriated the allowance instead of using it to recruit, pay and equip troops, Aurangzeb rose to his feet, a stern, straight-backed figure. 'You have betrayed not only your emperor but more importantly your god by breaking the tenets of the holy Koran which forbid theft and corruption. You have disgraced me and your religion before an infidel and the foreigners who are already insolent and contemptuous of our rule. If you had died you would have been a martyr. Now what are you? A cur, cringing and whimpering before your master. Because I am merciful I will not send you to your eternal punishment, but you and your family will surrender your property to the throne. To cleanse yourself of your sin you will make the *haj* to Mecca as a poor and humble pilgrim, living only by the alms you can beg on the way. Now get out of my sight!'

The governor, by now slumped on the floor, tried to stand but fell back. The two guards seized him by the arms and dragged him away, leaving a trail of yellow liquid in his wake. The coward had lost control of his bladder.

Aurangzeb turned to his silent courtiers and generals. 'Remember that man's fate. I will not let the acid of corruption eat into the ties that bind our state. I shall not be so merciful if any of you transgress. As for that traitor Shivaji, I have already despatched strong forces to wipe him and his insults to the Moghul dynasty from the surface of the earth. All of you are now dismissed to apply yourselves to your duties with renewed and selfless determination and vigour.'

Dusk had fallen and bats not crows filled the air as Aurangzeb returned to his personal apartments. Alone there he took out a key, unlocked a small ivory casket

15

and removed a piece of paper. Still standing, he re-read the letter he had received from Shivaji and shown to no one.

You Moghuls think you are fine soldiers but even the best of you could not survive for long in my lands. The territory of the Marathas is harsh and hard but it is ours. We love it and will defend it to the last of our lives and fortresses. Trespass here and you will drown in your own blood.

Such boastful and arrogant taunting might provoke other men into rash and hasty actions, as Shivaji doubtless intended it should him. But experience had taught him the value of keeping his emotions under control and concentrating on what mattered – in this case bringing those who defied him to justice. This he would achieve in his own time and in his own way, but when his victory came it would be absolute and for ever: a lesson to any other aspiring rebel upstarts.

Chapter 2

Begum Padishah

'What is it, sister?' Aurangzeb put down his silver and turquoise bound copy of the Koran and looked up at Roshanara. She was gasping for breath as if she had run all the way from the *haram* to his private apartments.

'Two *cossids* – messengers – have come from Agra . . .' she managed at last. 'They brought me a message from Jahanara.'

'Jahanara? She's not ill?'

'No . . . not Jahanara, but our father. She says he is close to death and begs me to persuade you to go to him. She says he has things he wishes to say to you . . .'

Aurangzeb stood up. 'What things?'

'Jahanara doesn't say, but she insists that if you don't come at once it will be too late.'

'Too late? For me or for our father?'

Roshanara blinked. Sometimes Aurangzeb's mind was hard to read. 'Perhaps for you both,' she ventured.

17

'He forfeited my respect many years ago. Besides, what could we possibly say to one another now? He will reproach me. I will tell him that I did what I did for the good of the empire. How will that benefit either of us?'

Tears were forming in Roshanara's eyes. How she wished Aurangzeb would put his arms round her, but that wasn't his way. He was staring straight ahead, his face as immobile as it was inscrutable. 'Do you remember how our father rescued me from a swollen river when I was a baby?' she asked. 'I recall nothing about it, of course – I was too young – but Jahanara does. When we were growing up she often told me how I was torn from our mother's arms when our wagon overturned in the water and was nearly washed away but he saved me. I owe it to him that I'm alive today.

'I've heard the story many times. And I've some good memories of our father of my own from when our mother was alive. But in the years after she died we both know things changed. We shouldn't be over-sentimental. I, in particular, as emperor cannot allow emotions to cloud my judgement.'

'But sometimes I think . . . I think . . . we might not have always been fair in our judgement of him. Maybe he was only doing what he thought was for the best.'

Aurangzeb took his sister's hands in his. 'It's natural that at a time like this we remember the ties which once bound our family, but we deceive ourselves if we think that what we did was wrong. Besides, it was I not you who decided how things must be, not for my own good or benefit but for the sake of the empire. I take full responsibility for it before the world and before God. You must remember what would have happened had I not acted. Dara Shukoh was not only a heretic and contemptuous of his brothers but weak and soft at his core. Given time he would have destroyed much of what our ancestors fought for while our father – blind to the faults of his favourite son as is the man who looks into the noonday sun – stood fondly by.'

Roshanara nodded. Her brother was probably right – he usually was. In all the years since Aurangzeb had seized the throne from Shah Jahan and made her First Lady of the Empire in place of her older sister Jahanara they'd never spoken of these matters. And she'd been content for it to be so. Her life had run smoothly and pleasantly. Position, wealth . . . most worldly things she'd ever wanted were hers. She ruled the *haram*. And though she sometimes indulged herself in ways she knew he wouldn't approve of she was discreet – very discreet! She was a good First Lady, just as she'd been a good daughter until she realised how little she mattered to her father compared with Dara and Jahanara. She shouldn't feel guilty. Wiping away her tears with the back of her hand, she asked, 'What will you do, Aurangzeb? Will you go to Agra?'

'I don't know.' Aurangzeb gently released his sister's hands. He realised he must think carefully. The news of his father's illness wasn't unexpected. How could it be? Shah Jahan was old, and as the regular reports from his jailers had informed him, had been growing increasingly frail over recent months. If he was honest, and he shouldn't conceal his true feelings from himself over the six years since he'd deposed and imprisoned his father, there'd been times he'd wished him dead. Or at least sincerely thought he did . . .

Yet now that his father's passing was becoming a reality

he wasn't quite so sure. Despite what he'd said to Roshanara, did he feel at least a little guilty about imprisoning Shah Jahan? Why had he never visited him in prison? Had it been because he couldn't trust himself in case his father showed him forgiveness, love even, and he was weak enough to relent towards him? But what could the outcome of any reconciliation have been? Shah Jahan back on the throne – or his brother Dara Shukoh's surviving son? No, he could never have allowed that to happen for the sake of the empire. But perhaps it had been something else: fear of what he might have seen in Shah Jahan's eyes. Contempt, not the love that in his youth he had craved and deserved from a father who reserved his affections for his heretic eldest son.

Even when he had sailed down the Jumna river from Delhi to pray at the Taj Mahal where his mother Mumtaz lay in her jewel-inlaid white marble sarcophagus he had not permitted himself a single glance up at the Agra fort as he passed almost in the shadow of its red sandstone walls, conscious that Shah Jahan might be watching from the octagonal tower of his prison, high on the battlements. Seldom a month had passed without a letter from Shah Jahan commanding, sometimes beseeching him to visit. He had disciplined himself never to reply without allowing at least a day or two to elapse to give him time to master his feelings. He'd told himself that the letters were tricks designed to make him feel guilty rather than the expression of a genuine desire to see him.

So he had never visited his father. And why should he go now other than as an outward show of filial piety? What purpose would be served by going to his father's deathbed? Only to stir up further the feelings of doubt, perhaps even of guilt, that were already creeping up on him, together with what was probably real sadness. Hadn't he just cautioned Roshanara against impulsive sentimentality? Breathing deeply, eyes closed as was his habit when thinking, he saw a way through.

'Write to Prince Muazzam. He's camped only twenty miles from Agra. Ask him to ride to the fort and report back to me how he finds his grandfather. By sending my son, I will be seen to be acting towards my father with honour and respect. And it will give me time to decide whether to go myself.'

'I will write at once.' Gratified to be taken, as she thought, into Aurangzeb's confidence, Roshanara turned with a swish of her stiff silk robe and hurried away to fulfil his wishes.

Alone, Aurangzeb sat down and picked up his Koran again. But though he opened it at the verses he'd been reading he could not concentrate on their holy message. By postponing any decision to go to his father he had made it unlikely that he would ever see him alive again, and avoided a confrontation in which he might not even have been able to control his emotions, never mind the outcome. For a moment he closed his eyes, but instead of darkness he saw as clearly as if she was here before him now the face of his oldest sister Jahanara, who had chosen to share their father's imprisonment and consequently he hadn't seen since his rebellion. How must she be feeling now, and how would she judge him?

• ◆ •

Three weeks later, dressed in the white of mourning, Aurangzeb rode slowly up the twisting ramp and through the first of the great spike-studded gates of the Agra fort.

Though many years had passed since he had last made that journey, the red sandstone battlements, the courtyards and the gardens were as familiar as when his father had taken the throne and lived with his young family here. Hadn't he and his brothers practised swordplay among those pillars over there . . . And all the time, waiting for them in her rosewater-scented apartments, their beautiful, loving mother . . .?

At the thought of Mumtaz's smile, Aurangzeb frowned. Her memory was always bitter-sweet, all the more so today when he had just come from the Taj Mahal where his father now lay beside her. Alone in the crypt he had wept, but whether for Mumtaz and the loneliness he felt after her death, for Shah Jahan or for himself he wasn't sure.

Aurangzeb raised his chin. No onlooker must see in his face anything but the fitting gravity of an emperor mourning his father. Glancing around, he confirmed that everything was as he had ordered when a messenger from Muazzam brought the news that he had reached Agra to find Shah Jahan already dead. White banners, not green, fluttered from the battlements. The fountains were still. Even the rose bushes had been shorn of their blooms. It should not be said that he had been lacking in respect towards the man who had been not only his father but once the Moghul emperor.

Reaching the many-columned Hall of Public Audience where a group of his white-clad courtiers and generals waited in silence to greet him, Aurangzeb dismounted and passed slowly between their ranks, looking to right and left as all bowed their heads, their right hands on their breasts in token of loyalty and submission. Reaching the marble dais on which his father's peacock throne had stood until he had had it removed to Delhi, Aurangzeb climbed the three shallow steps, turned, and raising his hands said simply, 'I thank you all for your attendance on me, your emperor, on this sombre day. Tonight, as you pray, I beg you reflect as I will do on the transience of this earthly life and that all we are we owe to almighty God to whom we must all answer whatever our position.' Then Aurangzeb turned and walked through the door held open by a *qorchi* that led to the private imperial apartments.

The white marble pavilions beneath their canopies of burnished gold gleamed in the fading light. For a moment, he imagined the graceful figure of his mother framed in one of the arches waiting for her husband and children to join her for the evening meal.

Later, he lay on a low divan against a silk cushion in the apartments prepared for him. Candle flames flickered in the mirrored niches as attendants placed dishes on the white cloth they had spread before him. Though he'd not eaten since before dawn he had little appetite and took only plain rice, *dal*, and chicken from the tandoor. He drank ice-cooled water from the Jumna which his *qorchi* poured into the drinking cup he carried with him everywhere. It was carved into a lotus flower from a piece of translucent white jade which would supposedly discolour instantly if poison were present.

When he'd finished, Aurangzeb went out on to the balcony. A full moon was rising over the ox-bow bend in the river, silvering the pearl-drop dome of the Taj Mahal. For some minutes Aurangzeb stared at the scene . . . unutterably beautiful, unutterably melancholy . . . then looked away. He could delay no further the meeting he desired and dreaded in equal measure. He clapped his hands.

'Majesty?' His *qorchi* stepped through the muslin hangings on to the balcony.

'Go to my sister, the Princess Jahanara. Convey my deepest respects to her and ask her to come to me here.'

As he waited, Aurangzeb paced the balcony, his long slender fingers clicking the green jade prayer beads that habitually hung from his belt, heart beating as if he were about to ride into battle. At last he heard movement behind him and heard his *qorchi* say, 'Majesty, she is here.'

'Thank you. Now leave us and see we are not disturbed.'

He turned to see a slight figure dressed in white muslin, a white shawl covering her head and leaving her face in shadow. Brother and sister looked at one another in a silence which Aurangzeb finally broke.

'How are you, Jahanara? Won't you let me look at you?'

His sister took a few steps forward and slowly pushed the shawl back from her face. She had aged more than he'd expected over the seven years since they'd last met and looked older than her fifty-one years. Her hair, drawn back from her brow in a thick plait, was almost pure white and she looked thin, her cheekbones jutting through her taut skin. The scars from the fire that had nearly killed her as a young woman remained on her left cheek and neck, but like the rest of her they seemed to have faded. Her eyes had dark shadows beneath them. Aurangzeb had rehearsed what he would say, but words wouldn't come as he gazed at the careworn figure. As he hesitated, Jahanara moved nearer and began to make the formal obeisance due to an emperor.

'No!' Aurangzeb pulled her to him. She didn't resist,

24

and when eventually he released her he saw tears on her cheeks and felt a prickling beneath his own eyelids that he struggled to control. 'Come and sit with me. You have been absent from my side for too long.' He mustn't be carried away. Jahanara had chosen to share their father's imprisonment when she could have remained as First Lady. And she'd loved the heretic Dara more than she'd loved him . . . that was what he'd always remembered when she came into his mind. It had given him the strength to ignore the fact that, in spite of everything, he wanted the approval of his eldest sister, who had in so many ways taken his mother's place.

'I am glad our father lies at peace beside our mother,' Jahanara said softly. 'I did everything that was fitting – the mullahs prayed all day and all night for the repose of his soul.'

'Thank you.'

'In his last moments, he told me that he bore you no ill will . . . that he forgave you.'

What did he have to forgive me for? For saving the empire from his incompetence and keeping it out of the hands of my degenerate brothers who would have ruined it? And I haven't forgiven him . . . he never appreciated me, Aurangzeb wanted to retort, but he held his tongue. Instead he asked, 'Did he say anything else?'

'He told me to beg you at all costs to keep on good terms with your sons and not to allow them to fight with each other. He spoke of *taktya takhta* – throne or coffin – the warrior code we brought with us from our ancient homelands on the steppes. He said it had plagued our dynasty since we first entered Hindustan. With almost his final breath he whispered to me that the greatest threat to our dynasty has always come from within – that if we do not take care we will destroy ourselves, leaving our enemies nothing to do but carry away the spoils of our once great empire. He said he had tried to end the rivalries, but failed.'

'Was that all he reproached himself with?'

'No. He worried that he had done wrong during his life . . . as we all have, of course.'

Aurangzeb felt her take his hand between her own. 'Do you think what I did was wrong?' he asked.

'You know I do. You violated your duty as a son . . . as a brother. You made Dara your enemy, not the other way round. And after you defeated him, you need not have killed him, or his son . . . or have turned against our other brothers.' She must have felt his hand stiffen in hers because she gripped it more tightly. 'But Aurangzeb, the past is the past. If our father whom you wronged so much could forgive you, so should I. Aren't we still brother and sister? I've never ceased loving you. Though I chose to stay with our father I did so because that seemed right to me – it was my duty as a daughter.'

Aurangzeb bowed his head so that she shouldn't see his face. The almost ecstatic relief that he was to be reconciled with the sister he had always loved was overwhelming. 'You will return with me to my court in Delhi, where you will have everything you could wish for. You will again be First Lady of the Empire as our father appointed you after our mother's death, and I shall appoint you Begum Padishah – Queen of Princesses. You will have your own mansion if you wish it . . . servants . . . the best jewels in my treasure houses . . .'

Jahanara smiled that gentle smile he remembered so

26

well. 'The best promises you can make me are not of titles or of luxury but to care for the empire and those of our family who are left. Please God this can be a new beginning for our house.'

Chapter 3

The Captive

S eated on a golden chair on the dais of the Hall of Public Audience in the Agra fort, with Jahanara watching through the grille high in the wall to one side, Aurangzeb felt content. The three months since his reconciliation with her had brought nothing but good news and now she and his entire court were about to witness his latest triumph. Outnumbered and out-manoeuvred on the battlefield by a 150,000-strong Moghul army, Shivaji, who had dared to sack Surat, had been forced to make terms. The Maratha leader had not only agreed to yield twenty-three of his fortresses and pay 400,000 rupees in compensation but in a few moments, together with his young son Sambhaji, would make obeisance before him and all the court.

A flourish of trumpets told Aurangzeb that the moment had finally come to give this pair of desert rats a taste of true Moghul magnificence. He had made them wait while he announced a large number of routine imperial edicts and dealt with a long list of petitions. Though he usually despised worldly trappings as inducements to vanity and sacrilegious pride, they sometimes had their uses and this was one of those times. He had dressed with particular care in robes of gold-embroidered cream brocade, with ropes of pearls, carved emeralds and blood-red rubies wound round his neck and wrists. Hanging from a diamond-studded belt about his waist was Alamgir – the sword that his great-great-great-grandfather Babur had brought from Ferghana – and on his hand gleamed Timur's golden tiger-headed ring. In his mind's eye he pictured himself: a figure of absolute earthly power and authority, forty-six years old and in his prime, Aurangzeb, sixth and God willing greatest yet of all the Moghuls. The image pleased him.

Flanked on either side by a line of six Moghul body-guards in green tunics and polished steel breastplates and carrying tall lances, Shivaji and his son were approaching through the ranks of courtiers, all turning to look with curiosity at the Deccan leader. The Maratha was at least six inches shorter than himself and far slighter. As Shivaji halted before the dais, his son a few paces behind him, instead of keeping his eyes modestly on the ground as befitted the vanquished he stared unblinking up into the emperor's face. Immediately, Aurangzeb turned his own head to gaze disdainfully into the middle distance. At another trumpet blast, Aurangzeb's steward stepped forward and held out a paper to Shivaji on which was written the oath of loyalty he was to take.

Conscious that Shivaji's eyes were no longer on him, Aurangzeb looked down again from his dais. Instead of reading the few lines aloud, the Maratha was scrutinising them, a frown on his face. Then he turned to the steward.

'These words are in Persian – a language I know well, as you can hear – but I would prefer to take the oath in my native tongue.'

Aurangzeb stiffened. Had defeat taught the man no humility? 'You will take the oath in Persian, the language of my court!'

'Very well.' Shivaji began to read. 'I Shivaji, leader of the Maratha clans, hereby affirm my loyalty to the Emperor Aurangzeb whom I acknowledge as my overlord and whom I will serve – as will my son Sambhaji – faithfully and honourably . . .' His voice was deep and his Persian fluid and faultless. Aurangzeb had heard that he had pretensions to be an educated man. When the oath-taking was over, acknowledged by Aurangzeb with a nod of his head, silence fell. The Maratha needed to understand his insignificance to the empire, and where better than here in front of all his court including the other vassal rulers he had summoned to Agra, like those orange-clad Rajput princes over there whose pride he sometimes found almost equally insufferable.

He gestured to his steward. 'Place my latest vassal behind those commanders over there so he may observe how we conduct business in my court and learn from it.' Shivaji turned to see that Aurangzeb was pointing towards the back of the hall where his most junior officers were lined up, and his face flushed. The sharp intake of breath from those assembled before him told Aurangzeb how well they too had understood his intention to humble this defeated upstart to whom he had behaved with such apparent magnanimity when others less far-sighted might have executed him. How much better a visibly humbled vassal than a heroic martyr who might inspire his people to future revolt.

Aurangzeb waited for Shivaji to take his place, but instead the Maratha shook off the steward's restraining hand and stepped forward to the very edge of the dais. 'Majesty, I am a ruler, like you. Noble blood runs in my veins, yet you consign me to a place amongst men of inferior rank. Why do you insult me?'

Shivaji was so close that Aurangzeb could hear the man's rapid breathing, see the anger in his eyes. The silence was intense. Slowly Aurangzeb rose. Willing his voice to remain calm, he said, 'You have just sworn an oath of allegiance to me, yet already you disobey and defy me.'

'And already you seek to humiliate me before the world. I will not stay here to suffer insult.' Shivaji turned abruptly on his heel and seizing his son by the arm began pushing his way through the courtiers.

'Guards, stop that man!' Aurangzeb ordered. 'Put him and his son under arrest. Faulad Khan, as governor of the Agra fort, you will be responsible for keeping him secure while I decide his fate.'

Shivaji flung him a contemptuous look over his shoulder but did not resist as guards led him and his son quickly away. Aurangzeb seated himself again. No one looking at his expression must guess the rage boiling within him. 'Let us turn to other matters – the report of the revenues from Bengal . . .'

• ◆ •

Shivaji carefully checked the contents of three giant wicker baskets nearly as high as his shoulder – loaves of *nan*, baskets of dried apricots and raisins, small sacks of rice and lentils – and smiled. Everything was as it should be.

'The poor of Agra praise your name every day, sire,' his steward Ekoji said as he closed the final lid. 'I will ask the guards if they too wish to check the baskets. Then I will order the bearers to load them on to the cart.'

'Excellent. And give the guards and bearers the usual coin. I want to be sure the food reaches those it's intended for. I hear the price of bread has risen even higher in the markets and that many of our faith are going hungry.' Shivaji said no more. Aurangzeb's eyes and ears were everywhere and he always chose his words with care.

Every afternoon for the last three months he had been sending Ekoji from the cramped quarters in the fort where they were confined to the fort bazaar, which his steward was permitted to visit, to purchase goods for distribution to the Hindu poor of Agra. Every evening just before dusk, Shivaji had been despatching three large baskets of provisions to a temple in the town. At first the guards had been reluctant to allow these acts of charity, insisting on obtaining the permission of the fort governor Faulad Khan. And the governor too had been suspicious, poking into the filled baskets himself for the first few days and inspecting them on their return to make sure no one was attempting to conceal weapons for Shivaji inside them. But just as Shivaji had hoped, these daily inspections had begun to bore the governor. He had become content to entrust them to the guards who – given the silver which Shivaji bestowed on them – were only too happy to comply.

Now they too were growing lax. Most days they barely glanced into the bulging baskets before allowing them to be loaded on the donkey cart that drew up outside the interior gate leading to the four rooms built around a tiny courtyard that were Shivaji's prison. Now the elderly, yellow-turbaned driver shook the reins and the cart trundled down the fort's winding ramp and out into the city towards the temple where the food was to be distributed. What fools the guards were, Shivaji congratulated himself. They hadn't discovered his messages hidden amongst the dried fruits and addressed to the priests of the temple. Nor had they found the priests' replies, rolled tight and tucked deep into the wickerwork, reporting that, just as Shivaji had asked, they had succeeded in contacting some of his commanders, asking them to wait with fast horses at an appointed place outside the city, ready for the moment when he could make his escape.

But when would that moment be? He'd been biding his time, waiting for the daily distribution of alms to become so routine that the guards lost interest altogether. He prided himself that patience was one of his strengths – but so too was knowing when to act. If the persistent rumours Ekoji had been hearing in the bazaar – that in the next few weeks Aurangzeb intended to despatch an army to Kandahar and send his Maratha prisoners with it into exile in Kabul, well away from their troublesome homelands – were true, the moment was fast approaching.

Returning from seeing the baskets despatched, Ekoji poured water for his master to drink into a brass bowl which he first handed to one of the few Maratha servants Shivaji had been allowed to retain to taste. Watching the ritual, Shivaji gave a wry smile. Early in his imprisonment he'd suspected Aurangzeb might attempt to poison him, or perhaps send an assassin to slit his throat. But nothing had happened. Aurangzeb had proved himself too astute to create a martyr by doing anything so crude. Shivaji now realised he was probably safe enough while still in the fort. Any attempt on his life would come somewhere on the road between Agra and Kandahar, well away from prying eyes and wagging tongues, and be carried out in such a way that it could be blamed on *dacoits* or rebels rather than the emperor. Another reason he'd decided he must escape before Aurangzeb could send him away.

Now it seemed the gods themselves might have intervened to save him. Just an hour ago, while Ekoji had still been in the bazaar, he had overheard the guards discussing something that he must tell his steward as soon as possible. As he took the bowl of water from Ekoji he touched the brass image of the elephant god Ganesh hanging on a thong around his neck. Ekoji acknowledged the gesture – a secret signal that Shivaji had something important to communicate that the guards must not overhear – with the briefest nod of his black-turbaned head.

Draining the bowl, Shivaji slowly crossed the courtyard to the small latrine, concealed behind a high wall where Ekoji quickly joined him. The two men waited a moment, ears straining, but no sound came from the courtyard. As Shivaji began noisily to urinate he whispered to his steward, 'While you were away I heard one of the guards say there is to be a feast and firework display tomorrow to celebrate the anniversary of the Moghul victory at Panipat which began their cursed conquest of Hindustan.'

'Yes, sire. I also heard people talking about it in the bazaar, and on my way back I saw green velvet tents being erected in one of the biggest courtyards. I suppose that's where the feast is being held.'

'Excellent. The entire fort will be distracted. It'll be a perfect opportunity to attempt the escape.' Shivaji bent to rinse his hands, pouring water from a wide-necked earthenware jar. There was no need to say more. They'd discussed the escape a hundred times – sometimes here in the latrine, sometimes in whispered conversations in the dead of night – going through every detail.

That night, lying close beside him on the divan they shared, Shivaji whispered the news to his son. It was the first time he'd spoken of his plan to the nine-year-old Sambhaji and he felt the boy's body stiffen. 'Don't worry. Just do exactly as I and Ekoji tell you and all will be well.'

The next day passed painfully slowly for Shivaji, but as the afternoon dragged by he began to catch the sound of excited voices from beyond the walls of his small compound – perhaps the first guests arriving for the feast? With the sun not yet beneath the horizon, the first fireworks screamed up into the sky, their trails of stars barely visible. The sound of cheering followed. With the celebrations under way he only hoped the bazaar was still open so that Ekoji, who had set off at the usual time, could make his purchases and the cart would be allowed into the fort to collect the baskets. While he waited for his steward's return he willed himself to sit still in the courtyard and not to pace or do anything else unusual to attract the attention of the two guards, slouched in the shade of a neem tree chewing betel. But at last Ekoji appeared in the gateway and behind him Shivaji saw the baskets, carried as usual by two bearers apiece. He began to breathe more easily. So far so good, though the difficult part was yet to come.

'Sire – the provisions are here. Will you inspect them as usual?' Ekoji asked.

'Yes, of course. But the noise of these fireworks and all the cheering is deafening me. Have the baskets taken into my room.' As the bearers carried their burdens inside, followed by the steward, Shivaji remained where he was, waiting in case the guards said anything, but just then came another explosion of fireworks and the two men jumped on to a stone bench to stand, backs to Shivaji, craning up into the sky to look at them.

Still Shivaji waited until all three baskets had been carried into the room where he knew Sambhaji was waiting and the bearers – dismissed by Ekoji – came out and also began staring up at fresh bursts of stars, golden in the fast darkening sky. Silently he began counting up to five hundred – the time he calculated it would take Ekoji to remove enough provisions from two of the baskets and hide Sambhaji inside one of them. Then he rose and, after stooping to flick some imaginary dust from his sandal, walked slowly inside.

'Quickly, sire!' Ekoji whispered. Shivaji climbed into the only basket that was still open – the one closest to the doorway. As he curled up inside, loaves and packages of food landed on his head and shoulders as Ekoji quickly piled in as many as would fit around and on top of him before closing the lid and calling, 'Bearers! Here!' Such was the noise now coming from outside that the bearers didn't seem to have heard. Shivaji felt Ekoji push past his basket as he went to the doorway and called again, more loudly. There was a lull in the fireworks and in the sudden quiet Shivaji heard the slap of the bearers' bare feet on the stone floor. Then he felt his basket begin to rise and braced his muscled arms against the sides as the bearers carried it back into the courtyard and lowered it on to the flagstones. Two further thumps told him the other baskets had arrived beside him.

'Do you want to look inside the baskets? I haven't

fastened their ropes yet,' he heard Ekoji shout to the guards. He closed his eyes. Surely time had never passed so slowly. Sweat was running down his back. How would Sambhaji be managing? He was a brave boy, but he was only nine . . .

Nobody spoke. What was happening? Perhaps any moment now the lid would be flipped back and he would feel fingers poking about, perhaps digging into his skin, grabbing his hair, dragging him out. But then the fireworks began again. Almost at once he felt the basket lurch. He was moving again. Transfixed by the latest display, the guards must have gestured to the bearers to carry the baskets away. Despite the noise of the whizzing, fizzing rockets Shivaji could just make out the rhythm of their feet and tried to count the number of steps. Eight, nine, ten . . . 'This Shivaji gets more generous by the day. I'd swear on my life this basket is the heaviest yet,' one bearer muttered. But all the time they were keeping moving . . . eleven, twelve, thirteen . . . they must be passing beneath the low stone lintel of the inner gate to where the donkey cart should be waiting. Through the fizz and whizz of the rockets his keen ears detected what was surely the jingling of a harness. The cart was there!

But then the bearers let his basket fall. For a moment it rocked wildly back and forth − if it tumbled over, the lid might come off and he would be revealed. He crouched down into an even tighter ball, holding his body rigid, willing the basket to stop swaying. 'Careful, you fools!' he heard Ekoji shout. 'If you want my master's coin don't be so careless. Now pick it up again.' The basket rose once more. Shivaji could barely suppress a cry of triumph as he felt it lifted yet higher to be put, he guessed, on to the cart.

His must have been the first, judging by the way the cart shook under him once and then again. A moment later the driver cracked his whip and Shivaji felt his basket tip forward slightly as the cart began its slow descent of the twisting ramp leading from the fort.

Soon, if all went well, they would reach the temple, where the priests would help him and his son disguise themselves as itinerant beggars before guiding them through Agra's narrow streets to the grove of mango trees beyond the city walls where his men would be waiting with horses. Then, the warm wind in their hair, they would ride hard through the darkness for the Deccan hills and home.

• ◆ •

Aurangzeb looked down from the battlements of the Agra fort on to the parade ground beneath, where the knotted whips were falling again and again on the naked flesh of the two guards. They were screaming, and the sand beneath their lacerated bodies was spattered with blood as they strained frantically against the hide straps securing their wrists and ankles to the wooden frames on which they were spreadeagled.

A hundred lashes was a just punishment. Because of those men's slackness the Maratha leader had escaped. As a consequence Shivaji would be a hero once more and he himself a laughing stock. And that wasn't all. The guards had only discovered Shivaji's flight this morning, although he and his son had clearly escaped the previous evening, concealed in the baskets of alms the Maratha had so cunningly been sending to the temple. His steward, who must have supervised their flight, seemed to have slipped away during the night together with Shivaji's few servants.

38

He had immediately despatched some of his best horsemen in pursuit but there was little chance they would catch up with the fugitives.

The screaming died away. Both guards appeared to have fainted. As the whips continued to rip into them – he'd ordered there to be no respite if they lost consciousness – their bodies dangled limply from the frames like slabs of meat from the butcher's hook. If they survived – and they probably would – they would bear the scars of the beating for the rest of their days: a fitting reminder of how they had neglected their duty. As for Faulad Khan the fort governor, he would be exiled to Kabul as punishment for his laxity.

Turning away, Aurangzeb walked slowly back to his apartments. After ordering his attendants to lower the *tatti* screens and then to leave him, he knelt on the hard marble floor to pray in the semi-darkness. As always, communion with his god, to him the one certainty in an uncertain world, brought solace. By the time he touched his forehead to the ground for the final time and stood up, his mind felt calmer, clearer. Shivaji had made a fool of him. But perhaps his escape had had a divine purpose. Maybe God was warning him that he was growing too proud and confident of his own abilities, and too lax in his religious observances towards the one truly all-knowing God? This wasn't the first time he'd asked himself how good a Muslim he really was. Sometimes at night, when sleep had eluded him, he'd pondered ways of proving his devotion to his faith – building more mosques, increasing his donations to the poor, sending more rich gifts to Mecca . . .

Yet all those things would give him pleasure. Now, for the first time, it came to him – for his actions to please

God he must sacrifice something he really loved. But what? The pleasure he found in women? Of his wives, Dilras Banu had died many years before and Nawab Bai held few attractions for him, but night after night in the warm arms of Udipuri Mahal he escaped the cares of the world. Would it serve God if he denied himself the delight of Udipuri's voluptuous scented body entwining itself around him? No. God had created women with a purpose – to be the bearers of sons. Though he already had four, one, Mohammed Sultan, had betrayed him during his war with his father and brothers and as a consequence would spend the remainder of his days in a dungeon. As for the other three – Muazzam, Azam and Akbar – at present, even if not without their faults, they were sources of some pride to him. But who knew what the future might hold? What if another of them proved a traitor, or any died of illness or in battle? To secure the empire's future he needed further sons; this was not the time for sexual abstinence. There must be other things he could give up. Music might be one. The sound of tabla and sitar always gave him sensual pleasure, but wasn't that frivolous and selfish? Music served no purpose except personal gratification. He would forgo it. And he would also cease wearing fine clothes and jewels except when occasions of state demanded it . . . a godly man had no need of such fripperies. Simplicity must be his personal watchword in future. Then surely his God would approve his denial and self-sacrifice and grant him victory over the unbeliever Shivaji.

The thought of the Maratha leader darkened his mood again. He could imagine him exulting over his escape . . . smirking and boasting to his followers of how he had outwitted his Moghul captors. Well, he and his people and all the others who shared his faith would soon have reason to repent his defiance.

· ◆ ·

Shortly after the end of morning prayers two days later, Aurangzeb entered his Hall of Private Audience where at his request his religious advisers, the *ulama*, awaited him. The black-robed, black-turbaned mullahs bowed and he gestured to them to sit in a semicircle around him on the thick red and blue carpet.

'As you know, the Maratha rebel Shivaji has escaped. His flight is an affront to me and to my empire. That is why I summoned you here. All rebels and malcontents will see Shivaji as a champion of their fight against Moghul rule. The unbelievers among them may in addition point to the faith they share with him, and to the aid priests from a local temple gave him in his escape, to urge other Hindus to join them in rebellion. I will not allow that to happen. After much thought I have decided the time has come to do what we have so often discussed – what some of you have so often pressed upon me – to demonstrate my power and authority to my Hindu subjects. I intend to show them how tolerant and benevolent Moghul rule has been by imposing some restrictions on their religion, with the threat of more if they support any rebellion.'

Many of the mullahs were nodding their agreement, some looking towards their leader Abu Hakim, a white-bearded scholar from Herat, who raised his hand. 'May I speak, Majesty?'

'Of course, Abu Hakim.'

'Your words bring us joy and demonstrate your abundant wisdom. We have long seen how the infidels have abused the freedoms and equalities granted them by your great

41

ancestor the Emperor Akbar – may his soul rest in Paradise. The Hindu "religion" – if we can call it such – is presided over by prating priests. I know from reports I receive that in the incense-filled gloom of their temples where they think themselves safe many have the temerity to preach sedition against your blessed throne. They denounce the Moghuls as foreign invaders and claim that you have no lawful authority over your Hindu subjects whom you and your ancestors have dispossessed of their lands – no right to tax or discipline them and that therefore they are free to ignore your orders and demands. Of course we will do all in our power to help Your Majesty make these wretched people understand the power and benevolence of your rule, and through that of our faith, of which you are such a magnificent example.'

Abu Hakim was a loquacious and fulsome flatterer, far too fond of the sound of his own voice, Aurangzeb thought, acknowledging the mullah's words with a bow of his head. His long and ponderous sermons were all too often designed to display his learning rather than to inspire the faithful. But as Aurangzeb had known when appointing him head of the *ulama* he was intelligent enough to divine his emperor's wishes and self-serving enough to find religious arguments to justify them. It was Abu Hakim who had assured him that by executing the heretic Dara he was doing God's work and would be rewarded not damned for his actions.

'Thank you, Abu Hakim. You and the other members of the *ulama* will be a great support if you guide your brothers in the mosques and madrassas across my empire to uphold in their sermons the lawful and benevolent nature of my rule and its adherence to the true path of

42

our faith. To demonstrate my authority over all my subjects, I intend to issue imperial *firmans* banning such Hindu festivals as Holi and Diwali. I will also order the destruction of holy places revered by the Hindus—'

'Not all of them, surely, Majesty?' asked a young cleric, who from the fierce look Abu Hakim shot him from beneath his bushy brows realised his mistake in speaking out and interrupting the emperor and now stared hard at the carpet in front of him.

'A sensible question. Certainly not. It would be impractical and unwise to attempt to destroy them all. I intend to begin with the temple at Mathura, which is a centre of Hindu pilgrimage and sited in an area where there have already been reports of discontent and of the molestation of some of my tax gatherers. If that does not teach my subjects to bow to the power of my authority, I will choose further temples to make examples of, perhaps those newly built or refurbished. And to demonstrate the supremacy of both my rule and our own religion in physical earthly terms, I will construct mosques on some of the sites where temples have been demolished.'

Aurangzeb paused, watching the effect of his words. He had taken the *ulama* by surprise but their expressions told him how much most of them approved. He would be the first Moghul emperor to apply his religion in his rule. All his ancestors, however great, had compromised. Some – Akbar especially – had acted as if they had no true religion at all. Others had paid only lip service to their faith, ignoring it in their worldly dealings and in their personal lives indulging themselves with wine and opium and other pleasures. He'd witnessed such behaviour while young when his grandfather Jahangir had demanded himself and

Dara Shukoh as hostages for their father Shah Jahan's future good behaviour following the fighting between the two men. Night after night in their grandfather's custody, they'd watched his empress Nur Jahan dissolve pellets of opium in cups of wine. With every sip Jahangir had defied his religion, fuddled his brain and hazarded his empire by allowing his scheming wife to rule in all but name.

'I have something else to say,' he continued. 'If I wish to uphold our religion as well as my authority before all my people I myself must be beyond reproach in my personal observance of my faith.'

'But Majesty – no one in this world could be a more pious and observant son of Islam than yourself,' said Abu Hakim.

'You're wrong. I can and must do more to set an example. I know that I am sometimes too lax. My love of music, for example, distracts my mind from my duties and dissipates my energies, encouraging me to be indolent. I therefore intend to ban the playing of musical instruments at my court. I will also restrict my wearing of extravagant garments and jewels even more strictly to the most important state occasions and urge my courtiers to do likewise. Such ornamentation is nothing but a manifestation of excessive personal pride and vanity that deflects us from a more spiritual life. I also intend to discontinue the vainglorious practice of having a court writer chronicle my life. God, my only judge, will have no need of such a record and nor do I. Now unless any of you have anything further to say, leave me. I will summon you again once the necessary *firmans* have been drawn up so we may discuss further how to put my plans into operation.'

Alone in his apartments that evening Aurangzeb felt some satisfaction. Though Shivaji's flight still rankled, perhaps it had proved a blessing, punishing his pride and pushing him to take firm action. He was also glad he'd found the strength to forgo the pleasure of music. Unlike his strictures on clothing and his abandonment of the court chronicle, it had cost him a real effort. Now having announced it publicly there could be no going back. But he had other legitimate pleasures left. Later he would go to Udipuri Mahal . . . The arrival of a *qorchi* interrupted such pleasant thoughts.

'Majesty, the Lady Jahanara is here. She requests the favour of a few words with you.'

'Of course. Show her in. Welcome, sister,' he said, as she entered still dressed in the white of mourning for their father, even though the prescribed period was past.

'Aurangzeb – thank you for seeing me.' She took his hands and gripped them a moment.

'You look well.' He smiled at her. It was true. These last months had indeed made a difference, but looking more closely he saw that tonight her expression was strained and anxious. 'What brings you here so late in the evening, Jahanara?'

'I had to speak to you as soon as possible. I've just heard something that I . . . well, that I couldn't believe: that you intend to ban Hindu festivals and will destroy some of their temples. One of my attendants said her husband heard a mullah announce it tonight at evening prayers, here in the Moti Masjid. Tell me it isn't true.'

'I cannot . . . it is true. I've been considering such measures for some time, but Shivaji's defiance proved to me that this is the right moment to demonstrate my authority

45

over the Hindus before others follow his rebellious example. It's my duty to show my subjects my tolerance is not without bounds and to protect the empire from any threat – internal or external.'

'But Hindus are the vast majority of your subjects. And most are good servants to our empire and loyal to you as they have been to our ancestors. Religion rarely has anything to do with rebellion. Just think how many of our enemies have come from our own religion – the sultans of Bijapur and Golcunda, the Shah of Persia and the turbulent Afghan tribes on our north-western frontiers. Compared to such enemies tell me what our loyal Hindu subjects have done to deserve this? Act against their religion and you will drive them straight into the arms of rebels like Shivaji. Can't you see you'll create the very threats you seek to avoid?'

Aurangzeb's smile stiffened. The reconciliation with his sister was still so recent, so fragile . . . he must be careful not to damage it. Yet she was challenging his judgement – something no one else would dare to do – and he could not allow anyone, not even Jahanara, to interfere with his decisions.

'I cannot agree with you. What I want to do is to show my power in a way that cannot be ignored, so that they will understand the enormity of my revenge should they join Shivaji in rebellion. You are a woman and have been living a secluded life. How can you understand the realities of ruling and the minds of our enemies as I do?' he said gently.

'But I do understand! Didn't I once assist our father in dealing with affairs of state? Didn't he give me our mother's own seal with which to issue *firmans*? Didn't he seek and

46

often heed my advice?' Jahanara's eyes flashed for a moment. 'I'd be failing in my duty to him and our ancestors if I didn't try to warn you. If you persist in using religion in support of your political ends you will destabilise, perhaps even destroy, everything the Moghuls have striven for, creating divisions where there have been none, divisions which will remain for generations. Didn't we consolidate our position in Hindustan by marrying into the houses of the great Hindu nobles rather than alienating them by discriminating against their religion? Doesn't their blood run in your veins – your sons' veins? Don't you yourself have a son by a Rajput noblewoman? Do you love Muazzam any less than the others because of it? Hasn't our dynasty and our empire prospered by being blind to a man's religion?'

'You allow yourself to be over-influenced by your liberal Sufi beliefs. You may find them a suitable philosophy, but they are far removed from my own convictions.'

'Yes, I'm a Sufi. I'll always be one and that leads me to believe in tolerance and respect for others. But that's not the main reason why I beg you to give up this plan of yours. I ask it because it is so dangerous to the continuity of our rule. Aurangzeb, who advised you? Was it the *ulama*? Perhaps the mullahs think too much about their own power and not enough about the general good and that of your realm.'

Aurangzeb's smile faded. 'It was my decision and mine alone even if I did discuss it with the *ulama*. Before God I know I am right, Jahanara.'

'When you were a child you were always so stubborn – you would fight far bigger boys if you thought yourself in the right. I loved you for your courage but I worried

47

about it as well. You see the world too simply when you have made up your mind – right and wrong are like black and white to you. You always expect the world to follow not just logic but your version of logic. What if your Hindu subjects do not bow before your show of power? You will be storing up trouble and resentment for yourself and your successors where there is no need.'

There were tears in her eyes now as she looked appealingly into his face, but the lack of emotion she saw there and the absence of any change in his expression told her as clearly as any words that she'd spoken in vain. Turning, she slipped quickly from the room. Aurangzeb was about to follow her – he knew he had hurt her, which was the last thing he wanted – but he checked himself. What more could he say or do? Jahanara should have known better than to question his judgement on worldly affairs, and she must learn.

Chapter 4

Rebels in the Dust

'Remember who Jani is – Dara's daughter! Why make the child of a traitor you loathed your daughter-in-law? Sometimes I don't understand you.' Roshanara shook her head.

But I understand you, Aurangzeb thought. Roshanara disapproved of the match between Azam and Jani simply because Jahanara had proposed it. She hadn't hidden her resentment at her sister's reinstatement as First Lady of the Empire. 'It's not fair,' she'd said, petulant and pouting as a child. 'It was me, not her, who was loyal to you! Who escaped from the Agra fort to your camp? Not Jahanara – me! Who told you how many guards, how many cannon our father had to defend the fort? Me!' He had sought to console her first with soothing words, then with a handsome gold necklace set with the finest Golcunda diamonds. She'd accepted it eagerly enough – why wouldn't she? She loved jewels. Yet since the court's return to Delhi she had sulked in her apartments in the *haram* and never visited Jahanara in her mansion. And now this . . .

'Sister, allow me to judge what's best for our family. Even while we were still in Agra, I noticed Azam's growing feelings for his cousin – and didn't you yourself remark on it?'

'Yes – as a warning! It never occurred to me you'd sanction their marriage.'

'Uniting Dara's daughter with one of my sons will strengthen my position, not diminish it. It will show the world I desire to heal past rifts,' Aurangzeb said, conscious of repeating almost exactly Jahanara's words to him.

'But you always told me you meant to marry Azam to the daughter of one of your important noblemen, or a foreign princess . . .'

'And I still can . . . Jani needn't be Azam's only wife.'

'At the very least you should have told me about the marriage instead of letting me hear of it first from others in the *haram*. How do you think that made me feel? How did it make me look in the eyes of the other women?'

'I'm sorry, it was remiss of me. I should have told you first.'

'I'm glad you recognise that now.'

'I hope in turn you will understand why I favour this marriage. In any case, I'm glad to see you, because I want to ask your help.'

'My help?'

'My treasurer tells me that the foundation I set up to care for the widows and families of officers who die in my service is badly in debt, even though I grant it thousands of rupees every year. It is either being badly mismanaged or someone is embezzling the funds. I can't think of anyone better suited to investigate and report back to me than you. Will you do this for me?'

'Yes,' Roshanara said after a moment. Her gratified smile told him his idea had worked. He had always known how to manage her. Ever since childhood she'd disliked being alone, craving company and attention and the feeling of being important – weaknesses that made her vulnerable to both flattery and slights. Until Jahanara's return to court, she had been diffident – deferential even – towards him, seeking always to please him. Latterly, however, she'd been allowing resentment and jealousy of her elder sister to dominate. From now on he'd make sure he visited her more often, paid her more compliments, particularly in the presence of others, and gave her more gifts. He smiled back. 'Now forgive me, I've many matters to attend to before evening prayers.'

Alone once more, Aurangzeb settled himself on a couch by the casement, closed his eyes, and linking his hands beneath his chin began to think. The wedding would take place in ten weeks and be as lavish as he could make it. His recent vows to wear simple clothes and spurn bright jewels were no reason to hold back from making this the greatest spectacle his subjects had ever witnessed. This would be magnificence with a purpose, designed to show the whole world the wealth and permanence of the Moghul empire and, above all, his own strong grip upon it.

• ◆ •

Aurangzeb watched from the highest step of Jahanara's handsome mansion within Delhi's Red Fort as the bride-groom's procession approached. Two hundred bearers, ten abreast, clad in tunics of Moghul green and carrying solid gold trays heaped with jewels, gold coin and precious spices – pepper, cinnamon and cloves – led the way, walking perfectly in step. A detachment of imperial cavalry followed in silver helmets and breastplates, the tails and manes of their black horses gleaming like silk.

Behind them the fourteen-year-old Azam in his coat of gold cloth was riding the long-necked, large-eyed, pale-coated Akhalteke stallion he had just presented to him as a wedding gift. Bred beyond the Oxus, Akhalteke horses were the swiftest, most enduring in the world. They had carried the Moghuls' ancestor Genghis Khan to victory, and their slender but muscled bodies were said to sweat not perspiration but blood. Azam was flanked by Muazzam – at twenty-four a husband himself – and nine-year-old Akbar, both in coats and turbans of silver cloth studded with diamonds flashing like fire in the sunlight. Aurangzeb drew himself up. Even if pride in worldly things was wrong, he'd not felt like this since the first time he'd mounted the peacock throne . . .

When the leading bearers were just forty feet away, trumpets on the mansion roof sounded the signal for the procession to halt. The bearers immediately stopped, trays held out stiffly before them. Then each row divided, five men taking three paces to the right, and five to the left. Behind them the bodyguard reined in and wheeled their mounts to either side. Azam on his pale stallion rode through the central aisle they'd created, his brothers just behind him. At the bottom of the mansion steps the three dismounted and Azam walked up the stairs to kneel before Aurangzeb. 'I ask your blessing, Father.'

'You have it. Now rise and followed me inside. Your bride is waiting.'

Though it was daylight, tall scented candles in golden candelabra burned in Jahanara's mansion. Their fragrance mingled with that of incense and of the garlands of *champa* flowers and white jasmine wound around the red sandstone columns. The ceremony would take place in a high-ceilinged, marble-floored chamber stretching the width of the mansion where the guests were already assembled. As Aurangzeb entered, his eyes flicked left and right to confirm that everything was in order. The wedding tiara that he'd tie on Azam's head was on a marble stand next to the flower-painted platform – a gift from his subjects in Kashmir – where Jani sat concealed beneath her veils of golden gauze embroidered with stars. Only her small bejewelled hands folded in her lap and her hennaed feet were visible.

Behind the dais was a screened area from which the royal women could watch, Jahanara among them. This wedding was not only a means of healing, at her prompting, past dynastic wounds but a way of smoothing over a more recent rift. Since Jahanara's disagreement with his treatment of the Hindus, he'd felt a distance between them – even thought she might not accompany him back to Delhi. Jani had shared Jahanara's years of confinement in the Agra fort, and from the way she spoke about her Jahanara clearly loved her like a daughter. Agreeing to the wedding and having it take place in Delhi had been his device to encourage Jahanara to return with the court.

As Azam took his place beside his bride, Aurangzeb nodded to the mullah to begin.

'Do you consent to take this man for your husband?' the mullah first asked Jani. Her reply from beneath the layers of spangled veils was a quiet but distinct 'Yes'. Next, at the mullah's prompting, Azam too gave his consent and recited the customary wedding prayers. Then Aurangzeb lifted the gleaming wedding tiara, the pearls on the gold wires trembling like blossom in the breeze, from its stand and placed it on his son's head. Finally he took a bowl of rosewater from his *qorchi* and briefly rinsed his hands before another attendant handed him a goblet of water which, as the wedding ritual required, he drained to confirm the holy union of bride and groom.

'Long life to the new husband and wife. May God smile on their union and bless it with many children!'

Jahanara's mansion was too small for all those who must be invited to an imperial wedding feast. Instead, he'd had a giant pavilion erected in the great arcaded courtyard of the fort facing his Hall of Public Audience. Making his way there past flower-filled gardens and fountains bubbling with rosewater he could already smell the sauces flavoured with saffron, butter and cream. The imperial cooks had been at work for weeks, ordering the finest provisions from across his empire – musk melons, sweet grapes and pome- granates from the orchards around Herat, walnuts and almonds from the Punjab, dried apricots and cherries from Kashmir, partridges, pheasants and quail from the imperial hunting grounds to be captured and carried alive to Delhi, subtle herbs from the northern foothills and hot spices from the south . . .

Kettledrums boomed and trumpets blared as, preceded by his bodyguard, Aurangzeb entered the pavilion and took his place behind a low table on the velvet-draped dais in the centre. Further drumming announced the entrance of the imperial princes, led by Azam. The bridegroom joined him at the table on the dais while Muazzam and Akbar seated themselves on a divan immediately below. They made a handsome trio. Muscular Muazzam had inherited the high cheekbones, long narrow nose and strong jaw of his Kashmiri Rajput mother. They looked far better on him than on Nawab Bai, whom he'd only married at Shah Jahan's insistence. Azam and young Akbar bore little resemblance to their Persian mother Dilras Banu – his principal wife until she had died following the birth of Akbar. But in both of them – especially Azam – he thought he recognised something of himself. For a moment he saw the face of his eldest son Mohammed Sultan. But for his treachery, he too would have been sharing this celebration, instead of a dungeon with rats. But Mohammed Sultan's fate was just before God and before the world. He had no regrets . . .

Settling himself against gold-embroidered cushions, Aurangzeb signalled the feast to begin. First to arrive were green-tunicked servants carrying great gold platters holding roasted peacocks, long bright tail feathers gloriously spread, and whole sides of roasted mutton and venison. Others followed with dishes of pulao scattered with fruits and nuts wrapped in gold leaf, pyramids of saffron-flavoured rice, fragrant fresh-cooked breads stuffed with almonds and raisins and tureens of silver and gold containing delicately sauced, long-simmered dishes that were the cooks' finest creations. Aurangzeb himself ate heartily, although he forced himself to stop before others did, to show no gluttony. Then, with crystal dishes filled with fruits and gilded sweetmeats still passing between the tables, he rose and made his way through the wooden screens draped with green silk that segregated the female members of the wedding party.

Jahanara, he was pleased to see, had set aside her mourning. Dressed in midnight blue, she was sitting on a cushion on one side of the bride while his daughter Zebunissa and his youngest sister Gauharara sat on the other. Jahanara looked happy, her eyes bright as she laughed at something Zebunissa said. But where was Roshanara? He glanced swiftly around. No, she wasn't here.

At his appearance Jani had modestly pulled her bridal veils low over her face but as he approached he heard Jahanara say, 'No need to cover your face before your father-in-law.' Slowly Jani pushed back the filmy golden gauze and looked up at him. How like Dara she was, the same oval face, the same thickly fringed dark eyes, those delicate cheekbones that had always seemed to him too girlish in his brother. What was she thinking? Did she appreciate his generosity in giving her an imperial prince for a husband, or was she remembering her father's fate? Jahanara would have told her to forget and forgive the past as she herself had done, and to be grateful for the present.

He smiled at her. 'Jani, I welcome you as my daughter. May God smile upon your marriage with my son and make it fruitful.'

'Thank you, Majesty.'

'To mark this occasion I would like to give you, my sisters and my daughter some gems I have myself selected from our imperial treasure houses.' At his nod five female attendants approached, each carrying a leather casket, domed lid open to reveal the diamonds, emeralds, rubies and ocean-blue sapphires sparkling inside — one casket, slightly larger than the others, for the bride, the others for his daughter and three sisters, except that one of his sisters wasn't here. 'Where is Roshanara?'

Gauharara answered. 'During the wedding ceremony she said she felt unwell – a headache, I think – and was going back to her room.'

'I'm sure the *hakims* would advise that her best cure would be to forget the headache and join us. Send a servant to say that I request her to come at once and that I'll wait until she does.'

Aurangzeb sat by Jahanara. Around him the women were murmuring among themselves, some coming forward to examine his gifts to the bride and the imperial princesses. The sweet scent of jasmine reminded him of Udipuri Mahal. Heavily pregnant as she was, his concubine could not be here with the noblewomen of the *haram* but she too would have wedding favours from him – jewels with which he personally would adorn her glorious body, ripening with the child she would soon bear him . . . But then from the men's section of the pavilion he heard raised voices. 'Majesty, there is urgent news,' his *qorchi* called from the other side of the screen.

Aurangzeb hurried from the women's enclosure. 'What is it?'

'A *cossid* – a messenger – has just ridden in. An army of Jats – perhaps twenty thousand of them – is ravaging the area around Mathura.'

Mathura was only ninety miles away on the road to Agra! What could have possessed the Jats? Aurangzeb knew what Jahanara would say – that his actions against their Hindu religion had turned the Jats' smouldering resentment of his rule into open insurrection. Well, if it had, so be it. It was for the best. It meant his policies were flushing his enemies out into the open, like rats from a burning barn. And he would destroy them as they deserved!

• ◆ •

The billowing cloud of red dust on the horizon was growing larger by the minute. Aurangzeb, sitting straight-backed in the howdah of his tall war elephant and shielding his eyes against the rising sun, gazed towards the horsemen approaching fast across the sandy, treeless plain. Soon he began to make out individual silhouettes and then the glittering tips of the leading riders' lances. The Jats, like the inexperienced rabble he knew them to be, seemed intent on flinging themselves headlong on to his own disciplined ranks. Let them come.

As soon as he'd heard of their rebellion he'd ordered his troops to be readied and then quickly despatched two armies, each double the reported size of his upstart opponents', to advance towards them – one from Agra and the other from Delhi. He had himself accompanied the latter force. They'd not made as speedy progress as he'd wished. The cannons he'd insisted – rightly, he still thought – should accompany them to give them an advantage over the Jats, who had none, had slowed their pace. When he'd ordered a night march in an attempt to make up for lost time some of the great white oxen pulling the guns had slumped in their traces. Exhausted by their daytime efforts they'd refused to rise however harshly their drivers beat them with their long whips. Artillery, infantry, baggage train and camp followers had begun to mingle with each other. As the increasingly disorganised ranks straggled through a patch of thick jungle, according to reports brought to him a pair of tigers had attacked a party of his outlying scouts and killed two of them.

Although he could scarcely credit it – tigers usually hunted alone – such rumours had only added to the growing confusion. He'd been forced to abandon the night march before all discipline was lost.

As he'd watched his officers riding hither and thither by the inconsistent light of a crescent moon, increasingly obscured by scudding clouds, his greatest fear hadn't been that the Jats would seize the opportunity to attack – he'd known them to be still too far off – but that they'd take advantage of the delay in his advance to disappear with their booty into the remote bush and desert between Mathura and the lands of the Rajputs before his forces could catch them. However, they had not. Gokla, their leader, had continued to raid Moghul garrisons and treasure houses. Then, evading the Moghul army Aurangzeb had despatched from Agra, Gokla in his insolence had ridden to confront the emperor himself, as eager for battle as he was.

Even if the force he commanded didn't have the four to one numerical superiority he had planned, with battle approaching Aurangzeb was confident that he had sufficient men to make Gokla regret his rashness. Beckoning two of his scouts close to his elephant, he shouted his orders. 'Go to my generals. Tell them to be ready to receive the Jat onslaught. Have them put horsemen in the front rank but let them only be a screen for a line of our best musketeers placed immediately behind them, together with those cannon that have kept up with our march and can be readied in time. As the Jats attack let the horsemen move aside to expose them to the withering fire of our musketeers and gunners. Then, when our enemies' charge is blunted and they are falling into confusion, let the horsemen get among them and cut them down without mercy. I will watch the progress of the battle from that low hill over there. May God be with us and victory ours.'

A quarter of an hour later Aurangzeb watched from his chosen position as the first waves of wildly yelling Jat horsemen, riding hard, heads down, lances extended, approached the screen of Moghul cavalry drawn up just as he'd ordered in front of his musketeers and artillery. Again, as he'd instructed, at the last moment, they wheeled away, right and left. As they did so, there was a loud crackle of musketry and a crash of cannons as the troops behind followed his commands. For what seemed to him an age, but could only have been a minute or two, white smoke obscured his vision. When it thinned, dispersed by a rising breeze, he saw that many Jat horsemen had fallen. Riderless horses were racing away, reins dangling. Others, wounded, were rolling on the ground or struggling like some of their former riders to stand on shattered limbs.

His own Moghul horsemen, identifiable by their green tunics, were rushing back into the melee, cutting and hacking as they went. But they were by no means having it all their own way. The weight of the Jats' reckless charge had been so powerful that it had broken through the line of Moghul musketeers and cannon in several places. In one, a rank of his musketeers had been scythed down almost to a man and their bodies lay twisted and bloodied on the ground. Nevertheless, others were trying to reload, feverishly using their long steel ramrods to push powder and ball down the barrels of their weapons. Elsewhere, to his disgust, some of his musketeers were already turning away, discarding their weapons as they fled in their haste to escape pursuing Jat horsemen. While he watched, one fugitive tripped and fell and as he tried to rise a Jat transfixed him with his lance, a just reward for his cowardice. But why would men on foot, whether musketmen or plain infantry, never learn that there was less risk to their wretched lives, never mind more honour to be gained, by standing with their comrades and facing horsemen rather than running, arms waving and screaming with fear, to be spitted by their mounted opponents like fowl for the cooking fire.

The musketeers were not the only ones in disarray. Jat horsemen had overrun several of the cannon, killing or putting to flight the gunners before they'd had time to reload. Now some of the enemy had dismounted and were heaving on ropes they had tied to the cannon, straining to turn the weapons round to fire into the Moghul ranks. How had so many Jats reached his lines so quickly? Perhaps some horses had carried two men. The Jats had certainly come well equipped with ropes, counting on success in capturing artillery pieces.

Aurangzeb's heart beat faster as he scanned the battlefield to see where the greatest of the mounting dangers lay. With an effort of will he kept his features expressionless and his movements and gestures slow and calm to avoid giving any impression of haste or disarray, never mind apprehension or fear, to the troops around him and unsettling them further. The immediate threat was soon obvious and it was rapidly approaching his own position. A tightly bunched phalanx of orange-clad Jat riders was carving its way towards him. At its centre, and flanked by two flag-bearers struggling to hold on to the shafts of the large orange banners straining behind them in the growing wind, he made out a heavily moustached figure gesturing towards him. It could only be Gokla, the Jats' leader.

Suddenly two Jat riders in the first rank stood in their stirrups and levelled their long-barrelled muskets towards him. He saw the puffs of white smoke as they fired but did not flinch or move in any way, knowing they were well out of range. 'Move forward!' he shouted over the din of battle to the two *mahouts* perched on his elephant's neck behind the great beast's ears. One of them, a grizzled and badly pockmarked veteran, used his steel *anka* – guidance stick – to prod the elephant down the low hill and towards the crush of battle on the plain. Raising its trunk and trumpeting, the elephant obediently began to descend the slope, its wallowing gait making Aurangzeb's gilded howdah sway. His mounted bodyguard also began to advance, taking closer station around him as they reached the bottom of the hill. 'Make sure all our banners are unfurled and our trumpeters and drummers sound the attack,' he shouted. 'I want our troops to see that I am going forward to confront our enemies. It will hearten any that are faltering.' There was a crack behind him as the green flags caught the wind, followed almost immediately by the blare of the trumpets and the urgent tattoo of the drummers' sticks on the taut camelskin of the drums mounted either side of their placid horses' necks.

Aurangzeb and his bodyguard began to close quickly with Gokla's onrushing horsemen. Then another Jat rose in his stirrups and levelled his musket. This time he was in range. The grizzled driver twisted and pitched forwards, from the neck of Aurangzeb's elephant, blood pouring from his shattered face. As its long-time *mahout* hit the ground the elephant loyally swerved to avoid him, causing the howdah to sway so violently that Aurangzeb had to grip the sides tightly to avoid being thrown out. Almost immediately the second driver slid into the place of the first and steadied the beast.

'Give me the first of my muskets,' Aurangzeb called to the bearer seated behind him. Quickly the man passed him the weapon. Gripping its ivory inlaid stock, Aurangzeb took careful aim at Gokla, who was now hacking with his curved sword at one of the leading Moghul bodyguards. Just as Aurangzeb fired the bodyguard's mount reared up and its rider fell, wounded by Gokla's last stroke. Aurangzeb's ball hit not Gokla but the head of the rearing horse which immediately collapsed, pinioning its wounded rider. Tugging hard at his reins, Gokla swerved away from the dying animal's flailing hooves and kicked his mount hard towards Aurangzeb's elephant, followed by several other grim-faced Jats determined to sell their lives dear.

'Hand me my other musket, and quickly,' Aurangzeb called to his bearer. The man swiftly passed it to him and the emperor again took careful aim down the long barrel. Just then his elephant stumbled over a body lying twisted on the ground and this time Aurangzeb's ball hit Gokla's own sweat-scummed black horse. Leaping from the saddle as the animal fell, now almost deprived of companions by Moghul swords and musket balls, Gokla rushed forward on foot, orange robes streaming behind him and curved sword still in hand. He was less than a hundred feet away from his quarry. Aurangzeb drew his own sword from its jewelled scabbard, but as he did so one of his bodyguard – a young Uzbek – flung himself from his saddle on to the Jat leader, knocking the sword from his grasp and pulling him to the ground.

For a moment or two the men rolled together in the red dirt, grappling for advantage. Then Gokla succeeded in freeing his dagger from the scabbard at his waist and thrust it twice deep into the Uzbek's groin. Blood spurted and the man doubled up, both hands clutching at his wounds, as Gokla struggled to his feet. Looking around and quickly realising that he was alone and must soon be killed or captured, the Jat leader pulled back his arm and hurled his dagger at Aurangzeb. Both his arm and his aim were good. The weapon flew straight, turning tip over hilt, and this time Aurangzeb twisted aside. Still the blade caught him a glancing blow just below the elbow of his left arm, which he'd raised to protect himself, before thudding into the gilded wood of the howdah's side.

Blood began trickling down Aurangzeb's arm and dripping from his fingers as two of his men grabbed hold of the now unarmed but still violently struggling Gokla.

'Don't kill him. Take him to the rear. I will deal with him later when we've secured the victory. Once news of his capture spreads it should make our task easier.'

'Majesty,' one of his officers called. 'Your wound . . . won't you wait for a *hakim* to dress it?'

'No. It's a scratch. Much better to exploit the Jats' disarray now their leader has been captured.'

Two hours later, with the noon sun high in the sky and the wind whipping puffs of red dust from the earth, two guards pushed Gokla to his knees before Aurangzeb, who stood a little distance in front of his scarlet command tent. He was now washed and dressed in his imperial robes, and the wound in his left arm had been neatly stitched and bound by the *hakims*. He had been right, of course. As news of Gokla's capture had spread many of his men had broken off the action and fled, but they had kept their discipline as they did so. Therefore to his chagrin, more seemed to have succeeded in getting away than he would have hoped, Jat riders again taking up a second man behind them. He had ordered his men to continue the pursuit, and if any villager was found sheltering a fugitive they were to burn down the whole village as a warning to other communities not to rebel against him.

Aurangzeb turned his gaze on Gokla. 'Have you anything to say before your Emperor as to why you rebelled against me?'

Gokla raised his battered face. His luxuriant moustache was matted with blood but there was unflinching defiance in his eyes. 'I acted as I did to defend my people against your oppression of our lives and now of our religion. We Jats do not recognise your right to rule over us. My only aim was to kill you. That's why I never let my men retreat when I could so easily have done so – why I advanced to meet you. To me you are the embodiment of evil. If I had rid the earth of you, my life would have served its purpose. My only regret – and it is deep – is that I failed.' Gokla tried to stand, but the two guards pushed him to the ground and pinioned him there.

Aurangzeb swallowed his rising anger. As emperor he should not be seen to engage further with the defeated rebel. To do so might seem to give Gokla and the intensity of his hatred a status they should not have. 'You, not I, will die now, your traitor's body hacked limb from limb and the pieces displayed over the Agra city gates.' Aurangzeb turned to the head of his bodyguard, standing just behind him. 'Let the execution take place immediately. And have my orders for the disposal of the body followed at once. I will not trouble myself further with this insignificant traitor, however insolent he may be.'

With that the emperor walked slowly back into his scarlet tent without a backward glance at Gokla being dragged away, still struggling and screaming defiance, to execution by his guards. Once he had calmed and collected his thoughts he must give thanks to God for his victory. Then he would begin to consider how best to recapture that other and more dangerous rebel, Shivaji.

• ◆ •

'Roshanara – I'm pleased to see you. You don't often visit me.' She must have heard the news that Aurangzeb had defeated the Jats and would soon be back in Delhi, Jahanara thought. But Roshanara looked anything but happy. Her cochineal-reddened lips were a thin line and her expression was strained and preoccupied. Waving away an offer of refreshment from one of Jahanara's attendants, she sat down and looked around her. 'Your mansion looks even finer than I remember – those embroidered silk wall hangings are new, aren't they? But Aurangzeb wouldn't want you to have anything but the best, would he?' Her voice seemed to crack.

'Roshanara. What's the matter?'

'How can you pretend you don't know!'

'Truly, I don't . . . tell me what's troubling you.'

Roshanara pulled a piece of folded paper from the silk purse hanging from her belt. 'This! This is what's the matter!'

'What is it?'

'A letter from Aurangzeb . . . and it's all your fault! I

66

know your influence over him. You're the only one he cares about or pays heed to, but did you have to use your position to interfere in my life? Don't look so innocent. You can't fool me. I know exactly what you've been up to . . . telling tales of me to Aurangzeb.' Roshanara was shaking with passion and her voice was full of bitterness.

'I don't know what you mean.'

'Don't you? It was bad enough when Aurangzeb brought you back to court and you took my position as First Lady without a thought for how I might feel . . . I . . .'

'Roshanara, I know that must have been difficult for you. I should have talked more to you about it, but I didn't know quite what to say, and to be frank I was a little embarrassed. At the same time I never thought you'd be quite so concerned—'

'Why was that?' Roshanara interrupted. 'I'll tell you! You assumed, just as Dara always did, that as the eldest you were entitled to every honour and could treat the rest of us like children, dispensing favours when you felt like it . . .'

At the mention of their brother, Jahanara looked away for a moment so her sister should not see the hurt and anger on her face. Roshanara made Aurangzeb's rising sound like a nursery squabble rather than a fratricidal war that brought bloodshed and death. Roshanara had always taken a narrow, self-centred view of things – perhaps she couldn't help it – and she was obviously upset. Mastering her own feelings, Jahanara knelt beside her sister and tried to take her hands, but Roshanara kept them resolutely folded in her lap.

'Criticise me if you want to, but not Dara,' Jahanara

said quietly. 'He's dead and you know how dear he was to me . . .' *as he should have been to you; he was your brother too*, she was about to add but instead said, 'Tell me what you meant just now when you accused me of interfering in your life.'

'I went to see Aurangzeb just before he left on campaign, but I expect you know that.'

'No, I didn't. Go on.'

'I told him how much he had hurt me by taking away my former position. He said he understood . . . that you and he would find other responsibilities for me . . . that he valued and loved me. I believed him, but now I find he didn't mean it . . . any of it!' A vein was pulsing in Roshanara's temple and tears had appeared in her eyes.

'Why not?'

'Because I asked him whether I could have my own mansion within the fort – as you have. He promised to consider it . . . even talked about which mansion might suit me . . . and then today a messenger brought this letter in which Aurangzeb says he cannot agree to my request . . . that unlike you I am not to be trusted to have my own establishment . . . that he has received reports of my behaviour while he's been away, of drinking parties in the *haram*. He adds that he's known for some time that I drink wine – that he had been prepared to turn a blind eye to it, but the recent reports of my excesses – how one night I had to be carried unconscious to my bed have decided him. He absolutely forbids me to drink wine or ever to ask him again to live in my own mansion! But that's not the worst of it . . .'

Though all the attendants had left the room and they were alone, Roshanara lowered her voice so that Jahanara had to lean closer to hear her. 'He says he's also heard that I've been taking lovers. He warns of the direst consequences if anyone brings him proof and informs me that he is dismissing some of my servants and appointing ones he trusts in their place, who will report back to him on all my actions. It's going to be like being in prison and it can only be your doing. You want to punish me because I didn't side with you, Dara and our father during the civil war. Before you came back Aurangzeb trusted me . . . relied on me . . . and now all that's changed.' Roshanara had given up whispering and her voice rose in strident accusation. 'When Aurangzeb returns I want you to go to him and tell him that your stories about me aren't true . . . none of them!' Her tears began to fall in earnest.

Stunned by her sister's accusations Jahanara tried to think. How could she make her understand that none of this was of her making? 'Listen to me,' she said at last. 'You've convinced yourself that I want to injure you in Aurangzeb's eyes, but in fact that's the last thing I want. During all those years of solitude in the Agra fort with our father to care for and only Jani for a companion, I longed for the days when we'd been a family – united and happy and loving. That time can no more return than the dead can rise, but I believed then and still do that we can salvage something of what we once were. That's why when Aurangzeb asked me to return to court I agreed despite my misgivings. I don't want to create more divisions – I want to heal our wounds so that the children of Shah Jahan and Mumtaz who remain can be a family again.'

Roshanara had stopped crying and was regarding her

intently. Encouraged, Jahanara tried again to take Roshanara's hands and this time she didn't resist.

'Sister, I swear on the life of our mother that whatever Aurangzeb has heard about you has nothing to do with me. But his harsh reaction to such spiteful gossip doesn't surprise me. Haven't you noticed how he's changing? His religious beliefs have always been orthodox and austere but now – as I think all the world can see – they are becoming more extreme and all-consuming. He's adhering more and more strictly to what he considers the true path of Islam. I believe his views are wrong. I've tried again and again to warn him that it's a dangerous path. It's narrow, it makes no compromises and no allowances for human weakness. But he won't listen to me – you may think I have great influence on him but I don't. So if he's becoming hard on you, it's because what he hears of your behaviour doesn't accord with the principles of our faith as he sees them. Look at how he has renounced music because he thinks the pleasure it brings is self-indulgent and therefore sinful. But none of this means Aurangzeb doesn't love you . . . he believes he is acting for your own good.'

As Jahanara released her hands and stood up, Roshanara brushed the remaining tears from her cheeks. Then, reaching for the tiny jewelled mirror she wore on a ribbon round her neck, she studied her face before carefully wiping away some streaks of kohl and standing up too. Had she made her sister understand, Jahanara wondered? But there was something she must ask her. Drinking wine was one thing, but for an imperial princess to take lovers . . . In the days of their ancestors that would have surely meant instant death by stoning. Even now, given Aurangzeb's hardening religious attitudes, who could tell what he might do if Roshanara was caught in fornication? She should try to caution her sister but must choose her words with care. Though she might have convinced Roshanara that she'd not been telling tales of her to their brother that was a long, long way from overcoming her hostility, let alone gaining her trust.

'Roshanara, there's something I must ask you. Please forgive me, but you mentioned that Aurangzeb had heard rumours that you have lovers. Have you . . . have you done anything that might cause people to believe this might be so?' Roshanara stared at her but said nothing and Jahanara felt her heart sink. 'Roshanara – please . . .'

'Please what? Tell you something that's none of your business? If I have lovers – and I'm certainly not saying I do – why shouldn't I? Just because the daughters of Moghul emperors may not marry is no reason for us to deny ourselves life's pleasures . . . Don't look at me like that. Who are you to judge? What about you and that Englishman – Nicholas Ballantyne? All the time you pretended to be so perfect, but I knew what you were getting up to. And that's why I told our father – not because I disapproved, but to punish you for being such a hypocrite. Just as you're being now!'

'Roshanara, you don't understand . . . I'm not judging, I'm just trying to help you. You must be careful . . .'

But her sister was no longer listening. Instead, she turned and swept from the room. Jahanara stared after her, but after a moment what she saw was not her sister's imperious figure but a young man with hair the colour of maize and eyes blue as the summer sky. Roshanara was wrong. She and Nicholas had never been lovers. Yet over the years since they'd parted she'd never ceased to think of him or wonder what might have been in another life . . .

• ◆ •

As Aurangzeb's chestnut stallion bore him through the great Lahore Gate into Delhi's Red Fort – his bodyguard preceding him, breastplates glinting in the afternoon sun, the main body of his troops behind – he gave silent thanks for the victory God had granted him over the Jats. Later, as the sun dipped below the horizon, he would ride on elephant-back through the streets of his capital to the Jami Masjid, proud atop its rocky promontory, and there pray in earnest. The sandstone mosque with its white marble inlay was one of the most beautiful in all the empire, as well as the largest. In his father Shah Jahan's time, five thousand labourers and craftsmen had worked for six years to build it at a cost of over one million rupees. It was one achievement of his father of which he could be truly proud.

Aurangzeb rode on into the fort's great courtyard. Later he would summon his officers and bestow gifts of money, horses, finely chased swords and robes of honour upon those who had distinguished themselves in the campaign against Gokla. But now his mind was fixed on Udipuri Mahal, who just four days ago had borne him a son – another sign that the heavens were smiling upon him.

As he made his way into the *haram*, door after door was flung open to allow him to pass and the cry of 'The emperor approaches' rang in his ears. When he reached the tortoiseshell-inlaid doors leading to Roshanara's quarters he did not stop. He had no wish to see his sister at present and she probably wasn't even there. She and his other sisters were most likely still on the *jali*-screened balcony from which the royal women could observe his ceremonial comings and goings. But Udipuri would be waiting for him . . .

Entering his concubine's apartments he at once caught the smell of the attar of roses that was her favourite perfume, just as it had been of his mother Mumtaz. Signalling to the *haram* attendants to leave, he pushed open the doors to her inner chamber and paused on the threshold. Udipuri was lying propped on a couch, her long dark hair tumbling over her shoulders as she looked down at the baby sucking lustily at her right breast. In her own distant country of Georgia, deep in the Caucasus mountains, women however noble did not employ wet nurses. How beautiful they both looked – the mother and the child feeding at her blue-veined, alabaster-pale breast.

'Aurangzeb!' Her eyes lit at the sight of him. 'Come and look at your son.' Cradling the tiny head, which was dusted with fine black hair, she gently removed it from her breast and held the child up to him. Deprived of his milk the baby began to cry, kicking tiny legs, as Aurangzeb took hold of him.

'I would like to call him Kam Bakhsh – the mullahs tell me it is an auspicious name.' He smiled at Udipuri. 'Would you be happy with that?'

She nodded.

Looking down into Kam Bakhsh's tiny, innocent, protesting face, as yet untainted by the evil of the world, Aurangzeb felt such joy that he caught his breath. Perhaps this son – so much younger than his brothers – would be the mainstay of his old age? Only God knew what the future held, for himself or for this child, but he prayed that his feelings for Kam Bakhsh would stay the same, and the boy would never know the coldness and rejection he had suffered at the hands of his own father.

Chapter 5

The Sorceress

'**M**ajesty, wake up. The *khawajasara* asks you to come immediately to your sister Roshanara's apartments!'

Aurangzeb felt Udipuri stir beside him as, forcing his eyes open, he blinked in the light of the candle the *haram* attendant was holding up. 'What's happened?'

'She's suddenly been taken ill, Majesty.'

'I'll come at once.' Getting up, Aurangzeb wrapped himself quickly in the robe another attendant held out and hurried through the silent corridors of the *haram* towards Roshanara's apartments. The tortoiseshell-inlaid doors were wide open. Beyond them a small group of women, Jahanara and Gauharara among them, were watching two turbaned *hakims* lean over the bed on which Roshanara lay. As Aurangzeb approached, his tall figure casting shadows in the flickering candlelight, one of the *hakims*, an elderly man with thick-lensed glasses, straightened himself and touched his hand to his breast. Aurangzeb saw that the other doctor, a younger man, was holding a steel basin to his sister's right wrist in which he was catching a trickle of bright crimson blood.

'What's the matter with her? Is it serious?' Aurangzeb could scarcely believe it. As far as he could recall Roshanara had seldom known even a day's illness in her forty-six years.

'We're not sure yet, Majesty. We only arrived a few minutes ago ourselves. What is already clear to us is that she has a very high temperature and is slipping in and out of consciousness. Her heart is beating much too fast. I have instructed my colleague to bleed her a little to try to slow her heartbeat. We will also prepare an infusion of poppy juice to soothe her and bring down her temperature.'

'Roshanara . . .' Aurangzeb knelt down on the other side of the bed and took her left hand in his. It felt heavy and lifeless as if her soul had already departed. Roshanara's eyes were closed, and, just as the doctor had described, her chest was rising and falling rapidly beneath the thin sweat-soaked sheet. As he squeezed her hand her eyelids fluttered. 'Roshanara . . . It's me, Aurangzeb.'

Slowly, as if it was a great effort, Roshanara opened her eyes. Although she was looking straight at him she appeared confused. 'Aurangzeb . . . is it really you?'

'Of course. You are ill, sister, but the *hakims* are here and say they will soon restore you to health.' But his voice lacked conviction even in his own ears. He needed no doctor to tell him his sister was very ill – that was all too obvious from her appearance.

'Aurangzeb . . . I want to speak to you alone. Please send the others away.'

76

Aurangzeb turned towards the silent group. 'Leave us for a few moments, please. You too,' he nodded at the *hakims*, 'but remain outside.' The younger doctor, who had just finished bleeding Roshanara, quickly bandaged her wrist with white muslin, picked up his leather satchel of instruments and followed the rest from the room.

'We're alone now, Roshanara.'

She'd closed her eyes again and as he stroked her thick hennaed hair back from her face she spoke once more, but so faintly that he had to lean close to catch the words. What was she trying to say? He thought he heard 'I'm sorry . . . so sorry . . . I didn't mean . . . you must understand . . .'

'Roshanara, don't upset yourself. Lie still.'

'No, I must speak . . .' Her voice sounded firmer and she opened her eyes again. Somehow she found the strength to haul herself a little higher against her pillows. For a moment the effort took her breath away, but then she continued. 'Aurangzeb, listen, please. I know I . . . I disappointed you. But I couldn't help myself . . . I drank because it made me feel happier. And I mustn't deceive you, not at a time like this, with death perhaps close . . . once or twice I did take lovers, just as you suspected . . . Don't judge me too harshly . . . all I ever wanted was to matter to someone . . . to be close to someone . . . to feel their warmth. However hard I tried – even when Jahanara was with our father in Agra and I was the one by your side – I suspected you didn't really need or care for me. You just tolerated me, despite everything I'd done for you. That wasn't fair of you, Aurangzeb. Even before Jahanara's release I felt you pushing me aside as if I was of no importance to you. I was lonely, as I've been for most of my life – ever since our mother died. Was I wrong to feel like that? Please . . . I feel I'm burning up inside . . . I don't think I've got much time. Do I matter to you as much as Jahanara? Tell me, please!'

Stunned, Aurangzeb could find no words. The stories about her taking lovers had been true . . . He realised he was no longer stroking her forehead. Stretching out his hand again he found it almost an effort to touch her, though her face looked agonised. Even now, when she should be begging God's forgiveness for her sins, her mind was on her rivalry with Jahanara, competing with her elder sister, beseeching him to say that she, not Jahanara, was the more important to him. A few soft words would ease what might well be her final moments on earth, but he could not, would not, lie, especially to a woman who had sinned so grievously.

Her eyes were fixed on him, waiting. He had to say something.

'Roshanara, you are completely wrong to think I'm not grateful to you. I am. You stood by me in my struggles consistently from the first when few others did. And of course I love you . . . you should not need to ask. I . . .' For just a moment he felt himself weaken, almost ready to say what she wanted, but then he steeled himself. 'I must go now, but I will pray for your recovery, as I will ask my mullahs to do.' Dipping the corner of a cloth into a bowl of rosewater beside him, he wiped the sweat from her face, then kissed her forehead and got up and made for the door.

'Aurangzeb . . .'

He heard her faint call but didn't look back. What more could he say to her? She was his sister and he loved her, but there was no more comfort he could give her. By her own admission, she was a sinner.

In the antechamber the little group was waiting, Jahanara standing slightly apart. Going to her, Aurangzeb took her hand. 'You will send me word at once if her condition changes, won't you?' Jahanara nodded. As she and the others returned to the sickroom, he made his way back not to Udipuri but to his own apartments, where he spread his rug on the marble floor and knelt to pray for Roshanara as he had promised. By the time he had finished a pale golden light was filtering through the shutters. Feeling the need for the sun on his face, he walked out on to his terrace as its golden rim rose above the horizon and a new day began. For a while he contemplated Delhi spread out before him, smoke from the first cooking fires spiralling into the early morning air.

In a short while he must attend his council. With his sister so ill, to say nothing of her shameful admission, he'd find it hard to concentrate on affairs of state. But he would. It was his duty and there were urgent matters to attend to, in particular reports of a strange sect – Hindu farmers and petty traders who followed some outlandish practices and were, or so one of his governors warned, preaching insurrection.

Going back inside he picked up the governor's report, intending to read it again before the council meeting. But thoughts of Roshanara jostled for his attention. Only a year apart in age, how close they had been as children – natural allies, just as the older Jahanara and Dara had been. Roshanara had had a pet mongoose which she had sometimes let him play with. Their misery at the death of their mother had bound them closer . . . Yet just now

Roshanara had complained of being lonely and had blamed him. When was it that he'd realised God had marked him out for some special purpose – that to achieve it he could have no confidants but must keep his own counsel, excluding Roshanara with the rest? But though he had schooled himself thereafter not to need or rely on anyone, that did not mean he did not love his sister. Surely Roshanara understood that? She could not blame him for her own breach of the bounds of decency. Her lusts, not any failure of his, were the cause.

'Aurangzeb . . .' He looked round to see Jahanara. 'It's over. She died in my arms, but your name was the last word she spoke. And in those final moments she smiled – such a sweet smile – and she looked to me just as she did when she was a child . . .' Tears were running down Jahanara's face as she stepped towards her brother and enfolded him in her arms.

• ◆ •

'Look, Majesty. It is true about their appearance.' The head dropped from the jute sack on to the white marble floor and rolled a little way before stopping, its open but sightless bulging eyes staring up at Aurangzeb. The head certainly looked very strange. Just as the travel-stained officer who had captured the man and executed him as a spy had told him, these people – 'Satnamis', he'd called them – shaved off all the hair on their heads, even their eyebrows. The spy had been dead some time – the skin on the head was mottled and the flesh beginning to rot. The sickly sweet stench of death caught Aurangzeb's throat.

'Enough! I had no thought to disbelieve you. Put the head back in the sack. One of my attendants will remove it and burn it.'

The officer – a bushy-bearded Baluchi – scrabbled to pick up the head, a task he did not find easy with no hair to grip. At last, however, he had it in the sack and a servant, holding it at arm's length, carried it from the room.

'What I find difficult to believe is not that such a strange sect exists – many erroneous beliefs spring up in Hindustan – but that people who joyfully eat anything and everything, pork or beef, fish or fowl, and who have such bizarre rituals in which men and women join alike, can ever pose any threat to our power, however locally or temporarily,' Aurangzeb said.

'Majesty, even though it is true they don't care what they eat and men and women alike live communally, the problem is that at Narnaul, not so far from us here in Delhi, they've found a fanatical leader – not a man but a straggle-haired old woman with blazing eyes who proclaims herself a sorceress. Her passion and her speeches are so compelling that she has succeeded in convincing her followers that her spells and potions will render them impervious to sword strokes and even musket balls if they do as she says. So strong is their belief in her powers that with her at their head and amulets she has fashioned and blessed on their arms they have overpowered not just one or two but several of our small garrisons. They did so from within, after entering by stealth, in disguise or more often through drains – even latrine drains. Believe me, Majesty, they don't care how they pollute themselves, really they don't.'

The officer drew breath for a moment but words were soon tumbling from him again. 'Their sudden appearance as if by magic, yelling that their sorceress's spells have enabled them to walk through walls and that they are inviolable, unmans and unnerves our soldiers and officials, Muslims and Hindus alike. They scatter and flee. So great is their fear of these Satnamis even though there are still only five thousand of them and nearly all are on foot that they are marching virtually unopposed on us here in Delhi, with more and more peasants joining them along the way. I captured the spy whose head I showed you in a village no more than thirty miles away. Their main body is reported only double that distance from Delhi. Excuse my urgent and dishevelled appearance before you, Majesty, but I fear we do not have enough troops to defend ourselves with our main armies away in the Punjab confronting the Sikhs, truly I do. I wanted to warn you as soon as possible so we take what measures we can.' The officer finally fell silent.

Aurangzeb looked sternly at him. 'Calm yourself, man. Our troops' fear seems to be contagious, clawing at your own heart. Whatever an officer's inner agitation he should not display it. You are right in saying that our main armies are confronting the Sikhs under their guru Tegh Bahadur. But so they should be. The Sikhs pose a much greater long-term threat to our rule. They are brave, well organised and well armed. Their beliefs – even if not our own – are more coherent than any ravings of the sorceress you describe.'

The officer straightened his shoulders but his expression remained anxious. 'Majesty, I did not mean to alarm you unduly or to appear excessively alarmed myself. I did not intend to question your deployments of the troops. I was worried – and I confess I still am – about how we should repulse these Satnamis.'

'Such decisions are for me. Now leave me to ponder them.' As the officer bowed and moved towards the door,

Aurangzeb added more softly, 'Thank you for your report and for your haste. The sooner I know of such threats the more effectively I can move to confront them.'

After the officer's departure Aurangzeb spent some minutes standing on the balcony of the room looking out over Delhi. The credulity of people amazed him – their ability to believe in omens, magic and the ravings of fakirs whose rantings had everything to do with their own diseased minds and nothing to do with the spiritual. It was his duty to show the people of Hindustan their errors and bring them to the correct path. Doing so would be central to his rule as he had already made it to his life. However, his immediate task must be to suppress the outlandish Satnamis and their sorceress quickly and completely before their rising spread and began threatening his suzerainty. How to achieve this when many of his best troops were away in the Punjab was the question. The officer's demeanour had shown him how quickly unease and near panic could infect the most loyal.

As he gazed across the city, turning over the possibilities in his mind, dusk began to fall and the orange light of cooking fires to prick the gathering darkness. Then it came to him. He would fight fire with fire to avoid a conflagration. If his people and soldiers believed in spells and charms he would show them that he could deploy them too. He would have his imams prepare prayers for the protection of his Muslim troops and have the Hindu priests do likewise for those who believed in their gods. 'Donations' would persuade any who were reluctant. Then he would have these prayers written on parchment and sewn on to flags to be paraded before his troops by the imams and priests before they left Delhi to confront the Satnamis and later carried at the head of the army which would leave the following day. He himself would take command to give further confidence. The force would consist mainly of horsemen for reasons of both speed and effectiveness against the mainly foot-bound Satnamis, most of whom until a few weeks ago were simple farmers.

• ◆ •

Seated once more in his gilded howdah atop his great war elephant, Aurangzeb waved his hands above his head as the signal to his horsemen to charge the Satnamis, who were still running hither and thither trying to grab their weapons. He and his troops had taken them by surprise as they were making camp for the night on the muddy banks of a sluggish tributary of the Jumna about twenty miles from Delhi. He had been right. The prayers prepared by Muslim and Hindu holy men had heartened his troops. They had covered the distance from Delhi in only six hours. Now his soldiers were showing no fear but cheering and yelling as they levelled their lances or drew their swords and kicked their heels into the flanks of their horses. Specially selected men – Muslims from Lucknow and Hindus from Rajasthan – were carrying their religion's prayer flags. He had prudently placed them not in the vanguard but in the middle ranks for fear of the effect the death of a banner-bearer or the falling of a blessed flag into the mud would have on his troops.

A few Satnamis fired arrows at the onrushing Moghuls. One of the leading riders somersaulted over the head of his horse as it collapsed, hit in the neck. Another swerved away, losing control of his mount as he grasped at the arrow embedded in his thigh. However, as Aurangzeb ordered his *mahout* to follow in the wake of his advancing troops, the first of his horsemen were already in the midst of the Satnamis, whose numbers seemed larger than the Baluchi officer's estimate. Most, however, looked to be armed only with spears and bows and arrows, or weapons roughly fashioned from agricultural tools.

Soon Satnamis were falling, some flattened simply by the weight of the Moghul horses' charge, others cut down by the riders' swords. Many were dying but none made any move to turn and run even when wounded. Despite a sword cut to his face, one near-naked and skeletal-looking Satnami slashed with his scythe at the legs of galloping horses as calmly as he must once have cut grass in his village fields. Two horses fell, sinews severed, before he was impaled on a Moghul lance.

Another man clad only in a loincloth, but taller and more powerful-looking, leapt at the neck of a Moghul rider's black mount and by sheer strength and willpower pulled horse and rider to the ground. Then, grabbing the dazed man's sword, he thrust it into his body. Other Satnamis tried to follow his example. By no means all succeeded, many being knocked aside or run through, but soon twenty or so Moghuls were down, some sprawled motionless in the mud at the river's edge, others dragging themselves away or trying to fight off the Satnamis swarming around them and relentlessly stabbing at them with spears and knives. Soon, however, the number of Satnami bodies strewn across the riverbank showed the battle was beginning to go the Moghuls' way. Yet still the remainder held their ground, only falling when cut through by several strokes.

Aurangzeb's war elephant was almost up with the first

rank of his men, only a short distance from the centre of the Satnamis' camp, when a dozen or so of them ran yelling out of a large tent. Unlike their fellows, several had muskets which they were trying to level towards him. Two of his bodyguards charged them, but one Satnami, better prepared or more skilled than his fellows, fired before they reached him. Hit in the head, one guard slumped over his horse's neck as the frightened animal swerved away, galloping in panic into the river where its rider fell to float face down in the muddy water. The other bodyguard – a tall man wearing a green turban rather than the usual steel helmet – was proving his valour. He had already disposed of all but three of the musket-carrying Satnamis, leaning from his saddle to hack into their bony naked torsos with his sword as they attempted to steady their long-barrelled muskets.

Wheeling his nimble mount, he knocked aside one musket barrel just as its owner fired then slashed the man across the head, slicing into his shaven skull. The second Satnami quickly reversed his ancient musket, swung it by the barrel and with the butt hit the bodyguard's horse across the windpipe. Whinnying in pain, the animal reared up and threw the guard, who landed at the Satnami's feet, losing his grip on his sword as he fell. The Satnami wielded his musket again, striking the bodyguard in the pit of the stomach. As the Moghul doubled up the Satnami aimed at his turbaned head, but he twisted away just in time. As he did so he pulled a dagger from his belt and buried its serrated blade to the hilt in the Satnami's naked thigh. The man didn't even seem to notice but again swung the musket butt. This time the bodyguard caught it and wrenched it from the Satnami's grasp. Then, struggling to his feet, he smashed it repeatedly with all his force into the Satnami's face, pulping his nose and knocking him out.

Meanwhile, the remaining Satnami had fired at Aurangzeb. The ball splintered the roof of his howdah. 'Charge that man before he can reload,' Aurangzeb shouted to the *mahout*, who hastened to obey, but before the elephant could reach the musketeer the fighting bodyguard had thrown himself at him, seizing his ankles and bringing him to the ground, and wrestled the musket from his grasp. Then with a blow of his fist he knocked him unconscious.

The fabric of the tent which had concealed the musketeers twitched and a small, gaunt-featured figure with long grey hair emerged, thin arms spread wide. Chanting over and over again 'I am magic! I am magic!' the sorceress walked steadily towards Aurangzeb's elephant, head held high and looking neither right nor left. Several of the bodyguards seemed to recoil. None moved to restrain her. She halted in front of Aurangzeb's elephant and looked up at the emperor. 'You cannot harm me,' she shouted. 'Any wound your weapons inflict on me and my followers will heal and we will rise again. But I can harm you where it will not heal – in your mind – and I will. I curse you to live long but never to know peace in either your family or your realm.'

Aurangzeb did not reply but quietly asked the bearer behind him for his musket. Taking it, he levelled it and took deliberate aim at the body of the sorceress. She did not flinch but began her mesmeric chanting again, her staring eyes fixed unblinking on him. For a moment Aurangzeb's mind froze, but then he recovered himself and fired. Blood welled from the sorceress's scrawny chest, crimsoning her worn and flimsy muslin robe, but her expression did not change, nor did her eyes flicker. She held her gaze on Aurangzeb and continued to chant as more blood seeped from her mouth and ran down her chin. Then she slowly sank to her knees before pitching forward, arms still outstretched, the last of her chants fading as her face hit the mud.

'Have her body carried through each of the towns and villages she and her fellows captured. Execute one of our Satnami prisoners in each place and leave their bodies to rot in chains so no one can doubt either that she is dead or that her followers are as mortal as any man,' Aurangzeb ordered. To his *mahout*, he said, 'Turn the elephant. We will begin the march back to Delhi.' But hard as he tried to concentrate on the many tasks that lay ahead as his elephant plodded through the dusk – defeating Sikh rebels in the Punjab, recapturing Shivaji, now steadily building his power in the south, and putting down a Persian-inspired revolt by lawless tribes on the empire's north-western frontiers – he could not stop the woman's words from echoing round his brain. No matter how often he reminded himself that she had been only a deranged infidel while he was a rational man and faithful follower of a religion in which such curses had no place, they would not go away.

• ◆ •

Sipihr looked uncertain, eyes watchful beneath the wedding tiara. But after twelve years' confinement in the fortress of Gwalior it was only natural that his nephew should be a little nervous, Aurangzeb thought, scrutinising him as the wedding ceremony in the main courtyard of the Red Fort drew to a close. Sipihr's angular, high-cheekboned face was nothing like that of his father Dara Shukoh, whom his sister Jani so closely resembled. Perhaps he looked more like their mother – the long-dead Nadira? Aurangzeb frowned. Try as he might he could remember almost nothing about her except that his brother had loved her to the exclusion of all others and she had died as she and Dara had fled his pursuing armies.

Once again, the wedding had been Jahanara's idea. 'By freeing Sipihr from Gwalior and allowing him to marry you will again be proving to your people that the days of conflict within our family are over. The marriage will discourage any who might seek to rekindle old rivalries among us,' she had urged him. However, this time it had taken him longer to decide. Dara had had many supporters. Within his empire there must be some only too ready to plot to place Dara's surviving son on the throne, so he had to balance the risks of freeing Sipihr against his desire to show Jahanara that he was doing what he could to heal the divisions within the imperial dynasty. But finally he had thought of a way of reconciling Jahanara's wishes with his own security. Though Sipihr would not return to Gwalior, he would not have his full freedom – at least not yet. Instead he would live with his bride on the island of Salimgarh in the Jumna river in Delhi. His life would be comfortable and he would lack for nothing, but he would still be cut off from contact with the world beyond and spies would keep constant watch on him.

The tall young woman sitting beside Sipihr draped in shimmering bridal veils woven with silver thread was his own daughter Zubdatunnissa – the first Moghul emperor's daughter to marry since the time of the Emperor Akbar. Again, this had been Jahanara's suggestion. 'It isn't fair that the daughters of an emperor aren't allowed to marry,' Jahanara had argued. 'Why should they be denied the happiness of husband and children?' He had not missed the echo of Roshanara's dying words, and he'd seen the sadness in her eyes – for herself, or for Roshanara, or for them both?

Till recently he'd never questioned the rule which the Emperor Akbar had introduced to limit the birth of potential rival claimants to the throne. But his mullahs had told him that it had no basis in the Koran. Furthermore, he could see that it might encourage sexual sin. Roshanara had blamed her fornication upon it. But most important of all, perhaps, the rule had failed in its purpose. It hadn't prevented generation after generation of imperial infighting. The more he'd considered it, the more certain he'd become that the best – indeed the only – way to preserve the stability of the empire was not through arbitrary and irrational laws but through strict and unwavering control based on the teachings of his faith over both his government and his family. Too many of his ancestors had grown weak especially in their later years – allowing themselves to be governed by wine, opium and even women when they should have been ruthlessly asserting their authority. He would not make that mistake. He would be as strongly in control at the end of his reign as at its start. Therefore it would be no threat to him for his daughters to marry.

Aurangzeb rose, gave his final blessing to the couple and made his way through the smiling wedding guests and out of the courtyard. The wedding party would continue feasting and celebrating for much of the night, but he had pressing matters to deal with. Judging by the ever more urgent despatches from his governor in Peshawar the rebels on his north-west borders were growing rapidly in strength and insolence, using weapons provided by the Persian shah – ever intent on wreaking mischief in Moghul lands – to raze villages and plunder the caravans of peaceful merchants.

Soon he must again ride out at the head of his armies. Yet God willing he was leaving behind him an imperial family more united than at any time since he had taken the throne. This wedding would be a potent symbol of that unity.

Chapter 6

Bandits of the North

A urangzeb tugged up his scarf to cover his nose and mouth. A strong north wind was whipping dust and grit into his face as he and his army ascended one of the many rocky passes leading up through the jagged purple hills to confront the Persian-inspired revolt in his Afghan territories. At least he had put an end for the present to the threat of the martial Sikhs in the Punjab. The head of their leader Tegh Bahadur now adorned the main gate of his Red Fort at Delhi. There was still Shivaji, of course, but the Moghul armies were successfully confining the Maratha menace to the Deccan, even if at a considerable cost in men and money.

The wind was not only full of dust but cold, and Aurangzeb pulled his fur-lined cloak closer around him. As he did so he remembered some words of his ancestor Babur, the founder of the Moghul Empire, which he had read as a child. Babur had written of his dislike of the heat of Hindustan and longing for the cool mountains and snow-fed rivers of his homeland in Ferghana beyond the Oxus. What a long way the Moghuls had come since those days . . . how they had changed. These bare, windswept hills were as alien to him as the hot plains of Hindustan had been to Babur a century and a half ago.

He was roused from his musing by a realisation that the riders ahead of him were slowing down, jostling each other as they strove to change formation before entering an even narrower section of the high-sided pass where no more than four could comfortably ride abreast. Half an hour later, as he followed them into the shadows on his imperial elephant – to realign the ranks had taken time and the vanguard was probably now over a mile ahead of him – Aurangzeb grew chillier still. Looking up, he saw that the rock- and scree-strewn peaks were blocking out the autumn sun. The only small patch of sky he could see suddenly filled with dark screeching birds. For a moment he thought he could see movement among the rocks above. And could that be the crackle of musketry? Or was it simply scudding cloud creating shadow and a distant low rumble of thunder? Then suddenly all around him his bodyguards were reining in, pulling back the heads of their horses, which were whinnying in alarm.

Aurangzeb was about to send one of the officers of his bodyguard forward to investigate when he heard a cry of 'Make way. I must report to His Majesty' and saw a young rider emerge from the chaos ahead of him, swerving and pushing his horse through the halted column. 'Let him approach,' Aurangzeb ordered, and his bodyguard moved swiftly aside. A moment later he was waving away the young man's attempt at a salutation of his imperial presence. 'We can dispense with formalities. What is happening ahead? Are we under attack?'

'Yes, Majesty. My father Yusuf Khan is the commander of the vanguard today. As we rounded a tight bend and approached the narrowest part of the pass a volley of musket shots rang out from the peaks. Several of our leading horsemen collapsed from their saddles. Two or three men – wounded, I think – were carried further up the pass as their horses bolted in fright. My father ordered the next ranks of the vanguard to dismount and prepare to receive an attack. In particular he told the musketeers to load their weapons ready to return fire. Then we all scanned the heights, trying to see where the firing had come from. We couldn't – until the attackers fired a second volley, killing or wounding several more of our men and causing more horses to bolt, adding to the chaos.

'My father ordered the musketeers to fire, aiming at the points where we'd seen the smoke from our enemies' last volley. Then he ordered some of our scouts to scramble up the steep sides of the pass to investigate. However, as they scrabbled for a foothold on the scree more shots came, this time from the peaks on the opposite side of the pass. Two of the scouts flung up their arms and fell backwards. One crashed straight back down on to the stony floor of the pass, smashing his skull. The body of the other rolled down the scree until it hit a rock and lay still. My father shouted to the rest of the scouts to return before ordering the remainder of the vanguard to retreat round the bend in the pass and take cover. Then he told me to come back as quickly as I could to report to you.'

'How many attackers were there?'

'I don't know. But each volley sounded as if many

muskets were being used. At least twenty or thirty men or horses fell each time. At the distance the attackers were firing from I can hardly imagine that more than one in ten of their shots would hit. So that would make at least three hundred of them.'

'From what you've said I'd guess even more. Is the pass blocked?'

'I think so – just before I left a scout who had skidded down a scree slope shouted that from the height he'd reached he thought he could see a barricade of tree trunks, branches and rocks round another bend, but he may have been mistaken.'

'I don't think he was.' Aurangzeb paused to think, but not for long. With an unknown but substantial number of attackers and the way ahead probably blocked it seemed obvious that a withdrawal from the pass would be sensible. 'Return to your father,' he told the young man. 'Tell him to order a retreat.' Then the emperor turned to members of his bodyguard. 'Ride along the column commanding other units to turn back, but warn them to withdraw in good order without losing touch with those to their front and rear. We must not allow any part of the column to be cut off.'

• ◆ •

That evening, as campfires were blazing on an expanse of flat ground at the entrance to the pass, Aurangzeb stood in front of his scarlet command tent waiting for his generals to assemble for a council of war. The withdrawal had gone as well as could be expected although he had lost more men – perhaps over a hundred in all. Most had been picked off by musket shots from the heights, a few killed by lone attackers who had rushed wild-eyed and hurling defiance from their hiding places in the rocks into his troops, slashing and hewing with their *tulwars* – Afghan swords – trying to kill or wound as many men as they could before, as was inevitable, they were themselves killed.

As the last of the vanguard had been leaving the pass under the command of Yusuf Khan, three horses had come galloping down the defile towards them. Each had a body in Moghul green thrown across the saddle, the wrists roped to the ankles beneath the horses' bellies. When Yusuf Khan's soldiers had caught the frightened animals and cut the bodies free, they found they were those of their comrades whose horses had bolted during the first attack. They had been terribly mutilated. In one case the severed genitals had been inserted in the mouth. In the other two the eyes had been gouged, the nostrils slit and the ears and tongue cut out. There had been no message on any of the bodies but even so the meaning was clear – the Moghuls' writ did not run among these wild men of the mountains.

The generals were now approaching. In the lead was Raja Jaswant Singh, the ruler of Marwar, one of his orange-clad warriors preceding him holding a blazing brand. Aurangzeb could not help but recall another Rajput general – Ashok Singh of Amber – who some years ago during his campaign even farther north against Balkh and Samarkand had defied his orders to withdraw in similar circumstances to those of the afternoon. Instead he had sacrificed himself and many of his men in a frontal charge on the enemy because of some bizarre notion of honour.

Aurangzeb had restricted his impositions on the Hindu religion to the lands under direct Moghul rule as yet, leaving his vassal states, foremost among which were those

96

of Rajasthan, to carry on as before. Prudence had dictated such an approach, but it would only be temporary. When the time was ripe he would exert his authority over the mettlesome Rajputs – a people he had long distrusted. Their mercurial personalities were as difficult to fathom as their 'death or glory' tactics were to fit into military strategies, and that was to say nothing of their infidel religious beliefs which led them to sacrifice their women on their funeral pyres.

None of the Rajput rulers had made any formal protest to him about his treatment of their fellow religionists, but his spies had told him of their misgivings. As a consequence he had incorporated more Rajput soldiers and generals into his army for this northern expedition against his fellow Muslims than he would have usually done. His purpose was to keep their minds and bodies occupied and well away from where any Hindu risings might break out. He had long suspected the loyalty of Jaswant Singh in particular. He had changed sides too swiftly and smoothly in the civil war for Aurangzeb to trust him entirely, even if he had done nothing since to cause suspicion.

'Come into the tent, Jaswant Singh,' Aurangzeb said now. The Rajput bowed and entered, swiftly followed by the other generals, and when all were inside Aurangzeb turned and went in himself. 'Be seated,' he told them. 'We must decide how best we continue our advance. But first, have we sufficient sentries and pickets placed to ensure the safety of our camp tonight?'

Jaswant Singh answered. 'Of course, Majesty. We have trebled the usual number of sentries and in addition horse patrols are riding the perimeter.'

'Good. And what do you advise for the morrow?'

Jaswant Singh again responded. 'From my experience of these hill tribes – and it is considerable – they may well melt away during the night. However, if they do not, to attempt to force the pass would be foolish. We must outflank or bypass them. It shouldn't be difficult. I recall from a previous successful campaign of mine here that there are many other routes through these hills.'

Aurangzeb smiled. Jaswant Singh's advice was good. How proud the man was of his military expertise and experience. His self-satisfied views had given his emperor an idea – one which the Rajput ruler would not like but would keep him out of harm's way and distant from the empire's centre of power for some years. When the present campaign was won he would cite Jaswant Singh's self-proclaimed experience in these hills and mountains to tell him he was well suited to the new post to which he was appointing him – the governorship of this rebellious north-western province.

• ◆ •

Jaswant Singh lay sleepless in his tent near the Khyber Pass as the winter winds howled around it, shaking the canvas walls. Aurangzeb's armies had quickly cleared the northern passes of the Persian-backed rebels and bandits, thanks in no small measure to his Rajputs. He had been surprised and dismayed by his appointment as governor but had been unable to find any reason to question his emperor's fulsome praise of his experience, and assertion that he was the best man for the job.

That was many months ago now. Once left in command he had discovered like so many of his predecessors how difficult it was to maintain complete control over the hill tribes. The tribesmen raided his outlying fortresses and ambushed his supply columns, disappearing on each occasion before he could engage them in battle. Their muskets outranged his own men's and they scrambled up and down steep hillsides like mountain goats. What's more, they committed the most barbarous atrocities on captured Moghul troops to intimidate others from pursuit in anything but the largest groups. Only their propensity to fight among themselves on any pretext prevented them from overrunning the province completely. His Rajput troops in particular hated the mountains, the climate and the local people in equal measure. He himself, like many others from the plains, had fallen prey to bouts of coughing which were becoming ever more frequent and intense.

The tent shook again, buffeted by fresh gusts. Jaswant Singh shivered. He felt cold to his bones despite the sheepskins piled on him and the brazier of burning charcoals in the corner of the tent. Closing his eyes he tried to recall the warmth of the sun on his face, how his great sandstone fortress of Mehrangarh glowed red at sunset above the endlessly, infinitely beautiful Rajasthani desert. Would he ever see his homeland again? Somehow he doubted it. Climate and disease were closing in on him. What an end for a son of the people of sun, moon and fire, condemned to battle the lawless tribes of this chill, bare land for an emperor he had never loved and only served through expediency, who had left him here while he himself returned to Delhi. Perhaps this was his divine punishment for giving his allegiance to Aurangzeb while Shah Jahan still lived? The irony was he'd sensed the emperor had never fully trusted him – not that the emperor seemed to trust anyone, and in particular no one of his race or religion.

And if he died here in these cold, distant mountains

what would happen to Marwar? His only son Jagat Singh who had accompanied him north had been killed six months ago, thrown by his wounded horse into a deep ravine during an ambush. Many princes of his house would like his throne. Unless he acted there might be civil war, and if that happened what an opportunity it would give the Moghuls to annex his lands. Gripped by anxiety, he started coughing again, bringing up some frothy crimson blood which he quickly wiped from his lips with the damp cloth that was now never far from his side. He mustn't delay. 'Bring me pen and paper,' he called to his servant.

Propped up with the sheepskins pulled around him, Jaswant Singh began to write a letter to his chief minister with a hand that trembled slightly, setting out his wishes for the succession. Two of his wives were pregnant. If one should bear him a son that child must be the next raja. If both had sons, his heir must be the first born. If no sons were born, his great-nephew must succeed him. When he had completed the letter and pressed his great embossed seal into the hot wax he'd dripped on to the paper, Jaswant Singh lay back as outside the wind continued to shriek. At least he had secured the future of his kingdom if death came for him soon, as he expected it must.

Chapter 7

Coronation of a King

Aurangzeb looked around at his counsellors sitting cross-legged before him in the Hall of Private Audience in Delhi's Red Fort, his two middle sons among them. It was prudent to invite Azam and Akbar to these meetings of his advisers. Their presence allowed him to assess their abilities as well as to instruct them in the art of government in a way that his own father had failed to do for him. Soon he might appoint them to governorships as he had done with their elder brother Muazzam, now in Gujarat. But he had more urgent matters to consider. Yesterday a *cossid* had brought news of the death near Kabul of Jaswant Singh.

'You all know why I have summoned you. Jaswant Singh is dead. I cannot pretend too much grief at the passing of a man of questionable loyalty, so I will not waste time in false sentiment but turn instead to the future administration of Marwar.' Aurangzeb looked at his treasurer, the grey-haired Abdul Asif. 'Have Jaswant

Singh's officials yet paid his overdue annual tribute to our treasury?'

'No, Majesty.'

'Then you will send officials to Marwar to take over the administration of the state until they have recovered what is due.'

'As suzerain of Marwar, what will you do about the succession to the throne?' Azam asked.

'The *cossid* who brought the news of Jaswant Singh's death also brought a copy of his last will and testament. In it he has the temerity to state what the succession will be rather than, as his treaty of vassalship requires, making clear his wishes but leaving the final decision to me as his overlord. In doing so he has shown an arrogance typical of himself and his race. Jaswant Singh did, however, die in my service and I shall not be vindictive. Two of his widows have given birth to sons in Lahore after their return from Kabul in the autumn. I will summon them to Delhi so that I can decide what is just. Meanwhile I will take the opportunity of the temporary appointment of imperial officials to oversee the administration of Marwar to show the Rajputs that they are not immune to my measures to demonstrate the paramountcy of my rule in our empire. The officials selected to go to Marwar must be strict Muslims and strong characters, loyal and committed to their duties and their faith. They will publish *firmans* restricting Hindu festivals as has been done elsewhere in the empire. What's more, I will command them to choose one celebrated Hindu temple and destroy it. It will serve as a warning both to the Marwaris and to the over-proud inhabitants of the other Rajput states to pay me the respect that is my due, and which was so lacking in Jaswant Singh's behaviour while he lived and in his testament.'

Akbar spoke. 'But Father, the Marwaris will be uneasy enough about the arrival of Moghul officials. If you pull down even one of their holy places, won't it look like an act of aggression, or even war? These people are our allies. Why provoke them, especially at a time when they are still in mourning for their dead raja and we already have risings against us – not only Shivaji in the Deccan, but elsewhere in the empire? Shouldn't we consider further before taking such measures?'

'You always find reasons to delay, not act. Can't we ever take a decision, brother?' Far more than the popular, equable Akbar, Azam seemed to have inherited their long-dead Persian mother's bold temperament, Aurangzeb thought. Azam was right. Akbar needed to learn that decisive action was often the only way. But impatient, impetuous Azam also had something to learn – to curb his tongue before the council. Imperial princes should not bicker in public. Frowning, he raised a hand. Reading the rebuke in his father's eyes, Azam fell silent. Then Aurangzeb turned to Akbar who was looking offended by his brother's comments.

'Akbar, you pose what seem to you valid questions, but ask yourself this: are the Rajputs truly our allies? They are not of our faith and only acknowledge our overlordship because they benefit from our generosity. After his initial victories over them, my great-grandfather the Emperor Akbar was too liberal with them – as was your grandfather, who sought only the most perfunctory oaths of allegiance and then only when a new Rajput ruler came to the throne, all of which simply encouraged their arrogance and pride. The Rajputs are an impetuous, ill-disciplined people. Instead of praising and conciliating them, our ancestors should have enforced our supremacy. With the death of Jaswant Singh and their affairs in disarray, this is an excellent time to remind the Marwaris of my authority over them. If they defy me, we, not they, will benefit. I hope you understand that, Akbar?'

'I do, Father,' Akbar replied quietly.

• ◆ •

Aurangzeb walked quickly past the bubbling fountains of the central courtyard of the Delhi fort towards the sandalwood gates of the *haram*. The two female Turkish guards at the entrance pulled open the gates and the soft fragrance of the women's quarters – rosemary, patchouli and musk enveloped him. He turned not towards the sensuous pleasures of Udipuri Mahal's red-velvet hung apartments but to the more austere rooms his sister Jahanara used when she visited the *haram*. He had come as soon as her attendant had brought him her request. He would be happy to see her. Jahanara was proving as diligent in her duties as the First Lady of the Empire as he could wish. She received the wives of ambassadors and vassal rulers in great state, charming them with her words and wit, and answered many petitions for charity from widows of officials and others who had fallen on hard times. She oversaw the *khawajasara*'s administration of the *haram* efficiently, while at the same time soothing the jealousies and calming the intrigues inevitable among so many women living together. Having her own mansion to retreat to probably eased the latter task.

Jahanara was standing looking through the casement as he entered the room. Hearing his footsteps, she turned round, head held high. To his surprise she was frowning and there seemed no warmth either in her smile or in her dark eyes. Without any pretence at formality or greeting she spoke first. 'I've heard rumours that not content with your move against Marwar and your restrictions on the Hindu religion you intend to reimpose the *jizya* – the tax on infidels the Emperor Akbar repealed – on all your subjects who do not share our faith. I couldn't believe it. It would be madness.'

Taken aback by her vehemence, Aurangzeb hesitated. However misguided, Jahanara was saying what she truly believed. Unlike others around him – even other members of his family – she wasn't motivated by self-interest. He tried to keep his voice level and calm. 'Yes, I intend to reimpose the *jizya* as the tradition of our religion requires. You should not criticise me for reimposing it but my predecessors for abolishing it.'

'Aurangzeb, how could you? And how could you not tell me in advance?' Jahanara was almost shouting. 'You are repudiating everything our forebears strove for. By abolishing the tax, they sought unity and harmony among our people. You forget this isn't a Muslim country – as I've told you before the vast majority of your subjects are Hindus – but you behave as if it were, provoking division and rebellion. If our ancestors had acted like you our empire would never have survived. You must listen to me . . . it's my duty to be frank. Persist in this and you'll alienate too many of your loyal subjects and bring down their wrath on our heads. You'll conjure a tempest in which everything will be swept aside. Why can't you see it?' Jahanara paused, blazing eyes fixed on him.

'I repeat, the reimposition of the tax is no more than the

105

orthodox tradition of our religion demands of a ruler and I am an orthodox Muslim ruler.' Hard as he tried, Aurangzeb couldn't keep the exasperation from his voice as he continued, 'I'm sorry I didn't tell you first but I anticipated your reaction and didn't wish us to quarrel. I apologise sincerely for that, but you should realise these affairs do not concern you. As a woman you should accept my guidance in worldly matters just as I so often accept yours in those which concern our family.'

Jahanara stepped towards him. For a moment he thought she might be about to strike him, but instead she dropped to her knees in front of him, looking up at him imploringly. 'Please, please reconsider! For my sake and for the sake of the dynasty.' She was clutching his leg now. 'If you persist you'll destroy our empire.'

There was nothing more he could say. To continue the argument would only deepen the void opening between them. Either of them might say things they regretted – things about the past better left unsaid. Aurangzeb disengaged himself as gently as he could from his sister's grip turned and walked stiffly from the room.

'Aurangzeb! Wait . . .' Jahanara called, but he didn't even turn his head.

•◆•

Aurangzeb took off his imperial diadem in Delhi's Red Fort and wiped the sweat from his forehead with a cloth. Then he took the jewelled cup containing cool water-melon sherbet which his young *qorchi* had poured for him from a long-necked jug. He had just returned from announcing the formal reimposition of the *jizya*. To avoid any outbursts of anger from among the Hindus his officials had made sure that the front ranks of the crowd

106

beneath the *jharoka* balcony from which he had made the proclamation consisted of the *ulama* and Muslim members of his court. There had been plenty of soldiers drawn from Muslim regiments on hand and the announcement had gone off with only a few shouts of protest from the very back of the crowd. He hoped it would do the same elsewhere.

He took a deep drink of the sherbet. The air on the balcony had been hot, still and humid. Even the birds had seemed to prefer clustering on rooftops to flying. The monsoon couldn't be far off, bringing the cooling relief of the rains. Suddenly he felt his body shake and sherbet slopped from his cup. He wasn't ill, was he? Overcome by the heat or even the strain of the occasion? No. There was another stronger tremor – an earthquake, and quite a severe one too. The jug of sherbet fell from the low table where the *qorchi* had placed it, spilling its foaming pink contents across the blue and brown Persian carpet. At the same time two hanging oil lamps fell, their glass shattering. Aurangzeb clutched at a pillar to steady himself as an ivory-inlaid mirror crashed to the floor and splintered. Outside he heard a thud. Part of the intricately carved sandstone railing around the balcony had fallen. An altogether louder rending sound followed as a jagged crack appeared in the sandstone lintel of the door to the balcony and much of the balcony itself disappeared, crashing twenty feet to the ground. The shaking was stopping but there were still several more thuds as parts of roofs or crenellated sandstone battlements finally toppled and fell.

Letting go of the pillar and moving to a casement, Aurangzeb looked out. The sky was dark with wheeling, squawking birds shaken from their lethargy. A chunk of battlement had landed on a white marble fountain smashing it and water was gushing on to the marble courtyard. Red roof tiles lay shattered on the marble paving. In one corner of the courtyard a worker – a gardener, it looked like – was lying propped against a wall while one of his fellows was unwinding his white turban, presumably about to use it to bind the bleeding gash in the man's lower leg. He appeared to be the only casualty in the small part of the fort Aurangzeb could see, but what about the *haram*, and indeed Jahanara's mansion? Given their construction was similar to that of his own quarters they too should be relatively undamaged, but he must find out. He turned to the *qorchi*, whose hand was shaking as he bent to pick up the fallen ewer.

'Leave that for now. Go and check for me on any damage to the *haram* and Jahanara Begum's mansion.' Then he remembered there was sure to be damage to the humbler buildings clustering around the walls of the fort. 'And have the officers of my bodyguard go into the city to inspect what has happened there.'

An hour later, reassured that the damage to the *haram* and to Jahanara's mansion was slight – there had been some panic in the *haram* but the one serious injury had been to an attendant whose leg had been so badly crushed by falling masonry that the *hakims* were about to amputate – Aurangzeb received the report of the chief of his bodyguard.

'Majesty, there has been considerable damage. Part of the northern gateway to the city has collapsed. The keystone to its arch crushed a donkey cart and its driver as it fell. A gatekeeper was so badly injured by a blow to the head that he has not spoken since and is not expected to live. A ten foot section of the city wall close to the Jumna has fallen down, the top of one of the minarets of a nearby mosque has collapsed and the back wall of a Hindu temple has split. Many small mud-brick dwellings are nothing but rubble, with some of their inhabitants trapped beneath. Elsewhere wooden debris and straw from roofs have fallen on to cooking fires and started blazes, some of which are out of control.'

'Send soldiers to help with the fires and pulling people from the fallen buildings. If necessary have more buildings pulled down to isolate the fires. Order my treasurer to distribute monies to those most in need.'

'I will see to it, Majesty – but there is something else you should know. Some of the Hindu population shouted at our men that the earthquake resulted from the anger of the gods at your reimposition of the *jizya*.'

'That is arrant, irrational nonsense. Hindu and Muslim alike have been affected – so have their buildings. I might as well say it is a warning from God to those of my subjects who are unbelievers to turn to the true path for the sake of their souls as well as their purses.'

'Majesty, what you say is of course correct, but if I may be frank many of these are simple people strong in their Hindu beliefs. No arguments, however rational, are likely to sway them.'

Aurangzeb nodded. He had been right before God to reimpose the *jizya* whatever the consequences. He would have his troops ready to contain any risings whether in Delhi or anywhere else in his empire.

• ◆ •

The bells in the temple of the Raigarh fort woke Shivaji just before dawn. His stomach was rumbling – not surprising since he had spent the previous day in fasting and in prayer – but the time for feasting and celebration was coming. He had been planning this, his coronation day, for over four months, overseeing every detail, however small, himself and even studying ancient Hindu texts so that he could identify and revive Hindu coronation customs that had almost been forgotten under Moghul oppression. To show how well he understood the sacred nature of kingship he had very publicly undertaken a series of pilgrimages to important shrines and undergone complex purification rituals. As a result, Brahmin priests had conferred on him the right to wear the sacred thread. In gratitude for their support, he was now feeding and housing fifty thousand Brahmins from across Hindustan whom he had invited to witness his coronation as king of the Marathas.

Shivaji rose, and with the help of his waiting attendants washed his hair and body in water from the holy Ganges that had been blessed by the priests. Then he dressed in a robe of purest white. The attendants hung garlands of flowers round his neck before decking him in armlets, anklets and necklaces of pure gold. When he was alone again he lit some incense and knelt before the small shrine in the corner, bowing his head. As he began to pray he felt a light-headedness that he knew had nothing to do with hunger . . . it was mingled excitement and anticipation, but also a sense of unreality. He could scarcely believe this day had finally come.

He was still at his devotions when he heard someone enter and looking up through the swirls of rising incense saw the tall, lean figure and intense dark eyes of the Brahmin priest Gaga Bhat.

110

'Come, sire. It is time.'

It had been a good idea to summon this renowned scholar and sage from the holy city of Varanasi to Raigarh here in the Deccan hills to consecrate him as king. Gaga Bhat's presence gave a holy authority to his rule over his own Maratha people and would surely encourage all those of the Hindu faith to rally to him.

Shivaji followed the priest into the courtyard and across to the temple. Within its precinct a low golden stool was waiting near a stone statue of Nandi draped with marigolds. His wife Soyra Bai and eldest son Sambhaji were standing behind the coronation stool, and his priests and chief courtiers were grouped around the pillared precinct.

As soon as Shivaji had sat down, Gaga Bhat approached with a golden bowl. 'Shivaji, with this water from holy mother Ganges I hereby consecrate you king of the Marathas. May your reign be long and just, so that your people bless you and the gods look favourably upon you.' Then, dipping a golden spoon into the bowl, he flicked droplets of water over Shivaji's face and head three times. His chief ministers approached next, bearing golden jugs also filled with holy water with which they sprinkled the new king, while sixteen Brahmin women, each carrying a golden tray with five lighted oil lamps on it, circled around him chanting hymns to drive away evil spirits.

A weighing ceremony – an ancient Hindu coronation custom which he was reviving – followed. Four priests, struggling a little under the weight, entered the precinct carrying a giant set of scales.

'Come, Majesty.'

At Gaga Bhat's prompting, Shivaji rose – his now damp robes clinging to him – and walked to the scales, where he seated himself cross-legged in one of the saucers. A pity I am so light, he thought, almost tempted to smile despite the solemnity of the moment. The poor who will receive these gifts would benefit more if I were a fleshier man. As the ceremony began, more priests loaded gold bars – the first of the seven precious metals he'd learned had once been traditional on such occasions – into the other saucer and he felt a shudder as he himself began to rise. Next came silver coin then copper, zinc, tin, lead and finally iron, and after them sacks of nutmegs and cloves, then salt, camphor and fine linens and last of all foodstuffs – everything from yellow bananas and ripe mangoes oozing sweet juice to sugar, butter and pungent bright green betel leaves.

The ceremonies in the temple precinct at last complete, Shivaji returned with his wife and son to his apartments to exchange his white robe for one of crimson silk heavy with gold embroidery. Soyra Bai, herself magnificent in rich silks and jewels, took off his plain gold jewellery and replaced it with so many bracelets and rings set with glittering gems that barely any flesh on his hands and arms remained visible. 'There! Now you look truly like the great king you are,' she said. Round his neck she hung jewelled necklaces and on his head – she was nearly as tall as he was and had no need to stand on tiptoe – she placed a crimson turban shimmering with pearls. Then, with his wife and son following and behind them a bearer with his sword, shield, bow and arrows, Shivaji, to the sound of trumpets and drums, made his way to his new throne room and entered at the precise moment dictated by his astrologers. As he mounted the steps to the octagonal throne, behind which Gaga Bhat was standing, attendants showered the waiting guests – the most important of the thousands in the fort and surrounding villages who would be celebrating his coronation – with tiny gold and silver lotus flowers.

'Hail great king!' Gaga Bhat called as Shivaji seated himself beneath the scarlet royal umbrella that the Brahmin had just raised. It was time for him to speak for the first time as a monarch.

He lifted his hands for silence. 'My people, I come before you here at Raigarh as your king. It is a sacred role – one that confers upon me a sacred duty to care for and protect not only my own Maratha people but also all my Hindu brothers. But how can I fulfil my duty when a foreign invader casts a shadow over our lands, our lives and our spirits? The Moghul tyrant forbids us to celebrate our religion in the ways we would wish. He seeks to tax us simply because our faith is not his. To him we Marathas are vermin – rats, he calls us – but we will show him we are lions. I pledge to you present here – and to all those suffering his vile oppression – that I will drive the Moghul out. Haven't I already proved I can outwit him? He had me in his power but I slipped through his fingers like the fine earth of this land to which he has no right. With your help I will be victorious and restore peace and justice to Hindustan!' Shivaji rose, and gesturing to the attendant carrying his weapons to step closer he grabbed his sword and circled it above his head. 'Death to the Moghul Empire!' he shouted, and all around rose echoing cries. 'Death to the Moghul Empire!'

Suddenly Shivaji heard a cracking and booming – surely not cannon fire? Looking over the heads of his subjects through the open doors of the throne room to

113

the courtyard beyond, he saw that rain was beginning to fall. The sound had been thunder. The long-awaited monsoon, that blessed rain that nourished Hindustan and its people, had come on today of all days. It was a sign from the gods that he, Shivaji, would wash away the Moghul Empire as if it had never been.

Chapter 8

The Ranis

A kbar bent low over his horse's neck to present the smallest possible target to the muskets of the red-turbaned Marwari soldiers he could see running from the tents of the camp they had pitched around the summit of a low, rocky hillock amid the dusty plain. All around him his horsemen were doing the same. He'd attacked from the east so the Marwaris would have the rising sun in their eyes as the Moghuls swept down on them. They'd been foolish to act so rashly. They should have known his father well enough to realise defiance never went unpunished . . . retribution was only a matter of time.

When Aurangzeb ordered Jaswant Singh's two widows to bring their newborn sons to Delhi, the Marwaris had at first seemed to obey. The ranis had begun the journey – even nearly reached Panipat. But then a Marwari messenger had brought word to Aurangzeb that one of the ranis had fallen sick and needed to rest before conti-nuing. A week later, Moghul scouts had reported that the

Marwaris had struck camp under cover of darkness and were travelling quickly back to their own lands.

Aurangzeb had at once ordered Akbar and a detachment of five hundred horsemen to pursue and apprehend the fugitives. It had taken Akbar a little more time than he would have wished to assemble his force and the fugitives had almost reached the borders of Marwar before his advance scouts had finally sighted them and sent him word. By the time Akbar had caught up with the scouts, who been concealing themselves behind a ridge eight miles east of the Marwari position as they awaited his arrival, the ranis and their entourages had been camped for three days in the same place and for some reason showed no signs of preparing to move again. Perhaps now they were almost in Marwar they thought themselves safely beyond Aurangzeb's reach, or perhaps one of the ranis was indeed ill. Akbar had considered offering the Marwaris the chance to surrender the ranis and their babies – according to his scouts, the camp's defenders numbered only sixty or seventy – but he knew the Rajput warrior code well enough to know that they would never agree. A surprise attack was the best way to keep his own casualties to a minimum . . .

With red sand flying around him and the first Marwari tents now barely fifty yards ahead, Akbar had no time for further reflection. The air began to crackle with musket fire. To his left one of his officers tumbled from his saddle and rolled over several times before disappearing beneath the horses of the men following. Another rider swerved away grasping at the bleeding wound in his thigh. As he'd expected, the Marwaris, though few in number, intended to sell their lives dear in defence of their ranis.

As his mount easily leapt some barrels stacked between two baggage wagons, Akbar extended his sword ahead of him ready to strike at any attacker. The thudding of hooves told him his bodyguards were with him. 'Highness, look out on your left!' one of them shouted. Dragging hard on his reins, Akbar wheeled his horse as a Marwari crouching in the shelter of some rocks hurled a spear straight at him. Just in time, Akbar flung himself forward and the weapon flew over him to embed itself in the side of a wagon, long shaft quivering. The guard bent from his saddle and with a single stroke sent his attacker sprawling back on the rocks, blood welling from his throat.

All around him he heard the clash of steel on steel. The fighting was fierce. From the corner of his eye Akbar saw a Marwari musketeer rest the long steel barrel of his weapon on the side of a wagon and take careful aim at a young Moghul *qorchi* who had been knocked from his horse and was staggering about dazed. Kicking his horse on, Akbar rode past the boy, pushing him to the ground and out of harm's way as he did so. At the same time the musketeer fired and the ball grazed his own cheek. Breathing hard, Akbar looked around. The Marwaris were beginning to fall back, most towards two white tents in the middle of the camp on the summit of the hill. They were larger than the rest. That must be where the ranis were sheltering . . .

Urging his mount on again, Akbar joined his men as they pushed towards the tents. A squat, powerfully built Marwari leapt from behind a pile of saddlebags no more than six feet away. As the man pulled back his right hand Akbar caught the glint of metal, but before the Marwari had time to throw his dagger the sword of one of his bodyguards sliced the man's cheek open and exposed his white teeth. He fell backwards, his face running with scarlet blood. Akbar gasped with relief. Such were the fortunes of war – he would have had no time even to duck.

By now thirty or so Marwari soldiers – perhaps all that were left – had formed a ring around the two white tents, their weapons turned defiantly towards the Moghuls as if urging them on. They hadn't a chance and would soon be dead . . . unless they would listen to reason. Akbar didn't want to add to the number of killed and wounded he could so easily have joined himself at least three times in the last few minutes.

'Halt!' he called to his men. Dismounting, he took a couple of steps towards the tents and, ready to leap aside if any of them tried to attack him, shouted towards the Marwaris, 'Why sacrifice your lives? You've fought honourably but you can see you're completely outnumbered. I promise we intend no disrespect to your ranis. Surrender them to us and I guarantee that they will be escorted to the imperial court in Delhi where they will be treated with every honour due to the royal women of Marwar.'

Silence greeted his words. The Rajputs seemed to grip their weapons more tightly.

'Listen to me.' Akbar tried again. 'Haven't Moghul and Rajput fought side by side for centuries? Aren't we brothers? Doesn't your blood run in my own family's veins? But resist further and you give me no option but to destroy you.'

At that moment, the flap of one of the tents opened and a woman emerged carrying a small child wrapped in orange cloth. The embroidered edge of her saffron sari was pulled so low over her face that Akbar couldn't make out her features, but he could see heavy golden bangles around her slender wrists and ankles.

'Please . . . let there be an end to the fighting. There has been enough death and I do not want any more wives and mothers to have to mourn the loss of a dear one as I have had to mourn the death of my husband, Jaswant Singh. I can do what these brave soldiers who would give their lives to defend their ranis cannot. I surrender to you. I heard you speak of treating us with honour just now. I will hold you to your word. I surrender myself and my son Ajit Singh into your keeping and ask my soldiers to lay down their weapons.'

The Rajput soldiers exchanged glances and one called out, 'How can we surrender to these enemies of our faith and traditions?'

'I am Hadi, my late husband's senior rani. You will do as I bid you.' The woman's voice, though young, was firm and authoritative. Truly these were a warrior people, the women as well as the men, Akbar thought, looking at the slim upright figure trying to calm the newly woken child, who had begun to cry and thresh about.

'Lady, I promise to honour every word I spoke.'

The flap of the other white tent rose and a second woman, wearing a purple sari pulled down over her face and as richly jewelled as Hadi, stepped out. 'I heard my sister's words and your reply and am come like her to surrender to you. I am Rani Shilpa. My child is inside the tent with his nurse.' Her voice sounded older than Rani Hadi's and she was shorter, but her bearing was just as queenly.

Akbar spoke softly. 'Please return to the comfort of your

tents until I have assembled enough camels to carry you, your women and your children to Delhi.' As the ranis re-entered their tents he quickly ordered his men to disarm the remaining Marwaris and to check the camp thoroughly to ensure that no others lurked elsewhere. While his troops tended their Moghul wounded he would allow the Marwaris to do the same for their comrades, and afterwards to cremate their dead.

The funeral pyres were burning low and the sun was starting to sink in the west by the time Akbar was ready to depart, the women and children riding in giant panniers on either side of the camels which his men had purchased from a nearby village. The remaining Marwari soldiers, some heavily bandaged, were riding weaponless on their own fine horses while his Moghul horsemen surrounded the entire column, on the alert to ward off any attempt by the Marwaris to rescue their ranis. Akbar was satisfied. Not only had he acted as a man of honour should, but his father would be well pleased with him for apprehending the fugitives and bringing them to Delhi.

• ◆ •

Three weeks later, the walls and minarets of Delhi at last took shape on the hazy horizon. Though the journey had been tediously slow, thanks to the slow plod of the camels and the need not to exhaust the women, Akbar's spirits were as buoyant as when he'd started out. No Marwari war parties had pursued the column and the only dangerous moment had been when a tiger, startled from some scrub by a patrolling picket, had come into the camp late one evening. Akbar, sitting beneath the awning of his tent and reading by the light of a burning torch, had barely had time to glimpse its striped tawny body and its great eyes shining like lamps before it had vanished again into the darkness.

As the column of horsemen and heavily laden, groaning and spitting camels passed beneath the Lahore Gate and into the fort, Akbar felt a pleasurable anticipation. Though he'd sent messengers ahead with news of his success, he looked forward to telling his father about it himself. Critical as the emperor so often was of all his sons, not just himself, even Aurangzeb should have no reason to do other than praise him. Halting the column in an inner courtyard, Akbar jumped from his saddle and threw the reins to a groom. Then he called to a *qorchi*. 'Send for guards from the *haram* to lead these camels to the women's quarters so the ladies may dismount in fitting privacy. Then have them taken straight to my sister the Princess Zebunissa in the *haram*. I have already written asking her to have suitable apartments prepared. And treat them with the utmost respect. These ladies are ranis of Marwar.'

Satisfied that he had done everything necessary to ensure the ranis' comfort and stopping only to rinse the dust from his face and hands and drink some water, Akbar hurried to his father's apartments. The emperor was seated cross-legged in front of his low desk reading, and looked up as the *qorchi* announced Akbar.

'So your mission prospered?'

'Yes, Father, though it took longer than I'd hoped to overtake the Marwaris. I was fortunate that having almost reached their borders they halted and pitched camp for some days.'

'Yes, you mentioned that in your letter. That did seem a little odd. Now tell me everything, especially about the camp – how many soldiers the Marwaris had, how much

121

weaponry, how long it took to overcome them. Leave nothing out. You know how I value detail.'

Akbar related all that he could remember and then waited for his father's congratulations, but Aurangzeb sat deep in thought, his brows locked in a frown. 'How many Rajputs did you say were defending the camp?' he asked at last.

'About seventy. No more.'

'Did it strike you as strange that the Marwaris should provide their ranis – and the potential heirs to the throne of Marwar – with so little protection?'

'No. Few in number though they were, the Marwaris fought like demons . . . I lost thirty men. I've always thought one Rajput equal to five of any other soldiers.'

'They are indeed good fighters, although they mistake vainglorious gestures for good tactics. But that's not why I'm concerned.'

'Concerned? About what, Father?' Akbar stared, an uncomfortable feeling in his stomach. His unease grew when Aurangzeb ignored his question to ask one of his own.

'You also said that having almost reached their borders, the Marwaris had halted. How did you know that precisely?'

'From my advance scouts. While one returned to me with word they'd found them, the rest concealed themselves and kept watch. By the time I and the main body of my force arrived, my scouts had been observing them for three days.'

'Again, didn't you think that was odd, not to say obliging of them? Why hadn't the Marwaris hurried on with all speed to one of their fortresses? They must have known

122

I'd send troops after them. Why stay where they were vulnerable?'

'Perhaps one of the ranis or babies was ill and needed to rest. The heat in the desert was ferocious, and—'

'Where are the women now?' Aurangzeb interrupted.

'In the *haram*, in Zebunissa's care.'

'Well then, I shall pay them a visit. It would only be courteous. You may come as well.' Aurangzeb rose and walked swiftly from the room. Increasingly uneasy, Akbar hesitated a moment then hurried after his father. He reached Zebunissa's apartments in time to hear Aurangzeb say to his sister, 'Send for the women. I wish to see them at once.'

'They will be tired . . . they've had little time to settle themselves . . .'

'No matter,' Aurangzeb said brusquely. 'Do as I say please, Zebunissa.'

'If you insist. I will of course fetch them myself.'

It wasn't long before Zebunissa returned with the two ranis, each now wearing a sari of bright yellow – the colour of Marwar – and each with her head covered by the rich folds of gold-edged silk.

'Bare your faces, both of you,' Aurangzeb said without ceremony.

Akbar listened in dismay. These were royal women. He had promised they would be treated with respect. Where was his promise now?

The women stood motionless. 'I am the emperor. I order you to bare your faces or I will have it done for you.' Aurangzeb's voice was cold.

Rani Shilpa was the first to obey, raising a hennaed hand to push the edge of her sari back from her face though she kept her gaze on the ground.

'Look at me,' Aurangzeb ordered. Slowly she raised her face. She was about thirty, Akbar thought, and handsome enough, with a round face and full lips.

'Now you.' Aurangzeb turned to Rani Hadi, who pulled back her sari and without waiting for Aurangzeb's order looked full into his face. With her oval face and large, lustrous eyes she was as beautiful as Akbar had imagined. Unlike Shilpa she did not seem intimidated by Aurangzeb's cold-eyed scrutiny.

'Which of you is the senior rani?'

'I am,' Hadi answered at once.

'You look very young. How long were you married to Jaswant Singh?'

'Four years.'

'He received a bad flesh wound fighting in my service in the Deccan some time ago. Where on his body was it?'

For the first time Hadi looked unsure of herself.

'If you were intimate enough with Jaswant Singh to bear him a son, shouldn't you know? I repeat, where was his wound?'

'It was . . . it was on his chest,' Hadi said after a moment.

Aurangzeb turned to Shilpa. 'What do you say? Is she right?'

'Yes . . . yes . . . his chest.' Shilpa visibly gulped then glanced at Hadi, who was looking fixedly ahead. Though Hadi's face was calm Akbar could see how quickly she was breathing.

Aurangzeb went right up to Hadi and stared at her. She did not step back but proudly met his gaze. He went next to Shilpa and subjected her to the same scrutiny.

'You may have deceived my son but you do not convince me for one moment,' the emperor said at last.

'What do you mean? We are ranis of Marwar. Your son promised we would be well treated. Instead you have violated our right to keep our faces hidden and now you insult us further.'

'An excellent performance, but there's no point in keeping up this pretence. As far as I know the only wound Jaswant Singh had was in his thigh. Who are you really? Well-bribed performers from the bazaars of Marwar?'

Hadi's eyes blazed. 'We are not ranis, it is true, but we are Marwari noblewomen deserving of respect.'

'If you wish me to treat you as such, tell me what happened. Defy me further and the consequences will be severe.'

'We are ladies-in-waiting to the two ranis. Out of love for our mistresses, when our scouts reported your son's troops were just a few days behind and gaining fast we agreed to impersonate them. While we made camp and waited for your troops to catch up with us, the true ranis, their sons and the bulk of our forces were riding deep into the Marwari hills, beyond your reach. We have acted with honour. Kill us if you must, but spare the babies, who are our own sons and so young you cannot blame them for their role in the deception.'

As she finished speaking, Akbar glanced at his father's face. As so often he found it hard to guess what he was thinking but at last Aurangzeb said, 'Very well, I believe you. Zebunissa, have these women confined to their apartments and well guarded while I decide what to do with them. Akbar, come with me.'

As he followed his father back to his apartments, Akbar's spirits fell further. What a fool he'd been to be so taken in by those women. If only he'd questioned them at the time he might have discovered the truth and just been able to catch up with the real ranis and their children. Alone with his father, he waited for the criticism to fall on him but to his surprise, though pensive, Aurangzeb did not look angry. Pouring two cups of pomegranate juice, he handed one to Akbar and gestured to him to sit.

'I hope this will be a lesson to you,' he said, in so mild a tone that Akbar was surprised. 'Though you thought you had fulfilled your orders, in fact you had not. Why? Because you failed to put yourself into the mind of your enemy, which is the first rule of warfare. Instead you naively believed what you wanted to believe, saw what you wanted to see, and so the Marwaris tricked you as easily as a nurse tricks a child by pretending to hide a sweetmeat in one hand when all the time it is in the other. You are a grown man. It is time you learned to think more deeply . . .'

Akbar listened dutifully as his father continued to lecture – contrasting his son's behaviour unfavourably with his own at the same age, driving the message home with example after example of his own shrewdness and foresight. Slowly resentment began to overtake relief in Akbar's mind. His father was right – he should have shown more common sense, but Aurangzeb didn't need to talk to him as if he was some young *qorchi* who had never tasted battle. At the same time he began to realise how distasteful the mission of pursuing women and children had been to him, and how glad he had been when the supposed Rani Hadi had surrendered to him to save more bloodshed. Probably his relief had blinded him to the possibility of a trick.

'. . . so what would you do now, Akbar, if you were I?'

'Send a force to capture the real ranis and bring them here to Delhi?'

'That's a lazy answer. You've neither given yourself time to think nor listened to what I've been saying. I told you always to try to work out what others might be thinking, and that applies as much to your family as to your foes. Knowing me as you do, you should have asked yourself whether I would really do something so obvious. You should have considered what other options there might be and which one would be most likely to appeal to me.'

'But why aren't you going to pursue the ranis?' Akbar was nonplussed.

'Think for once! It won't be long before the two ranis quarrel and with their respective factions rip Marwar apart as each tries to thrust her own child on to the throne. In so doing they will weaken Marwar further and destroy its ability to resist us.'

'But in that case why did you send me to arrest the ranis in the first place?'

'For two reasons. First, if I'd taken no action I would have looked weak. Second, I wished to provoke the Marwaris into spilling Moghul blood. I was secretly delighted when the ranis decided to defy me and return to Marwar. I even provoked their flight – sending agents into their camp to spread rumours that I intended to imprison the ranis when they got to Delhi and have their offspring murdered. And the stratagem has worked even better than I'd hoped. By killing some of your troops and then deceiving you the Marwaris have given me all the justification I need to invade their lands. We have indulged these proud Rajputs too long, according

127

them a status and prestige they don't deserve. I intend to teach them humility and obedience and to make their lands a full part of our empire. You, my son, will be the agent of my victory. You will return to Marwar, this time at the head of a large invading Moghul army, and you will conquer it.'

Akbar said nothing. For the moment, misgivings about his father's scheming against the Marwaris faded in the joy of being given his first major command.

Chapter 9

Kingdom of Ghosts

The heat was so intense that, shaded though he was by the leather canopy of his war howdah, Akbar's head was aching. The monotonous orange desert, unrelieved by a green leaf or a single bright flower, held no charms for him. Two weeks had passed since he had led his 20,000-strong army into Marwar – two weeks during which not a Moghul musket had been fired or sword unsheathed. Instead he seemed to have entered a land of ghosts – every village, every mud fort was deserted, every well filled with stones. The only living things had been pariah dogs and a few peacocks fluttering shrieking in alarm into the branches of the low dusty trees.

But soon he and his troops would reach Marwar's great fortress of Mehrangarh, for centuries the pride of its rulers, to which he was certain the main Marwari forces had withdrawn. Four days ago he had sent messengers demanding its surrender, but its defenders had sent them away empty-handed. What were the Marwaris planning?

To fight him beneath the fortress walls or to force him into a siege? Probably the latter – it could take months to dislodge them . . .

An hour later Akbar's war elephant – swaying so much as its feet sought a purchase in the deep soft sand that Akbar had to cling to the howdah's gilded sides – crested some high dunes and there in the distance was Mehrangarh. In the shimmering haze he found it hard to tell where the cliff ended and its steep grey walls began. As he stared at it, a sweating scout rode up, horse blowing hard. 'Highness, a small group of riders – about six – are heading across the plain from Mehrangarh towards us. They've almost reached the foot of the dunes but you can't see them from here. Should we intercept them?'

'I want to take a look at them for myself. Fetch me a horse.' A few minutes later, mounted on a bay horse and accompanied by two bodyguards, Akbar followed the scout down through the dunes until they reached a projecting tongue of rock from which three more scouts were peering. Dismounting quickly, he joined them. 'Look, Highness, down there!' said one.

Akbar followed his pointing finger. Yes, almost immediately below them the riders were just beginning to climb into the dunes. They must know his army was on the other side . . . the cloud of dust would have been visible for miles. So what did they want? He studied them carefully. Their clothes were pale orange, almost the same colour as the sand. They were obviously too few to fight, and since they were making no effort to conceal themselves they were hardly likely to be spies. They must have come to negotiate. 'They're Marwaris, I'm sure.' Akbar turned to the scouts. 'My guess is that they wish to talk.

130

But watch them and send word at once if you see anything suspicious. It's possible they've been sent to distract us while their main force attacks, but I hardly think so – from this vantage point we'd see their troops before they got anywhere near us.'

Returning to the column, headache forgotten, Akbar sent a detachment of troops to meet the riders, disarm them and bring them to him. Then, remounting his elephant, he waited impatiently in the sweltering heat. Half an hour later his men returned with the Marwaris, whose magnificent black horses were foamy with the effort of climbing the dunes. Akbar didn't need the daggers, swords and spears that his men had taken from them and were now spreading out on the sand to tell him these men were warriors. Their bearing was enough. 'I am Akbar, son of the Emperor Aurangzeb. Tell me who you are and what your purpose is.'

The riders exchanged glances. Then one more richly dressed than the others, with a heavy gold chain round his neck and plugs of gold in his ears, spoke. 'We are envoys of Marwar. We bring an answer to your demand that we surrender our fortress.' Reaching into a silk bag tied to the pommel of his saddle he extracted a folded paper which, at a gesture from Akbar, he handed to a *qorchi*.

Akbar took the letter and studied the elaborate wax seal: a Rajput warrior on a rearing horse – then broke it open. He'd expected words of defiance, insult even, but the message, written in excellent Persian, read simply, *You demand our fortress. Take it if you wish. It is yours.* It was signed *Durgadas Rathor, Regent of Marwar.* The Marwari nobles had chosen the true Rani Hadi's son as their raja and appointed Durgadas as regent until the

131

boy was of age. No one could speak with more authority for Marwar.

'You know the contents of this letter?' The riders nodded. 'And this is all you have for me? No other message?'

The man with the gold earrings said, 'There is nothing else.'

'Very well. Tell Durgadas that I accept the surrender of the fort as I hope soon to accept the surrender of Marwar's forces so that together, to the benefit of all, we can return peace and tranquillity to these lands. My men will escort you back to the plains, where your weapons will be restored to you and you may depart without hindrance.'

As the Marwaris rode off, his father's words returned to him: *put yourself into the mind of your enemy*. Why had the Marwaris handed over their principal fort without any conditions? Did it mean the war was over before it had begun? He wouldn't be foolish enough to take the apparent yielding of Mehrangarh at face value. While he and most of his men remained here, he would order a strong vanguard with plenty of musketmen to cross the plain and if they met no resistance to advance into the stronghold itself and search it thoroughly.

He watched from a vantage point in the dunes as an hour later the first of his vanguard reached the base of the cliff and began a cautious ascent of the steep, winding path leading to the fortress four hundred feet above them. He braced himself for the flash of a cannon or the crack of a musket from the battlements, but before long ten burning torches – the agreed signal that his men had secured the fort – shone from the ramparts.

Dusk was approaching and the air was mercifully cooler

by the time Akbar, still mounted on his war elephant, approached the fortress's two-storey gatehouse. Carved into the stone lintel he noticed the same Rajput rider on his mettlesome horse as on Durgadas's seal. The stonework looked ancient. How many centuries had the Marwaris been masters of this place? Far longer than the Moghuls had been the masters of Hindustan . . .

Passing beneath a second gateway, Akbar saw to his left a whitewashed wall on which was a row of small red palmprints. He knew what they were – marks left by royal widows on their way to die in the flames of their husbands' funeral pyres. *Sati*, it was called. Would that have been Hadi's and Shilpa's fate on Jaswant Singh's death had they not been pregnant? As a boy, one of his favourite stories had been how his namesake the Emperor Akbar, learning that a widow was to be burned at Fatehpur, had ridden to save her.

No one was to be seen in the shadowy stone-paved courtyards or on the narrow, ornately carved balconies jutting above his head as Akbar rode into the heart of the sandstone fortress, noting its thick concentric walls, the sharp angles designed to frustrate an attacking force and the spikes on the gates placed to prevent elephants from crashing through them. Passing through yet another gate he entered a large open area around which were grouped some elegant pavilions – presumably the royal living quarters.

Installed in what had once been Jaswant Singh's apartments, Akbar tried to relax. Mehrangarh was his but he couldn't shake off the feeling that somehow the Marwaris were tricking him again and that, as before, he was blind to their schemes. He had worried about being forced to

133

undertake a long siege of Mehrangarh. Maybe what he should worry about now was being besieged himself. But that couldn't happen. Only five thousand of his troops were billeted in the fort. The remainder were encamped around the base of the cliff. Looking through the casement he could see the red lights of myriad cooking fires pricking the darkness. He'd ordered the watch to be trebled and thrown a curtain of pickets all round the base of the cliff. No, the Marwaris could not take him unawares here.

So what did they mean to do? Tomorrow he would send out more scouts; there might be someone in the jumble of mud-brick buildings below the cliff who could tell him something. Then he remembered the few elderly attendants who, because of their frailty, had chosen to remain in the fort. Maybe one could give him a clue about the whereabouts of the Marwari armies. Going to the door, he called to a *qorchi*. 'I was told that several Marwari servants have stayed here. Bring them to me.'

When the *qorchi* returned, he was shepherding three old men, their wrinkled faces anxious. 'Don't be afraid,' Akbar said quickly. 'Tell me who you are.'

The one who looked the oldest answered. His back was so curved that he stood barely four foot tall. He was leaning heavily on an ivory-headed stick and his head jutted forward like an old tortoise's. 'We were retainers of Jaswant Singh until our infirmities made it impossible to serve him any longer. He allowed us to live on in the fort and receive food and a pension.'

'I am also a generous man, as you will find if you answer my questions.'

At Akbar's words, the tortoise-headed man glanced at his companions – a tall skinny man whose head was dwarfed by his loosely tied red turban and one whose filmy eyes seemed unable to focus. 'I was once my late master's steward. I will answer you if I can.'

'All I want to know is this. Where are the Marwari armies?' Even as he asked the question Akbar wondered why he was bothering. Why should the old man tell him anything that might injure his own people, even if he did know?

But to Akbar's surprise the old man grinned, showing more gum than teeth. 'So you want to know where our soldiers have gone. You'll find out soon enough, so where's the harm in my telling you? They've gone into the Aravalli hills – all the troops and their families, taking all the royal treasure . . . you've occupied an empty fort, but you haven't taken Marwar.' The old man's smile turned into a chuckle.

When he was alone again, Akbar sat deep in thought. Not even his father had foreseen this. Contrary to Aurangzeb's assertion about Rajput foolhardiness and futile courage, the Marwaris had no intention of sacrificing themselves in battle unless they had to. How could he truly defeat an invisible enemy? He could already imagine his father's critical face . . . hear him disparaging his failure. He must take the fight to the Marwaris in their hills.

• ◆ •

The sun was beating down from a cloudless sky and sweat was running into Akbar's eyes as the wheezing snorts of the foul-breathed camels of the baggage train at the rear of his two-mile long column slowly faded from his ears. He had ridden back to check that the baggage train was keeping up with the rest of the column, and had been glad to find that only a few stragglers and sick animals were falling behind into the desert, where the circling vultures would soon be feasting on the animals and in all probability some of the men also.

Suddenly he heard three trumpet blasts – the alarm signal he had agreed with his commanders. They came from his vanguard, hidden from his view behind some outcrops of the Aravalli hills. Kicking his horse forward and shouting to his bodyguard to keep close order, he galloped along the column. With the bay's hoofs pounding on the stony ground he rounded one of the outcrops to see ahead of him a squadron of saffron-clad horsemen emerging from the heat haze, sun flashing on their drawn swords, about to smash into his leading troops.

Moments later, the Moghul vanguard, which had been travelling at little more than walking pace, reeled backwards under the weight of the Marwaris' charge. A number of Moghul horses reared back on their hind legs. Others, struck in their flanks, collapsed, either throwing their riders or pinioning them to the ground. Three Marwaris surrounded a Moghul standard-bearer. He unhorsed one with a slashing sword stroke but in doing so he had to drop the reins and so lost control of his mount. As the animal skittered sideways, another of the Marwaris thrust his sword into the flag-bearer's neck. The man fell from the saddle but his left foot caught in the stirrup, and as his frightened horse galloped away it dragged his body behind it, the head bumping along the ground. One of the Marwaris dropped briefly from his saddle to pick up the fallen Moghul standard and rode off with it, yelling in triumph.

Elsewhere, a regiment of Moghul musketeers who had been marching behind the leading horsemen had had little time when the alarm was sounded to load their weapons, never mind to steady them on the tripods they carried strapped to their backs or to take careful aim. Some of the speedier amongst them got shots off, knocking two or three Marwaris from their saddles before the Marwari horsemen encircled them, scything them down like harvest corn.

All this time – perhaps no more than five minutes – Akbar was pushing his sweating horse towards the fighting, urging it on with hands and heels, head bent close to the animal's neck. Then, with shouts and the noise of battle all around him and his blood pounding in his ears, he was crashing into the melee, his green-clad bodyguard beside him. He slashed at a heavily moustached Rajput rider, opening a bloody gash in his thigh, but was thrown back in his saddle as a Rajput lance dented his breastplate. Made of the best steel, it held. Akbar cut again as another Rajput rode at him swinging his long straight sword. Akbar's own hasty stroke missed but it was close enough to make the Rajput swerve away before he could get a blow in. The man wheeled his horse and charged at Akbar again, sword now extended in front of him like a lance. Before he could reach him the sharp blade of one of Akbar's body-guards sliced into his neck with such force that his head spun from his body while his orange-clad torso remained upright for some moments before it fell. Akbar noticed that another Marwari horseman was losing control of his mount, and as it bolted across his path he grabbed at the rider's flowing saffron robe. Succeeding in grasping a handful, he held on and jerked hard. The Marwari fell backwards from his saddle beneath the hooves of Akbar's mount, which reared up in terror. Clinging to the bay's neck, Akbar stayed in the saddle but took a little time to calm the frightened beast, which by now was bucking violently.

When the horse was quieter, he looked around for another target only to see that the Marwaris were breaking off the action and galloping away less than an hour after the attack had begun. A few were stopping to take up a wounded or unseated comrade. As one held on to his reins with his left hand while he tried to scoop up one of his fellows with the right, a ball from a surviving Moghul musketeer hit him in the back. He flung up his arms and fell from his horse on to the comrade he'd intended to rescue, heels drumming the sandy earth in his death agony.

No one could doubt the selfless bravery of the individual Rajputs, Akbar thought as he looked around him, eager to gather his men to pursue his fast disappearing enemies. However, there was so much confusion, so many men and horses wounded, that it was over an hour before he had assembled enough well-mounted troops to start. Another hour later and he was well into the undulating sandy hills, only to find the tracks of the Marwari horsemen diverging. They seemed to be splitting into smaller groups.

'Should we ride after the largest band?' Akbar asked the chief of his bodyguard.

'I advise against it, Highness. They may be trying to lure us even deeper into the hills where they can reunite and ambush us again. Besides, the sun is dropping. It will not be long until it is dark.'

Akbar nodded. The man was right. Better return to the main column and send out scouts in the morning to try to locate the Marwari bands. He could imagine his father's reaction when he reported his losses, but better suffer that than lose more men and perhaps his own life by being caught in a nocturnal ambush.

• ◆ •

'Majesty, a *cossid* has just arrived with a despatch from your son Akbar.' Aurangzeb's young *qorchi* bowed. With a sigh the emperor put aside the returns from his tax collectors in his eastern provinces. They had not made happy reading. As elsewhere in his dominions, revenues were lower than they ought to be. He feared rampant corruption was to blame. His governors and their officials seemed to believe that he was preoccupied with rebellions and foreign incursions and they were far enough from his eye to be able to take bribes or to turn some of the monies they gathered into their own purses without being detected. When he sent inspectors from his Delhi treasury to investigate they usually reassured him all was well, but most men were venal and true loyalty a scarce commodity and they too were probably bribed. The only solution would be to make an imperial progress himself to probe and question and perhaps to persuade some junior official to reveal his seniors' wrongdoing either for reward or to lessen his own punishment.

But he could not be everywhere. He had come here to Ajmer to be close to Rajasthan and Akbar's operations against Marwar. While there had been no disasters, the campaign was not going as well as he would have wished. That said, he had heard nothing from his son for some time so perhaps the *cossid*'s report would contain better news. 'I will read the despatch at once,' he told the *qorchi*.

'I have it here, Majesty.' As he spoke the young man took a sealed paper from the battered leather pouch he was holding. Aurangzeb took it and quickly broke the seal. Ignoring the formal personal salutations with which it began, in order to get to the meat of the message he started to read. The further he got, the greater the furrow in his forehead.

Akbar's campaign was going nowhere. His letter began by relating the Marwaris' fighting methods. They struck without warning, now here, now there, almost always in relatively small bands but large enough to kill or wound numbers of his troops before they disappeared again. Their attacks often took place at dusk to allow them to escape pursuit more easily. Moghul soldiers weren't used to fighting an enemy that behaved like bandits rather than a proper army. He couldn't tempt the Marwaris out from the hills on to the plain to face him in a pitched battle where his greater numbers and superior equipment, in particular his artillery, could be brought to bear. His men were increasingly reluctant to pursue the Marwaris into the hills, wary of fighting in such terrain for fear of ambush, a fear in part justified by experience. They were growing ever more cautious, clustering together in close order. His scouts and patrols were falling back on the main column at the first hint of danger, so he couldn't get sufficient intelligence to close with the enemy. When he seized a fort he usually found it deserted. His men were increasingly unwilling to be left to garrison such places for fear of a Rajput attack. Akbar summed up his predicament: *Our army's superior numbers and equipment are nullified by the Rajputs' tactics and their greater knowledge of their homeland's terrain. I must confess – and as I do so apologise – that I am far from securing the victory I would wish to win for you.*

Aurangzeb paced his scarlet command tent for almost an hour, turning over and over his options for action.

Not only the rebellions elsewhere – Shivaji, who'd had the gall to proclaim himself king of the Marathas, was still marauding through the Deccan from his mountain fastnesses – but also the need to overhaul his administration and bring corrupt officials to justice meant that he must end Marwari resistance quickly. Was Akbar capable of doing that on his behalf? He wasn't sure. His son was by all accounts a competent enough general, not given to rashness as Azam could sometimes be. He was unlikely to hand his father a disaster but was he any more likely to bring him a decisive victory? Was he showing himself weak? How committed or dedicated was he? He had written of his wish to win victory for his father's sake but he should want it for himself and his future. From the reports he had received, his son preferred to consult extensively with his officers, weighing their opinions and debating with them before deciding what to do. Such a desire for consensus made him popular, but efficiency and decisiveness were more important in a commander than popularity.

After much thought Aurangzeb called to his *qorchi* for pen and paper and began to write to Akbar. His first words were of admonition.

You shame yourself and me by admitting your men are reluctant to follow you. A Moghul prince should not allow his men to influence, never mind dictate, how and when they will fight. A leader must lead and you seem reluctant to do so. The Marwaris' tactics are not new as you seem to believe but akin to those both of Shivaji and of the tribesmen on our north-west frontiers. Didn't I myself successfully lead our men into the hills and passes beyond Peshawar to suppress the vermin preying on our Kabul merchants by dint of determination and the severe punishment of captured rebels?

I believe you have not shown yourself strong enough in spirit to command this main attack on the Marwaris. Instead, Muazzam will leave the governorship of Gujarat to take over the command of your army. However, I intend to give you an immediate opportunity to redeem yourself and prove my reservations groundless. Reports are reaching me that the Mewaris are rising to make common cause with their cousins and co-religionists in Marwar. I am assembling two armies to enter Mewar and crush them – one to advance from the east, the other from the south. You will return here to take up the command of the southern army. Your brother Azam will lead that advancing from the east. I myself will oversee the whole campaign. I pray God that in your new command you will not disappoint me further.

Glad that he had made and communicated his decision, Aurangzeb quickly closed his letter, not with any formal or personal farewell but simply with his signature, followed by the words *Emperor of Hindustan by the grace of God.*

Chapter 10

'Beware Aurangzeb'

S hivaji watched the orange flames still rising into the star-filled evening sky from the small Moghul fort on a promontory overlooking swampy ground where a tributary of the Tapti river joined the main channel. When he and his men had appeared from the hills two days before, the Moghul garrison had succeeded in closing the heavy gates in the fort's double brick walls before the vanguard – commanded by his son Sambhaji – could charge through them. However, they had thereafter offered little resistance, keeping up only a most desultory fire over the next forty-eight hours on his own forces whom, reluctant to waste lives by a frontal attack, he'd ordered to test the defenders' resolve by siege. The Moghuls had been only too pleased to accept the offer he had made today, under flag of truce, to permit them to go free if they surrendered the fort and their arms. He had been careful to keep his word and to prevent his men from molesting or even taunting the surrendering soldiers – better they told their comrades of his leniency if they returned to Moghul service, which he suspected not all would. Their stories would encourage other Moghul troops to question the need to resist his attacks too vigorously.

The burning of the fort and of those supplies and weapons he did not need would soon be complete and it would be time to supervise the distribution of booty to his troops. Then, with his son Sambhaji beside him, he would preside over a victory feast. He usually looked forward to such occasions but today he did not feel well. His head was aching and his many mosquito bites – the insects were everywhere in this marsh – were itching and suppurating. Although the evening was growing chill and he could see some of his troops pulling blankets around their shoulders, he felt hot, and touching his brow he found it running with sweat. Also, following the excitement of the surrender, his heart had not resumed its usual steady rhythm but was beating quick and shallow in his chest. He fancied he could almost hear its hectic pounding.

No matter. He would soon feel better. Turning, he ducked inside his tent to prepare himself for the victory ceremonies ahead. It seemed a little cooler inside. That was good. His attendant had left a pottery bowl of water on a stand. He picked up the cotton cloth placed next to it and was bending to dip it into the water, ready to wipe the perspiration from his face, when suddenly the bowl seemed to rise to meet him, spinning as it did so. Blood pounded in his head and, losing consciousness, he fell forward on to the bowl, which toppled from the stand and broke just as he too hit the ground.

When Shivaji opened his eyes again, he saw Sambhaji, his

hakim and several of his attendants looking down on him. 'What happened?' he asked.

'You collapsed and lost consciousness for about three hours,' the *hakim* replied. 'One of your attendants found you, put you to bed and then called me.'

Shivaji tried to sit up but the effort was too much and he sank back. The thin cotton sheet over him felt wet. So did his garments. Had they tipped water over him to revive him? He touched his face. It was beaded with sweat but at the same time he was shivering. He must have a bad fever. With difficulty he focused his eyes again on those looking down on him. Their concern was obvious. 'How ill am I?' he asked, his breath coming in shallow gasps. 'Tell me the truth . . . I must know . . . am I about to die?'

'I . . . I don't know, sire. But you are, I think, very ill . . .'

Shivaji closed his eyes, willing his body to regain its strength. He still had so much to achieve. But he could feel his fingers and toes beginning to lose sensation. Was this how death felt when it came to claim a man? Somehow he'd always imagined his end would come on the battle-field . . . an honourable warrior's death, not an end like this, shuddering with swamp fever . . .

Opening his eyes again, he gestured to his son to lean closer. 'I may not have long, Sambhaji. Listen carefully. I have taken great strides in my journey to free our people and our religion from Moghul oppression . . . but there is much, much further to travel and I fear I must leave you to complete the journey alone. The road will not be straight, but promise me, my son, that you will renounce all distractions to travel it as quickly as you can, gathering

145

the people of Hindustan behind you as you go.' Breathing was growing ever more difficult. 'Together you will form an irresistible tide, washing away the Moghul menace. Remember everything I taught you . . . avoid pitched battles . . . hit hard and hit quickly, now here, now there, be as elusive as a shadow and their great lumbering armies will never catch you . . . and always beware Aurangzeb . . .' The light faded from Shivaji's eyes. His body gave a convulsive twitch as his great soul left it, and he lay still for ever.

Sambhaji bent and kissed his father's damp forehead. 'I will remember.'

•◆•

As was usual with him when battle was imminent, Aurangzeb sat calmly in the gilded howdah on the back of his trusted war elephant. Two *mahouts* sat one behind the other on the animal's neck and behind the emperor in the howdah were his bearer with his muskets and a green-turbaned guard. Around the elephant was a squadron of his mounted bodyguard, all experienced men and devout Muslims. The attention of every one of them – like his own – was on Muazzam's army forming up in front of them, ready to attack a Marwari fort in the Aravalli hills.

Under Aurangzeb's guidance Muazzam had applied torture to one of his captured prisoners – something Akbar had scrupled to do. The hot iron had dragged from the young Marwari scout the information that the Marwaris were intending to congregate at this fort prior to launching another attack on his own troops. Again on his father's advice, Muazzam had not moved to attack at once but first sent his own scouts to alert him when the Marwaris'

146

assembly seemed to be nearing completion. Then he had marched his troops quickly to their attack positions.

Aurangzeb had been pleased that Muazzam had been prepared to act decisively but also with due prudence – unlike Azam, who had advanced quickly west into Mewar where his impatient and impulsive tactics had led to reverses and heavy casualties. Aurangzeb had despatched his son to Bengal as governor and replaced him with a trusted Uzbek. Akbar's advance into Mewar from the south had been slower but – somewhat to his father's surprise after his failure in Marwar – relatively successful in capturing and holding territory.

But now all Aurangzeb's attention was on Muazzam, who from the howdah of his command elephant had just started to wave the green flag which was the signal to fire for the few cannon he had been able to get through the hills quickly enough to take part in the action. They had been mainly manhandled across the broken country by their Turkish gunners. Any damage they did to the fort's walls would be welcome, but the smoke from their firing would be even more useful to provide cover for his advancing foot soldiers. Some had muskets to pick off any Marwari who showed his head over the fort's parapet. Others, in groups of four, were to carry storming ladders and yet others pots of powder to be placed against the gates and ignited to bring them down. So important had he and Muazzam thought smoke was to protect the attackers that they had also ordered as much as possible of the sparse brushwood in the area to be cut and piled into bonfires to augment the smoke from the artillery.

The cannon began to fire and orange flames appeared in the brush bonfires. Before the smoke did its work of concealment Aurangzeb saw that cannonballs had already knocked several stones from the wall by the gates. Soon the musketeers began to march into the thickening smoke, quickly followed by the ladder-carriers and the foot soldiers who would climb them. The men carrying the pots of gunpowder, one on either side of a yoke across their shoulders, were still waiting to be ordered forward.

Soon Aurangzeb heard the crackle of musketry as orange-turbaned Marwaris poked musket barrels through loopholes on the battlements and the Moghul musketeers returned fire. A Marwari fell head first, arms and legs whirling. The top of a ladder appeared against the fort walls above the smoke. Soon a Moghul foot soldier could be seen on it, about to climb on to the battlements. Two Marwaris rushed towards him and pushed both him and the ladder away from the wall to collapse back into the smoke and fighting below. The same process was repeated two or three times before a Moghul soldier managed to scramble on to the battlements. He was helping up a comrade when a Marwari knocked him from the walls with a sword stroke and despatched his fellow too before himself falling, hit by a musket ball.

The drifting smoke was clearing. The amount of brush the troops had been able to gather had not been great, and since the cannon could scarcely fire without hitting their own men there was no smoke from them either. As the smoke thinned, Aurangzeb saw bodies lying around the base of the fort walls. Some Moghul musketeers were sheltering behind a pile of them as they fired up at the battlements. Then several flashes came in quick succession, followed almost instantly by a deafening series of bangs from near the fort's gates where the cannon had already knocked away some of the masonry. The powder-carriers had done their work. The explosions flung bodies as well as stones and pieces of wood high into the air. As the smoke dispersed one gate could be seen partly shattered and hanging from only a single hinge. The wall beside it was also breached.

Moghul foot soldiers were now scrambling over the rubble, trying to force entry to the fort. The Marwaris were still fighting hard. Several of the Moghul solders fell, some hit by musketeers on the battlements, others spitted by long lances wielded by Marwaris who had rushed to the crumbling wall. Muazzam was waving some Moghul horsemen forward to attempt to charge across the breach. In moments they were kicking their horses on. In their onward rush they trampled some of the Moghul dead and even knocked down beneath their hooves some wounded men trying unsuccessfully to drag their shattered bodies to safety. Two volleys of musket fire followed in quick succession from the battlements. Horses and riders alike crashed to the ground, adding to the piles of bodies. The surviving Moghul riders wheeled away to regroup and attack once more.

Moghul musketeers had succeeded in picking off many of their Marwari counterparts as they exposed themselves on the battlements to fire on the charging horsemen, so when the Moghul riders attacked again the crackle of musketry was much less. Even so, the horsemen failed to get across the mounds of rubble and human and animal dead and wounded and so wheeled away again to re-form once more.

Before they could do so a mass of orange-clad men

149

appeared at the breach, some mounted, some on foot. Scanning the battlements, Aurangzeb saw they were now deserted and Moghul foot soldiers were climbing unchallenged on to them. Then the fort's battered gates were pushed aside and more Marwaris appeared. Almost instantly, together with the men clustered at the breach, they began to ride and run at the Moghul ranks, waving their weapons and yelling their war cries as they came. The Marwaris were insanely sacrificing themselves, Aurangzeb thought, just as Ashok Singh and his men had done so many years ago beyond the Oxus. The Moghul musketeers and gunners were knocking the Marwaris down as they ran but several got among the cannon, spearing some of the Turkish artillerymen before being killed themselves. Soon few Marwaris were left standing.

Ten or twelve Marwari horsemen suddenly seemed to notice the emperor in his command howdah and began to charge towards him. Moghul musketeers immediately emptied several saddles. Then his bodyguard rode at the survivors, quickly engulfing them and leaving them all strewn on the ground, dead or dying, long before they could reach his own position. What infantile, irrational fools these Rajputs were, Aurangzeb thought.

That evening, he and Muazzam sat quietly in the emperor's scarlet command tent while their men celebrated outside. Their victory had been so important – it should open Marwar to his armies – that Aurangzeb would for once turn a blind eye to any consumption of alcohol by his soldiers, something he would normally have punished with a flogging. He began to doze, as with advancing age he was becoming increasingly prone to do after meals, but he woke with a start as his *qorchi* entered. 'A *cossid* has arrived from Delhi with a message that he has been told to bring to you in person immediately on his arrival.'

'Bring him in,' Aurangzeb said, standing up.

Moments later the *qorchi* ushered the messenger in. Travel- and sweat-stained, he bowed low before Aurangzeb before handing him the despatch pouch.

'Thank you for your haste. Go and join my men's celebration of their victory. You have deserved it.'

As the *cossid* and the *qorchi* left, Aurangzeb took out the despatch, broke the seal and read. A smile quickly replaced his normally austere expression. 'Rejoice, Muazzam. Shivaji is dead of fever.'

'I do. It is great news for our empire. But will Sambhaji continue the struggle against us?'

'We must assume so. But he's said not to be the leader his father was. It'll take him time to assert his authority, and he may not be able to keep the Marathas united. Certainly the death of that infernal infidel Shivaji will eliminate any risk of the Rajputs and the Marathas making common cause against us.' Aurangzeb's smile broadened. Events were moving his way. God was surely on his side.

• ◆ •

Akbar cupped his eyes against the sun. Yes, there in the shimmering heat haze were the roofs and building of the small Mewari town of Desuri. His scouts had reported it abandoned by enemy troops. He intended to make it his base while he rested his men and prepared for his advance on Kumbhargarh – one of the last strongholds of the Rana of Mewar. His march into Mewar had gone well, pushing the Mewaris back into their heartlands. He had tried hard to limit the damage he and his men had done to the fields and property they had crossed or

151

occupied. He hoped the rebellion would soon be over and that – if he had been as mild as he could in suppressing it – the reconciliation with the Mewaris he so desired would be easier to achieve. Whatever his father thought, Rajput support had been essential to the Moghuls' rise to greatness and he wished they could be allied once more to their mutual benefit. His aunt Jahanara certainly believed so. Her affectionate letters to him often included quotations from the writings of the Sufi teachers to back up the belief they both held that Rajputs and Moghuls, Hindus and Muslims, could once again live in harmony after a little time had elapsed to allow tempers to cool and memories to fade.

He could only wish that he found the much more frequent despatches his father sent to him as congenial as his aunt's letters. The latest missive from Aurangzeb had arrived that morning. In it his father gloried in Muazzam's advances in Marwar, exalting his son's determination to crush his opponents and his sternness in silencing any dissent. At the same time, Aurangzeb seemed to be taking for granted his own successes in Mewar. He certainly lavished no praise on him, rather exhorting him to greater efforts and offering unwanted advice on the conduct of his campaign and the need for harsh treatment of the Mewaris. His removal from the command of the army in Marwar still rankled, too. His father's rebukes about his preference for listening to advice and consulting others had been unfair. As in so many other matters, not least in religion, Aurangzeb seemed to think that there was only one way to do things – his own. His father often took what was meant to be helpful comment as criticism bordering on sedition. He preferred to surround himself with those who shared his interpretations of both military tactics and holy texts rather than those who might make him think again. In doing so he lost touch with much of his empire and many valuable sources of advice.

Still, once he had taken Kumbhargarh his father would surely have to acknowledge his virtues. But first he must occupy Desuri. He walked over to where Tahavvur Khan, the officer whom Aurangzeb had originally placed in charge of this arm of the attack on Mewar, was standing. Tahavvur Khan had not seemed to resent him being placed over him. But then he'd been hardly likely to. They had known each other all of their lives. Tahavvur Khan's mother had been one of Akbar's wet nurses and the two were milk-brothers – a tie sometimes said to be stronger than blood. Certainly they enjoyed each other's company and trusted one another completely. What's more, Tahavvur Khan's military expertise had contributed much to the success of their campaign, as Akbar freely admitted in his reports to his father.

'Can we move into Desuri?' Akbar asked.

'Yes. I've had scouts check for ambushes and the like and they've found nothing – no sign of Mewari troops or indeed anybody much else either.'

'Good. Let's get going.'

Less than an hour later, they rode through the open gates into the dusty town square of Desuri, deserted except for two pale-furred pariah dogs scratching themselves vigorously in the shade. The two men smiled at each other in mutual satisfaction at their progress. It struck Akbar that he felt more at ease with Tahavvur Khan than with his father or indeed any other male member of his family.

Three days later Akbar was resting on a low divan in a

high-ceilinged room in one of the largest houses they had found deserted in Desuri, which he had made his head-quarters. The walls of the room were hung with fabrics in the vibrant red, yellow and orange colours so loved by all Rajputs. In three of the corners were niches of mirrored glass with candles in them, in the fourth a statue of one of their Hindu gods. Akbar had ordered his attendants to disturb neither it nor the offerings of incense and now faded marigolds still spread in front of it. He sat up as his *qorchi* came in.

'Sire, an envoy has arrived under flag of truce from the Rana of Mewar.'

Akbar's heart leapt. The ambassador could only have come to discuss peace terms – the peace he himself so ardently desired. He would not be unduly harsh.

'Have Tahavvur Khan and my other senior officers join me and then I will receive him.'

'Sire, he says his explicit instructions from the rana are that he must see you alone.'

'Does he say why?'

'No, but he did beg me to repeat to you that this was the rana's personal instruction to him.'

Akbar's first instinct was to refuse. He did not want to have secrets from Tahavvur Khan in particular. But perhaps the rana's pride was so great that he wished to sound him out in private about possible terms before opening any formal discussions.

'Very well. Inform him I will see him in private.' Then another thought struck him. 'But tell him he must submit to a thorough search for weapons before I do so.'

Half an hour later the Rajput envoy, a tall white-moustached man of over fifty, elegantly dressed in an

154

orange turban and tunic and white pantaloons, was shown in by Akbar's *qorchi* and bowed low before the prince. When his *qorchi* had left Akbar spoke first. 'You are welcome as an envoy of the rana. Despite the present hostilities between us I have not lost my admiration for both him and his people.'

'He will be glad to hear it, Highness.'

'Now tell me why he has sent you to me.'

'He asked me to say nothing but to pass you this letter, to leave you to read it and then to bring back any response you wish to make.' He produced a sealed paper from his tunic.

'Why doesn't he wish you and me to discuss relations between our two peoples?'

'To be frank, he fears that in your father's empire walls have ears. I can say no more.'

Akbar frowned. What could the letter contain? If he wanted to find out, he would need to agree to the envoy's proposition. He could see no reason not to do so. 'Very well. Hand me the letter. I will have you taken to some comfortable quarters in the town but you will understand that I cannot allow you to leave them, since if you did you would be able to observe my army and its equipment.'

'I understand, Highness. I will wait as long as you wish for any response you may care to give in any form you desire.'

When the envoy had departed Akbar broke the seal and began to read. As he did so his eyes widened and his heart beat faster.

I write because it grieves me that we are at war — a war which is not of Mewar's making. Why do we shed the

155

blood of our people who for so long have been allies not enemies? I think that you may share my feelings and hope you will not think me presumptuous when I say you are well named. Like your namesake and great ancestor the Emperor Akbar, whose revered memory will live for ever in Hindustan, your valour and your sense of justice are well known. The Great Akbar was a friend to all men of honour, regardless of race or religion. He extended his hand to his Hindu subjects, repealing the heinous laws against them. I have heard that you are unhappy that your father has reimposed many of them.

The Great Akbar was a particular friend to the Rajput states. He recognised that we, like the Moghuls, are a warrior race. He placed us in command of his armies. He took wives from among our princesses. You yourself have Rajput blood. Your great-grandfather the Emperor Jahangir was the son of a Rajput princess, as was your grandfather Shah Jahan.

I am sure you understand these things and that in your heart you desire peace between the Moghuls and the other Rajput states as much as I do. What a pity, many of us Rajput rulers say, that your father Aurangzeb sits on the throne instead of one who would restore justice and harmony to the children of the sun, moon and stars and reign as gloriously and justly as the Emperor Akbar.

I write in friendship and in the hope that you will agree to meet me to discuss how best we can work together to resolve the divisions between us and improve the fortunes of us all. I eagerly await a reply from one whom until recently I regarded as my friend not my enemy and hope to do so again if he proves, as I believe, the salvation of the empire.

156

Akbar read and re-read the letter. Pleasure at being compared with the Emperor Akbar mingled with a rising excitement at the rana's final sentences. Could the rana be suggesting they allied themselves against Aurangzeb to depose him and replace him with Akbar? Though he did not say so in so many words, that seemed to be what he meant and of course explained the envoy's insistence on absolute secrecy. Akbar was surprised by his own willingness even to consider such a proposition. He would never have contemplated such a course of his own volition even if he believed, as the rana seemed to do, that he could make a better job of ruling than Aurangzeb and repair the divisions his father had caused . . . would he? But could he be sure that that was what the rana meant? What's more, was he deceiving himself if he thought he could get the support of the Moghul Empire's armies and courtiers? He couldn't be certain . . . he needed another opinion. Who better to consult than his milk-brother Tahavvur Khan?

'I agree that what the letter seems to be suggesting is an alliance against your father,' said Tahavvur Khan quietly half an hour later as they rode alone around the town walls. They had decided that in the open on horseback was probably the best place for such a sensitive discussion.

'And what do you think I should do about it?'

'I think first you should consider whether the rana is setting a trap for you, drawing you into a conspiracy he can expose to your father and so destroy you and your campaign.'

'He is an honourable man. I cannot believe he would do such a thing,' Akbar said, concealing what was now a worrying thread of doubt contending with the ambition

157

that once awoken seemed hard to suppress. 'Do you think I would have any support if I marched against my father?'

Tahavvur Khan said nothing for a while. 'I believe you would,' he said at last. 'I know you would have mine. But don't be hasty.'

'I am grateful, Tahavvur Khan. You've often been right in urging caution on me in military matters. However, if I don't act now I may never have another chance. Shouldn't I at least agree to meet the rana to see what he has to say?'

'And what if your ever-suspicious father learns of the meeting? He has spies everywhere. We both know he appointed officers – Iqbal Beg and Hanif Khan to name just two – to your headquarters solely to report back to him. Do you want to share the fate of your eldest brother Mohammed Sultan – to spend half of your life in a cell and then die there?'

Akbar thought for a while. Tahavvur Khan was right about his father's network of informers. Then an idea came to him – one he congratulated himself that even his devious and subtle father might have been proud to have thought of. 'No one here except the two of us knows the content of the rana's letter, though many will know that a Mewari envoy has arrived and will be speculating about what he wants. I will burn the letter and then let it be known that the rana has written suggesting a meeting to discuss the terms of his surrender. Then I will write to my father telling him that I have agreed to such a meeting. That way he will have no grounds for suspicion and there will be no need to plan a secret rendezvous with the rana.'

After a moment Tahavvur Khan nodded. 'That could well work, and the prize merits any remaining risk.'

Less than an hour later, back in his room Akbar sealed his short letter to the rana simply agreeing to a meeting without commenting on its purpose. The contents could do no harm even if they fell into his father's hands, since Aurangzeb would already have received the other letter he had just written informing him that the meeting was to discuss surrender terms. After handing both letters to his *qorchi* for despatch, Akbar went to a candle burning in one of the room's mirrored niches and carefully burnt the rana's letter to him. To ensure its complete destruction he collected the debris and ground it beneath his heel. And that, he realised, was what he was seriously contemplating doing to his father's rule!

Chapter 11

Taktya Takhta! – Throne or Coffin!

'Look! The Rana of Mewar has brought only a single adviser, as we both agreed we would,' Akbar said with relief to Tahavvur Khan, pointing to a tall figure on a dark horse. Jewels glittered on his bridle in the morning sun as the rana approached the small palm-fringed oasis midway between their two armies which they had chosen as their meeting place. The single rider with him looked younger than he would have expected, but that was the rana's business. The rana slowly dismounted in the shade of the dusty palms and walked, with his companion keeping a few steps behind, towards where Akbar and Tahavvur Khan were standing beneath the canopy erected by some of Akbar's men the previous evening.

As Akbar took a step forward to greet the rana, to his surprise the rana bowed low. 'Let us leave aside formalities,' Akbar said. 'I am eager to hear what you have to say to me. We can speak frankly here, well away from prying eyes and ears, so that we both clearly understand the other's intentions.'

'I will certainly be explicit. I have come on behalf of the Regent of Marwar as well as myself. We both think that you have much of your great namesake Akbar about you in your tolerance and regard for all the people of your empire.'

Akbar smiled, despite himself flattered once more by the rana's praise. 'I only wish I could measure up even to a small extent to the greatness of my noble ancestor, whom I too so admire. Compared to him I'm nothing.'

'Your modesty becomes you, Highness, but allow me to be the best judge. You ask me to be frank. I will explain my purpose in coming. Your father's bigotry against his Hindu subjects will ruin the empire, turning long-time allies like the Rajput kingdoms into foes and dissipating wealth and resources to the detriment of all in futile internal disputes. By doing so he will leave Hindustan vulnerable to foreign invaders. He is too sure of his right-eousness and of the absolute nature of the strict beliefs which lie behind it, and indeed too stubborn, to change. Besides, his recent actions against us and our fellow Hindus mean that many will no longer willingly accept him as their ruler. Therefore, although we believe that the states of Hindustan are stronger under Moghul overlordship than when they are fighting amongst themselves, he must be replaced, and you, Akbar, are the natural choice.'

Akbar was too overcome by the confirmation of the rana's intentions to respond at once. The rana's letter had roused ambitions within him he'd scarcely known he had. His discussions with Tahavvur Khan and the long debates he had had with himself had only deepened his desire to fulfil them. But now that the time had come to voice them he hesitated. While his mind raced, Tahavvur Khan spoke instead. 'Forgive me, but how can we know that you will honour your promises?'

The rana's dark eyes flashed. 'Hasn't the word of a Rajput always been good? But if you doubt me, the young man beside me is my son. I will surrender him into the prince's custody, if he wishes, as a pledge of my sincerity.'

Akbar spoke at last, his mind now fully made up. 'I too think my father is damaging the empire by his actions. Emboldened by your words and your expression of belief in me, I am prepared to lead you and the many others that Tahavvur Khan here and I think we can attract to our banner from elsewhere in the empire to depose him.' There. He had said it. Taken the irrevocable step of agreeing to oppose his father who he knew would never forgive him as he had never forgiven Mohammed Sultan. He felt not the jolt of fear he had anticipated but a new strength and confidence. He would show his father he had been wrong to belittle him, to deride his tolerance and desire to compromise and unite the people of the empire for its greater good.

'I accept your offer of alliance,' Akbar continued. 'Together we will restore the Moghul Empire to the proud position it held in my ancestor Akbar's time. I know Rajputs are men of honour. Therefore I do not require your son as a hostage for Rajput sincerity.' As he finished speaking Akbar walked forward and embraced the rana. Releasing him after a few moments, he said, 'We should begin to plan our campaign, should we not? As a first step I will rally as many of my own army to our banner as I can. And Tahavvur Khan and I have reason to hope that it will be all of them, don't we?' His milk-brother nodded.

'Once I know you have succeeded in that, I will in turn bring my own army to join you and arrange for forces from Marwar, and any other Rajput states I can persuade, to rally to you,' the rana said. 'We must act quickly. Our scouts tell us – and you must know, I am sure – that your father has left Muazzam's army and returned to Ajmer. With your brother Azam's departure to take up his position as governor of Bengal there are fewer than eight hundred soldiers with Aurangzeb. Your own more numerous army is much nearer Ajmer and your father than any others. You have a great opportunity to seize him and take the throne almost before he realises what is happening, and certainly before many more lives are lost.'

• ◆ •

Akbar returned to his cool room in Desuri. Two hours earlier, he had received the near unanimous support of his officers for his alliance with the Rajputs to topple his father from his throne. He had gone on to appear before his troops. They had cheered him lustily as, standing in the howdah of his war elephant, he had promised them rewards when he was emperor and as a token of what was to come announced a feast that evening before they left Desuri the next morning.

However, he had just heard that Iqbal Beg and a few of his horsemen had galloped away – presumably to take news of his rebellion to his father. Hanif Khan had brought the report of their departure together with protestations of his own loyalty, of his opposition to Aurangzeb and disgust at Iqbal Beg's action. He had not believed him entirely. Hanif Khan would merit careful watching and he would ensure that he received it.

It had been inevitable that news of his rebellion – he must be frank with himself: it was as much a rebellion as Aurangzeb's had been against Shah Jahan – must soon reach his father. If it hadn't been Iqbal Beg it would have been someone else. And what did it matter? His father would not have time to summon extra troops before he himself reached Ajmer with his Rajput allies. What he must do in all honour, however, was to write to his father himself explaining why he was doing what he was doing. He sat down in front of his low desk and took out a piece of paper. If he was quick and used a relay of imperial *cossids* his letter should reach his father even before Iqbal Beg.

· ◆ ·

The setting sun was shining through the casement of the audience hall in the Ajmer fort and its many pillars were casting long dark shadows across the white marble floor as Aurangzeb read his son's short letter. It was the first he'd heard of Akbar's rebellion and he could hardly credit what he was reading. But it was Akbar's writing and it was his seal. The more he thought about it, the more a cold anger took control of him. How could his son – who could not even conduct a successful campaign against Marwar – think himself better fitted to rule than his father? How dare he be so traitorous as to join forces with the Rajputs – the enemies of his father and his faith? He'd always believed Akbar too pliant and weak even to stand out against his father's opinions in private, never mind to rebel. It could only be the treachery of the Rajputs which had raised delusions of greatness in him.

164

His letter was full of spurious and sanctimonious comments about the need for unity between Hindus and Muslims and the repeal of the *jizya*. Akbar's reverence for his namesake and the wateriness of the Sufi beliefs to which he adhered had clearly made him only too susceptible to pious Rajput pleas for a return to former times of so-called equality and religious tolerance.

But could his son be a greater dissembler than he had ever considered possible? Perhaps this was not an impulsive rebellion prompted by slippery Rajput subtlety. Perhaps Akbar had been planning it for some time. Had he dared to involve his brothers? Thoughts of his own scheming – how he had persuaded his brothers Murad and Shah Shuja to join with him against Dara Shukoh and their father by promising them a share of the empire – occurred to him. How easily they had grabbed at his false promises.

Surely the cautious, diffident Muazzam – so careful in obeying his father's guidance in the campaign against the Marwaris, so reluctant to speak in council – would not be so easy to seduce from the path of filial duty, if only because of a well-founded fear of the consequences?

But what about Azam? Unlike Muazzam, Azam was Akbar's full brother and nearer to him in age. He could be hot-tempered and impulsive even if his marriage to Jani seemed to have settled him a little. But from his commanders' reports he knew that Azam was already well beyond Allahabad with his forces, travelling down the Ganges towards his new post of Governor of Bengal. All this argued that Akbar's brothers were probably not involved and that the rising was as much to do with the Rajputs as with his son. He would make them suffer for their temerity.

As he began to think more calmly about the situation and his options, he realised with something of shock that Akbar's forces, allied to the marauding Rajput bands, might well be able to cut him off from reinforcement. Better therefore he garrisoned the Ajmer fort and stayed in it than sallied with his men in any direction. The fort was strong and even his eight hundred men should be able to put up a good defence against their much more numerous opponents. He would release gold from the Ajmer treasuries to stiffen his troops' resolve. He would immediately summon Muazzam to march to join him and his forces but without telling him the reason. His son's reaction would soon show him whether he was complicit in the rebellion.

He must also think about how best to win more adherents and in so doing disrupt the plans of Akbar and his infidel allies. Battles were fought in men's minds as well as on the battlefield. With his subtle brain and with God on his side he would prove more than a match for any rebels. A knock at the door interrupted his thinking. A *qorchi* appeared. 'Majesty, Iqbal Beg is here. He insists on seeing you at once. He has, he says, news of the greatest import.'

'Tell him he has been too slow. I know all about the treachery of my son, and I am dealing with it.'

Alone in his room in the Ajmer fort later that evening Aurangzeb was eating a simple meal of spiced lamb from the tandoor accompanied by yoghourt and *nan* bread. As he chewed he was turning over in his mind how best to defeat his son's rising when the hangings over the shadowy entrance to the room twitched and a shrouded figure appeared. Who could it be, unannounced and at this time?

His hand went to the dagger he always wore but almost at once he saw it was his sister, Jahanara, who had joined him at Ajmer on his return from Muazzam's camp.

As she stepped further into the room and the light she lowered the shawl which had partly concealed her face. There were tears in her eyes and her hands were in constant distracted motion. 'Aurangzeb, I've just heard about Akbar. I've always thought him so honourable . . . tell me it isn't true. I don't think I could bear it . . . not this . . .' The words were tumbling from her.

'It's true. Akbar has rebelled.'

'What will you do? We can't let our family be engulfed once more in blood and hatred . . . we can't . . . we mustn't . . .'

His strong-minded sister was the nearest to hysteria he'd ever seen her.

He took her by the wrists. Her whole body was shaking as he looked her straight in the eye. 'Calm yourself. Trust in me. I am already planning his capture. All will be well.'

'How can it be?'

'Because I will make it so. I'll not allow Akbar or any other upstart to threaten me or put my empire at risk. He will suffer the full consequences of his actions.'

'Akbar is your son, but you're talking about him as if he was a stranger.'

'He is a stranger to me now.'

'Aurangzeb, please . . . don't be so cold. Show him some mercy.'

'Why should I? He has rallied the infidel Rajputs against me and means to have my throne. Sit down by me and let me tell you what he has done. Then see if you think he deserves anything but the severest punishment.'

As he described what he knew of the rising and its supporters, his sister's agitation seemed to subside. Her hands no longer clenched and unclenched but lay still in her lap. Some time passed after he'd finished speaking before she responded. 'Forgive me. I shouldn't have come to you in such an agitated state. I'm grateful to you for telling me what has happened . . . but . . .' she paused, as if choosing her words with care, 'there are things I must say, though I know you won't want to hear them.'

'Go on.'

Jahanara began, speaking slowly and deliberately while the fingers of her right hand twisted a corner of her shawl. 'Akbar is wrong to rebel. Completely wrong. Nothing can justify a son's defying his father in this way. I will tell him so, just as all those years ago I told you when you raised an army against our father. And I—'

'But that was quite different. When I moved against our father I did so for the salvation of the empire. He was weak and under the influence of Dara and his self-serving heretical views. It was my duty before God.'

'We will never agree about that, but this isn't the time to re-open old wounds. You talk about duty. Isn't it our duty to prevent present and future discord? I can help you . . . if we act together we can stop this rebellion almost before it begins. Let me go to Akbar's camp . . . I will make him see how misguided he has been—'

'No. I absolutely forbid it!'

Jahanara's heart sank. Aurangzeb's face was set in the obstinate expression she remembered from the days of their childhood. 'If you won't allow me to do anything then please take the first step towards a reconciliation yourself, before it is too late. If you do, I'm sure Akbar and indeed the Rajputs will respond. They probably already regret their rashness.'

'If I do what you ask I will look weak. It isn't for me to approach rebels. It's for them to surrender and submit to their just punishment so that all the empire – all the world – understands what happens to traitors.'

'Even if their leader is your own son?'

'The more so, since he is breaking not only the bonds of loyalty that tie a subject to his ruler but those that bind a son to his father. I won't give you false hopes – the best Akbar can expect is to spend the rest of his life confined in Gwalior fortress as his brother Mohammed Sultan did.'

'Think what you are saying. Act not just as a ruler but as a father too. You once believed, rightly or wrongly, that our father had no regard for you or your opinions. Akbar may well feel the same about you. I know he's been unhappy because you criticise him so much. If you'd shown him more love, more belief in him, he might never have listened to others more ready to praise him. I've often wanted to speak to you on his behalf, but knowing you as I do, and fearing I'd do more harm than good, I held back. I blame myself for not trying harder.'

'It would have made no difference. Akbar deserved condemnation much more often than praise. I was merely trying – and it seems failing – to set him on the true path.'

'Even if that was your intention, if you'd been less severe he might have been less susceptible to Rajput flattery. Kam Bakhsh is the only one of your sons you ever show any warmth to.'

'That's because he's a child. When Kam Bakhsh grows up I'll expect him too to show obedience to me and deference to my views.'

'I can see from your expression that I'm exasperating you, and I know what I'm going to say now will annoy you further. I've said it before but I must say it again. Some blame for this rebellion lies in your treatment of your Hindu subjects. Don't you see that if you showed greater tolerance your rule would be easier, both you and your subjects like the Rajputs would be more content?'

'What do ease and contentment have to do with ruling? Right and duty are what matter.'

'But duty is exactly what I am talking about – your duty to rule well, to bring well-being to all your people, not to punish or even some might say persecute some of them.'

'I punish no one who doesn't deserve it.'

'When did your view of the world become so bleak? As emperor you have the power to do so much good, yet you choose to spread shadow. I'm sorry if my words hurt you, but if our mother were here she would say the same. You are so quick to condemn, so slow to praise . . . so harsh and unforgiving that people fear you, your sons included. Your courtiers and commanders won't speak in council until they know your views. Then, rather than speak their minds and give good advice, they merely obsequiously agree with you.'

Aurangzeb said nothing. Emboldened, Jahanara continued. 'Please, Aurangzeb – even if you find it hard to forgive Akbar, do whatever you can to end this rebellion without bloodshed. It would be more than I could bear if our family were to be ripped apart once more . . .' Try as she might, her voice was starting to crack. 'Please . . . I beg you . . .'

'Jahanara, your feelings do you credit. You've sacrificed

much of your life to trying to keep our family together. I know that, even if at times I've not appeared to. However,' Aurangzeb took a deep breath, 'in seeking to blame me for what has happened you betray a woman's ignorance of a man's world. I am the emperor and I alone must take decisions, however painful. Akbar and his infidel allies must and will be punished without mercy.' He paused, then added more softly, his eyes directed at the floor and not at his sister, 'Now, since it would be fruitless and only cause us both more hurt to debate further, it would be best if you returned to your quarters, please.'

Jahanara rose and walked slowly from the room. Back in her apartments, needing comfort, she picked up one of her books of Sufi teachings, but her eyes were brimming with tears and wouldn't focus on the words. All her life she'd worked to keep her family together but time and again she had failed. Whoever would have thought that the children of Shah Jahan and Mumtaz, born of such great love and who had endured so much together, should have come to this?

Chapter 12

Emperor Akbar the Second

'Majesty, your council awaits.'
The words of the Raja of Amber, resplendent
in his court robes and glittering jewels, sounded sweet in
the 23-year-old Akbar's ears. Shaded by a large white
umbrella held by an attendant, he walked across the sandy
ground towards his tent, accompanied by the raja and
Tahavvur Khan. Drawing closer, he saw that his Rajput
allies had decked it in scarlet – the traditional colour for
a Moghul emperor's command tent. As he approached the
low gold throne on a velvet-covered dais erected beneath
the awning, the Rajput rulers drawn up in two lines on
either side prostrated themselves before him as one.

Although he relished their gesture and the confidence
and reverence it displayed towards him, he was conscious
of the pride and status of the Rajputs themselves and
knew he must not wallow in the glory of his new position. He quickly motioned the rulers to rise. 'Even if I
am your leader I owe my position to your support and

encouragement. You are my brothers-in-arms. Together we will re-order the Moghul Empire and restore it to its former united glory from its present splintered state. But before we can do so we must subdue the forces of division embodied in my father and his bigoted and self-righteous supporters. What do we know of their latest movements?'

The Rana of Mewar spoke. 'All reports from our scouts agree that Aurangzeb remains at Ajmer and has no prospect of reinforcement before we can reach him. Ajmer is after all only three or four days' march from here.'

'Nevertheless, the Ajmer fort is still strong.'

'But many of the townspeople are of Rajput stock and we believe sympathetic to us. With their help we should be able to infiltrate the defences and seize your father.'

'And kill him as he well deserves for his treatment of our people,' a burly officer standing two ranks behind the rana added.

'Silence, Ravi!' The rana turned and fixed a steely eye on him. 'Such matters are not for you to judge but for your betters.'

'You should know,' Akbar said, 'I could never agree to my father's execution. He must be confined in comfortable circumstances.'

'Apart from a few hotheads like Ravi behind me who are better suited to the battlefield than the council chamber, we knew before we approached you that you would be too compassionate to countenance his death. We agreed that we would accept his imprisonment.'

'I am glad of that.'

'But we would beg you that however comfortable his confinement it should be in some remote place well away from the centre of power. If allowed to remain in Agra or Delhi he is sufficiently subtle and devious to contrive ways to stir up dissent. Far better he should be hundreds of miles away.'

'Have you somewhere in mind?'

'A fortress deep in the Rajasthani desert, or the fortified city of Jaisalmer, perhaps? He will find few supporters among the hardy and devout Hindus who live there.'

'Majesty,' Tahavvur Khan interrupted, 'we are all agreed on the principle that your father should be imprisoned. The location is a matter for the future. First we need to capture him. And whatever the rana may say, that may not be as easy as we think. We must act quickly.'

'You're right, of course, Tahavvur Khan. Rana, when can your troops be ready to march to cut off Ajmer fort from reinforcement and to seize my father?'

'First light tomorrow.'

'My own men too. Give the necessary orders. We will march at dawn tomorrow to create a new dawn for the Moghul Empire.' Akbar smiled, pleased not only with his choice of words but with his first taste of imperial power.

• ◆ •

'Send Wazim Khan to me.' Aurangzeb told his *qorchi* as he sat beneath the shade of a spreading neem tree in the main courtyard of the Ajmer fort. The son of one of his old viziers, Wazim Khan was becoming an increasingly trusted confidant at the centre of his network of spies and informers. He only wished the rest of his advisers and senior officers were as efficient, ingenious and discreet.

A few minutes later the stout, black-clad figure of Wazim Khan appeared, puffing a little from his haste to reach his master. 'Sit next to me.' Aurangzeb waved him to take his place beside him.

When Wazim Khan had wiped his brow and settled cross-legged next to him, the emperor asked, 'What news of Akbar and his Rajput allies?'

'On the move towards Ajmer in great strength.'

'As we expected. When we met a couple of days ago you were going to identify astrologers in my son's camp who might be susceptible to bribery to suggest that according to their star charts it would be inauspicious to attack Ajmer before the new moon in twelve days, thus gaining us precious time.'

'Yes. I sent messengers at once and they already report some success.'

'How any man of reason can credit their nonsense is beyond my understanding. However, let us hope they are believed and the advance is postponed. If it is, some of our reinforcements might be able to reach us before they attack. What do we know of their progress?'

'*Cossids* have confirmed that loyal troops are hurrying by forced march to your side from several directions, but they are all still some way off and many may not even arrive by the new moon.'

'Do the loyal troops include those of Muazzam?'

'Yes, Majesty, with your son riding at their head. He should be among the first to reach you. My spies in his headquarters tell me that although some of his young officers urged him to join his brother he told them he put his loyalty to you and his faith first.'

Aurangzeb sighed with relief. His sons were not uniting against him. 'Good. I will reward him with new responsibilities and with some of the estates that previously belonged to his brother. But provide me with a list of those in Muazzam's camp who argue treason against me. When the time is ripe I will deal with them severely.'

'Of course, Majesty. Is there anything else I can do to help forestall Akbar's advance? I've already asked your officers to send scouts disguised as travellers to attempt to get into his camp and discover his plans. Your officers tell me too that their men rejoiced at the bounty they received from the treasury on your orders, and that they are well drilled and in good heart, even if few in number. The quartermaster reports our armouries are well stocked with powder and musket and cannon balls and the granaries and water tanks full, so we should be able to withstand a siege if we must.'

'I'm glad to hear that. I have no other task for you at the present. I have had one or two more thoughts but I need to think more about how to disrupt Akbar's advance before I take even you into my confidence.'

• ◆ •

'How impressive they are.' Akbar was standing beside Tahavvur Khan and the Rana of Mewar in the open howdah of his war elephant as the first ranks of his horsemen approached, orange pennants fluttering on their lance tips. Most of his thirty thousand horsemen were Rajputs from Amber and Bikaner as well as from Marwar, and Mewar, and more were arriving all the time. They were magnificently dressed in tunics and turbans of the most vivid oranges, yellows and reds, their banners with their symbols of sun, moon and fire billowing behind them. Mounted drummers and trumpeters were playing blood-stirring martial music. The morning sun was glistening on their swords as in unison they unsheathed them and placed them to their lips as they paraded past Akbar's elephant. Even though they rode in ranks fifty horsemen wide they took nearly an hour to pass.

The artillery followed, first powder wagons covered by oiled cloth and other carts carrying cannonballs, next the long-barrelled cannon on eight- or even ten-wheeled limbers. Most of the oxen pulling them had red and yellow ribbons on their horns. The gunners – many of them Turkish mercenaries – marched beside their weapons, their ramrods over their shoulders. Akbar was amused when he noticed two or three Europeans, faces burned red by the sun, amongst them riding astride the cannon barrels waving their plumed hats towards him.

After the guns had passed – sufficient to begin a siege of Ajmer if necessary, as he said to Tahavvur Khan – the foot soldiers appeared through the clouds of dust the cannon had raised. As in all armies, they were the least impressive units. Many were barefoot and equipped only with old-fashioned weapons such as spears and bows and arrows. Even so, they appeared better disciplined than many he had seen and they cheered him lustily as they passed.

Once the review was complete, Akbar descended from his elephant. Still accompanied by the rana and Tahavvur Khan, who seemed to be less talkative and full of humour than usual, he walked across to a makeshift wooden platform. There the other Rajput rulers and his own senior Moghul commanders awaited him. More junior officers clustered around the platform, all sweating in the oppressive, humid heat. Dark clouds which had been piling the horizon all morning were now covering half the sky. The storm could not be long delayed. Akbar climbed nimbly up the rough steps on to the platform and asked the Rajput rulers and his own senior officers to gather behind him in a semicircle. Then he took a few steps towards the front of the platform, raised his hand for silence and addressed the upturned and expectant faces of the junior officers below.

'I and my brothers-in-arms,' he said, with a gesture designed to embrace all those standing behind him, 'have been impressed today, not only by the discipline and equipment of your units but also by the heartiness of the salutations that you and your men have directed towards us. Here at Deorai we are only ten miles from the Ajmer fort. Our scouts tell us that my father's eight hundred men have received no reinforcements. Tomorrow we will march to surround the fort and force my father and his few supporters to surrender. I've already had messages of support from Hindus, Muslims and Sikhs alike, so once my father is in our custody all other opposition will vanish. Victory will be ours and the empire united once more.' As Akbar spoke, lightening flashed across the camp and unseasonable rain poured from the purple thunder clouds.

Chapter 13

The Smooth-Tongued Counsellor

A kbar tossed and turned. Once or twice in the night he had woken to hear rain beating on the roof of his tent and the wind howling around it. A hand was on his shoulder, gently shaking him. 'Majesty, the Rajputs have gone.'

It must be part of a dream – one of those dreams in which the worst fears and anxieties come to the fore. He must wake up and find it wasn't true. He opened his eyes and tried to rub the sleep out of them and reality in, but he didn't succeed. The voice belonged to one of his young *qorchis*, who was now holding his silk robe out to him. He put it on over his nightclothes and followed the youth to the entrance of the tent. Peering from beneath the awning across the puddles to where the Rajputs should have been preparing for battle he heard none of the noise and hubbub so typical of those brave and high-spirited warriors, saw no smoking cooking fires, no weapons piled for action. What was more, nearly all the Rajputs' tents seemed to have disappeared.

How could this be? A jug was standing on a table beneath the awning and Akbar poured some water over his head in another attempt to wake himself from this horrible fantasy. The liquid was morning-chill and wet but the scene before his eyes did not change. It had to be reality. Akbar shuddered. The Rajputs had deserted him. His ambitions were dust; his life worthless if his father captured him. As he stood dumbfounded, trying to understand what had happened, a single orange-clad Rajput emerged from one of the few remaining tents and walked towards him. Akbar recognised him at once as Jaginder, one of the younger sons of the Raja of Amber, someone he'd known most of his life. Jaginder threw himself on the wet ground before him, but Akbar at once gestured to him to rise. 'No need for that. What has happened?'

'Most of my fellow Rajputs have departed. I volunteered to remain with some of our horsemen to tell you why. Knowing you as I do, I had too much faith in you to believe the reason for their leaving.'

'What do you mean?'

Haltingly at first and keeping his eyes on the ground, Jaginder began. 'A party of pickets sent out by the Raja of Bikaner to keep the camp safe while you were reviewing the troops yesterday came across two unarmed men sneaking towards the camp. When approached, they quickly and quietly surrendered. Asked what they were doing they confessed almost unprompted that they were your servants returning to you with a letter from your father replying to one you had sent him. They handed over the letter – sealed with Aurangzeb's seal – to the pickets, who brought it to the Raja of Bikaner. He broke the seal, and after reading the contents immediately summoned his fellow rulers to a council meeting which I attended with my father. There, flushed with rage and without any preliminaries, the Raja of Bikaner burst out, 'I have long worried whether any Moghul can truly be our friend, but I have kept my counsel, acquiescing in your support for Akbar for the sake of the unity of our people. But now my worst suspicions are proved, here in this letter from the father to the son. It is definitely the emperor's own hand – I know it well from his letters to me. It begins, "Well done, my courageous son. You deserve my congratulations on the skill and cunning you have displayed in entrapping the uncultured and barbarous Rajputs." The letter went on to detail what Aurangzeb said were the plans you and he had to betray us today . . . how you would lead our columns in front of some of your father's largest cannon concealed in brush and scrub between here and the Ajmer fort.'

Akbar's head was swimming, trying to come to terms with what Jaginder was saying, still trying to convince himself it was reality. 'It is a lie, a damned lie,' he burst out, voice trembling. 'I've not corresponded with my father. I'm a man of honour. It's another of his treacherous schemes . . . don't you see?'

'Yes, Majesty, I do, and that's why I'm still here. And by no means all of the council believed the contents of the letter at first, but the two captured men, when questioned before the council, added extra details such as the signal you would give to your father's gunners by having the *qorchi* riding next to you drop the standard he was carrying just before you swerved away from the column,

181

allowing the cannon to open fire on us. By this time nearly everybody was convinced. My father however suggested we confront you to give you a chance to defend yourself. He even sent an officer to speak to you, but your captain of the guard insisted you were sleeping and had given strict orders not to be disturbed, particularly not by any Rajputs, all of whom were to be denied access to your inner enclosure. When the officer returned and reported what the captain had said it further fuelled the council's suspicions. Eventually they agreed that we would be safer to withdraw for the moment rather than to risk all by accompanying you to Ajmer. Some, like my father, were for staying close by, but others were for retreating back to their kingdoms. During the night, under the cover of the storm, most broke camp. My father is only a few miles off in the protection of the hills west of here. I can't say for sure about the others.'

'But what about my other troops . . . my original Moghul army . . .?'

'Seeing our preparations for departure and hearing our story, some of them, fearful you had trapped them into betraying your father and they would be punished for it, went to the personal camp of their general, your friend Tahavvur Khan. But they found him gone. Now certain of a plot, many of them have already left and most of the remainder are preparing to do so – many, I understand, to surrender to your father. Others, including most of the foreigners, are going off in small groups, some after looting what they can carry from the baggage train.'

Akbar turned to his young *qorchi*, who had been standing beside him all the time. 'Fetch the captain of my bodyguard.'

The boy disappeared but was soon back. 'He has gone, Majesty.'

Akbar nodded. He wasn't surprised. His father had clearly suborned him. The man's refusal to allow anyone to see him was part of the plot, designed to increase, as it had indeed done, the Rajput leaders' suspicions. Still in a daze, he gestured his *qorchi* and Jaginder to follow and walked across the muddy ground past abandoned weapons and equipment towards Tahavvur Khan's camp. Some of the few remaining soldiers greeted him. Most, though, scuttled away on seeing him, obviously intent on departing.

Entering Tahavvur Khan's tent, Akbar found many of his milk-brother's possessions gone, but propped on a low table was a sealed and folded paper marked with his name. Fingers trembling, he opened it.

My milk-brother, I implore your forgiveness for deserting you. By doing so I know I forfeit my honour. However, I had no alternative. Last night, your father's smooth-tongued adviser Wazim Khan came to me in disguise. When we were alone, he began to talk not of surrender terms for the Ajmer fort as I had expected but about a message your father had asked him to deliver to me. The emperor wanted me to know that in view of my treachery he had had no alternative but to seize my wife – who as you know is expecting a child – my two young sons and my parents. Wazim Khan showed me their rings in proof of their confinement. If I did not return my loyalty to him, the emperor would have them all killed, together with my brother – my parents' only other child – and his family, wiping my blood line from the earth. As you can imagine, I wanted to kill Wazim Khan, but I knew

183

*I must not. He was deaf to all my pleas but began to
alternate descriptions of the torture my family would be
put to before being killed with blandishments and offers
of rewards, claiming that all I would be doing if I accepted
them and went over to Aurangzeb would be returning
to my proper path of duty. He told me too that I was
not the only one being approached . . . that he had heard
that the Rajputs would abandon you. He assured me
your father had promised that he would pardon you when
you were captured. That I would be doing you good
rather than evil in leaving you. I weakened and I agreed.
I felt I had no choice for my family's sake. All day during
the review I wanted to say something to you but I
couldn't. Forgive me.*

Akbar threw his letter aside. He could scarcely blame
Tahavvur Khan or the Rajputs. His father had stooped to
tactics he himself would never use and had outwitted him.
The rift between Hindu and Muslim, Rajput and Moghul,
had been too deep for him to heal fully in the short time
he had had. Aurangzeb had found it only too easy to
reopen the scar. However, he would not give in. For one
thing, he did not believe his father would pardon him.
That was just another lie to suborn Tahavvur Khan. Hadn't
his father always been most unforgiving to those closest
to him? Aurangzeb had captured his own brother Murad
in the civil war by deceit, and had him killed. His eldest
son had died in a prison to which Aurangzeb himself had
condemned him. Even if Akbar had lost his army he would
not allow himself to suffer such a fate.

Moreover, if he gave in he would be surrendering for
ever his ambitions not only for himself but for the empire,

leaving it to crumble among the divisions and suspicions, religious and personal, that his father loved to promote. Instead he would redouble his efforts. His ancestors Babur and Humayun had experienced far greater setbacks before fulfilling their ambitions. So too had his grandfather Shah Jahan. He would draw on their experience and his own reserves of courage and continue to strive to reunite the empire as his namesake the Emperor Akbar had originally done. Turning to his young *qorchi*, he said, 'Summon any men that remain loyal. We will ride immediately to join the Raja of Amber if' – and here he turned to Jaginder – 'he will protect me.'

'He will, I assure you, Majesty.'

'Then we depart at once. What cannot be packed in a few minutes we must leave behind.'

• ◆ •

'Have you heard anything yet?'

At the sound of his sister's voice Aurangzeb turned to see Jahanara come through an arched doorway on to a secluded section of the battlements of the Ajmer fort, from which he was looking across the plain below towards where riders from Akbar's camp should appear. He prided himself on his straight back, but his 67-year-old sister was now stooped and leaning on an ivory-handled stick, a brown woollen shawl pulled around her against the morning chill. 'No, nothing.'

Jahanara's face was drawn. Akbar's rebellion had tormented and weakened her in brain and body. She had confessed to him that worry for himself and the unity of the empire contending with her love for her nephew were preventing her from sleeping. After a moment or two, unable to quell his own impatience, he began to pace the

185

battlements, his eyes returning to the horizon, which was now in places obscured by squalls of rain. Then from the haze two riders emerged, galloping towards the ramp which twisted its way upward from the plain to the gateway of the fort. Surely the expected messengers?

After ten more long minutes of uncertainty the horsemen appeared, wet from the rain and streaked with dirt, accompanied by the neatly groomed Wazim Khan in his freshly laundered dark clothes. His plump face was creased into a broad smile. 'Your plans worked, Majesty. Nearly all the Rajputs have fled, together with much of the rest of Akbar's army. Tahavvur Khan and many other deserters are waiting for your permission to come in and surrender.'

Aurangzeb's shoulders relaxed and he dropped to his knees in prayer. 'God be thanked for bringing the idea to me. A just cause and a strong mind have overcome a well-armed but weak-willed and traitorous crew.'

'And what of Akbar?' Jahanara asked, her concern clear in her voice.

'I assume he has followed the Rajputs?' Aurangzeb asked Wazim Khan, who nodded. 'Very well. When Muazzam returns – and he should do so in two or three days' time as he is riding ahead of the main body of his army – I will send him in pursuit of his brother, to bring him back in chains to Delhi.'

While her brother thanked the messengers, and issued further instructions to Wazim Khan, Jahanara stood in silence, unable to keep out of her mind the stories she had heard of Dara Shukoh's being paraded in rags on a tattered elephant through Delhi to his death after his capture by Aurangzeb's forces. Please God that did not happen to Akbar. When the three men had left she quietly spoke. 'Aurangzeb, I am grateful that your stratagem has prevented the shedding of blood. I had feared for our family and for our friends among the Rajputs as well as for our own men . . .'

'You are too generous-hearted,' Aurangzeb broke in. 'No matter how many Rajputs had died it would have been of little account, and the outlaw wretch Akbar is no family of mine. But we should be grateful that none of those faithful to God and the empire will now die today, and give thanks to God for it.'

Hearing the contempt in Aurangzeb's voice, Jahanara held back the arguments she had been formulating for pardoning Akbar and the Rajputs as a sign of a renewal of unity within the empire. Her words would be wasted at present. Better to bide her time, perhaps even to enlist the support of Gauharara, Jani, Zebunissa and maybe Udipuri Mahal in a kind of female petition. She simply said, 'Beyond sending Muazzam in pursuit of Akbar, what else will you do next?'

'I will accept the submission of those who deserted Akbar, but in time I will make sure the officers among them are posted to where they can cause little trouble. I will reward Tahavvur Khan as I promised and do so openly so that all can see I keep my word and will trust any such promises I have to give in future. But I will have him closely watched. His heart will still be with Akbar and his treachery will corrode his soul. Who knows what he will do? I will never be able to trust him.'

'You would not have killed his family would you?'

'Perhaps not the women – but they would all have been reduced to the direst poverty, made servants performing

187

the humblest of tasks. Executing the males would have given me no joy, but you must never make threats which you are too weak-hearted to carry out.'

Brother and sister were still together, seated at their morning meal, an hour later. Although Aurangzeb was eating the breads and vegetables with relish, Jahanara was not. She was toying with her food, pushing it around her plate and crumbling the bread between her fingers. How could she eat when she was so worried about where Aurangzeb's victorious scheming had left Akbar and the empire? Hearing Wazim Khan announced, she looked up. She disliked this smooth-tongued man who by his counsels of deceit had worked his way into such a position of trust in her suspicious brother's mind. He had some partially burned papers in his hand and he was no longer smiling.

'Majesty, you should see these. Some of our men found them while searching your son's abandoned tent and galloped immediately to bring them to us. The prince must have been in too much of a hurry to burn them properly.'

'What are they?'

'Letters to him from his sister Zebunissa.'

A chill of apprehension quivered through Jahanara's slight frame.

'Let me see them.' Aurangzeb rose from the low table at which brother and sister had been eating, took the letters and then raised the eyeglass he now often wore on a green ribbon around his neck and used to read when the light was low, as it was now. Moments later he threw the letters to the floor. 'More treachery, and from an unlooked-for source!'

'What does Zebunissa write?' Jahanara asked mechanically, even though she had already guessed.

'She offers Akbar support, encourages his rebellion and looks forward to his victory.'

That Zebunissa held such views was no surprise to Jahanara. Her niece shared many of Akbar's tolerant opinions, which were so close to her own. But how foolish she had been to encourage rebellion, and how much more foolish to commit her encouragement to paper. What could she say to assuage the anger blazing in Aurangzeb's eyes? 'Brother, Zebunissa has been stupid – no, more than that, disloyal to you in encouraging her brother – but do not judge her too harshly. Fraternal love is strong, as you and I know despite our differences. It caused Roshanara to side with you against our father. Even if you think Roshanara was right to do so, perhaps now you will understand a little more how he felt.'

Aurangzeb had smiled faintly when she spoke of fraternal love, but her comparison between Zebunissa and Roshanara had caused him to frown again. She'd been wrong to make it but hadn't been able to help herself. She must change course if she was to succeed. 'We may be being too ready to prejudge her betrayal of you. Our father once wrongly accused me of a liaison with the Englishman Nicholas Ballantyne, confining me without even giving me a chance to defend myself before him. At least bring Zebunissa in front of you to explain herself.'

'No. These letters make her guilt absolutely clear.' After a moment he added more gently, 'Sister, I cannot see her for fear she may soften my heart and prevent me inflicting the punishment that is right and just and will serve as an

189

example to any, however near or far from me in blood, whether male or female, who may consider treachery.'

Jahanara said no more. What would be the point? She must accept that the slim hope she'd cherished of joining with Zebunissa and other royal women to plead success-fully for Akbar had crumbled into nothing.

• ◆ •

Two days later Jahanara was again at table with Aurangzeb. He had invited her to join him and Muazzam, who had that morning ridden into the fort with five hundred horsemen. Since Aurangzeb had learned of the disper-sion of much of Akbar's army he had begun gathering forces for the pursuit of Akbar. And within just a few hours of reading Zebunissa's letters to Akbar he had had her taken from Ajmer in a closed howdah on elephant-back to imprisonment in Gwalior. As she had kissed her weeping niece, Jahanara had whispered that she would do all she could to win her father's forgiveness for her. She had also pressed into her hand a Sufi volume, with the wish that it would bring her comfort. Soon but not yet she would petition Aurangzeb to allow some of Zebunissa's best-loved possessions to be sent after her to ease her confinement.

She herself had little appetite for the meal. In truth, since finding out about Zebunissa she'd eaten almost nothing and had vomited back what little she had. She'd heard officers talk about the weaker-minded of their men becoming literally sick with fear at the prospect of battle. She too must be sick with fear – not of action but for the future of her family. She must do what she could to prevent her fears from becoming reality, even if in truth she could do little.

Looking up from her almost untouched food – *dal* and a little roasted lamb – she saw Aurangzeb wipe his mouth with a cotton cloth, fold it and place it on his cleared plate and then turn to Muazzam. 'I must congratulate you again on the speed with which you have reached me, as well as upon your success in Marwar.'

Muazzam smiled – a smile less diffident than usual when he was with Aurangzeb. 'Thank you, Father.'

'Now I wish you to prove your loyalty further. You will pursue that treasonable wretch Akbar, capture him and bring him back to Delhi. If the only way to seize him is to kill him, do so without compunction. I can parade his dead body through Delhi as well as his live one.'

Jahanara froze. Muazzam's expression changed and a pulse began to throb at his temple. 'Yes, but I will do my best to persuade him to surrender. I would not wish to kill him . . . he is my brother.'

'You are wrong. He is no longer your brother. His actions, like those of Zebunissa, have put him out of the family.'

Muazzam was looking down at the table with its spread of rich foods. 'I will obey your commands, as I've always tried to do in Marwar and elsewhere.'

'Good. Now I suggest you go to begin your preparations so that you can leave in pursuit of Akbar as soon as possible.'

Muazzam stood up, hesitated a moment, then bowed to his father and moved towards the door.

Jahanara rose too. Leaning on her stick she followed her nephew to the door where, pulling him close, she embraced him. As she kissed his cheek she whispered into his ear, 'For my sake and your own, as well as our dynasty's,

191

do not be over-eager. Take time in your preparations and the pursuit.'

As he left there was relief on Muazzam's face. His aunt might just have provided him with a solution to a tormenting dilemma.

• ◆ •

'I think we'll have light long enough to get our men over the river ahead before we camp for the night, don't you, Jaginder?' Akbar wiped the sweat from his brow with the back of his hand and stood in his stirrups to peer over the dry scrub towards the wooded riverbank.

Jaginder nodded. 'Our scouts report the banks slope only gently and at this season the river is fordable easily enough.'

'Good, then let's press on.' Akbar smiled. He and Jaginder had grown closer as they had journeyed swiftly south with the remnants of his army and the 500-strong escort of Rajput horsemen Jaginder's father, the Raja of Amber, had provided. Even if his force was small he had no doubt all were loyal to him, having spurned frequent opportunities to slip away. Their commitment and unity had helped them outdistance the pursuers his father had sent after them. A few days ago they had all been further heartened when an envoy he had sent to Sambhaji had returned with the news that the Maratha ruler had agreed to his offer to join him in the Deccan and make common cause against Aurangzeb.

Together we will show him that men of different races and faiths can work together for the greater glory of Hindustan, Sambhaji had written. How good it would be to share his mission with a ruler of like mind. With Sambhaji's support as well as that of Jaginder's father he should be

192

able to persuade other Rajput states to rise again in his support when an opportunity presented itself. Together they should be able to attract more allies from among the empire's other vassals as well as entice officials and commanders from what could only be lukewarm attachment to his bigoted father. But he must not get ahead of himself. His first task was to rendezvous with Sambhaji and establish their all-important relationship.

'Jaginder, take fifty of your Rajputs across the river to secure a foothold on the far bank from which we can rig ropes across the river to help men with weaker mounts to cross.'

Jaginder immediately turned, called to one of his junior officers to follow with his men, and kicked his horse through the scrub into the trees fringing the river. In scarcely more than fifteen minutes one of the Rajputs returned with a message from Jaginder that preparations were advanced enough for the main body to begin to follow. Akbar quickly ordered his men to form up five abreast and start to cross.

With his bodyguard around him he positioned himself near the front of the column. As they entered the trees, a flock of birds, disturbed as they began to settle on their roosts for the night, rose screeching into the air. Just as his scouts had reported, the slope of the riverbank was gentle and the ground firm beneath the bay's hooves. As he urged his mount into the slow-flowing water, which could only be three feet deep, a pair of Sarus cranes silhouetted against the setting sun flapped lazily above his head. Soon he would be across and soon after that able to eat and rest his aching limbs after what had been a particularly long and tiring day in the saddle.

His horse skittered a little, tossing its head, perhaps unsettled by the water washing around its flanks, however softly. He tightened his grip on the reins and bent to whisper some words of gentle reassurance into its ear. As he did so, he heard a crack and immediately felt a stinging pain in his thigh. He put his hand to it to find blood. There were further shots. What was happening? Had he been wrong about the loyalty of his men? Had one or more simply been patiently staying with him on his father's instructions, waiting to dispose of him?

No. More shots followed as he scrabbled to unsheathe his sword. Then with a great yell a troop of horsemen burst from the woods on the far bank and galloped at full pelt into the river, raising great splashes of water, and attacked his men. A young Rajput pitched from his horse into the shallows to float face down, hit by a ball fired from the pistol held in the hand of one of the leading attackers, a heavily bearded man riding a chestnut horse. As one of Akbar's bodyguards kicked towards him, instead of attempting to reload his pistol the man reversed it and grasping the barrel threw it hard towards the bodyguard, by now only feet away. The bulbous steel butt caught the guard's mount between the eyes. Whinnying in pain, it reared up, throwing into the water not only its rider but also the bodyguard next to him, whom it caught full in the chest with its hooves before regaining its footing. It struggled out of the water shook itself and then galloped away reins dangling, still neighing in distress.

The bearded attacker was almost on Akbar, who by now had freed his sword. The man slashed wildly at him with a scimitar, shouting 'Zindabad Aurangzeb – Long live Aurangzeb – and death to all traitors to him.' Akbar raised

194

his own sword just quickly enough to deflect the scimitar's blow and before the man could recover his balance and strike again thrust his sword into his armpit. Despite the blood pulsing from the wound his opponent tried once more to attack, but his strength was draining away with his blood and Akbar easily parried his stroke before striking deep into the man's abdomen, causing him to double up and pitch from his saddle into the water.

All around him Akbar heard yells and the clash of steel on steel as well as the occasional cracks of pistol and musket shots. Suddenly he felt himself propelled backwards from his saddle as his horse reared. He hit the water arms flailing but succeeded in keeping hold of his sword hilt. Trying to avoid his horse's hooves he struggled to ground his feet on the river's muddy bottom. Then he saw two yellow protuberant eyes just above the surface about ten feet away. A pair of sharp triangular-toothed jaws opened and tried unsuccessfully to clamp on to his horse's leg – a crocodile drawn by all the blood, animal and human, in the water. It must have been what had spooked his mount, causing it to throw him in the first place. Now the crocodile was turning towards him, opening its mouth once more. Flinging himself forward and using all his strength he thrust his sword between its teeth and deep into its gullet. Blood spurted. The beast's armoured tail thrashed the water for a moment and then it lay still. But another crocodile was gliding towards him. He struck out again and it sheered off.

Then he heard shouts and splashing behind him and felt strong arms tugging at him. Jaginder and one of his bodyguards had bravely ridden back into the river and were hauling him towards the bank. Reaching it, he scrambled a little unsteadily to his feet, water pouring off him. He was still grasping his sword in his hand, and looked around for another horse so that he could continue the fight. However, those of the attackers who could were urging their horses from the water and galloping away into the gathering dusk with some of his men in pursuit. The river water was red with blood and several bodies were floating in it. As he watched, a crocodile glided sinuously towards one and bit into its thigh with its gaping jaws. A high-pitched scream followed. The man was still alive. His arms were now vainly clawing the water as the crocodile pulled him beneath its surface. Thank God he would soon be dead. There was nothing he could do for him, but he must help any others who still lived.

'Any men with a dry musket or pistol shoot these vile beasts! The rest help get any survivors from the water.' He himself ran into the river again and grasping one of the ropes swam towards a man struggling feebly towards the bank. He could be no more than twelve feet away. Gripping the man's outstretched hand, he was pulling him to shore when he heard a musket shot and the water churned less than a body's length away. A large crocodile had been approaching, unseen by him but not by a Rajput on the bank who, having been one of the first to cross, had been able to keep his musket and powder dry. Moments later Akbar was back on the bank with the man he had saved. He didn't recognise him and he was wearing Moghul green. He must be one of the attackers. He had a wound in his upper arm which had penetrated skin and creamy white fat deep into red muscle, and was slowly recovering after vomiting volumes of dirty water. 'Why did you attack us?' Akbar demanded.

'We are the garrison of a Moghul fort ten miles or so away. Our commander is a zealous supporter of the emperor. Warned of your approach, he ordered us to ambush you, hoping for reward.' Now that he was out of the water blood was welling from the wound in the man's arm. 'What do you intend to do to me?' he asked, his whole body beginning to shake.

'To have my *hakims* sew and bind your wound and free you to take back word to the emperor that I – the son whom he calls a degenerate wretch – saved you and that my own life was previously preserved by a Hindu Rajput and a Muslim member of my bodyguard. Tell him that shows how all who live in Hindustan can work together and will again after I have replaced him on the throne.'

As Akbar turned away he could feel blood running down his leg from the wound in his thigh to join the water in his boot – he too must get to the *hakims*. He knew that while such gestures as freeing the soldier and entrusting him with a message about the empire's unity were easy and popular he was far, far away from achieving his ambitions. While his father lived he must be constantly on guard. All he could do was strive for what he believed was right. How far he succeeded would depend in great part on his alliance with Sambhaji. He must make sure it worked.

Chapter 14

'Farewell My Brother'

'Y ou owe me an explanation. I gave you command of one of my best-trained, best-equipped armies. I expected before too long to be thanking God for your victory over your traitorous brother and for either his death or his capture. What I certainly did not expect was that you would return to Ajmer with him still at liberty and his troops in the field. Why have you done so?'

Muazzam could feel the expectant air in the audience chamber where despite the late hour his father had ordered his advisers and commanders to gather. Why was his father humiliating him like this? He might at least have allowed him time to change his mud-spattered riding clothes. And why make him appear before the full council as if he were some disgraced official instead of his son? He had been away for over five months. Surely after such an absence any father would wish their first meeting to be in private.

Raising his chin he addressed Aurangzeb, sitting

stiff-backed and granite-faced on a low gilded throne before him. 'Father, as I reported in my despatches, I tried to advance quickly but Akbar with his remaining forces and Rajput allies had too great a start. I split my column and rode ahead with my swiftest horsemen, leaving the artillery and most of the baggage behind, but fast as we rode we couldn't catch up with them – my scouts were tracking them but they were always two or three days before us. I hoped that when my brother learned I'd divided my army – he must have had spies observing our pursuit – he might be tempted to turn back to attack me, but he was too shrewd to take my bait.

'Even so, I persisted. I waited for my main force to catch up, then pushed on after him into the Maratha hills. But soon the season was against me. Every day was hotter than the last. The local people were sullen and resentful, abandoning their villages at our approach and taking their cattle and food stores with them. Fresh water was hard to find. Someone – perhaps my brother's forces or perhaps their local supporters – had poisoned many wells and waterholes with dead animals. The captain of my body-guard, Sayid Aziz – you know what a strong man he was – died vomiting blood and soiling himself after drinking tainted water.

'When the rains came, instead of relief they brought more problems. The earth turned to mud, slowing our progress, and diurnal fever and other diseases spread through my camp – the *hakims* could do nothing. Soon we were only managing two or three miles a day. When nearly half my men were ailing or already ill and many dead I decided that continuing the pursuit would be reck-less, not to say wasteful of human life. In their condition my men could not have been certain of withstanding a concerted attack by Akbar and the Marathas who, I was told, had joined him in strength. And so, reluctantly, I gave the order to retreat northwards. I knew you would be displeased and disappointed, therefore I rode ahead so I could report to you in person as quickly as possible. My main force will arrive within the next month. Then you will see for yourself their poor condition and depleted numbers . . . I did everything in my power to fulfil your orders, but I could see it was impossible and that my men were dying needlessly.'

Aurangzeb sat immobile, not a hint on his face of what he was thinking. Muazzam's heart beat faster. Had his father guessed? Aurangzeb had a way of delving deep into men's minds until he had laid bare their innermost thoughts. But he had been so careful . . . told no one of his true intentions . . . not written a single word to his aunt that might fuel his father's suspicions. Every day, with every lurch of his war elephant on the long tramp south, her urgent, whispered words had echoed in his head. *For my sake and your own, as well as our dynasty's, do not be over-eager. Take time in your preparations and the pursuit.* And he had obeyed because in his heart that was also what he wanted. Akbar was foolish and conceited with it – why should he think himself any more entitled to the Moghul throne than his brothers? – but Akbar was neither bloodthirsty nor hard-hearted, too much the reverse in fact if he wanted to seize the throne. He couldn't believe Akbar would have killed him if his plot had succeeded, and he himself would not be his brother's executioner if he could avoid it. And the searing, suffocating heat and then the drenching monsoon rains had been much more than a pretext for his slow advance and decision to withdraw. His men had truly been exhausted and ill.

Someone coughed nervously behind Muazzam and he could hear others shuffling their feet, but Aurangzeb said nothing. Prolonged silence was a device of his father's. He'd seen him use it countless times . . . making people so nervous they'd break the silence, even if it meant blurting out something ill considered that might incriminate themselves or at least show a weakness for Aurangzeb to exploit. But his father wouldn't intimidate him. Even if he suspected him, he could have no proof.

At last Aurangzeb shifted a little on his throne and leaned forward. 'You say you did everything in your power, but you did not. If you had you would have delivered to me dead or alive the traitor who once called himself my son. Instead, though you know the Deccan almost as well as I do myself, you allowed him and the Rajput traitors he is associating with to evade you and join forces with the Marathas. You were neither decisive nor determined enough in pursuing the campaign. Even worse, you abandoned it without seeking my permission. The first I knew was the brief message you despatched by *cossid* telling me you and your forces were crossing back to the north shore of the Narmada river.'

'Father . . .' Muazzam began, but Aurangzeb raised a finger on which was the only jewel he now regularly wore – Timur's heavy tiger ring. In the candlelight the gold glinted warmly, but his father's dark eyes as they gazed relentlessly into his were devoid of any emotion whatsoever. Determined though he was to resist, the need to escape that look was too great and Muazzam dropped his eyes to the floor. Having stared him down, Aurangzeb spoke.

201

'I repeat that you have been too cautious. That is not a quality I can tolerate in any of my generals, let alone a son. This was your opportunity to impress me but all you've proved is that you do not have the talent or courage to lead an army, let alone rule an empire.'

What did that mean? Had his father been considering him as his heir but now changed his mind? He had little time to ponder as Aurangzeb continued, 'I am removing you from your command and will find you some less demanding post more suited to your mediocre abilities. I see now that the only way is for me to lead the pursuit of my criminal son myself. Leave me. When I have decided your future, I will tell you.'

As Muazzam turned to go, he thought he glimpsed something – the flash of an eye perhaps, or the soft gleam of pearls – behind the grille set in the wall to allow women of the imperial family to observe council meetings. Had his aunt Jahanara been watching? If so, she would know he had honoured her whispered request to be tardy in hunting Akbar.

• ◆ •

'I'm glad I'm going with you. You know how much I hate it when you leave me behind.' Udipuri Mahal smiled up at Aurangzeb as she stroked the lean curve of his cheek with a finger. Though the years were passing, she was still beautiful. Sometimes he wondered if the joy he felt in possessing her sumptuous, satin-skinned body was a sin and he should not make love to her so often. But Udipuri was the one person who brought him peace. Her love for him still shone as brightly and honestly as when he had first taken her for his concubine. That was why he could not leave her behind

202

at Ajmer . . . God would understand how much he needed her unconditional, unquestioning love as he confronted the campaign ahead.

Udipuri pressed closer until he felt the yielding softness of her breasts, but this was not the time for love-making. In a few hours he must ride out at the head of his army to complete what Muazzam had failed to do – the capture of his son and the conquest of the Marathas. Taking her by the shoulders, he stooped to kiss her full red mouth. 'I must go. I still have many things to do before we leave, but I'm glad that at the end of each day you will be waiting for me in the *haram* tents.'

As Aurangzeb left the room and made his way through the *haram* quarters, his mind was already turning towards his new wider-bore cannon – he must make sure they had been properly mounted or their limbers would break. As he approached Jahanara's apartments he saw that the doors were open and one of her attendants was waiting just outside. 'Majesty, your sister asks if she may see you before you leave the *haram*.'

'Of course.' Aurangzeb passed through the sandalwood doors into Jahanara's rooms. If he was honest he had been avoiding being alone with her these past weeks. She'd said no more about Akbar's rebellion, but every time he saw her her face looked pinched, haunted even, and despite himself her obvious misery galled him. Why couldn't she at least try to understand the necessity for his actions instead of closing her mind to his arguments?

Jahanara was sitting by the casement, wrapped in a pale shawl. As he entered she picked up her ivory-handled stick and prepared to rise.

'No. Don't get up on my account.'

Jahanara settled back. 'It's good of you to see me, especially when you're so busy. When do you leave?'

'In three or four hours, as soon as I'm satisfied that everything's ready.'

'I will pray for you while you're away, but there's something I should tell you. These past few weeks I've felt my strength ebbing.'

'What do you mean? Are you ill? Why've you said nothing? Should I summon my *hakims*?'

Jahanara smiled and shook her head. 'I've no ailments any *hakim* can treat . . . I'm not ill but I'm weary, Aurangzeb, so weary . . . weary of life. Sometimes I barely have the strength to rise in the morning.'

'I will send *hakims*, whatever you say. They must have potions that will soothe and invigorate you. My campaign, God willing, will be short and when I return to Ajmer you'll be better.'

'Perhaps, though my heart tells me that we may not meet again on this earth.'

Aurangzeb felt his stomach clench. Kneeling beside her, he took her hand. The bones beneath the thin dry skin were fragile as a bird's. 'Sister, God doesn't allow anyone to know the length of their days.'

'I know that. But if I'm right, there are things I must say in case I never have another chance. No, don't interrupt. You must listen, if not for my sake, then for the sake of our mother who loved us both. I ask you yet again to spare Akbar and Zebunissa. Find it in your heart to forgive them.'

'Before God I can't. Akbar has gone too far. I can't forgive him. Neither can I overlook Zebunissa's treachery.'

'So the wheel is in motion once more and can't be

204

stopped. *Taktya takhta* – throne or coffin – that's what you've always believed, isn't it? I was foolish to hope I could prevent it but it was my duty – my holy duty, indeed – to keep trying, just as I again beg you to remember that your Hindu subjects have the same claim to your care and protection as the Muslims, though I know you will not listen. But I've something else I want to say . . . that whatever our differences I love you. I always have, ever since you were a small boy who thought there was a single simple solution to every problem and you knew it, and if others would not listen you tried to impose it with your fists. I pray you will find peace both in this life and the next.'

Jahanara leaned forward and he felt her lips brush his forehead. Tears pricked his eyes as, struggling to control his voice, he whispered, 'Please understand. I can't follow the path you want – not out of lack of love or respect for you but because my religious beliefs and the harsh realities of the world of men compel me otherwise.'

'I know what you feel, and why. It is the relentless inevitability of it all that makes me so sad.'

'Jahanara, I . . .' A trumpet blast echoed from the parade ground. The shrill sound was a welcome saviour. 'I can't stay any longer. But I will send you my best doctors and every day I'm away I'll pray that your health returns.'

'And I will pray for your safety and your happiness as I will pray for the safety and happiness of every member of our family. God go with you, Aurangzeb, my brother.'

Aurangzeb kissed his sister's lined forehead, stood up, hesitated a moment and then, resisting the urge to look back, walked quickly from the room, out through the *haram* and down the stairs into the courtyard. His favourite elephant, trunk painted red for war and canopied howdah strapped to its back, was standing patiently beneath the shade of a neem tree. Grooms were saddling horses and the musketeers of his bodyguard were checking and loading their weapons. Aurangzeb caught the smell of warm horse-flesh, of freshly oiled saddles and bridles, of gunpowder and of men's sweat – all the familiar smells of war. As he breathed deep he realised with relief that he was back in his world, where decision and action – not amorphous, ambiguous emotion – were paramount.

Three hours later, as kettledrums boomed from the upper storey of the gatehouse, Jahanara and Gauharara stood together on a *jali*-screened balcony on the high walls of Ajmer as their brother rode out to join the long lines of horsemen and foot soldiers drawn up outside the fort. Jahanara took hold of Gauharara's hand. How many times had she watched those she loved depart to war? How many times had she pondered the futility and the waste of it? As the final minutes before Aurangzeb's departure had passed, she'd wondered whether he might come to her again, or whether she should seek one last brief meeting. But she knew each had said all they had to say. Nothing could reconcile their opposing views of their religion or of the nature of empire and family duty.

As the vanguard moved south, led by Aurangzeb, an unseasonable thin drizzle began to fall, dampening the earth. Jahanara leaned on her stick, watching until Aurangzeb's elephant carried him over the brow of a low hill and he was finally lost from view. Raising an unseen hand, she waved and whispered, 'Farewell, my brother . . . peace go with you and all our people.'

• ◆ •

'They slaughtered members of my baggage train. There can be only one punishment – death beneath the elephant's foot – and I want it carried out immediately.' At Aurangzeb's words, six of the eight Marathas kneeling before him, hands bound tightly behind their backs, began calling out for mercy. Another – the youngest by the look of him – started rocking back and forth, eyes clenched tight, retching. The remaining Maratha, yelling defiance, tried to struggle to his feet, but two soldiers kicked him to the ground. Even so, the man – strongly built, with a scarred face and long hair hanging loose – glared up at Aurangzeb. Suddenly he spat a gob of yellowish, viscous phlegm which landed just above the hem of Aurangzeb's green robe and ran slowly down, leaving a snail-like slimy trail. A soldier raised the butt of his musket but Aurangzeb shook his head. 'Don't waste your strength against these vermin who offend before God and man when their death is so close.'

'You call us vermin, but what are you?' the straggle-haired man shouted, spittle still flecking his lips. 'You're nothing but a foreign invader seeking to impose your will on a land that isn't yours – a land that has never belonged to your people. Who are you Moghuls? Just a set of bandits from the wildernesses beyond the northern mountains who saw a chance to invade as a thief sees an opportunity to steal . . . and whom, led by Sambhaji, we will banish from our lands.'

Aurangzeb looked down at the man, noting the tight-clenched muscles in his neck, the veins standing out on his sweat-beaded forehead. Such passion, such defiance, such belief in a cause at the very moment when his life was about to be painfully extinguished was worth reflecting on. What made this man believe Sambhaji was a leader worth dying for? According to his spies, Sambhaji was more sybaritic and less driven than his father. But were his spies telling him the whole truth, or only reporting what they thought he most wished to hear? Sambhaji must have some qualities if he could inspire such courage and self-sacrifice. If so, it would be a mistake to under-estimate him and he must find a means to get to understand him better. He would talk to Wazim Khan about redoubling his efforts to infiltrate the Maratha camp to learn more about Sambhaji.

From of the corner of his eye Aurangzeb saw the massive grey shape of the execution elephant approaching, guided by a single *mahout* perched on its neck. Lifting his head, he saw that a few feet away some of his men were tipping from a bullock cart the slab of rock that served as an execution stone. Its surface was streaked brown with dried blood and it had iron rings at each corner. As soon as the stone was in position, Aurangzeb signalled to the captain of his guard. 'That one!' He pointed to the man who had spat at him. Probably the Maratha thought he was taking revenge for being spat at. He wasn't. He was respecting the man's courage by allowing him to die first.

Soldiers quickly stripped the man, who was silent now, and stretched him belly up across the stone, tying his wrists and ankles to the four rings. The elephant's shadow fell on him as the beast raised its foot, then at the *mahout's* command brought it slowly down. As his guts spilled, the Maratha screamed like a wild animal. Aurangzeb took a cloth from the young *qorchi* by his side and held it to his nose to block out the nauseating stench of noxious gases and human faeces. The *qorchi* himself suddenly squatted down and Aurangzeb heard him vomit but said nothing.

He was only young. In time he would learn that distasteful though they were such acts were necessary if a ruler was to inspire fear and thus maintain his authority.

By the time the remains of the seventh man were being removed from the stone on to an oiled cloth spread on the ground, ready to be rolled up and carried away to a burial pit dug well away from camp, the air had grown fouler. The last prisoner – the youngest – was shaking like an old man with palsy as soldiers yanked him to his feet and one hacked carelessly at the rope binding his wrists, slicing his skin with his steel dagger so that blood streamed down his right hand. The soldiers were about to rip off his clothes when Aurangzeb raised a hand.

'Wait. I've something to say to him.' He spoke slowly and deliberately. 'There is no reason why, young though you are, you should not die too. But I might offer you the chance to live.'

The young Maratha stared at him, still shaking.

'In return for mercy I want information about Sambhaji. I want to know everything, from what he likes to eat and drink to what makes him laugh, to how he talks to his men. Make me feel that I know him . . . that I am there in his camp with him. Can you do that?'

'Yes . . . yes, I can.'

'What is your name?'

'Santaji.'

'Well then, Santaji, convince me. For all I know you might never have met Sambhaji.'

'I was among his bodyguard for nearly two years until just before the rains my elder brother died of spotted fever and my father asked Sambhaji to allow me to return home.'

'Where is your father now?'

'He . . . he . . . was the second to die here.'

Aurangzeb considered. The fact that Santaji had just witnessed his father's execution would make him want revenge. He might therefore seek to mislead him. On the other hand his abject terror, the hope lighting his eyes as he'd grasped that he might not have to die, suggested that above all he wanted to live.

'Very well, we will see. Every day my officers will question you and report back to me. If I am satisfied with what you say, I will make your imprisonment easier. If not . . . well, remember what you have seen here today.'

Aurangzeb walked briskly to his horse and, waving away the groom who hurried forward to assist him, mounted with ease. He could no longer leap into the saddle as he could as a youth, but he was still agile enough, he reflected with no small satisfaction as he trotted off to inspect the picket lines around the perimeter of his camp.

That evening, as he rose from his prayers in his command tent, he was surprised to see his *qorchi* waiting by the entrance flap. He must have come in so quietly he hadn't heard him. 'Majesty, Iqbal Karim, your sister the Lady Gauharara's steward, has just arrived from Ajmer with a letter he insists he must give you at once.'

'Very well.' Iqbal Karim must have been just outside because within moments he was bowing low and holding out the letter. The wax bore the imprint of a leaping fish – Gauharara's seal. Aurangzeb broke it open and began to read. *Dear brother, our beloved sister Jahanara is dead . . .*

Struggling to maintaining his composure, he said quietly, 'Thank you, Iqbal Karim. Now leave me. I will send for you later.'

Once he was alone Aurangzeb let the letter fall and

dropped to his knees. Tears rolled unrestrainedly down his cheeks as he began to recite prayers for the repose of Jahanara's soul in Paradise. He barely heard the words as he spoke them. All his thoughts were for the sister whom of all his siblings he had loved the most . . . the one who had comforted him after their mother's death . . . the only one whose opinion of him had mattered. She had been so full of fear about the future – afraid for him, for the family, for the empire – she had seemed to lose the will to live. He'd seen it in her eyes, heard it in her voice. If only he'd been able to offer her some comfort, some hope, but he hadn't been able to. The only way to relieve her anxieties would have been to go against his conscience and betray his beliefs, and that he could never do.

The thought calmed him a little and after a moment's hesitation he picked up Gauharara's letter and read on.

After you left, our sister seemed to grow ever weaker, scarcely leaving her room where often she dozed away the day. In her waking moments she read Sufi writings and verses from the Koran and occasionally some of her beloved Persian poetry. Her appetite shrank to almost nothing. We could hardly persuade her to eat even a bowl of thin broth or a little boiled rice. She would always listen to the hakims' advice, smile and nod, then after they had left go on exactly as before. Ten days ago, she almost stopped eating altogether. I watched her fade before my eyes. I wanted to write and tell you but she absolutely forbade it. You know how forceful she could be, despite her gentle ways.

The day she died, her breathing was so fitful and shallow that her attendants called me to her just before dawn. Jahanara was herself until her final moments.

Speaking softly but distinctly, she told me to be sure to tell you her love for you had always been complete and unconditional, even though some of your actions had distressed her. Then she seemed to become a little agitated. Lifting her head slightly from the pillow she asked us to beg you to act with such love towards your own family – towards Akbar and Zebunissa, for whom she said she asked your mercy one last time – and towards those she called your wider family – your subjects – irrespective of their creeds and conditions. Once she had said those words she let her head fall back, and turning to the west breathed her last with an expression of perfect peace on her face.

Our sister left a letter asking to be buried in Delhi in a small grave open to the sky, just as old Muslim tradition decrees and as our ancestor Babur lies buried on the hillside above Kabul. She left some personal bequests but asked that her remaining possessions be sold and the proceeds shared between the Muslim and Hindu poor of Agra and Delhi. I am making the necessary arrangements.

May God give you strength in your grief as I pray God to relieve my sorrow. She was always the best of us.

Aurangzeb folded the letter carefully. As he knelt, wrapped in silent grief, he remembered something Jahanara had once told him – that Hindus had a name for a good and noble character: 'A Great Soul'. Those words fitted Jahanara perfectly.

Chapter 15

The Imperial Cockerel

As he rode beneath the gateway of the palace-fortress of Burhanpur Aurangzeb glanced up at the battling war elephants carved on the sandstone lintel. He hated this place, just as his father had done. That had been something they'd agreed about. He could almost hear Shah Jahan, half crazed with grief at the death of his empress, endlessly repeating lines from a chronicle of Akbar's time: *They told the great emperor that Burhanpur was a place of sinister reputation, ill-omened and dark, where no man could prosper . . .*

Though the sun was not yet beneath the horizon and the day had been unrelentingly humid and hot, Aurangzeb shivered. In those days, only twelve years old and naive, he'd hoped to comfort his father and be comforted by him in turn, but Shah Jahan had behaved as if the pain and sorrow of a loss that had afflicted the whole family was his alone.

Of course he'd been back to Burhanpur several times

since his mother Mumtaz's death but somehow this time was different. The nearer he'd approached, the more he'd begun to dread his arrival. So strong had this feeling become that he'd not let even Udipuri Mahal accompany him. Instead, he had left her twenty miles away with most of his entourage at the hilltop fortress of Asirgarh.

Was this sense of foreboding because of Jahanara's death? Probably. These past six weeks since he'd learned of it so many images from the past had crowded in on him. Most potent of all were memories of that summer's night, here in Burhanpur, when their mother's screams of agony filled the air. Through the half-open door of his mother's room he'd seen Jahanara, tears running down her face and long hair loose, stroking Mumtaz's brow, trying to soothe her. Jahanara had glanced around to see him watching horror-struck and rushed to close the door, but too late to stop him seeing Mumtaz screaming and threshing so wildly that her closest attendant, Satti al-Nisa could not hold her still. And he remembered his father, recalled from the battlefield, pushing past him as he ran in his riding clothes to her room and how again the door had been slammed shut on him. He'd sat huddled against a pillar in the courtyard until his mother's cries had stopped. He'd told himself that was good – that everything would be all right – the silence meant that she'd given birth to the new baby at last. But then wails of grief had told him that it wasn't all right at all . . .

He'd never entered his mother's rooms again. As soon as her body had been removed to its temporary burial place across the Tapti river, Shah Jahan had ordered the entrance to be blocked up. In all the long years since, those apartments on the third floor of the fortress palace overlooking the

214

shallow waters of the Tapti had lain silent and unvisited, holding their memories, their ghosts.

Now for the first time that seemed wrong. He had often prayed for his mother beneath the teardrop dome of the Taj Mahal but never here, where her soul had left her body. He would have the rooms opened up at once. Dismounting in the courtyard, he called for the steward of Burhanpur.

Two hours later, red dust hanging in the air and griming the pure white mourning garments in which he'd dressed, Aurangzeb knelt to pray in what had been his mother's apartments. Hangings, ragged now after more than half a century and bleached pale by the sun, fluttered at the casements. Mice and termites had long ago damaged the rugs and furniture and the fusty stink of bat droppings tainted the air. Even so, he gazed about him with a kind of wonder, seeing the rooms not as they were now but as they had once been, softly furnished and lit by scented candles. Something on the floor caught his eye. Stooping, he picked it up, and wiping away the crusting of dust found that it was an ivory comb. His mother's? He had often watched her attendant Satti al-Nisa comb her long silken hair scented with the attar of roses his mother loved.

Suddenly he felt he was choking. Dropping to his knees, he bent forward until his forehead pressed against the grimy sandstone floor and began to pray – at first for his mother's soul, then for Jahanara's and Roshanara's . . . and almost before he realised it he found himself praying not only for his father but for his brothers Murad, Shah Shuja and Dara Shukoh – something that in all these years he had never done. What had made him do that? He didn't

215

know. Only God who could see into men's hearts and minds would understand.

• ◆ •

Akbar lay back against the yellow silk bolster and took another swallow of wine. It warmed his stomach, just as the welcome he, his men and Jaginder's Rajputs had received from Sambhaji, now reclining by his side, on entering the Maratha homelands had warmed his heart and stiffened his resolve. For the moment at least he was beyond his father's reach. Poor Muazzam . . . he'd never come even close to catching him and he could imagine how his father would react. Aurangzeb had always thought Muazzam over-cautious and diffident, criticising him in public for it, just as he criticised all his sons except young Kam Bakhsh. Yet he'd never thought his father would be so vindictive towards his daughter. The news of Zebunissa's imprisonment had shocked him. He also felt guilty. After all, her support for him had brought their father's vengeance down on her. When he was victorious – as he would be – one of his first acts would be to ride to Gwalior himself and release her. She would become First Lady of the Empire, just as his aunt Jahanara had been . . .

Two acrobats, naked except for loincloths and their lithe, smooth-muscled bodies gleaming with oil, entered the room and bowing before him and Sambhaji began leaping and twisting and tumbling as if their bodies were boneless. As one flew threw the air, somersaulting three times, Sambhaji dipped into a leather pouch by his side and flung gold coins to them. Next came a squat barrel-chested man with a shaven head, followed by two men straining beneath the weight of a brazier

216

of glowing charcoals which they carefully lowered to the floor. The shaven-headed man pulled a dagger from his sash, the blade seemingly cocooned in layers of crimson fabric. As Akbar craned for a better look, the man thrust the dagger into the brazier until the fabric burst into flames. Then, circling the dagger two or three times above his head until the flames streamed out, he threw back his head and with one fluid movement inserted the flaming blade slowly into his mouth. Cheered on by Sambhaji and his commanders, he continued until only the metal hilt was visible. Then he withdrew the still burning blade, accompanied by a gush of flame, and handed it to an assistant. Next he took two further daggers from his sash and repeated the process, except this time they disappeared simultaneously into his gaping mouth. Akbar grinned at Sambhaji. It was a very long time since Aurangzeb had allowed the Moghul court to witness revelries like this and he applauded loudly as the fire-eater and his assistants bowed low and withdrew. But it seemed the entertainment wasn't over yet.

'My minister has something special for you . . . you'll like this.' Sambhaji's handsome, beardless young face looked mischievous. As he spoke, attendants doused the torches burning in brackets around the walls and the room that had been bathed in light was suddenly dark as ink. Panic seized Akbar's wine-fuddled mind. Heart pounding, his hand went for his dagger. Any moment he expected to feel a blade slashing across his throat or sliding through his ribs. Could it be treachery? Or one of his father's assassins? The emperor had agents everywhere. He tried to get to his feet but collided with Sambhaji in the darkness.

217

'Patience!' the Maratha said. Then, clapping his hands twice, he shouted 'Now!'

A door creaked open and a silhouetted figure appeared, followed by two more both holding five-branched candlesticks. As they came closer and the candlelight grew stronger, Akbar saw that the leading figure was a woman, her hair flowing loose over her shoulders, and wearing a clinging robe of some material that sparkled in the lights he could now see were carried by two boys. His heart began to resume its normal beat.

Approaching the dais on which Sambhaji and Akbar were standing, the woman bowed low. 'Welcome, Layla,' Sambhaji said. Layla's garment, shot through with what looked like silver threads, was almost transparent, revealing high full breasts, a tapering waist and opulent hips. At a nod from Sambhaji she began to dance, lit only by the candles held by the boys, with no music to guide her.

She barely moved her feet but swayed her body like a tree caught in the breeze. Then she began to revolve. In the flickering light Akbar saw her breasts and buttocks quiver and shake as she ran her hands over them, caressing her own soft flesh. She knew her power and revelled in it. His heart began to race once more. The silence in the room was intense . . . there couldn't be a man present who didn't want to possess her. Now Layla was coming towards him, Akbar realised. Sinking to her knees before him, she leaned back and raising her arms ran her hands through her richly hennaed hair. She was so close he could see the rise and fall of her breasts and the outline of her nipples.

'You like her, don't you?' Sambhaji whispered. Akbar nodded. 'Then go with her and together celebrate our alliance and the sweet days that lie ahead for both us and our peoples. You will find she is more than willing.'

Layla stood and held out her hand to Akbar. 'My lord.' She smiled, parting her full red lips slightly as she did so. To cries of encouragement from Sambhaji's men, he allowed her to lead him from the room to the apartments Sambhaji had prepared for him nearby, smelling the heady scent of her – *champa* flowers mingled with sweat. He could barely wait for the doors to close behind them before taking her in his arms. 'Patience, Majesty . . .' Layla whispered. Stepping back from him, with one swift, fluid moment she pulled her shimmering robe over her head and let it fall to the floor.

Akbar had never seen such a perfect body and for a moment wonder was stronger even than desire. Then Layla's laugh reminded him he was staring like a dumb-struck schoolboy. He pulled her to him again, running his hands along that sinuous waist and down over the satin swell of her hips. Layla's hands were also at work, pulling at his tunic. 'Wait. Let me undress you, Majesty . . .' Reluctantly letting go of her, Akbar stood, eyes closed, blood throbbing, as she deftly unfastened the clasps of his tunic, the buckle of the jewelled belt at his waist and the waistband of his breeches. When he was as naked as she was, he felt her begin to caress him with her fingertips and her tongue – pointed as a little cat's – licking the hollow of his throat.

She had asked him to be patient but that was impossible. Picking her up, he carried her to the low bed and laid her on it. She drew him down beside her and continued her caresses as he entered her and began to thrust. At the moment of climax he threw back his head, laughing with the joy of it. This was the start of a new life – a life beyond his father's shadow in which he could achieve anything he wished.

•◆•

'What do you think? Should we attack?' Akbar glanced at Sambhaji, who grinned back.

'Why not? My father wouldn't have hesitated . . .'

'Neither would mine.' Akbar muttered. Devious and slippery as a snake though his father could be in his scheming, no one could doubt Aurangzeb's courage on the battlefield or his ability to spot and take a military opportunity. These past months since joining Sambhaji, Akbar had been hoping for such a chance to strike against the advance Moghul forces moving forward from Aurangzeb's base at Burhanpur. Soon he would show his father his true worth.

He wriggled forward a little on his stomach to get a better view of the squat mud-brick fort a thousand feet below the high ridge on which he and Sambhaji were lying. Sitting on a low island in the middle of the Tapti river, a mile or so from the bottom of the ridge, it looked old but still strong. Yet according to reports brought by two of Sambhaji's men who had entered the fort disguised as itinerant hawkers, the garrison left behind a month ago while the main advance Moghul force probed further south wasn't large – no more than a hundred and fifty at most. The river, wide but shallow, should be easy to ford and there seemed little need to worry about artillery. Those narrow old walls with their slits belonged to the days of arrows, not cannonballs. The only place where cannon could be positioned on them was the flat top of the gatehouse, but there was no sign of any even there.

'When shall we attack? Tonight?' Akbar asked.

'Why not? We outnumber the defenders at least two to one. And there won't be much light – it's a new moon – so we should be able to take them by surprise.'

Action at last. Sometimes these past weeks Akbar had wondered whether Sambhaji – hospitable and welcoming though he was – shared his determination to confront the Moghuls as soon as possible. But that was unfair . . . he had just been waiting for the right moment, and when scouts had reported that the Moghuls had occupied this fort and deposited a large amount of supplies there he'd not hesitated. How good it would feel to win a first victory over his father's troops. Aurangzeb would never think his son daring and imaginative enough to bypass the advancing Moghul force to attack a fort his commanders thought they'd left safe and secure to the rear . . .

Even though it had been midday when they reached the ridge, the remaining hours of daylight passed with agonising slowness for Akbar as his own troops and the Marathas made their preparations in their makeshift camp concealed among trees below the ridge overlooking the fort. Each time Akbar scanned the sky, the sun seemed not to have changed position. To distract himself he rehearsed over and over again the plan that he, Sambhaji and their commanders had agreed. It was simple enough. As darkness fell they would move up to the crest of the ridge with their equipment. A little later, when most in the fort would be thinking only of food and sleep, they would descend on foot in small groups – horses would make too much noise – wade across the river to the island on which the fort stood and assemble under cover of a grove of mango trees about two hundred yards from the gatehouse. Then – assuming that they remained undetected – two men would creep forward to place a large sack of gunpowder as close as they could get to the gates. Simultaneously, others in groups of ten, each including two musketeers to provide covering fire, would position themselves around the perimeter of the fort, keeping tight to the walls, ready to scale them. At the agreed signal – a single trumpet blast – the men with the gunpowder would light the fuse that would quickly detonate it, hoping to blow the gates off their hinges. With some of his best men, Akbar would at once charge towards any breach while under Sambhaji's direction the other troops would assault the walls.

As the last of the apricot glow drained from the western skies, Akbar began to make the steep climb to the crest of the ridge with his *qorchi* by his side carrying his long sword and his bodyguards close behind. There was just enough light for him to make out Jaginder's long-shanked Rajputs, their weapons strapped across their backs, and Sambhaji's Marathas, some of whom were carrying ropes coiled over their shoulders, others manhandling scaling ladders or carrying bags of gunpowder and musket balls.

From the crest of the ridge, the Tapti glinted faintly beneath the pale sliver of the rising moon while the dark mass of the fort itself was almost invisible except for the occasional orange prick of light from the gatehouse and living quarters. The only sound was a far-off tinkle of bells as somewhere a herdsman was late in driving his flock home for the night. Akbar breathed deeply. Soon Sambhaji arrived. 'Betel?' the Maratha whispered, holding out a silver box, but Akbar shook his head, eyes fixed on the shadowy scene below.

'All seems quiet down there, but my father has eyes and ears everywhere so I've sent a couple of my scouts unarmed and dressed as country people just to make sure. We don't want to walk into a trap.'

'Are you afraid of him?'

'What?' Akbar, who had been lying on his stomach, sat up, taken aback by the question.

'Sometimes when you talk about your father you sound in awe of him.'

'I'm not frightened of him but I do know what he's capable of. You shouldn't underestimate him either.'

'I don't. But I've never forgotten how my father outwitted him by having us smuggled out of the Agra fort in baskets of sweetmeats!' Sambhaji chuckled but Akbar didn't join in. How could the younger man understand how he felt about his father when he and his own father Shivaji had been so close? For a moment he felt a pang – jealousy? No, that was too strong for it – regret perhaps. If Aurangzeb had been a different kind of father he wouldn't be on this ridge, alienated from his family and friends like Tahavvur Khan and reliant on those who in other circumstances would have been his enemies. But this was no time for such thoughts. Akbar looked up into the night sky, trying to judge the hour once more. At that moment there was a noise behind him. Looking round he saw Ashok, one of the scouts he had despatched to the fort.

'What did you discover down there, Ashok?'

'All seems calm and quiet, Majesty. They've closed the gates as usual for the night but there are no guards outside and they don't appear to suspect a thing. And I re-checked the ford – the water's barely waist high at its deepest.'

Akbar exchanged a look with Sambhaji. 'Then let's go!'

As whispered orders passed along the ranks of waiting men, the first groups began to move over the ridge and down the slope towards the fort. Akbar and his men went first. His every instinct was to hurtle down the steep hillside as fast as he could run and he had to force himself to move cautiously, taking care not to dislodge stones or rocks. As he picked his way, he started as the hooting of an owl followed by the shriek of its small victim pierced the night, both sounds seemingly magnified by the soft enshrouding darkness.

After half an hour Akbar reached the riverbank, where he waited for his men to gather around him. At any moment he expected to hear cries of alarm and to see torches flare on the fort battlements but there was nothing, even when two of his men dropped a metal box containing grappling irons. Then, following Ashok, Akbar and his men waded into the warm waters of the Tapti. Ashok had done well. The fording place was indeed quite shallow – it wasn't hard to hold muskets and powder horns above the water – and with a sandy river bed and barely any current there was little danger of slipping or of raising too many of the splashes that might betray them.

Reaching the island, Akbar and his companions made for the assembly point beneath the mangoes' dense-leaved, spreading branches. Soon the rest of his soldiers, the Marathas and the Rajputs had joined them and two of Sambhaji's men were moving stealthily towards the gate-house, bent double under their sacks of gunpowder, long fuse and tinder box, while two others, similarly equipped, stood ready in reserve in case some mishap befell their comrades. Still all was quiet.

Meanwhile, beneath the mango trees, the ropes and ladders were being readied by the ten-man units who swiftly crept away to take up their places beneath the fort walls. A low call – not an owl this time but an agreed signal from the men with gunpowder that the sack was in place – showed that they were ready. Nodding at Akbar and with a whispered 'Good luck', Sambhaji moved off to join one of the assault teams beneath the fort's walls. At Akbar's signal, his trumpeter gave the single blast. Almost immediately shouts came from within the fort. Moments later torches appeared on the battlements. Then an explosion split the air. Akbar's ears were ringing and he was choking on dust. The men with the gunpowder had done their work.

'With me!' Sword in hand, Akbar ran into the dust and acrid smoke around the gatehouse. The blast had shattered the mud bricks on one side of the gatehouse and one of the two iron-bound wooden gates was flat on the ground. As he ran, he heard cries as other attackers flung their ropes and grappling hooks over the walls and began quickly scaling their ladders. Then he tripped over a pile of rubble and as he stumbled forward what could only have been a musket ball whistled above his head.

Regaining his balance, Akbar saw in the semi-darkness only a few feet away a musketeer wearing a green tunic half concealed behind some jagged brickwork – part of the half-demolished wall adjoining the gatehouse. He was concentratedly ramming powder and ball down the long barrel of his gun, ready for a second shot. As Akbar drew his dagger and pulled back his arm, the man looked up. Akbar gasped to see a grizzled face he remembered well.

In his younger days Karim Khan had been one of Aurangzeb's inner group of trusted bodyguards. Akbar hesitated, almost about to lower his arm until he saw Karim Khan, who clearly recognised him too, return grim-faced to the task of reloading his musket as fast as he could. Akbar hesitated no longer but threw the dagger, catching Karim Khan in the throat as he was levelling his musket again. As his blood pumped out, the veteran pitched forward and his musket clattered to the ground by Akbar's feet.

Leaping over Karim Khan's still twitching body, Akbar ran as hard as he could towards a group of his men a few yards ahead who were trying to fight their way deeper into the fort. A young officer was outdistancing his comrades as he raced, sword outstretched, towards an interior gate when suddenly he spun round and fell with a scream, dropping his sword and clutching at his neck. Swerving to put enemy musketeers off their aim, Akbar joined his men already hewing and hacking at the Moghul troops who were now rushing from their quarters, struggling to pull on their equipment. Sometimes slipping on pools of blood on the flagstones, Akbar helped his men push the outnumbered but resolute Moghuls slowly back, until at last they burst through a wide archway into the fort's inner courtyard. He glanced around, body taut and ready to confront the next defender, but most seemed to have disappeared again into the fort's buildings while a few were throwing down their weapons in surrender.

Fighting was still continuing unabated on the battlements and as Akbar looked up a man pitched head first from them to splatter his brains on the flagstones – friend or foe he couldn't tell in the moonlight. His own men and Sambhaji's Marathas looked to be having the best of the fight up there. Sambhaji himself, more easily distinguishable because of the white plume in his helmet, was at their head fighting a bear-like man nearly twice his size, nimbly evading his slashing scimitar until, suddenly darting forward, he dodged beneath the man's raised arm to thrust his sword into his burly chest. His adversary staggered about for some moments, then also crashed arms flailing to the courtyard below.

Akbar saw one of his officers run down some steep steps from the battlements and rush towards him. 'Majesty, the governor of the fort has barricaded himself in one of the towers with some of his men, but he has just shouted that if you promise to spare the lives of himself and his remaining soldiers he will yield the fort and all the supplies it contains. He insists it must be you who gives his word and not Sambhaji.'

'Tell him Sambhaji and I are one, but I agree to his terms on a single condition. He must also surrender every Moghul banner in the fort to me. I am emperor. It is fitting.'

• ◆ •

I have taken your fort and these banners just as I will take the throne. With my allies whom you have wronged as you have wronged me I will fight until I have won justice for myself and your oppressed people. Akbar.

Aurangzeb almost smiled. 'If I'd ever needed proof that Akbar is naive and foolish, it's here in this letter. Can he really imagine that his capture of one insignificant, barely defended little fort would leave me quaking?'

'What is it? What does he say?' Udipuri Mahal sipped

227

from the glass that he knew probably contained wine as well as sherbet. Despite his strict beliefs he could not bring himself to challenge her about it. Once when he had done so she'd claimed that wine had been invented in the land of her birth, Georgia, and that its taste reminded her of her homeland and it seemed to guard her against the colic to which she was prone. Neither had he refused her pleas to be allowed to join him at Burhanpur. Since the night he had opened up his mother's apartments he felt he had dispelled some of the brooding memories and air of ill omen that hung over the place, helping him to shake off the melancholy torpor that had gripped him since Jahanara's death.

'Akbar crows like a cockerel over one tiny victory and he has the gall to send me some banners which he seized as trophies. He is as arrogant as he is stupid and conceited.'

'I know he has transgressed and I would never defend him, but I don't like to hear you speak so harshly of your own flesh and blood. It makes me fear for Kam Bakhsh if our son should ever offend you.'

'I love Kam Bakhsh – you know I do – but when he becomes a man he must learn the lessons Akbar has not: to obey and to be dutiful. Don't look so anxious. I hope Kam Bakhsh will not grow up to disappoint me, but his fortune lies in his own hands, in the choices he makes. Make him understand that and you will be doing the best any mother could do for her son . . . especially when he is an imperial prince.'

Udipuri took another sip from her glass. He had rarely seen her lovely face so pensive but she must understand the realities – that he was an emperor, holding the fate of millions in his hands. Pity and compassion even towards his own family were weakening and womanly emotions – something Jahanara would never acknowledge.

'What will you do now – I mean about Akbar?' Udipuri asked.

'What I came here to do. March out with the main body of my army and join my advance forces. At their head I shall defeat him and put an end to his arrogance once and for all. We leave Burhanpur in three days.'

Chapter 16

Enemies Under Islam

'W azim Khan, bring in the deserter – and reassure him he has nothing to fear. I will keep every promise you've made on my behalf.' Aurangzeb smiled as his trusted spymaster bowed and hurried as fast as his ever-increasing girth allowed to the entrance of the scarlet command tent. From what Wazim Khan had already told him, he and his assembled commanders were about to learn the truth about the marriage of convenience his traitorous son had made with Sambhaji.

Since he'd led his forces south from Burhanpur six months ago, he'd pushed almost unopposed into the Deccan as far as the banks of the Godavarj river, where he was now encamped with his army. But what had he really achieved? Nothing except to exhaust his men and empty his coffers. Akbar, Sambhaji and their forces had remained hidden in their barren hills, refusing battle and making only occasional hit and run raids. Even useful intelligence had been difficult to find. Yet now Wazim Khan's mixture of threats and promises seemed to have worked again, just as they had with Tahavvur Khan, who was now languishing, reportedly guilt-racked and in declining health, in an obscure post in northern Kashmir.

Wazim Khan soon reappeared followed by a slim young man with a neatly trimmed beard who prostrated himself as the spymaster spoke. 'Feroz Beg, Majesty. He was with your son just a few days ago.'

'Rise, Feroz Beg, and for the benefit of those present who do not know, tell them who you are and what position you held in the rebellious wretch Akbar's service.'

'I . . . I am the only son of Mohammed Beg, your old assistant treasurer. Our family came with your great ancestor Babur from Ferghana.'

Aurangzeb nodded. That Mohammed Beg's last years might be harsh ones if his son did not cooperate had been one of the key levers Wazim Khan had employed. 'And your place in the rebel camp?'

'A counsellor. Akbar would also sometimes use me as an envoy to sound out potential allies in foreign courts.' Feroz Beg's voice was hesitant and difficult to hear.

'Speak up. Any other duties?' Aurangzeb knew Wazim Khan had first begun to work on Feroz Beg after he had been revealed as one of those who'd tried to suborn one of Aurangzeb's own generals. Just in case the loyalty of any of his commanders might be wavering, he wanted them to realise he was aware that Akbar had contacted some of them. 'Sometimes I approached members of your own court . . . but latterly only to help Wazim Khan discover traitors to you, I swear, Majesty.'

'I believe you.' Aurangzeb looked round his assembled commanders but few met his eye. He turned back to

231

Feroz Beg. 'Now tell me the state of affairs in Akbar's camp.'

'These past months Akbar and Sambhaji have grown increasingly dissatisfied with each other as they've withdrawn further into the Deccan hills in the face of your advance. In particular Sambhaji's caution tries Akbar's patience . . .'

'How do you know?'

'Just six weeks ago,' Feroz Beg's voice became stronger, less hesitant as his confidence increased, 'I attended a private council of war – one of only a dozen or so present besides Akbar and Sambhaji. Akbar was propounding his plan to advance once more from the Deccan hills into your territories to confront you, appealing as he went for as many allies as possible to join him. He even mentioned sending me to the Rajputs to encourage them to join him again. He was full of enthusiasm, conjuring pictures of rapid advances, easy victories and the disintegration of your armies in the face of their combined assault. Sambhaji was doubtful. He kept asking how many allies Akbar had already secured, demanding whether he – Sambhaji, that is – could be sure enough of victory to commit his troops to exchanging the protection of the hills they know so well for the hot plains and desert where they would be more vulnerable to the stronger and more heavily armed Moghul forces. Akbar replied that he should believe in their mission to take the Moghul throne from you to the benefit of all the people of Hindustan.

'Sambhaji laughed. "That grand mission of yours may be why you might wish to advance but it doesn't explain why I should. Why should I risk everything my father gained by one great attack, planned more in hope than in realism? I may not have inherited my father's military brains but I know he would never have done as you suggest, and nor shall I. We must take smaller, surer steps."

"'But that will take too long," Akbar protested.

"'Time is surely on our side. We are much younger than your father. The longer he rules, the more he will alienate the people, making our task easier. The longer we keep his army here, the worse its morale will become, and the greater the burden of the taxes he will have to raise to support it," Sambhaji retorted.

'These exchanges continued for some time, growing ever more heated until an exasperated Sambhaji accused Akbar of stupidity and reckless optimism. Your normally placid son roared at him, "At least I prefer to fight rather than find reasons not to." Incensed, Sambhaji rushed at Akbar and swung a fist at him. Akbar ducked and wrestled Sambhaji to the ground where they rolled around like nothing more than two young schoolboys until we, their advisers, pulled them apart. Later they were reconciled, formally at least, recognising that they needed each other. However, Sambhaji is committed to a policy of attrition and remains reluctant for the present to undertake anything more than brief raids beyond the Deccan. Akbar has grown more listless and despairing. Indeed, he has lost so much heart that he has begun to talk of going to Persia to seek help from the shah as your ancestor Humayun did. He even suggested I might be his envoy.'

'If my son does go to Persia, he will prove himself even more a traitor than he has already,' was Aurangzeb's only outward response. Inwardly, part of him was a little relieved to hear that Akbar might flee Hindustan. It would spare him the dilemma of whether to execute him when he captured him, as he surely would if he remained in the Deccan. But another part was calculating how much support the shah and Akbar's dead mother's powerful Persian relations might give and how much mischief they might foment together on his always turbulent north-west frontier. Consciously putting such thoughts aside, he asked, 'How are Sambhaji and Akbar managing to fund and arm their troops at the same time as evading my own armies?'

'By the help of Bijapur and Golcunda, Majesty. The Bijapuris are providing the Marathas safe passage through their territories and sanctuary from your pursuing forces when they need it in return for a cut of the booty they seize from your lands to help refill their depleted treasuries. The Golcundis are sending the products of some of their diamond mines to fund local purchases of horses as well as the latest cannon and muskets from the English at the new settlement on the coast they call Bombay. The Golcundis see the Marathas as a first line of defence against you.'

'I'd heard rumours to this effect.' Aurangzeb thumped the arm of his chair with his fist. 'Is there no solidarity between the followers of Islam?'

'Both rulers believe you are a greater threat to them than Sambhaji. What's more, they regulate neither their own lives – nor the policy of their states towards their neighbours – according to the ordinances of our religion. They have other priorities.'

'What do you mean?

'The ruler of Golcunda, Adil Hasan, like many of his predecessors is utterly lax in his religious observances and gives himself over to licentiousness, indulging his every desire and squandering his great wealth in dissolute revelries.

234

I can give you an example I myself witnessed, when I was sent on a mission to Hyderabad. On Friday – though it was the holy day – Adil Hasan watched from a balcony as what must have been a thousand dancing girls entered the square, scantily clad in diaphanous *cholis* and tight-fitting pantaloons. As they began to dance to the beat of Golcundi drums, gyrating and thrusting out their hips, Adil Hasan ordered the large barrels of palm wine set up in each corner to be broached and jugs to be filled with the contents and passed to some of his favoured soldiers and courtiers clustering around the square. They immediately began greedily to quaff the strong liquor.

'As the darkness fell, attendants lit tall candles and the drumming grew louder and more insistent whereupon the women began to sing, some cupping their breasts wantonly with their hands. Becoming aroused, the men began to move towards them and the women opened their *cholis* fully, revealing their breasts glistening with sweat. Soon men and women were copulating openly and unashamedly. Others cavorted naked in the square's fountains which were also bubbling with palm wine. Such a scene of lust I have never witnessed before, Majesty. Even Adil Hasan joined in. He and one of his concubines stood at the front of the balcony and began to explore each other's bodies with their hands, probing, caressing—'

'Enough of Golcunda! No need for any more details of such ungodly immorality. Why does Bijapur assist Sambhaji and Akbar?'

'The ruler Sikander is a weak youth and as Bijapur's treasuries empty the divisions within the ruling family are deepening. Most of the rival factions see the Marathas as potentially useful allies in their internal struggles as well as protection against you. They are competing with each other to offer Sambhaji and Akbar concessions and assistance in their fight against you in return for their support. Sikander himself believes Maratha help is the best way of retaining his throne.'

'These rulers will learn not to consort with upstart traitors.' Aurangzeb rose to his feet. 'I have decided. We will conquer both Golcunda and Bijapur. This will both cut off their backing for the impious mountain rat Sambhaji and my traitorous son and at the same time extend and enrich our empire.'

At once some of Aurangzeb's commanders began to shout, 'God is great. *Zindabad Aurangzeb*. Long live the emperor!' The rest quickly joined in, clenched fists raised in the air, acclaiming his decision unquestioningly.

But as the noise subsided Muazzam, who had been standing by his father's chair throughout the discussion, said quietly, 'Father, remember what slow progress I made in the south. Even though as you often suggest much of the blame may fall on my shortcomings I truly believe that not all should. The terrain is harsh. The Marathas are united and fierce in their loyalty to Sambhaji and have time and again proved themselves good fighters. So too by reputation are the soldiers of Bijapur and in particular Golcunda. I think we need a large army to make sure of success – even larger than we now have for our campaign against Sambhaji. Acquiring such a force will take time and perhaps mean raising more taxes, which will cause our people further pain and perhaps even rouse discontent among them.'

'Muazzam, why must you always be so timid? You should know me well enough to realise that my outburst

236

against the rulers of Bijapur and Golcunda and my decision to expand our territories at their expense were not as spontaneous as they might have appeared. I have been pondering war against them for some time, assessing the relative strength of our forces with the help of Wazim Khan's reports. Our present armies will be sufficient, I assure you.'

Looking his son hard in the eye, he added, 'Only I can lead the main force in the first assault, which will be against Bijapur. But I have decided to give you a chance to redeem yourself by commanding a preliminary expedition to test the strength of the Golcundi fortresses, their forces and their resolve.'

• ◆ •

The crack of his cannon echoed around Aurangzeb's head. Only their barrels protruded from the protection of the earthworks he had had constructed and only then when they were about to fire on the great stone bastions of Bijapur. Once they had done so, his gunners, sweating and stripped to the waist, worked hard to restrain their recoil with thick ropes and then to ram powder and cannonballs down their barrels. Next they manhandled the cannon on their heavy limbers back into the firing position before putting the taper to the firing hole once more.

In the past six weeks since his army had begun besieging Bijapur there had been few occasions when cannon barrels had burst, either from heat or because of faults in their casting. Both his gunners and the foundry workers must know their business. Even so, the need to build new limbers and to train additional men, as well as the time it had taken to haul the heavy cannon and the other siege equipment laboriously through the Deccan hills after the

237

monsoon, meant it was nearly a year since he'd decided to subdue Bijapur and Golcunda once and for all and annex them to his empire before turning his attention to Akbar and Sambhaji.

Through the wisps of drifting cannon smoke he could see the crenellated walls of Bijapur and above them the white marble domes of the tallest of the celebrated palaces. The city's walls looked to be proving resilient although pockmarked by cannonballs in places, particularly where they were built out to protect the main gatehouse through which the twisting ramp led into the city. In addition to its strong walls Bijapur was surrounded by a half-filled moat. What's more, warned of his approach, the Bijapuris had cleared a considerable area of flat ground bordering the moat, burning off grass and shrub so that the area could be swept by musket and cannon fire from the walls. Therefore he had had to position his own cannon further back than he'd wished to keep them out of musket range, which meant the cannonballs from even his biggest cannon were losing some of their impetus before they hit the stone walls. The Bijapuris had also had plenty of time to stock the food and munitions stores within the city and the monsoon had filled their water tanks. They only fired back at his lines when they were sure of a target, thus conserving their ammunition supplies. If he wished to secure an early victory before either Golcunda or the Marathas could send aid if they were so minded he would need to make a frontal assault.

He turned to Wazim Khan, who was standing a short distance away. 'Have you any ideas how we might fill in the section of the moat that fronts the gate so that we can launch an attack with some hope of success?'

'My first thought, Majesty, is that we would need either darkness or smoke to provide cover for any such attempt.'

'Smoke is insufficient and subject to the vagaries of the breeze. Darkness it would have to be.'

'The full moon is in a few days. Its light will be a problem we'll need to bear in mind.'

'I suppose so. I hope we can get started before then.'

Wazim Khan said nothing for a minute or so, but then replied, 'Majesty, the moat is a difficult obstacle but I have one idea. In our work together we've many times proved the power of reward. Money is a potent lure for rich and poor alike. We've a great many destitute and near starving labourers among our camp followers for whom we've no employment now the camp and earthworks are completed. Why not offer them a few coins for each basket of earth they succeed in throwing into the moat?'

'Interesting. As you say, we have little other use for the labourers so there can be no harm in making the offer. And you're right – they will risk their lives more willingly with the promise of reward than if we urge them out from our lines at lance point. But to have any chance of success they'll need to advance in a body and in darkness.'

'Of course, Majesty. And we will need to have musketeers and gunners to provide covering fire if they are spotted from the walls, as must be likely.'

'It is worth trying. We will launch such an expedition just after midnight tomorrow. That should leave enough time to dig out sufficient earth for the purpose.'

Wazim Khan had been right, Aurangzeb thought as he stood in the semi-darkness thirty-six hours later. Thousands of camp followers eager for the coin he had offered had assembled with full baskets of earth. Even some of the local people had joined them. Many were clad only in loincloths, nearly all were barefoot and thin-faced. Several were glancing towards the open chests full of coin he'd had positioned near the assembly points, well guarded of course, so that they could see the reward for success.

In the time since his announcement he'd refined his plans with his officers. The first rank of labourers would be paid if they dumped their earth on the flat ground halfway towards the moat to provide shallow breastworks to which musketeers would run forward to give covering fire in addition to that from the cannon. The next rank would pile their earth three quarters of the way to the moat so that the muskateers could advance further. It would only be the third and subsequent ranks – there were at least twelve of two hundred men or so each – who would throw their dirt into the moat of Bijapur itself.

'Give the order to begin,' Aurangzeb said to one of his officers. A few minutes later the first labourers started to run out from the Moghul lines on their spindly legs. Most were carrying basketfuls of earth on their heads but others were working in pairs, carrying larger wicker baskets between them. As far as he could see in the gloom, the leaders had already covered about a quarter of the distance to the moat but then torches flared into light on the walls of Bijapur. Soon afterwards musket shots crackled, followed by the crash of Bijapuri cannon. Immediately, his own musketmen and artillery opened counter-fire.

By the light of the frequent cannon flashes he saw several labourers fall, spilling their loads. One or two rose and began to limp back towards the Moghul lines. The rest lay still or writhed in their death agonies. Some of the uninjured at once dropped their baskets and turned to flee. Many still eager for reward, ran on into the drifting smoke and darkness, seeming to release their earth as ordered at the halfway point between his lines and the moat before turning. Groups of Moghul musketeers crouching low and clad in black to make themselves difficult to see, rushed forward to take up firing positions behind the small earth mounds the labourers had created. The second rank of earth-carriers ran out quickly. Several collapsed, a few stumbling over the bodies of the first, most hit by musket or cannonballs. A third and a fourth rank broke cover, running hard. More and more twisted and fell but still many ran from his defences, only a few refusing to move forward. Aurangzeb found it increasingly difficult to see in the darkness and drifting smoke how far they were getting towards the moat, but the advance looked to be going well.

• ◆ •

Four days later Aurangzeb sat alone at breakfast in his scarlet command tent. His plan had only partly succeeded. Perhaps a hundred labourers had managed to empty their baskets of earth into the moat that first night. As he'd promised, he'd rewarded them, as well as those in the first two ranks who'd placed their dirt where ordered. Their efforts had raised a small hillock-like island in the scummy waters that half filled the moat. He'd ordered a second wave of earth-carriers forward the following night, doubling the previous night's promised rewards and sending with them elephants pulling logs to be pushed into the moat, but this time the Bijapuris had been ready. Fewer labourers had reached the moat and all but one of

241

the elephants, hampered by the weight of the logs, had been struck down by cannonballs. Their mangled corpses now littered the flat ground bordering the moat. The one elephant that reached the moat had been hit in its belly by a cannonball and toppled in. The growing stench of death from the bodies of men and elephants was everywhere but at last the piteous cries of the wounded were growing less. He'd felt he'd had no choice but to forbid rescue attempts because of the risk that so many more lives would be lost.

He stood up from the low table at which he'd been eating and began to pace the tent, which was growing increasingly airless as the sun rose higher in the sky. What should be his next move? For the moment he could think of nothing beyond patiently waiting for hunger to weaken the bodies and minds of the defenders while keeping plenty of scouts posted to warn of any approaching relief forces.

A *qorchi* entered and bowed. 'Wazim Khan to see you, Majesty.'

Immediately, Wazim Khan bustled in, slightly out of breath and wiping his fleshy face with a cream cloth. 'Majesty, there is a commotion around the gatehouse of Bijapur.'

'What sort of commotion?'

'Two or three Bijapuris emerged on their side of the moat and appear to be making preparations to cross. They've carried out some kind of raft.'

'Order our men to hold their fire,' Aurangzeb said as he moved past Wazim Khan out of the tent into the sunlight. Two men were being poled on the raft across the moat by four others. From a distance the two looked

242

like envoys. It could only mean the Bijapuris were ready to come to terms. The very act of sending out envoys would be a blow to morale, showing the people of Bijapur how little faith their leaders had in their ultimate victory. 'If they are indeed ambassadors tell them I will not negotiate but I will be merciful if Bijapur surrenders. There will be no massacres, no rapes of decent women and no looting of private homes.' As Wazim Khan moved towards the Moghul front line to carry out his instructions, Aurangzeb could scarcely contain his joy as he turned back to his tent. But he did so with difficulty knowing he must keep any outward rejoicing until he was absolutely sure of Bijapur's intentions. Otherwise he ran the risk of appearing foolish and premature in front of his men.

Towards midday, as Aurangzeb watched from beneath the awning of his command tent, the two envoys – for they had indeed been envoys – emerged from Bijapur's defences again. They were followed by ten men straining to carry a more elaborate boat which they placed on the moat's scummy, bloodstained and evil-smelling waters. Then a slight figure appeared, dressed all in white, and seated himself on a low stool in the middle of the boat before the ten men began poling it the short distance to the Moghul side of the moat. Reaching it, the figure seemed to slip as he scrambled ashore near the bloated corpse of the dead elephant but he quickly regained his feet and his poise. It could only be Sikander. Two green-turbaned Moghul bodyguards took station on either side of him and led him towards the Moghul lines past putrefying corpses upon which vultures were feeding, tearing flesh and sinew with their hooked beaks. Ten minutes later Sikander was approaching Aurangzeb's tent. Stopping five yards short of where Aurangzeb was standing, he held out in both his hands an emerald-encrusted gold staff and in a high-pitched but firm voice said, 'I hand this, my ancestors' staff of office, to you as token of my surrender to you of Bijapur and its territories.' As he spoke he bowed low.

Aurangzeb noticed that Sikander's right forearm was heavily bandaged and blood was slowly reddening the dressings. 'Did one of our musket balls teach you to submit?'

'No. One of my uncles, Iqbal Aziz, tried to kill me last night with his dagger. With my guards' help I fought him off and he is now dead, but as my *hakims* stitched and dressed the wound I knew he would not be the last to make such an attempt on me and that riven as it was by jealousies and ambition Bigapur must surely fall. However despicable it may sound to you, I realised I hold my life sweet – sweeter than my throne – and want to enjoy it longer. Therefore I decided that against the laws of nature and kinship my life would be safer if I put myself and my realm immediately in the hands of you, a stranger and an enemy to my people, than if I remained any longer with my disloyal and warring family.'

Aurangzeb turned to Wazim Khan standing behind him. Iqbal Aziz had been one of several members of the Bijapuri royal family to whom they had sent messages promising substantial reward and position if they would assist the Moghul cause. None had replied but Iqbal Aziz must have listened. By his action and subsequent death the Moghuls had secured their victory without even having to pay the promised fee.

Chapter 17

The Bi-Daulat

'Y ou did well to drive Adil Hasan and his Golcundi forces from the city, Muazzam,' Aurangzeb said to his son as they sat side by side in a cool inner room of Adil Hasan's marble palace in Hyderabad. Earlier that day Aurangzeb had joined Muazzam in the city, bringing with him the vanguard of the army which had defeated Sikander and brought Bijapur within the boundaries of the Moghul empire.

'Thank you, Father.' Muazzam smiled. 'My task was made easier by Hyderabad's lack of defences. In truth, once Adil Hasan realised the strength and determination of my army he made an orderly retreat with most of his troops and their equipment as well as nearly all the contents of his treasuries. Many of the inhabitants followed him with their possessions. Only a few – mainly the poor – remained in what was almost a deserted city by the time I entered nearly three weeks ago and had the mullahs read the *khutba* in your name

245

in the mosque in the Charminar to confirm you as the city's new ruler.'

'Your modesty about your achievements becomes you. You've also succeeded in securing the city. I've already noticed the measures you are taking to raise earthworks on the banks of the Musi river and elsewhere in case of counterattack.' Muazzam beamed, basking in his father's rare praise, as Aurangzeb continued, 'however, we cannot rest here too long. As soon as the main body of my army joins us, we must press the advantage you've gained. Where have Adil Hasan and his forces gone?'

'He has retreated to the fortress of Golcunda five miles from here with the bulk of his armies and, so I am told, all his wives and concubines. He's also sent some of his troops to defend the diamond mines.'

'We mustn't be distracted by the mines. Capturing the Golcunda fort and Adil Hasan has to be our priority. What do we know about the fort?'

'It's built around a conical four hundred foot high granite hill and is enclosed within a double ring of strong stone ramparts, each with several stout sixty foot high bastions protruding from them and positioned to allow effective crossfire against any attack on the walls. The single entrance is by a twisting ramp which passes through a series of interlinked gatehouses.'

'Food and water supplies?'

'The fort has a reasonable water supply but according to reports it may be insufficient for the number of people crowding within it. They have had time to lay in enough food for some months if they ration it properly.'

'We must surround the fortress as soon as we can and then I think try the defenders' resolve by some initial assaults to see if we can avoid a long siege. From what I know of Adil Hasan's licentious behaviour I cannot believe that he will prove a determined leader, or that his men will follow him devotedly. You've surprised me by your resolution so far, Muazzam, and as a result I will allow you to lead the first part of the campaign so you may convince me further of your merits.'

• ◆ •

Six weeks later Aurangzeb with Wazim Khan at his side watched as under a leaden and lowering sky Muazzam rode to give the order for the Moghul armies' cannon to fire on the walls of Golcunda. His son had conducted the campaign to cut off the fortress skilfully, feinting as if to make an immediate head-on assault and then despatching strong, swift-moving forces like the horns on the buffalo's head to complete the encirclement before the Golcundis could take effective action against them. His men had even succeeded in finding and severing one of the buried clay pipeways which connected water reservoirs in the hills with the fortress. As the summer heat built up, life would grow increasingly hard for those crammed within the fortress, eking out water and food and almost certainly arguing how it should be shared.

Aurangzeb turned to Wazim Khan. 'With experience Muazzam seems to be maturing as a commander, showing calmness and authority in making decisions, particularly when reacting to setbacks or the unexpected, don't you think?'

Wazim Khan nodded. 'He is blooming under the approval you have shown him recently, Majesty. Praise boosts confidence, a good thing in all but the most rash and conceited.'

247

The boom of Moghul cannon prevented any further conversation. Seventy of them had fired in near-perfect unison. White smoke billowed across the battlefield, obscuring both the walls of Golcunda and the Moghul positions even before the answering thunder of the Golcundi cannon reached Aurangzeb's ears. As gaps slowly appeared in the drifting smoke, Aurangzeb saw that the walls of Golcunda seemed intact, except near the main gatehouse where a few stone blocks had been dislodged from the top of the battlements and toppled on to the ramp below. The Golcundis had had some success too. The bronze barrel of one of the largest Moghul cannons had been knocked from its twelve-wheeled wooden limber by a Golcundi ball. As it fell it had pinioned two of its gun crew beneath its weight. A group of their comrades were struggling to pull it off their legs, but as far as he could see as the smoke closed in again with no success.

'Wazim Khan, have them bring my war elephant. Even though I will keep my word to leave the command to my son, I cannot bear to be this far from the action.'

A few minutes later, Aurangzeb's elephant was nearing the forward Moghul lines. As Aurangzeb peered through the smoke ahead, trying to see the fighting, wounded men began to emerge from it, passing him as they made their way to the rear. Some had their arms round the shoulders of their fellows. Others were supporting themselves on makeshift crutches as they limped along. Bearers carried the more badly wounded on stretchers roughly fashioned from branches. On one, a bearded man was screaming loudly as he attempted to hold in the red-blue intestines spilling from a great gash in his belly.

'May God speed him into the next world,' Aurangzeb murmured. 'There is nothing any *hakim* can do for him in this.'

Within a few minutes more Aurangzeb was passing through one of his cannon batteries. 'Quick as you can to reload. The lives of the rest of the army depend on you!' he shouted to the gunners, who returned him a cry of 'Long live the emperor!' without pausing as they bent their naked and gunpowder-streaked backs to the task of reloading the cannon. A short distance beyond the battery Aurangzeb ordered his *mahouts* to halt beside a young Moghul officer sitting straight-backed on his grey horse on a raised hillock, his even younger *qorchi* trying to control his own skittering mount at his side. 'What is happening here?' he asked.

'Majesty, your son has commanded me to wait here until he sends back word of the success of an assault he has launched towards the gatehouse. If all goes well, as I pray it will, I will lead up reinforcements, musketeers and foot soldiers, from your Bengali regiments so that—'

A great crash cut off his words. Aurangzeb's howdah shook and his elephant reared its head and trumpeted. Despite himself Aurangzeb closed his eyes, and as he did so warm liquid splashed his face and some pieces of soft spongy material clung to it. Reopening his eyes, he wiped his face with the back of his hand. The liquid was blood and the spongy material flesh from either the officer or his grey horse. Both were sprawled in the dirt, bodies shattered and bloodily torn. One of the *mahouts* had fallen from Aurangzeb's elephant and was lying motionless on the ground but had no obvious injury. The young *qorchi*'s horse had bolted with him. There must have been more than one cannonball to have done so much damage. Like his own men, the Golcundi gunners were obviously accomplished enough to fire in coordinated salvos.

The second *mahout* quickly settled Aurangzeb's elephant. Should he wait with his bodyguard in the dead young officer's place or press on towards the action, Aurangzeb wondered. Then above the sound of battle he heard hooves close behind him and two other officers rode up. The first – a much older man with a patch over his left eye – bowed low in his saddle as he said, 'Majesty, we saw our colleague fall and have come to replace him.'

'You know your orders?'

'Yes, Majesty.'

Aurangzeb nodded. The *mahout* who had fallen had regained his senses, only knocked out by his fall. Scrambling a little unsteadily to his feet, he reached up and taking the extended hand of his partner regained his place behind the elephant's ears. A sudden breeze had blown up as Aurangzeb gave the order to move forward once more. Moments later another deafening crash burst above his head and liquid again splashed his face, but this time it was rain, not blood – the sound had been thunder. The driving rain and wind dissipated much of the smoke, allowing Aurangzeb to see further ahead.

At first he thought his son's troops had stalled in their advance towards the ramp leading to the gatehouse. They were clustered in groups, taking advantage of any limited cover they could in the rough ground leading up to the fort. Then he saw green Moghul banners moving behind a series of small hillocks a little behind them. Suddenly Muazzam and a large body of horsemen burst into view. They were charging up the slope towards the ramp, banners streaming behind them, and as they rushed forward the remainder of his troops leapt up and followed, yelling war cries. The only exceptions were groups of musketeers sheltering behind several carts that had been brought up under cover of the smoke and overturned. They were maintaining a steady fire to keep down the heads of the Golcundi defenders on the battlements.

Despite their efforts, the Golcundi cannon and muskets continued in action. A cannonball blew apart one of the carts behind which ten Moghul musketeers were crouching, throwing splintered pieces of wood and the body of a musketeer high into the air. Meanwhile the Golcundis' own musketeers were concentrating their fire on nearer targets – the charging Moghul horsemen. Several of the horses crumpled, pitching their riders to the ground. Through the rain and the remnants of the smoke Aurangzeb saw one standard-bearer lose his grip on his large green banner as he fell. It caught around the front legs of his neighbour's mount, bringing it down too. Another rider and his horse crashed over them. Those following swerved to avoid the tumbled bodies but yet more riders and horses fell. As they approached the base of the ramp twisting up towards the gatehouse only a small group remained, but they were still galloping hard, heads bent low over their horses' necks, urging them on. Aurangzeb could no longer see Muazzam. Had his son fallen? No. There he was, just behind the leading attackers, sword glinting in his hand, the remnants of his bodyguard around him.

Moments later, a trumpeter by Muazzam's side put his instrument to his lips. Aurangzeb was too far away to hear the call but its meaning became clear almost at once as all

251

the surviving Moghul horsemen turned and began to gallop back towards their own lines. The trumpeter let go of his trumpet, threw up his arms and slid backwards from his saddle. Another banner-bearer fell too as a riderless horse, reins dangling, swerved across his path. His son and his men still had some way to go over exposed ground to reach the Moghul lines when, the rain squall having passed, drifting smoke again obscured Aurangzeb's view. He prayed that Muazzam would survive. Though the attack had not succeeded he had borne himself like a true Moghul prince.

• ◆ •

'You showed true courage and leadership, Muazzam. No blame can attach to you for the failure of the attack.'

Two hours after he'd safely reached his own lines and with some superficial wounds to his left knee and forearm bound and dressed, Muazzam stood before his father in the emperor's scarlet command tent. 'Thank you, Father.' He drank from the glass of sherbet he held in his right hand. 'I did my best, and so did my troops, who fought bravely. I regret the loss of so many of them, particularly my milk-brother Umar Khan. He was so badly burned by flaming oil the Golcundis tossed from the battlements as he tried to ascend the ramp that he died screaming in agony shortly after we regained our lines. It was horrible . . . he had lost most of the skin and hair from his head.'

'His soul will rest in Paradise tonight, as will those of all the faithful who have died for us today. I will ensure his wives and children are well provided for.' Aurangzeb paused for a moment and then continued, 'But turning back to our campaign, if it is to succeed quickly we must think of measures other than frontal assault. I will ask

Wazim Khan to join us. He often has good ideas on such matters.'

'Before you do, may I suggest something privately?'

'Of course.'

'What about negotiation – talking to the Golcundis?'

'If they wish to surrender the fortress and their lands I'm ready to listen, but I've seen no evidence that they are.'

'No, I mean a more equal negotiation.' Muazzam took a deep breath, dropped his voice almost to a whisper and continued. 'You know Adil Hasan's vizier's wife is a relation of my own wife? He contacted me through the two women, asking "Why should believer kill believer? Why should so many faithful souls fly to Paradise? Why should so many widows and children weep? Could we not discuss some compromise?" I responded that I did not wish lives to be sacrificed unnecessarily either and would be prepared to put some compromise terms to you if we could agree them. I even outlined some. I decided not to tell you until I had gone a little further in the discussion, but Umar Khan's death and your praise for my leadership today have emboldened me.'

Aurangzeb's face contorted with rage. His clenched fist smashed into his son's face, knocking him to the floor where he lay stunned, his jaw cut to the bone by Timur's tiger ring which his father was wearing and his crimson blood dribbling on to the Persian carpet on which he lay. 'Guards!' Aurangzeb roared. 'Here at once! I have a traitor for you to remove.'

• ◆ •

Two hours later, as darkness was beginning to fall, Aurangzeb walked briskly between two lines of his bodyguards to a platform in front of his command tent, before which about thirty of his most senior commanders had hastily assembled. Stern-faced, he spoke immediately. 'I have summoned you here to witness me pronounce judgement on a traitor. Bring him!'

The assembled officers gave an audible gasp as they turned to see two burly guards drag Muazzam, his hands and ankles bound, towards the platform. When they reached its base, they threw him roughly to the ground, which was still muddy from the day's intermittent rain squalls. Muazzam lay there unable to stand, his jaw dark red with congealed blood from his wound.

Aurangzeb gestured down at him. 'This *bi-daulat* – this wretch – has admitted to me, boasted almost, of entering into treasonable communication with our Golcundi enemy, have you not?'

'Yes,' his son muttered. Then, mustering his strength, he raised his head. 'But only because I thought it was for the good of the empire and of our dynasty.'

'How dare you pretend to know what is in the best interests of the empire in matters of such importance! Only I can decide that – not you, not my highest officials or commanders . . .'

'I am truly sorry, Father. My motives were the best.'

'Your sorrow and your motives are as irrelevant as your relationship to me, which I now disclaim. Have you anything further to say before I sentence you? You do know that a traitor's punishment is death?'

'Yes, and if that must be my fate I accept it. I will die loyal to you and the empire.' Muazzam's voice was calm.

Aurangzeb hesitated. In the first rush of anger he had intended to execute Muazzam, but now the moment of

254

irrevocable public decision had come he was not so sure. He had imprisoned, not executed, his son Mohammed Sultan for joining his uncle Shah Shuja and fighting against him in the civil war which had led to his own coming to the throne. His son Akbar's flight, first to Sambhaji and now – as his spies had told him a few weeks before – to Persia had saved him from having to decide his fate. Both Mohammed Sultan's and Akbar's crimes had been pure treason, whereas Muazzam had merely been presumptuous, acting in what he thought was his father's interest, even if in doing so he had unjustifiably usurped his authority. On the other hand, Mohammed Sultan and Akbar had been young when they'd sinned. Muazzam was older – over forty – and had seemed to be showing greater maturity. Where did these conflicting arguments lead him? Suddenly and unbidden the memory of Jahanara pleading for her nephew Akbar came into his mind. If Jahanara were alive now, she would plead with him for Muazzam too, he knew.

'Muazzam, you deserve to die but I will be merciful. You will be imprisoned in Gwalior. Guards, get him out of my sight.'

As Aurangzeb spoke, another squall of rain swept through the camp, large drops splashing his cheek like tears.

Chapter 18

A Dish of Sweetmeats

'**W**azim Khan, that is most useful intelligence. If it's confirmed it'll offer the best chance we've had of ending this siege in all these past eight months. Tell me more about this Afghan . . .'

A sudden ear-shattering explosion outside his command tent interrupted Aurangzeb. The ground shook beneath his feet and he gripped a tent pole to steady himself as a hail of objects hit the tent roof. What was it? An earthquake wouldn't produce missiles. As soon as the tremors subsided Aurangzeb hurried from his tent to discover what had actually happened. From the elephant lines he heard the beasts trumpeting. Several of his commanders were emerging from their own tents and looking around, seemingly bewildered. Clods of earth and stones were everywhere. Then he saw the cause.

Four hundred yards in front of him was a great crater in the ground. Half that distance away a small group of dirt-streaked and bloodied Moghul engineers were staggering from the narrow, low entrance to the tunnel they had been digging towards one of the Golcunda fort's largest bastions. On reaching it, the intention had been to pack as much gunpowder as possible beneath its foundations to bring it crashing down, to make the breach in the Golcundi defences that was so necessary to Moghul success. Something had clearly gone wrong, but what?

'Bring me any of the engineers who are fit enough to speak,' Aurangzeb told Umar Ali, the long-serving head of his bodyguard. A few minutes later a small but thick-set man, garments, face and hair all covered with dirt, was led up to him.

'Did some of your gunpowder explode as it was being carried through the tunnel?'

'No, Majesty. It was the Golcundis.'

'What do you mean? How?'

'They must have detected our tunnel either by the sounds our labourers made as they dug or moved through it or because the ground has subsided slightly along the line of the tunnel. They then dug a counter-tunnel to intercept ours and blow it up before we were ready to detonate our own explosives beneath the bastion.'

'I see.' Aurangzeb nodded. The Golcundis must still be well organised and disciplined as well as determined and alert if they had positioned watchers and listeners to detect tunnelling. It made the Afghan Wazim Khan had spoken about even more important and he must learn more about him. But he must first show gratitude and support to the tunnellers. He could only imagine how hard it must be to crawl belly almost to the ground along low narrow tunnels with barely enough props to support the roof while pulling bags of gunpowder, constantly fearing a

257

spark detonating the powder or an earthfall behind, blocking the only escape from a slow suffocating death.

'You and your fellows have acted with great bravery and loyalty to our cause. I will make sure that those of you who have survived are rewarded and compensated for any injuries, and that the families of the dead are cared for.'

'Thank you, Majesty.' The man bowed low.

Aurangzeb turned and moved swiftly back into his tent with Wazim Khan at his side. Even before they had seated themselves he asked, 'The Afghan – you say he is second-in-command of the Golcundi troops in the fort and yet he may be willing to betray the fortress to us?'

'Yes, Majesty. His name is Rashid Khan. You remember we intercepted one of the messengers who slip out of the fort at night? Rather than simply seizing his messages and killing or imprisoning him, I bribed him to continue his work but to show us each message he carried. Well, one of them was from Rashid Khan to a cousin commanding troops around one of the diamond mines. In it he lamented that he had ever joined Adil Hasan's service, even though he'd risen high and profited much. He feared the fort could not expect relief. No Golcundi army was strong enough so no commander would risk his troops in the attempt. Although it could resist for a long time yet, the fort would eventually fall. He himself might well be killed and even more certainly he would lose all the riches he had amassed. I arranged for our messenger to take a reply purportedly from his cousin sympathising and telling him that he had heard from prisoners of his that the Moghuls might be prepared to offer a reward to anyone able and willing to give them access to the fort and suggesting that if he were interested he should reply through the same messenger. His cousin would then make an approach to us. He replied encouragingly and at once, so I've come immediately to you to suggest you might write yourself offering him a pardon and a reward.'

'I agree I should write, but how confident can we be that he will not lead us into a trap? What do we know of him and his character?'

'Well, he's been a mercenary most of his life. Mercenaries as a group have a greater attachment to their own well-being and wealth than to any temporary master. I believe he himself has changed allegiance at least once before. He has no family within the fort – no one to think of or to protect other than himself. We already know from his original letter that he thinks ultimate defeat is inevitable.'

'All that is reassuring, but we should still seek a way for him to surrender the fort which will not expose too many of our men if he should betray us. That said, I'll write now and offer him a pardon and one of those large *jagirs* – estates – in the north of the Punjab we've seized from the rebellious Sikhs.'

• ◆ •

A few bats swooped low as just before dawn thirty members of Aurangzeb's bodyguard led by their commander Umar Ali, all dressed in black with their faces blackened with charcoal, crept towards the Golcunda fort from the left of the Moghul front lines. None wore any kind of steel breastplate or chain mail for fear that it might clink and betray them, particularly if they fell. Five of them were bowed under the weight of small barrels of gunpowder. They were heading not for the ramp leading to the gatehouse of the Golcunda fort but to one of the largest eastern bastions. There the Afghan general had agreed to admit them through a small iron-studded door at the base. When all was ready he would open it just enough for the light of a lantern inside to guide them towards it.

The thirty men moved swiftly and silently in single file, only occasionally stumbling in the gloom over a stone or the root of a long dead tree. Soon they were making good progress to the bastion and passing near where a cluster of five or six corpses of Moghul labourers lay putrefying. They had been shot down earlier that week by Golcundi musketeers on the battlements as they dug in a vain attempt to find a tunnel the Golcundis were rumoured to be using to bring in supplies. Suddenly a pariah dog, who had been feeding unseen in the darkness on one of the bodies, rushed ears back and snarling towards the Moghuls and buried its teeth in the thigh of one of the leading soldiers. With a superhuman effort he clenched back a cry, and swiftly pulling out his dagger thrust it twice into the dog's scrawny neck, killing it almost instantly. Then he, like the other guards, dropped to the ground, to lie motionless in case anyone on the fort's walls had heard either the dog's snarls or its dying whimper. But they were still some distance from the fort and all remained quiet.

Cautiously, Umar Ali stood and motioning his men to follow began to creep forward again. Now, with dawn a purple smudge on the horizon, they were beginning to climb over the rough, hard granite on which the fort was built. Umar Ali peered at the fort, looking for the gleam of lantern light that would lead them to the door. Nothing. Perhaps the emperor had been right to warn him they might be being enticed into a trap. But wouldn't the Golcundis allow them into the fort before falling on them?

Then a light appeared at the base of one of the tallest bastions little more than a hundred yards away. Gesturing to the rest of his men to conceal themselves as best they could, Umar Ali picked his way swiftly over the rocks towards the light. When he was already in the shadow of the walls he smelled a foul stink and his feet sank into some soft, sticky mess – a latrine outlet must be just above. Extracting himself he hurried on and quickly reached the half-open door, which was no more than four feet or so high. As he drew closer it was opened fully and, hand on his sword hilt and hairs prickling on the back of his neck, he ducked inside to find himself in a simple dungeon-like room with only a single other occupant – a tall hawk-nosed man holding a large lantern.

'I am Rashid Khan,' the figure said.

'And I am Umar Ali, the head of the Emperor Aurangzeb's bodyguard. You are alone?'

'Yes, and so are you. Where are the rest of your men?'

'Nearby. I came ahead to check that there was no trap.'

'I assure you there isn't, but don't take my word for it. Take the lantern and check for yourself.'

The lantern held high in one hand and his other hand still on his sword hilt, Umar Ali moved quickly around the circular windowless room, peering into the dark shadows. Once he started as a small animal – probably a rat – scuttled across his path but the room was otherwise empty, not even a piece of furniture behind which an attacker might lurk. He took several steps up the interior stone staircase leading from the room, the only other access apart from the door through which he had come. A strong door at the top was bolted securely from inside so no one else could enter. Turning back to Rashid Khan, he said, 'I'm satisfied. I'll signal my men to join us. I agreed that if all was well I'd open and close the door quickly three times to produce flashes of light as a signal.'

Soon the rest of Umar Ali's soldiers had crowded in. 'Where's the best place to position these gunpowder barrels to do the maximum damage?' Umar Ali asked.

'Against the outer walls near the door.'

Umar Ali's men began heaving the barrels into position and fitting the fuses. When they were in place Umar Ali said, 'Once they explode several regiments of our best troops are ready to dash towards any breach.'

'Good. But do you have long enough fuses to allow us to escape the blast?' the Afghan general asked.

'Yes, I believe so. But you must show us where we go from here.'

Rashid Khan nodded and Umar Ali signalled to his men to light the fuses. Four of them began to fizz as soon as the sparks were produced from the tinderboxes but the man lighting the fifth dropped his box and with shaking hands began to scrabble for it in the semi-darkness on the floor.

'Follow Rashid Khan, the rest of you. I'll finish this work,' Umar Ali said. Immediately the general led the Moghuls up the staircase. Umar Ali heard the sound of the door bolts being drawn as he bent to look for the tinderbox. He quickly found it and lit the fifth fuse. The others were already burning quite close to the powder barrels and after checking the fifth was fizzing properly he ran quickly to the staircase and climbed it two steps at a time. Fresh air blew down towards him from the open door at the top. He was quickly through it into the flat area between the two sets of circular ramparts and running towards where in the rising light Rashid Khan was beckoning from the cover of some rocks. Just as he flung himself down beside him, the powder barrels exploded. The bastion seemed first to teeter like an unsteady drunk and then with a roar and crash collapsed into a mass of dust and rubble. A block of stone thudded into the ground next to Umar Ali but Rashid Khan was already on his feet again, waving the Moghuls to follow him through the dust and smoke towards the inner circle of walls.

As Umar Ali and his men ran forward musket and cannon fire erupted from both the inner and outer battlements, seemingly directed not at them but at Moghul troops who must already be advancing towards the breach in the outer wall created by the bastion's collapse. In the confusion and smoke, Umar Ali and his men reached the inner wall undetected and flattened themselves against it. Rashid Khan whispered to Umar Ali, 'There's a small inner guardhouse in one of the bastions about three hundred feet round the curve of the wall to the left. I will go alone and order the guards inside to leave it and advance to defend the outer wall. If any disobey or linger outside we must kill them. Once in the guardhouse we must barricade ourselves in until your main force reaches us.'

'I understand.' Umar Ali nodded as Rashid Khan moved off. He found himself wondering how the Afghan could so completely reverse his loyalties, callously speaking of killing soldiers whom he commanded and who no doubt believed him loyal to them. He himself could never do that . . . the Afghan must have little conscience and be deeply selfish. Nevertheless, he was delivering all he had promised his new master the emperor and he and his men must follow his instructions.

A few minutes later, Umar Ali saw the Afghan reappear waving another lantern as a signal to approach. Still keeping close to the wall, he and his men crept round the curve of the rampart, weapons in hand. They encountered no one and swiftly entered the small guardhouse to find the Afghan alone. The only signs of previous occupants were a couple of open bed rolls with rough blankets thrown back and a half-eaten crust of bread on a long trestle table. The guards must have followed Rashid Khan's instructions and headed for the fighting.

Immediately, Umar Ali ordered his Moghuls to barricade all entrances to the bastion. They quickly fell to work, overturning the table against the outer door and slamming shut bolts. Climbing to the level of the battlements, Umar Ali looked through a large firing slit towards the breach in the outer walls. In the ever-increasing dawn light he could see Moghul banners waving and foot soldiers climbing over the debris. The Golcundis were still fighting hard. Slowly, though, they were being forced back, ducking as they ran from the cover of one pile of debris to the next.

Then a large group of Moghul horsemen appeared in the breach. One twisted and fell wounded from his horse as he attempted to leap over the rubble. The horse of another refused the jump and pitched its rider over its head before galloping back towards the Moghul lines, reins dangling. But soon, despite further losses, more and more horsemen were succeeding in clearing the debris unscathed. Wheeling their horses, they attacked the Golcundi defenders in the rear, bending low from their saddles, hacking and slashing at their backs. Under attack from two sides, the Golcundi retreat quickly turned into a rout as those who could disengaged themselves from the fighting and ran back towards the inner ramparts on which Umar Ali was standing. Moghul horsemen followed in hot pursuit. Several riders fell, either themselves or their horses hit by musket balls fired from the battlements.

'Unblock the bastion entrance once more! Fire on any retreating Golcundis. Do everything you can to attract the attention of our own attacking riders. Get them through the bastion as fast as you can into the inner courtyards. And bring our banner to me!' Umar Ali shouted down the staircase to his men below. One of them, who had on his orders worn the banner wound around his body beneath his dark garments, ran up the stairs and together he and Umar Ali waved the green flag through the musket slit.

Soon Moghul riders were jumping from their saddles and running towards the bastion. Glancing back towards the breach in the outer ramparts, Umar Ali saw that the fighting had virtually ceased. Moghul troops were arriving in ever increasing numbers, either on foot or on horseback. Most pressed quickly on towards the inner ramparts. Some paused to bend over fallen comrades, checking whether they still breathed and if they did trying to bind their wounds and comfort them. Then another group of mounted men appeared in the breach. Even at a distance he recognised many of them as members of his own command, the emperor's bodyguard. There at their centre was the emperor himself, breastplate gleaming and mounted on a black horse. Despite his near seventy years he was clearly eager to join his troops in their moment – his moment – of triumph. Umar Ali ran quickly down the staircase ready to greet his emperor and lead him into the heart of the fort.

Half an hour later, with Umar Ali and the rest of his reunited bodyguard around him, Aurangzeb entered a large stone building. Newly captured prisoners had informed them it was where Adil Hasan's private quarters were, and that he had retreated there as the fighting began to go against his forces. In truth, nearly all the Golcundi soldiers had now discarded their weapons and surrendered. Moghul troops were tying their hands, herding them into groups and making them squat on their haunches on the ground.

As the first of Aurangzeb's bodyguards crossed a marble-pillared courtyard two musket shots rang out. One of the guards collapsed, clutching at his calf from which blood was streaming. His fellows ran towards the pillars from behind which the shots had come. A bear-like Golcundi rushed from the shelter of one, swinging his musket around his head by its long barrel like a club. His first blow would have shattered the skull of the leading Moghul had he not ducked beneath it. Before the man could strike again, another bodyguard's sword caught him across the throat and nearly decapitated him.

Meanwhile, the second Golcundi musketeer had left his hiding place, thrown down his weapon and, swerving to evade his pursuers, disappeared through a curtained entrance from behind which the sound of music and singing could be heard. As they followed him through the curtain a bizarre sight greeted Aurangzeb and his guards. A man dressed in elaborately embroidered cream robes and wearing a red turban sparkling with diamonds with a white egret's feather at its crown was sitting calmly on

266

a gold throne in the middle of the room, delicately eating sweetmeats from a silver salver. Around him twenty dancing girls, white jasmine flowers in their hair and clad in the flimsiest of muslins, gyrated and sang to the music of five musicians standing behind the man who could only be Adil Hasan on his throne. Aurangzeb strode through his bodyguard towards him.

Before he could speak Adil Hasan did so, a half-smile on his face. 'You are, I think, the Emperor Aurangzeb. Come and join me in my pleasures for a while. I will savour every moment I have left to enjoy them and store each in my mind as a glorious memory to solace me as I endure whatever fate you have in mind for me.' As he spoke he gestured with his beringed hand to his musicians, who immediately increased the tempo of their music. The dancing girls began to twirl and spin more quickly, their scanty garments whirling round their bodies.

'Seize all these degenerates,' Aurangzeb roared. 'Put them in the deepest dungeons you can find!'

Just after sunset that evening, after completing his prayers, Aurangzeb walked to a balcony where Wazim Khan was looking down on the Moghuls' victory celebrations. 'We can be proud, Wazim Khan. The Moghul Empire is at its greatest ever extent. There are only a few remaining Golcundi forces to deal with and the Marathas to suppress. Then I can return north with my armies to set about restoring order to the administration of my lands, rooting out the corruption and venality that flourish in my absence, depleting our treasuries and authority.'

'This has indeed been a great day of victory for you, Majesty,' Wazim Khan said. 'Do you require me further this evening?'

'No. I have no more need of you tonight. The exertions of the day have tired me. I will go to the sleeping quarters of my command tent that my attendants have erected in the courtyard. You should join the celebrations.'

Towards midnight, Aurangzeb was still, to his surprise, unable to sleep. Though his body was tired, his mind was still pondering how best to subdue the remainder of Golcunda and in particular seize the diamond mines as quickly as possible with the least expenditure of money and lives. Could he suborn some of the remaining Golcundi commanders as he had the Afghan general? According to Wazim Khan, Rashid Khan had a cousin in the Golcundi forces defending the diamond mines. Might he be susceptible to an approach? What was the man's status? How senior was he? Wazim Khan would be sure to know, as well as to have other advice on how to proceed. There was no time better to consider his options than the present.

Rising from his bed, Aurangzeb walked towards the entrance of his command tent and called to one of the two tall guards standing alert and straight-backed just outside. 'Have Wazim Khan come to me.'

Nearly a quarter of an hour passed before Wazim Khan appeared. His hair and face were wet with sweat and he stumbled slightly as he ducked into the tent and again as he bowed – he must still be full of sleep.

'I have been thinking of our forward campaign and I want your advice.'

'Yes, Majesty . . . I will do my best . . .' Wazim Khan's voice was unsteady and he passed a hand across his perspiring brow.

'What more do you know of the commanders of the

remaining Golcundi forces, and in particular Rashid Khan's cousin?'

'Majesty . . . yes, Majesty . . . their commanders, of course . . .' Wazim Khan seemed dazed. Realisation suddenly dawned on Aurangzeb and he strode across to his dishevelled adviser. Yes. He reeked of it!

'Wazim Khan, have you been drinking alcohol?'

'No, Majesty . . .' Then, as the knowledge that he could not deny it penetrated his fuddled brain, Wazim Khan said, 'I'm sorry . . . Majesty . . . yes . . . to celebrate our great victory . . . Majesty, forgive me . . .'

'Tell me how often you drink, and be truthful. You above anyone should know how many sources of information I have to call on if need be.'

'From time to time, Majesty . . . no more than once a week, I promise. It makes me less . . . less constrained in my thinking. Some of my best schemes have . . .' Wazim Khan's voice tailed off.

'How could you! How dare you go against my strict prohibitions? Don't you owe me loyalty in all things?'

'I am loyal, Majesty . . . I found that Afghan . . . remember . . . please . . .'

Aurangzeb turned away in disgust. If Wazim Khan could disobey his prohibitions in his personal life, how could he trust him in affairs of state? Disloyalty and disobedience were cankers which having gained access to a man's mind could soon spread through its every part.

'You will receive five lashes before the whole court for your misconduct. Then you will return to your family estates where you will remain until further notice.'

'No, Majesty . . . I beseech you. Please, no . . . ! What of my dignity and my honour . . .?'

269

'You should have thought of them before you disobeyed.'

As the two tall guards he'd called from their post outside the tent led the stout, shambling figure of Wazim Khan away, Aurangzeb turned back towards his sleeping quarters. Why could he trust no one? Why couldn't those closest to him not simply obey his instructions unquestioningly and accept that he knew best what was good for his empire and all its subjects, themselves included? That was why he was emperor. That was their duty. What sin had he committed to be so ill served so often?

Chapter 19

The Executioner

'Majesty, forgive me for asking your *qorchi* to rouse you but my news cannot wait. Two of my scouts have located Sambhaji – he's at Sangameshwar!' Kamran Beg sounded breathless. Aurangzeb had seldom seen his chief scout so excited.

'Sangameshwar? What is it? A fortress?'

'No, Majesty. It's a palace set amid pleasure gardens where the Shatri and Sonavi rivers converge – small and with very limited defences. My men just wandered in. It belongs to Kavi-Kulesh, one of Sambhaji's generals. He invited Sambhaji there as his guest. My men spent several days in Sangameshwar disguised as peddlers of ribbons and other gewgaws. According to what they heard, Sambhaji passes his time in pleasure with Kavi-Kulesh. He has only a few troops with him.'

'Why has he brought so few?'

'Because he only intended to stay a short time. He left the bulk of his forces at a place called Devrukh, some

271

distance away, to re-equip, reprovision and train. But so great are the attractions of Sangameshwar he has already been there a month and shows no signs of moving on.'

Aurangzeb closed his eyes to think. All this fitted with other reports he'd had of Sambhaji. Though as brave in combat as his father, unlike Shivaji he was happy to entrust the task of preparing and planning to his officers. Another question struck him. 'How did your scouts track Sambhaji to Sangameshwar?'

'It was . . .' Kamran Beg hesitated a moment, looking a little awkward. 'It was Wazim Khan who originally suggested he might be there. During one of his last inter-rogations of Santaji, the young Maratha captive you spared, the youth said that Sambhaji liked Sangameshwar . . . even that he himself had spent time there with him.'

So, Wazim Khan had been crucial . . . Not for the first time since dismissing his former spymaster, Aurangzeb found himself regretting he was no longer by his side. His mind had been acute and his advice always shrewd, even if his flesh had proved weak . . . And now it seemed that Wazim Khan had presented him with a chance not to be missed. 'Kamran Beg, you must be familiar with the terrain between here and this Sangameshwar. How long would it take our troops to get there?'

'Sangameshwar is a hundred miles south-west of this fort. A well-mounted and equipped troop of horsemen could be there in two days and snatch Sambhaji before any help could reach him – I stake my life on it!'

'Would one troop be enough?'

'The place is barely defended. Besides, a smaller force would attract less attention as it entered Maratha territory.'

'Very well, Kamran Beg. You are a good fighter and officer as well as my chief scout. I place you in command of the mission. Take the Maratha prisoner with you. His knowledge of Sangameshwar may be valuable. As for you, succeed in this task and your reward will be great. If you fall, you will die a martyr for our cause and our faith. Glory awaits you either way.' As Kamran Beg hurried away to prepare Aurangzeb smiled wryly. His chief scout would indeed live or die by the accuracy and quality of his scouts' observations and of his own advice. That was how it should be.

• ◆ •

'We'll halt here on the edge of this wood. Tether your horses to the trunks of those trees. You, Ibrahim Ali, choose four of your men to stay and guard the horses. The rest of you, prepare to go forward on foot,' Kamran Beg ordered. In the fading light the horsemen went quickly about their work, drinking deeply from their large leather water bottles before resecuring them to their saddles and checking their weapons. Kamran Beg walked among them, making sure everything was in order. When all was ready he gave a grunt of satisfaction. He had been wise to dress his men as Marathas – the clothing had not only disguised them on the journey but should help them get into the palace.

'Fetch Santaji. I want him with me,' he told one of the horsemen, who returned a few moments later with the young Maratha. Kamran Beg gripped his shoulders and looked into his face. 'Listen. The hours ahead will decide your fate. If I find you've lied about anything you've told me about Sangameshwar, I'll cut your throat. Do you understand me?'

Santaji nodded.

'But before we begin, I'll give you one last chance. Is everything you've said true?'

'Yes, sir.'

'Very well. You will be at my side the entire time – my eyes and my ears as we find our way into the palace. Hold out your hands.' Taking his dagger, Kamran Beg cut the ropes binding the youth's wrists. 'This is only so you don't attract attention. Don't try anything. Now let's go.'

The sixty men moved quietly through the wood, the only sound an occasional crunch of a twig or rustling among fallen leaves as a snake slithered off. The rising moon gave some light but Kamran Beg was glad when the trees thinned and it became easier to see. As they emerged on to open ground, he thought he made out the glint of water ahead. The Sonavi or the Shatri? He wasn't sure which, but it didn't matter. He wasn't intending to try to get into the palace from the river-bank. The two scouts who'd found Sambhaji had reported that Kavi-Kulesh had built a high marble terrace in the angle where the two rivers became one before flowing towards the sea, and that behind the terrace was first the palace and then the pleasure gardens through which visitors made their approach – something Santaji had confirmed.

They were moving quickly now across fields sprouting with newly planted wheat. Soon they reached a stone wall about six feet high at the far side. Leaving half a dozen men behind to keep watch, Kamran Beg ordered the rest to scale the wall. Dropping down, they found themselves on soft thick grass and at the same moment caught the heavy scent of flowers. Still led by Kamran Beg, who had

274

a hand on Santaji's elbow, they crept cautiously forward into a densely planted rose garden, thorns scratching their flesh. Pushing their way painfully through, they emerged into an open space where one tall and four smaller marble fountains played silver in the moonlight. Through more dark foliage ahead Kamran Beg made out some small lights piercing the gloom – one here, one there – not many. After giving a low whistle – the signal to halt – he whispered to Santaji, 'What are those lights? Pickets?'

'No, sir. I don't think so. There are pavilions in these gardens where Kavi-Kulesh's men sometimes come to listen to music or watch dancing girls. At night the servants always light torches and candles in them, just as they do throughout the palace and along the terrace, so that the river water sparkles with light as if diamonds floated upon it.'

Kamran Beg pulled a face. This Kavi-Kulesh seemed to think himself living in a paradise on earth – just as the ruler of Golcunda had – and God willing he too was about to learn his mistake. 'Show us the quickest way through the gardens to the palace but avoiding the pavilions, Santaji.' The young man nodded and gestured to his right. At another signal from Kamran Beg – a double whistle this time – the Moghuls moved forward again. Sure enough, from somewhere over to their left came the sound of voices. Turning his head, Kamran Beg saw through some bushes the outlines of a small columned structure. Burning flares were stuck in the earth around it, and he caught the sound of a sitar and of rhythmic drumming. These people had no idea. If this was a Moghul palace, intruders would never have got to the wall unchallenged, let alone been allowed to climb over it into the palace grounds.

Complacency, though, would be a mistake. Sambhaji

might love pleasure but he wasn't a fool. Neither was his host Kavi-Kulesh, whose fame as a general was widespread. If any word of the Moghul raid had reached them – Aurangzeb was not the only one to have spies and scouts – this quiet might all be an illusion designed to lure the Moghuls to destruction. Careful always to keep Santaji close, Kamran Beg signalled his men to quicken their pace and the sounds of music began to fade.

Keeping low and creeping through yet more fragrant-flowered bushes, they soon saw almost directly ahead of them a low white building. It could only be the palace of Sangameshwar. Along its flat roof, flames lit the night sky from braziers positioned every few feet. More light shone through the deep casements of its two storeys and also through a central gateway whose doors were wide open so that the paved semicircular courtyard in front of the palace was also lit by an orange glow. Kamran Beg again signalled a halt and gestured his men to crouch down. By the moon's position, it was still early – perhaps no more than about nine o'clock. No need to rush. His keen eyes quickly took in the two Maratha guards by the gateway. Their muskets rested against the wall and they were squatting down, talking. A few minutes later, two men, arms around each other's shoulders, strolled out of the palace, said something to one of the guards at the gates which caused the man to laugh loudly, then went back inside. For a while nothing more happened except that one of the guards got up and, turning his back on his comrade, urinated copiously before hunkering down again.

But then from out of the darkness somewhere behind and to the right of the palace came the sound of iron-bound wheels grinding over the paving stones. Peering in that direction, Kamran Beg saw a large cart drawn by a team of six oxen approach round the corner of the palace. From its direction, it must surely have come from the river. As the driver cracked his long whip, the cart, loaded with what looked like barrels and sacks, turned sharply to pass through the gateway unchallenged by the guards, who barely gave it a glance. A few minutes later a second well-loaded cart appeared out of the darkness and followed the first through the gateway into the palace.

'Those carts – are they bringing goods from the river?' Kamran Beg asked Santaji.

'Yes, sir. Supplies for the palace are landed at a jetty about half a mile away and brought up by cart. The boats sometimes arrive late because the strong currents and rapids near the confluence delay them.'

'Where are the carts unloaded?'

'In the palace's central courtyard, where steps lead straight down to the cellars.'

After a few minutes the carts re-emerged and headed back towards the river. Kamran Beg thought for a moment. His plan had been to infiltrate his men into the palace in small groups, relying on the darkness and their disguise, but now he had a much better idea . . . 'Can we reach the jetty quickly through the gardens? I don't want to lose the cover of the bushes and trees.' Santaji nodded. 'Excellent – lead us there.'

Less than a quarter of an hour later, some of Kamran Beg's soldiers wiped their bloodied daggers on the grass while others dragged the bodies of the Marathas from the two carts they'd just ambushed into the undergrowth. Quickly, Kamran Beg ordered ten men into each cart –

277

two to sit up on the driver's seat and the rest to hide among the barrels and sacks. Then, despatching his remaining soldiers back to their hiding place opposite the palace gateway telling them to be ready to rush into the palace at the first sounds of fighting, Kamran Beg pushed Santaji into the first cart and climbed in after him, pulling an oiled cloth over both of them.

One of the men on the driving seat cracked a whip over the oxen and the cart was off, trundling up the path from the river and round the corner of the palace towards the gateway. How ironic, thought Kamran Beg. When he himself was just a child Shivaji and Sambhaji had been smuggled out of the Agra fort in baskets. Now he was smuggling himself into a palace to recapture Sambhaji. One or two minutes more and they'd be in the courtyard . . . Fingers curled around his dagger and body tensed, ready to spring if they were challenged, Kamran Beg waited. He heard a guard call out something and one of his men reply – Santaji had told them what salutation to use. It seemed to have worked. The cart turned sharply into the courtyard and halted.

'Stay where you are!' Kamran Beg whispered to the men around him. 'We must give the other cart time to get here.' But almost at once the low bellows of oxen and the creaking of wheels behind them told him the second cart had arrived.

But then Kamran Beg heard a cry, followed by a shriek. Flinging back the oiled cloth, he jumped down. One glance at the second cart told him what had happened. Two of his men were standing over a Maratha guard who was sprawled face up on the ground, his throat cut. He must have looked into the cart, seen them and tried to

278

raise the alarm. 'Out of the carts, everyone! Sharp now,' Kamran Beg shouted, looking quickly around.

Sure enough, the Maratha's cry had been heard. About ten of his comrades were running into the courtyard, weapons in hand. Confused by the disguise of Kamran Beg's men they wavered for a moment giving the Moghuls the advantage. As a tall, white-turbaned Maratha hesitated, Kamran Beg flung his dagger, hitting the man in the right eye so that he tumbled screaming to the ground, blood spurting through his fingers as he clutched at his face.

'Up there! Look out,' called a young Moghul. Kamran Beg ducked as a Maratha aimed a musket at him from the upper gallery that ran round all four sides of the courtyard. The shot hissed over his head to splinter the side of the cart he'd just leapt from. The Maratha was already reloading but the young Moghul pulled out a pistol he'd had strapped to his side and discharged it, hitting the man in the arm so that he dropped his musket, which fell to the courtyard below with a clatter.

A few yards away Ibrahim Ali was fighting off two Marathas. Ducking beneath their sword slashes, he deftly kicked the feet from under one of them, sending the man crashing back into his fellow. As the two men lay tangled on the ground, Ibrahim Ali thrust his sword into the belly of the first. Then, as the second struggled to stand, with two quick strokes of his scimitar he hacked off his head, which landed among some red-hot charcoals spilled from a brazier tipped over in the fighting. Moments later the man's hair burst into flames and the stench of singeing human flesh filled the air.

By now, the troops sent by Kamran Beg to wait opposite the palace entrance were running into the courtyard, weapons drawn. Blood on some of their swords told him they had disposed of the two guards outside the gate. 'To me! Quickly now!' Gripping Santaji and glancing over his shoulder to make sure his men were following, Kamran Beg headed for some thick marble columns supporting a wide balcony projecting over the courtyard. They should provide cover while he assessed how many defenders there were. But peering round one of the columns he saw the courtyard now seemingly deserted except for half a dozen bodies – four lying motionless in pools of dark red blood and two still showing a little life. None of them, as far as he could see, were his own men. He scanned the upper gallery, but could make out nothing except dancing light and shadows from the many torches burning in the brackets.

'I don't understand. Where are the Marathas? And how many are there?' Ibrahim Ali, scimitar still in his hand, echoed his thoughts.

'I don't know. Perhaps some have fled and some have gone to warn Kavi-Kulesh and Sambhaji.' Kamran Beg turned to Santaji standing back flattened against a pillar, eyes wary. 'Where are Kavi-Kulesh's private rooms?'

The youth hesitated, then gestured towards the gallery. 'Up there.'

'Take us!' Leaving ten men to keep watch in the court-yard below, Kamran Beg and the remainder followed Santaji up a broad, shallow flight of sandstone stairs that gave on to the marble-floored gallery. A trail of dark red blood showed the route by which the wounded musketeer had fled but Santaji led them in the opposite direction before turning abruptly to the right through a doorway carved with what looked like human figures. Warriors in

280

combat? No . . . looking more closely, Kamran Beg saw muscular men and high-breasted, round-buttocked women, limbs intertwined and joyously copulating. The walls of the wide corridor they were moving along were garishly painted with more scenes of vigorous love-making, some of the images life-sized. But what interested Kamran Beg more were the double doors of polished wood at the far end of the corridor.

'Kavi-Kulesh's apartments are through there,' Santaji whispered.

'What are they like? How many rooms?'

'One great oval chamber with two semicircular curtained alcoves on either side and at the far end a marble bath-house.'

'Any windows?'

'One above each alcove. None in the bath-house.'

Kamran Beg considered for a moment. Behind the double doors all seemed quiet. If anyone was there they had been warned. He and his men must not walk into a trap, especially as there was apparently just one way in and one way out – though he only had Santaji's word for what lay beyond that door. 'You go first and try the door,' he said to the young Maratha. 'Remember that if you call out a warning or try anything, one of my men will shoot you.'

Santaji swallowed hard but said nothing as he walked slowly down the corridor, Kamran Beg and his troops close behind. Reaching the doors, he pushed them. To Kamran Beg's surprise they swung smoothly open to reveal a great chamber just as Santaji had described. It was empty except for several low tables, pushed over so that the dishes of food and cups of sherbet had spilled among the yellow and red cushions and bolsters lying all over the richly embroidered rugs. Then from the corner of his eye he saw the pale muslin hangings covering the entrance to the left-hand alcove move.

He strode across and with the tip of his sword ripped the muslin away. Two beautiful young women, by their scanty but delicate attire probably dancing girls, stared back at him their eyes round with terror.

'Santaji, come here! Tell these women we mean them no harm but I want to know where Sambhaji and Kavi-Kulesh are.'

Santaji quickly translated what Kamran Beg had said, listened as one of the women gasped a reply, then turned back to Kamran Beg. 'They are of Kavi-Kulesh's household. She says that Kavi-Kulesh and Sambhaji were here but left after telling them to stay hidden behind the curtains in the alcove. She didn't see where they went.'

Kamran Beg looked at the women. The one who had spoken – tall, with long curling hennaed hair and full red lips – returned his gaze, though the rapid rise and fall of her heavy breasts betrayed her nervousness. Was she speaking the truth? Probably.

If so where was Sambhaji? Many years as a scout had taught him the value of intuition as well as logic. Everything suggested that Sambhaji couldn't have gone far – he'd had no time. The unlocked doors had been meant to deceive the Moghul intruders into thinking their prey had fled the palace. Well, perhaps he had. Or maybe he hadn't . . . Kamran Beg thought quickly. 'Ibrahim Ali, station men in the corridor outside to keep watch and warn if anyone comes. The rest of you, search every inch of this room and the alcoves. Rip down every hanging.

Break up every bit of furniture a man could hide in. Pull up every rug. Tap every wall. Look for any sign of where they might be concealing themselves.'

But half an hour later, with the once magnificent pleasure chamber in ruins and sweat running off his men's faces, they'd found nothing. They'd also searched the bathhouse, ripping tiles off the wall and jumping down into the empty five foot deep bathing tank, but it looked solid enough. And all the time silence, except for their own grunts as they laboured. Neither had the men stationed outside or those posted in the courtyard below seen or heard anything. The whole palace seemed to be deserted, not even an attendant, let alone a guard remaining . . . Sambhaji had made fools of them. At the thought of facing Aurangzeb and confessing that all he'd captured had been two dancing girls Kamran Beg's heart lurched against his ribcage. Aurangzeb did not like failure. He must redouble his efforts. They would pull the whole palace apart if necessary.

But not for a moment or two. His men's hair, beards and clothes were damp with sweat. One or two had flesh wounds . . . Why shouldn't they clean themselves a little before continuing their labours? 'You've been doing little enough. Fill the bathing tank with water,' Kamran Beg ordered Santaji. To his surprise the young Maratha hesitated. 'Didn't you hear what I said?'

Santaji nodded, went to the bronze wheel on the bathhouse wall and gripping it with both hands turned it until water began streaming down a carved stone chute into the bath. Kamran Beg went back into the main chamber to talk to his men, and on his return was surprised by how long the bath was taking to fill. And its floor wasn't level. At one end the water was four or five inches deep but at the other the tiles weren't yet covered. Peering more closely at the shallow end, Kamran Beg noticed that along the bottom edges where the bath's floor and wall tiles met, and around some of the floor tiles themselves, there appeared to be no plaster. Water was clearly leaking through the joints. Bad workmanship . . .?

Then, above the noise of running water, he thought he heard an odd, muffled sound. Rats, perhaps, somewhere in the pipework through which the water drained when the bath was emptied? 'Quiet!' he ordered, and kneeling down on the edge of the pool he leaned over and listened. Nothing . . . whatever it was had stopped. But then he heard Santaji shout 'Please, stop! You're drowning them!' Looking up, he saw the young Maratha run to the bronze wheel and haul it round to turn off the water. Kamran Beg got up and gripped Santaji by the shoulders. 'Explain yourself. What did you mean? Who are we drowning?' he asked, though he thought he knew the answer.

'There's a cavity under one corner of the tank – Kavi-Kulesh built it as a hiding place. I saw it when I was here before . . . I don't know if they're there but just now I heard something and had to speak – the hiding place was never meant to be used when the bath is filled. Water leaks in.'

'Show us how this cavity opens.'

Santaji got down into the bath and in the far corner of the shallow end gripped the edge of one of the malachite floor tiles, rectangular and a little larger than the rest, digging his fingers beneath its edges. Straining so that the sinews stood out on his neck, he prised it loose. Then, after handing it up to one of Kamran Beg's men, he squatted again and with far less effort this time pulled up a second slab. Leaning over, Kamran Beg gasped as he saw what Santaji had revealed – a tiny chamber directly beneath the shallow end. There, almost up to their necks in water, crouched two men, swords in hand.

'Take them alive!' Kamran Beg ordered.

The first – the older of the two – came quietly, dropping his weapon to the ground as he was pulled out by his hair. But as Kamran Beg's men grabbed the second man he tried to stab at them with his sword, slashing one of them across the cheek before being overwhelmed and disarmed. Water streaming from his sodden garments, he glared round, but it was not on the smiling Kamran Beg or the Moghuls gripping him tight that his eyes fastened but on Santaji. 'I know you! You're a Maratha, yet you betrayed me!'

'Sambhaji . . . sire . . . I knew the cavity would fill with water. I thought you and Kavi-Kulesh would die . . . I had to speak!' Santaji stammered.

'Don't lie. What did they bribe you with?' Sambhaji stared unblinking at Santaji.

'They promised me my life, but I never meant to be a traitor . . .'

At Sambhaji's contemptuous laugh, Santaji darted forward, pulled a dagger from the scabbard in the sash of one of the Moghuls holding the Maratha leader and drew it across his own throat. Blood pumped from the ragged cut as the young man tumbled forward on to the fast-crimsoning marble floor, where for a moment his body twitched, then lay still.

Glancing down, Kamran Beg saw that his boots were spattered with blood. 'Take the body away and give it due burial rites. But first despatch two riders to the emperor on our fastest horses. Their message to Aurangzeb is simple – that, God be praised, his enemy Sambhaji is finally in our hands.'

• ◆ •

Flies buzzed around the two filthy figures in their garishly striped garments and pointed hats as the mangy camels on which they were tied plodded onward. Through the heat haze the dragon's teeth battlements of the fort of Bahadurgad where Aurangzeb would be waiting took substance on the horizon. For a moment one of the figures looked up, then let his head fall on his chest again. Aurangzeb's orders concerning the captives' treatment had been explicit. For the first two days, until Kamran Beg and his men were well clear of Sangameshwar and the Maratha lands, they were to travel at night, their prisoners concealed amongst them, in case of any rescue attempt. But on the third day, as the party re-entered Moghul territory, instead of being taken immediately to the emperor, Sambhaji and Kavi-Kulesh were to be publicly paraded through the villages dressed as court clowns, objects of ridicule and derision, before they were brought to him at Bahadurgad.

Also on Aurangzeb's orders, Kamran Bag was denying the captives food and giving them just one cup of water a day. By now their lips were cracked and dry and they sometimes looked near fainting. Nevertheless they were keeping their expressions impassive, whatever insults his men offered them.

As the dusty procession passed beneath the fort's gatehouse two hours later and a kettledrum boomed in salute, Kamran Beg breathed a deep sigh of relief. His mission was over. He had succeeded. Leading his men into the fort's rectangular courtyard he saw that a large wooden platform had been erected at the far end. On the left-hand side stood a brazier piled with burning charcoals. In the centre a man in hide trousers and a tunic that left his brawny arms bare was honing a long blade. He was one of the imperial executioners. Kamran Beg had seen him at work before. More knives of differing sizes, blades glittering in the sun, were laid out on a table beside him. To his right were two stout upright wooden frames, both about six feet high and placed side by side. Facing each other in neat rows at either end of the platform were some of Aurangzeb's chief commanders and nobles.

Conscious of the many eyes upon him, Kamran Beg gave the signal to halt and he and his weary men dismounted. As grooms led their horses away, trumpet blasts from above caused some of the tired animals to skitter about. Looking round, Kamran Beg saw Aurangzeb, plainly dressed, step out on to a carved sandstone balcony fifteen feet above the courtyard and directly facing the executioner's platform. Giant banners of Moghul green fluttered on either side of the chair on which he now settled his tall, lean frame. An attendant standing behind the chair immediately began to cool him with a giant peacock feather fan.

'Welcome back, Kamran Beg. You and your brave men have done a great service to my empire. You have brought me the infidel son of that infernal infidel Shivaji, and the degenerate who was harbouring him. Bring them forward where I can see them properly.' Four imperial bodyguards ran to where the prisoners were still hunched and bound on their camels. Hauling them down, they dragged them to the open space beneath Aurangzeb's balcony, then threw them to the ground.

'Now you are where you belong, in the dust – a fitting place for those who have disregarded the true God and defied me, his faithful servant. Only one thing might save you, Sambhaji. Recognising your error and converting to Islam.'

'The Hindu gods are the only true ones. Your god is false. How could any true god have allowed you to commit the crimes you have?' Sambhaji shouted up at him through his cracked lips.

'Be under no illusions, then. You will both die. But first you will tell me everything I want to know – the locations of your hidden treasuries, the names of any Moghul officials or commanders who took bribes from you in return for information, and anything else I, your rightful ruler before God and man, demand.'

Sambhaji's face as he continued to look up at Aurangzeb on his balcony held nothing but defiance and contempt. 'Whatever happens to me, my people will cleanse Hindustan of you and your empire . . . I see you smile. Why? Because through guile and treachery you have me in your power? You're the real failure. Ask yourself what you have really achieved during your detested reign? Nothing! Your empire boils with rebellion. The name of my father whom you never subdued will live on in Hindustan because he was a hero and an inspiration to our people. Yours will only be spoken when it is cursed by those who remember your wickedness and oppression!'

'Silence!'

'No, I won't be silent! You think I'm afraid of you – a

288

man who murdered his own brothers and can't command the respect of his own sons? I know what Akbar thinks about you – he often told me – including how you falsely use this God of yours to justify your every malicious act against those of my faith. Akbar knew you for what you are – "the holy hypocrite" he called you, just as I do! And like him I despise you and all those who do your dirty work. In your next life you will return not even as a worm or a rat but as a flea or a tick . . .'

'Enough!' Aurangzeb was on his feet. 'I've listened to these ravings long enough. Executioner, begin your work. Start with the miscreant Sambhaji and take your time. But whichever parts of his body you cut first, leave his tongue till last. Before this is over he'll tell me everything I wish to know. Only then will I ask you to rip it out so I don't have to listen to his craven cries for mercy!'

'I'll never beg you for anything – I'd sooner bite out my own tongue,' Sambhaji shouted up as two guards seized him under the armpits, dragged him struggling to the platform and threw him on to it. Then, at a signal from the emperor, one of his most senior commanders, who had been standing in the front row of those watching, stepped forward. In his hand was a long piece of paper from which he began to read in a voice loud enough not only for Sambhaji but for Aurangzeb on his balcony and everybody else in the courtyard to hear.

'Sambhaji, you are a heretic traitor who has conspired against the Emperor Aurangzeb and his people, spilling the blood of the innocent by your crimes. Before you meet your end, you must answer for those crimes and answer the questions I have for you. The longer you take to answer, the longer and more painful will be your ordeal.'

'I'm not a criminal, but a patriot, and I'll tell you nothing!'

'Very well.' The commander nodded and the executioner advanced on the slight figure of Sambhaji, who by now had managed to struggle to his feet. Taking hold of his victim by the collar of his clown's coat with his left hand, the executioner swung his right fist into his stomach. If the man hadn't been holding him up, Sambhaji would have collapsed. Instead he dangled in that relentless grip like a broken puppet. The man punched him again and this time Sambhaji choked up a mixture of blood and phlegm.

'Here is the first question. Where are the main Maratha treasure vaults? We know from informants that six months ago you moved a large amount of gold and jewels to new locations.'

'I'll never tell you and you'll never find them,' Sambhaji gasped.

'I repeat my question. Where is your treasure?'

'You must be deaf. Didn't you hear what I just said?'

The commander nodded again and the executioner released Sambhaji so that he collapsed forward on to the platform. Then, leaning over him, with a few sweeps of his dagger the executioner cut his dirty garments from him. Sambhaji's wiry body bore several marks of battle. A long, now faded scar curved from his left breast across his stomach and almost down to his groin. His left thigh was scored from hip bone to knee. The executioner pulled him to his feet by his long hair and hauled him towards one of the wooden frames, then bound his feet and hands to each of the four corners so that his body was spreadeagled, helpless.

The commander was consulting his list of questions again. 'We know you tried to bribe members of the imperial court. Whom did you contact?' His voice rang out crisp and authoritative.

'Aurangzeb. I offered him one rupee to get out of Hindustan,' Sambhaji gasped, face pressed against one of the wooden struts so that his voice was muffled.

At a third nod from the commander, the executioner moved across to the wooden bench and, taking his time, selected a knife with a very long, very thin blade. Then, stepping up behind Sambhaji, with an almost surgical delicacy he made a long vertical incision down his spine, then a horizontal cut across. Sambhaji's body twitched visibly as rivulets of blood began to trickle down but he didn't cry out. Next the executioner altered the angle of the knife and slowly inserted it beneath the skin where the two cuts intersected in the small of Sambhaji's back. Then, with a kind of scything action, he began to ease the skin and its layer of fat away from the muscle and sinew beneath. Sambhaji at last let out a single high-pitched cry.

When he had stripped a flap of skin about nine inches long and three inches wide, the executioner stopped and looked at the counsellor, who repeated his question about conspirators at the Moghul court. But it was clear from the way his body was sagging that Sambhaji was barely conscious. The executioner flung a bucket of cold water over him and he seemed to jerk back into life. Again his inquisitor repeated the question but Sambhaji only shook his head.

Kamran Beg's stomach heaved and he had to turn aside to retch as the executioner prepared to wield his knife once more. As he tried to steady himself, he realised he wasn't the only one nauseated by the horror taking place on the platform. Behind the emperor, his chief bodyguard Umar Ali was biting his lips and staring hard at the ground.

While the executioner, expressionless and methodical, continued his gruesome work, Aurangzeb turned his gaze on Kavi-Kulesh, waiting his turn. If he was any judge of character the general might be willing to speak even if Sambhaji was not. Not that the answers to the questions his counsellor was reading out were in reality of any great importance. Through his own spy networks he was well aware of the identities of those of doubtful loyalty who needed watching. As for Sambhaji's treasuries, now that Golcunda and Bijapur were no longer financing the Marathas, what did they matter? Compared to Moghul wealth they were like a single grain of sand on a beach. What did matter was the public humiliation of Sambhaji – his absolute and public submission to Aurangzeb's will. Even if it took days he wanted that satisfaction so that everyone within his empire would understand that despite the passing of the years their emperor remained a potent force whom only the most reckless – or foolish – would defy.

• ◆ •

But it seemed that he would be denied that satisfaction after all. Two weeks later, Aurangzeb again sat on his balcony watching as the executioner dismembered Sambhaji's and Kavi-Kulesh's corpses – a pile of raw flesh and bone barely recognisable as human – ready to be insulted the final time by their heads being paraded through the villages of the Deccan. Somehow through days of constant torment both Sambhaji and Kavi-Kulesh had found reserves of strength and courage to resist him.

When the news of Sambhaji's capture had first reached him he had dropped to his knees and given thanks to God that his empire was secure and his triumph complete. Now, though, it didn't feel like total victory and he wondered whether he might have created another hero to the Marathas alongside Shivaji.

Chapter 20

The Emissary

Your Majesty, I, Sir William Norris, write to you from aboard the ship Scipio, *two weeks out of Mauritius bound for England, my beloved homeland. However, I am so weakened by frequent bouts of the flux that although only in the forty-second year of my age I fear I may not survive to see those shores again. Therefore I hope you will forgive my framing as a letter the report of my embassy to the great Moghul Emperor Aurangzeb on which I departed Britain in the autumn of the Year of Our Lord, 1698.*

For the benefit of any of your advisers whom you may care to consult and who are not familiar with my remit, my purpose was to persuade the emperor to grant more privileges to the traders of our country. In addition I was to seek on your behalf fulfilment of previous promises made by him to protect our merchants from the depredations both of corrupt officials and marauding robbers masquerading as rebels.

After a long voyage, the discomfort and tedium of which

I cannot begin to describe, I landed on 25 September 1699 at Masulipatan on the east coast of Hindustan where your consul Pitt greeted me warmly. However, complications in arranging my onward mission such as engaging suitable interpreters and permissions to cross Moghul territory ensued, resulting in considerable delays. Eventually, wearied by them, I decided to take ship again for the trading port of Surat on the west coast of Hindustan in August 1700. I arrived there four months later.

With the help of the English merchants who reside there I was able to complete my preparations for my journey to the emperor relatively speedily. He was, I was told, campaigning near the fortified city of Burhanpur on the Tapti river in the Deccan. After a hazardous journey often crossing territory in reality in the control of the Marathas who, praise be, showed themselves most courteous to me, I reached Burhanpur only to find the emperor's camp was somewhat further south. Although already in poor health, I immediately set out again and on 17 April 1701 reached the imperial camp. It was outside the Panhala fort which the emperor was besieging in an attempt to retake it from the Marathas ten years after he had first seized it from them.

Even though he had 150,000 troops and at least the same number of camp followers with him, the siege was making slow progress. It had already been under way for some months and rumours were rife which I later understood to have proved true that the emperor, despairing of military victory, was planning to suborn and bribe the fort's commanders to turn the fort over to him. The vast Moghul camp was nearly thirty miles in circumference I was told and contained 50,000 camels and 30,000 elephants as well as 250 bazaars. Be that as it may, it was in most places knee-deep in mud and large pools of scummy green water abounded around which mosquitoes buzzed in great numbers. Many of the emperor's courtiers and generals were ill. I myself soon contracted a fever which turned my stools to rice water. One of the few of the emperor's courtiers who seemed well disposed to my mission gave me opium mixed with the soured milk he called 'lassi' which affected a transient cure but the affliction has continued to return with greater frequency and intensity, hence my fears for my survival, but I must not trouble Your Majesty further with the details of my illness.

Immediately I recovered the half of my health and strength I began assiduously to petition for an audience with the emperor. On several occasions corrupt courtiers asked me for money to arrange an interview and when paid failed to meet their part of the bargain. The only excuse I can offer for their behaviour is that like most of the Moghul soldiery they have not been paid or rewarded by the emperor for their services for many months and in some cases years. The whole camp lives off the surrounding land, much to the distress of the local people who are all the more encouraged to support the Moghuls' enemies.

Not surprisingly, given the emperor's advanced age – he is in his eighty-third year – speculation and scheming about the succession is rife. Supporters of Prince Muazzam – released by his father five years before my visit from imprisonment in the fort of Gwalior where he had been confined by him for consorting with Golcundi enemies of the empire – begged me for support, offering trading concessions if and when he came to power. Although I was courteous, encouraging them to believe in the benevolence

296

of the English, when I met the prince who is himself no longer young I found him seemingly broken in spirit. While this may be a pretence, designed to deflect any further malice of his father, I rather doubt it. The emperor rules all his sons – and indeed his daughters – with an iron rod. He even briefly imprisoned his purported favourite son – his youngest who is named Kam Bakhsh – for what was officially announced as 'misconduct' but an informant told me was drunkenness. He only released him – so it was said – when his mother, the emperor's favourite consort Udipuri Mahal, pleaded on her knees with him, telling him her son's behaviour was her fault. He had only been following her bad example.

I first saw the emperor himself when he passed through the camp, being carried on a litter to view the siege works. He appeared all over white, in his dress, in the colour of his turban, as well as of his hair and his beard. He was a stately figure who looked at no one, reading as he was all the time from what I was informed was his holy book, the Koran, eyes steadfastly on it, never diverting from side to side. Many praise his piety but the strictness with which he imposes the religious dogmas he upholds on those of other faiths alienates the loyalties of many others.

When I eventually obtained the favour of an audience with him, on 28 April to be precise, he was courteous, thanking me for Your Majesty's presents and sending you his wishes for the continuance of your rule. However, after such a preamble he told me starkly that I should not expect from him the friendliness and freedoms which his grandfather the Emperor Jahangir bestowed on my predecessor Sir Thomas Roe, telling me he was no man for drinking foreign

297

spirits nor for discussing outlandish philosophies deep into the night.

He promised me he would look the more favourably upon our requests if we cleared the Indian Ocean of the scores of pirates – many from England and our colonies – who infest it. He remained particularly incensed at the depredations of Henry Avery who a little since off Bombay seized the Moghul vessel Ganj-i-Sawai *– part of the pilgrim fleet to Arabia – and made off with goods to the value of £200,000 by his account. He also complained of pirates' more recent capture of the* Queddah Merchant *and other trading vessels. I assured him we shared his interest in ridding the seas of pirates and said that although, despite our best efforts, we had unfortunately not captured Avery we had taken William Kidd who had attacked the* Queddah Merchant. *The emperor seemed little convinced by my protestations of our maritime strength and willingness to employ it to mutual benefit and dismissed me with the command to discuss my requests with his officials.*

I spent many sessions with these venal men. Nearly all sought from me tokens of friendship and goodwill – or to put it more bluntly bribes. Despite the emperor's prohibitions on alcohol many expressed a great desire for alcohol and in particular what they called 'the North British Spirit'. After much expenditure of both time and funds, I obtained in protracted discussion with them a number of concessions in the reduction of taxes and of customs dues as well as promises of protection for our merchants and goods. However, I doubt not that these latter will only be fulfilled in practice if more bribes are extended.

Overall from my experience of these last months I

298

conclude that the Moghul Empire is losing its cohesion among a plethora of internal enemies. Foremost are the powerful Marathas who have survived the death of their ruler Sambhaji and after a period when their power was fragmented have regrouped under a new leader, Rajaram – the younger son of Shivaji and brother of Sambhaji – to pose a continually growing threat which keeps the emperor and his armies bogged down in the south. Just before I left I was told Rajaram had died but his widow had succeeded in placing his young son – just a boy – on the throne without bloodshed.

There are also many rebels elsewhere – in the north, per exemplum, the Sikhs of the Punjab and the Jats. The Sikhs, I am informed, have their own faith which centres on the oneness of God. Since Aurangzeb executed their leader – or as they call him their guru – Tegh Bahadur in 1675, the Sikhs have strengthened their mutual bonds under the leadership of Tegh Bahadur's son, Guru Gobind Singh, who has battled with the Moghuls and other neigh-bours several times. While I was in Hindustan much conster-nation was caused among Moghul commanders by the news of a great congregation of Sikhs at Anadpur in April 1699 on the day of their annual harvest festival. There Gobind Singh founded a body of Sikhs called the Khalsa. All members would henceforth bear the name 'Singh' which means lion, live in spiritual union and defend themselves and their religion against all who try to oppress them. As I left Hindustan the Moghuls were preparing to send a great expedition against the Sikhs.

The Jats, too, are brave fighters, adept at the hit and run attack. They recently raided the vast mausoleum of the great Emperor Akbar near Agra carrying off much of its golden

299

adornments and furnishings. All the time, the Persian shah remains a constant threat on the north-west boundaries of the empire, looking for any opportunity to extend further his lands at the expense of the Moghul Empire.

Pressure grows on Aurangzeb's empire not only from these rebels and invaders but also from the corruption of officials in his distant provinces who, believing the emperor preoccupied with the Marathas, feel free to extort monies unfairly from the suffering people of Hindustan. The costs of the constant wars the emperor fights eat up all the monies and more that do reach the Moghul treasuries and the emperor is forced to raise taxes, increasing the burden on his people.

In my opinion, the powerful personality of the emperor alone holds his realm together. He is feared and respected in equal measure. Despite his advanced years none doubt the acuity of his brain and his ability to fathom the minds of others and thus to anticipate their actions. As is essential to his personal safety, he takes care to win the loyalty of his closest attendants and bodyguards and indeed many of the common people by small acts of kindness and attention, surprising them by his interest and knowledge of their lives.

When he dies I foresee another debilitating conflict for the throne. Which if any of his four surviving sons will succeed I cannot say. As I have previously recounted Prince Muazzam appears to me a mere husk of a man. Prince Akbar remains in exile in Persia and is, I am assured, given hospitality but no military support either by his mother's Persian relations or by the shah who, I am told, puts no trust in him. Akbar's full brother Prince Azam who is his father's newly appointed governor in Gujarat is by common report too impetuous and rash to sustain a successful campaign. The main qualification of the younger Kam Bakhsh is that he is thought to be his father's favourite and, as such, may have his path smoothed for him. However, from my acquaintance with him he seems callow and indolent, even if of equable humour. Indeed, it may be that one of Aurangzeb's many powerful generals may overcome them all and take the throne. Whatever the case, the inevitable confusion and in-fighting will create the potential for us to employ the growing profits from our trade with the country to suborn the governors of territories of interest to us to further establish England's position in this rich and vast country where the central authority is teetering on the brink of collapse.

I much fear my waning strength will not allow me to write further for the present. I will resume my task if God grants me the favour of prolonging my life. If not, I, Sir William Norris, your loyal subject and ambassador to Hindustan, salute Your Majesty and commend my wife to your gracious care and sustenance.

Chapter 21

'Hindustan is Our Land!'

'Have my war elephant prepared, Umar Ali. I intend to go to the front line to launch our new assault. It will hearten the troops to see me. This fort of Wagingera should not have detained an army as large as this as long as it has. My commanders should have overrun it well before I arrived from Burhanpur.'

'Majesty,' Umar Ali replied, 'I will of course order your war elephant if you require it. But permit me to ask, Majesty, whether you feel that you are strong enough for this so few days after your arrival? And, Majesty, even if you wish to signal the assault from the front line, do you need to do so from elephant-back? In your howdah you will make an obvious target for Maratha gunners and musketeers. Using a palanquin would be both more comfortable and less dangerous.'

'I appreciate your concern but I remain, God be thanked, vigorous enough for the task. I will use a war elephant. Although it may make me a more obvious target it will

302

equally allow many more of our troops to see me and that is my whole purpose.'

Half an hour later, dressed in Moghul green, Aurangzeb handed his gold-capped walking stick to the young *qorchi* at his side and with the youth's support began to climb the steps that led to the platform from which he would mount his war elephant. The great beast, his favourite elephant – a male named Thunderer – was standing calmly in front of the platform. His two *mahouts* were sitting one behind the other behind its ears. Umar Ali, his beard now growing white, was standing behind the green velvet padded imperial seat in the howdah holding an ivory-handled, six foot long musket. To allow more troops to see him. Aurangzeb had had the howdah's canopy removed. One of the mounted bodyguards, who would follow immediately behind his elephant, would carry a large umbrella to be passed to Umar Ali to shield him from the sun if necessary as they returned.

Slowly Aurangzeb reached the top of the platform and with the help of Umar Ali clambered into the howdah and settled himself into the seat. Guided by the leading *mahout*, Thunderer began to move with the slow wallowing gait with which Aurangzeb was so familiar. Soon he was passing one of his rear cannon batteries where he stopped for some moments to urge the gunners to great efforts. Then he reached the lines of horsemen, musketeers and infantrymen, all readied for action. His chief *mahout* turned Thunderer, guiding him with his steel *anka* along the massed ranks as Aurangzeb greeted his soldiers who in turn shouted '*Zindabad Aurangzeb!* Long live Aurangzeb!'

A few minutes later he approached a group of his senior officers assembled at his request to greet him. Thunderer halted in front of them, and with the aid of Umar Ali Aurangzeb slowly stood and then, disengaging his chief bodyguard's supporting arm, turned to the officers. Some failed to meet his gaze. Others shifted from foot to foot, clearly ill at ease, as well they might be, he thought, given their previous conduct of the siege. He spoke loudly and clearly. 'Today I wish you to attack the fort in full force and with courage in your hearts, confident in the strength of our cause and of our arms. Up to now you have trifled with these Marathas. Now show them who is master and prove to me your true worth. Capture this fort this day!'

One by one and then together in a rush not to be seen to be backward, his officers shouted their support. Aurangzeb held up his hand for silence. 'It is now your task to return to your regiments to inspire your men with the same renewed courage and heart you have shown me by your acclamation. In half an hour, in the view of as many of our men as possible, I will give the signal for the attack to begin with a single shot from my musket.'

Thirty minutes later Thunderer climbed slowly up a small hill in full sight not only of many of Aurangzeb's own men but also of the Wagingera fortress. The fort was set on a much larger hill and protected on two sides by cliffs which fell steeply to a wide, swift-flowing river below. It was not large, but its thick stone walls had proved themselves stout. Thunderer halted on the flat hilltop. Two mounted bearers unfurled their great, gold-embroidered green banners behind the elephant. 'Help me to my feet again, Umar Ali,' Aurangzeb ordered.

His chief bodyguard did so and then passed him his musket, which had battle scenes carved into its ivory stock. 'Do you wish to steady the barrel on my shoulder, Majesty?'

'No. I can hold it myself.' Aurangzeb was as good as his word. Using all his strength to keep the musket level, he fired a single shot towards the fort.

Immediately, shots rippled from along his front lines, his cannons opened fire and his horsemen began to advance cheering and flags fluttering as their mounts broke into a gallop. They were quickly followed by foot soldiers, some of whom were carrying long scaling ladders.

As Umar Ali helped Aurangzeb settle himself back into his padded seat once more, a cannonball buried itself in the earth of the hill nearby, sending up a shower of dirt which spattered Aurangzeb and his elephant. The well-trained Thunderer scarcely moved but one of the banner-bearers' horses reared, nearly throwing its rider. Through the thickening smoke Aurangzeb saw that the bodies of several of his horsemen, including at least two other flag-carriers, were already sprawled on the ground, hit by Maratha musket and cannon balls before they had got even halfway to the fort. A few riders were falling back, wounded. Others though were already beneath the fort walls, several standing in their stirrups, reins in one hand as with the other they fired pistols at the defenders on the battlements. Some were slowing to allow musketeers they had carried behind them to slip to the ground and ready their weapons.

A frightened horse suddenly bolted, carrying its Moghul rider over the cliff behind the fort as he struggled in vain to rein it in. More than a dozen Moghul musketeers collapsed dead or injured before the first of the foot soldiers ran up. They too had suffered casualties. Numbers of them were lying still on the steep slope leading up to the fort and a few others were crawling or limping back towards the Moghul lines. However, those who had reached the walls quickly raised scaling ladders and began to scramble up. The Marathas on the battlements pushed off the first few ladders, sending them crashing back with the Moghul soldiers still clinging to them on to their comrades beneath. Two or three Marathas fell with them, pitching from the battlements, hit by the harassing Moghul musket fire from below.

But the Moghuls were showing the great heart he had demanded. Such were the ever-increasing numbers reaching the fort that quickly more ladders were readied. The men on them succeeded in climbing on to the battlements. There they could be seen fighting hand to hand with the Marathas, slowly pushing them along the walls and despite more casualties isolating them in small groups. They had already captured one of the main cannon platforms and several of his men appeared to be trying to turn a cannon so they could fire it into the fort. Nearby another Moghul soldier tied the staff of a great green and gold Moghul banner to one of the crenellations of the battlements and it fluttered proudly in the wind.

'By the grace of God the fighting is going in our favour,' Aurangzeb said. 'My head is beginning to throb in the heat. Umar Ali, let us return to my command tent. Take that umbrella. I want no more of this sun.'

That evening in the *haram* tent, Udipuri Mahal looked across at Aurangzeb as he reclined on a divan, eyes half closed, his head resting on a silk cushion. 'You look exhausted, and so you've every right to after all your efforts today,' she said gently.

'Yes, I'm tired. But it was worth it. My presence spurred my men to greater effort. We captured the whole fort in less than two hours, even if its commander and some of his troops did get away through an underground passage we found. I'll make sure Wagingera is properly garrisoned this time. The Marathas won't recapture it or my commanders will have me to answer to.'

'I am pleased at your success. But be careful to spare yourself too much exertion.'

'That might not be entirely possible. I have decided something which I wish to tell you before I announce it to my commanders. I'm going to take some of my army north, back to Agra and Delhi. I've been in the south twenty-three years, pushing my empire's borders outwards to their greatest extent ever. I'll summon Muazzam to command the large forces that will remain here. He's a competent enough general and now obedient to his orders to a fault. His task will be to consolidate our positions, not to seek more territory. Azam can remain in Gujarat.'

'Why decide all this now?'

'Many reasons. There is unrest in the north. The Rajputs grow ever more insolent and the Sikhs ever more defiant. The Jats have even raided my mother's mausoleum in Agra. And what's more my own officials, believing themselves out of my eye, have become corrupt and venal. I will make examples of the worst of these men – that and my presence will cow the remainder into better behaviour and thus produce more of the revenues I need to sustain my armies.' Aurangzeb, who was sitting up straight now, paused and then continued, 'And to be truthful, I yearn to see the familiar landscapes and buildings of the north, to pray at my sister Jahanara's grave in Delhi and again at my mother's tomb in the Taj Mahal – and perhaps at my father's there too.' Aurangzeb paused again.

307

To Udipuri Mahal's surprise his expression was more melancholy than she'd seen before and one or two tears began to appear in his reddened eyes and run slowly down his lined cheeks into his white beard. He brushed them quickly away. 'I've been thinking more about him as I've grown old. My grief when I heard of Akbar's death in Persia last year, and before that at the news of the death of Zebunissa in her imprisonment, surprised me. Age has made me realise how unequal the bonds are between a parent and a child – how as the child grows it detaches itself from its parent, caught up in its own plans and ambitions, feeling it knows best. The parent still feels the bond and sees them still as children, failing to understand why they will not follow his guidance. Even though I have no doubt . . . none at all . . . that I was right . . . entirely right . . . to act as I did against my father, I am beginning to understand a little more how he may have felt.'

A wan smile crossed Aurangzeb's face as he finished speaking, and Udipuri moved over to him and put her arm around his shoulders. After some minutes' silence she asked, 'May Kam Bakhsh accompany us north?'

'Yes, if you wish.'

'I'm grateful. He is dear to me and I believe he is to you. I often worry that for that reason his brothers may conspire against him, particularly when he is away from your protection . . .'

'While I live – and I do not intend to die quite yet – I will allow no such conspiracies.'

A smile transformed Udipuri Mahal's fleshy features, reminding Aurangzeb of how she'd looked in her youth. Sleep slowly overcame him as she cradled his head against her breast. She stroked his thin white hair and arranged some strands over a scar from one of his battles, then began to sing a night-time lullaby from her native Georgia. Tomorrow she would order her servants to begin packing her chests while keeping aside for the journey those clothes and jewels that she knew best pleased her husband, even if some of the garments would need alteration to accommodate her growing girth. For his sake she would pour away the small stock of alcohol she'd secreted and which she knew he abhorred and try to stay entirely sober until they reached the north. Even if he still showed some of his familiar vigour, Aurangzeb was eighty-seven years old and he would need her to be his comfort on this arduous journey. Kam Bakhsh too would have a chance to show his abilities and demonstrate his worth as a successor to the throne when the time came, as surely it would . . .

• ◆ •

Kam Bakhsh was charging bravely at the head of his horsemen, splashing into the waters of the shallow river which glinted golden in the late afternoon light. Shading his eyes, Aurangzeb watched as one of the riders behind his son flung up his arms and fell from his white horse into the water. However, Kam Bakhsh was now through the river and halfway to the small, disused fort on the hill beyond. In places its mud walls, never high, seemed to have crumbled in the rains bringing them low enough for horses to jump. Soon the Marathas who'd escaped to the fort following their surprise attack on the vanguard of the Moghul column as it trudged slowly northwards would be killed or captured. The deaths of those of his men who had perished would be avenged. This was only the latest of the ambushes that had dogged his two-mile-long column, further delaying its already slow progress and forcing constant vigilance on every man in it. But now as the slope of the hill grew steeper Kam Bakhsh, on his chestnut charger, was outdistancing his bodyguard and nearing the fort walls. Then suddenly his horse crumpled and he pitched from the saddle to lie still on the ground.

Four or perhaps five of his bodyguard pulled hard on their reins, bringing their mounts to a sudden halt – so sudden that one of the horses reared. Quickly they dismounted and bent over the prince. The rest of the Moghuls charged on up the incline towards the fort. Two fell as their horses failed to clear the mud walls but the others did so successfully and disappeared from sight into the fort's interior.

'Send out *hakims* to bring my son back to the column, Umar Ali,' Aurangzeb shouted, 'and ensure no word of his fall reaches the women. They were travelling in purdah at the back of the column and when we were ambushed the guards will have surrounded them so that Udipuri Mahal will not have seen what has happened. She must only learn of it from me and then only when I know the extent of my son's injuries.'

Never since Humayun's time had a Moghul prince died in battle. Pray God he would preserve the life of Kam Bakhsh. At the time of his youngest son's birth he remembered thinking that an emperor needed several sons in case of the death or treachery of one or more. Since then he'd endured the treachery of Akbar. Was he now to suffer another's death? He would soon find out. One of the bodyguards who had clustered around Kam Bakhsh had remounted his horse and was galloping back towards the camp. Soon he was dismounting in front of Aurangzeb, who could read nothing from his face.

'My son – how is he?'

'We cannot be sure, Majesty. A Maratha ball hit his horse, not him, but as he fell he lost his helmet and his head struck the stony ground hard. He is bleeding from his nose, his mouth and one of his ears. He has lost consciousness but he is breathing and one of my comrades thinks he saw his eyelids flutter once. The *hakims* said it is better to leave him where he is for now. They have called for ice and blankets.'

'But if you leave him there, what about the Marathas?'

'Those who could not flee from the fort in time have already been taken prisoner. Everything is quiet again.'

'How many have you captured?'

'About twenty-five, Majesty.'

'Guard them securely. I will deal with them later. Now I must go to my son. Umar Ali, bring me a palanquin.'

Ten minutes later the six bearers laid down the green-curtained palanquin beside the group surrounding Kam Bakhsh. Aurangzeb could see little through the clustering bodies. Umar Ali, who despite his own near sixty years had run beside the palanquin, helped Aurangzeb to his feet.

'Let me see my son.' Those immediately surrounding Kam Bakhsh stood back. As he looked down on him, Aurangzeb saw that Kam Bakhsh still seemed unconscious. The blood had stopped flowing from his nose and mouth but at least three of his front teeth were shattered and a broken bone protruded bloodily from his left wrist. A dark-clothed *hakim* was holding a block of ice wrapped in a cloth to his grazed temple and swollen and purple left eye. But praise be to God, his son's chest was rising and falling rhythmically. He was breathing well.

311

'Has he moved at all?' Aurangzeb asked the *hakim*.

'He opened his eyes two or three minutes ago and even seemed to smile, but since then he has relapsed into unconsciousness.' As he spoke, Kam Bakhsh's head moved slightly, his eyes opened again and he appeared to look at his father.

'Kam Bakhsh, can you hear me?' Aurangzeb asked. But his son didn't reply and a new dribble of blood ran from his lips into his dark beard – perhaps a movement of his head had caused a cut to reopen. His eyes closed again. Another few minutes passed, then Kam Bakhsh's eyelids flickered and he opened his eyes once more. This time Aurangzeb was sure they were focusing on him. 'Kam Bakhsh . . .'

Before he could say more Kam Bakhsh's bloodied lips moved. 'Father?' he said softly but distinctly.

Despite his ageing joints Aurangzeb dropped immediately to his knees. 'Praise be to God!'

Two hours later, leaving Kam Bakhsh sitting up in a newly erected tent with his broken wrist set and Udipuri Mahal at his side, Aurangzeb had himself taken by palanquin to the riverbank. There the two dozen Maratha prisoners, their arms and legs tied, were being guarded by the same number of his bodyguards. Once he had alighted, with the aid of his stick he walked the short distance over to the captives. Nearly all of them looked at him unabashed.

'You are all traitors to me, your emperor. You and your kind have long plagued my rule. Today you have wounded my son. Nothing can save you from death, but if you convert to Islam your end will be speedy and as painless and dignified as possible, by the sharp sword of the executioner. Knowing that, do any of you wish to convert to the true faith?'

There was no response.

'Well then, you will be taken one by one to that cannon over there. You will be tied across its mouth and the cannon fired, blowing you to pieces. Then I will have any of your heads that can be found cemented into a tower to serve as a warning to any others who pass by and are contemplating challenging my authority. Guards and gunners, begin your work!'

As the sun began to set in a blaze of crimson across the river, two tall guards seized a long-haired Maratha and began dragging him towards the cannon. The prisoner did not resist but kept his head high, and as he passed near Aurangzeb shouted, 'Hindustan is our land. We will be victorious in the end against you and all other foreign invaders. Whatever pain and dishonour I suffer now, old man, your descendants will endure tenfold.' One of the guards hit him hard in the pit of the stomach and he doubled up but uttered not a single audible groan. Reaching the cannon, already loaded by the three gunners standing beside it, the guards bent him over its mouth and roped his arms and legs to the barrel in a deadly embrace. He still did not struggle or cry out. The chief gunner put the taper to the firing hole and the cannonball blew the Maratha to pieces, scattering blood, flesh and bone far and wide and sending his head bouncing towards the river.

'Call the palanquin-bearers. I need see no more of this,' Aurangzeb told Umar Ali. What more could he do to break the spirit of these people?

• ◆ •

'I must rest for some days. I fear I'm at the limit of my strength and need time to recuperate before we move

313

on towards Delhi, as I'm determined to do. Give the necessary orders, Umar Ali,' Aurangzeb said as his chief bodyguard knelt beside his travelling palanquin in the dusty courtyard of the fortress-palace of Devapur.

'Yes, Majesty. I'll tell your commanders so that they can secure the necessary supplies and make more permanent arrangements for the troops than the bivouacs so many use when we're moving on every day or two.'

'And do make sure my officials and commanders in the provinces know . . .' Aurangzeb broke off, racked by a bout of persistent coughing. After spitting a globule of phlegm into the porcelain cup he now kept at his side covered by a muslin cloth he continued, his voice hoarse and low, 'Let them know I am here so that reports reach me quickly in the event of trouble.'

'I will, Majesty. Do you wish me to help you from the palanquin to the rooms which the attendants you sent ahead have, I know, already finished preparing for you?'

'For once I'm too weary to walk. Have the bearers take me in the palanquin and send word ahead for the servants to prepare some iced water. Even though I do not sweat I feel as hot as if I'm burning up inside.'

'Of course, Majesty. The ice-house, I'm already assured, is well stocked. Udipuri Mahal has sent word she is awaiting you in your rooms. I'll also make sure the attendants have fitted the *tattis* to the casements and fed them with water.'

'Good. Now have the bearers move me inside into the cool.' As he finished speaking, another burst of coughing shook the emperor's thin frame.

He'd never seen Aurangzeb so prepared to show himself so frail before his staff, Umar Ali thought as he gave the necessary orders. He must indeed be ill.

Later that day Udipuri Mahal bent over Aurangzeb as the raucous cries of roosting peacocks filled the still evening air of Devapur. Her husband was tossing and turning in the fitful sleep into which he'd fallen soon after reaching the white marble apartments readied for him in the fort. Hs breathing was regular if rapid and seemed to rasp through his dry throat. She moistened his lips once more with the water from the silver bowl at his side. She too was tired and her eyelids began to close, but she suddenly jerked awake when she heard Aurangzeb say softly but clearly, 'Mother, help me. I suffer. There are snakes everywhere . . . snakes in my brain . . . snakes in my family . . . poison dripping from their fangs. Don't leave me for the snakes to bite. Help me! Help me!' He was tossing and flinging his arms around. His eyes were open and his eyeballs rolling wildly. He was growing delirious. He wasn't going to die, was he?

'Summon the *hakim* and fetch one of the emperor's imams to pray with him,' she told a young *qorchi* standing behind her. Then she took a lump of ice from the large bowl nearby and held it directly to Aurangzeb's forehead. As the water from the melting ice dribbled down his face into his white beard, Aurangzeb for a moment struggled even more violently but then lay on his back and grew still. She hadn't killed him with the shock of the cold ice, had she? No, his chest was still rising and falling.

Suddenly he looked at her. 'Udipuri Mahal, is that you?'

'Yes,' she said, 'I'm here. All will be well.' Almost before she'd finished speaking Aurangzeb's whole body seemed to grow wet with sweat, soaking dark patches into his pale garments. Praise be to God the fever had broken. He might yet live. Udipuri Mahal kissed his damp cheek. He would have no immediate need of the prayers of the dark–clad imam who had just entered.

In the cool of the early morning two days later, Udipuri Mahal was again sitting bedside Aurangzeb's bed. He had just awoken, and she was about to dip a spoon into a silver bowl containing an infusion of water, honey and herbs which the *hakims* had prepared to soothe his persistent racking cough when he said, 'No more need for that. Pass me the bowl. I will sip from it myself.'

With a smile she handed the bowl to him. He took it with a hand which only had the trace of a shake. 'Raise me up on my pillows,' he said after he'd drunk and returned the bowl to her. With little gasps of effort she lifted him until he was almost sitting upright in the bed. As she placed some thick brocade cushions behind his back he said, 'Now hand me my Kashmiri shawl. Quickly! There is a morning chill.'

Delighted that he was regaining some of his old authoritative manner, she said as she passed the shawl to him, 'I'm glad you seem to be feeling stronger.'

'I am. This morning I will resume kneeling for my prayers. This afternoon I will have myself dressed and carried to the Hall of Private Audience to preside over a meeting of my council.'

'There is no need to exhaust yourself by attending a council meeting.'

'There is every need. I wish to – and I will – attend a council meeting every day from now on. It will demonstrate to my counsellors not only that I live but that I am in my full mind and can rule effectively. During the night while I lay awake for a while I remembered how fifty years ago the news that my father, then only in his mid-sixties,

316

was very ill led me and my brothers to believe he was no longer fit to rule and the time was ripe to launch our bids for the throne. I will have no repetition of that. What's more, I will write to Muazzam and Azam reassuring them that I have recovered my health.'

Udipuri Mahal nodded, pleased not only at his reviving health and spirits but also at the news that he would attempt to stem the fervid speculation and scheming about the succession that, through her attendants and other members of the *haram*, she was sure she was even more aware of than he was. She would now have time to persuade Aurangzeb further of the merits of Kam Bakhsh as a successor. She must safeguard him as well as comfort her husband.

•◆•

The rains had come and gone, leaving Devapur and the surrounding countryside glowing many rich shades of green, yet still the imperial court was here, Udipuri Mahal thought as she looked out over the fort garden, where fountains bubbled amid the green of fruit trees and the blooming of the first roses. Each time Aurangzeb had begun to talk of resuming the long journey – over a thousand miles by the route he intended to take – towards Delhi, another bout of illness had overtaken him, frustrating his plans. However, apart from when the fever had first struck he had never failed to attend his daily council meetings, even though sometimes it cost him so much strength that he spent all the remainder of the day in his bed. Although these displays of willpower had drained him, they had served his purpose, stifling the most overt scheming about the succession. He had even executed a general who'd foolishly been heard boasting that he and his army would be the deciding factor in who would mount the throne.

At the moment he was better than for some while. His cough had eased and his appetite grown. The day before he'd again begun talking of moving on. This time she had been more encouraging than previously. If he was to make the journey, this would be the best time of year to travel, with days growing cooler and little chance of rain or stifling humidity.

One of her attendants, a tall young woman, entered, cutting into her thoughts. 'Madam, the emperor requests you go to him.'

'He's not been taken ill again, has he?'

'I think not, madam. I was told a *cossid* had arrived just before he called for you – perhaps there is some news he wishes to share with you.'

Quickly checking her appearance in the small silver mirror she always kept near at hand to ensure she looked her best for her husband, Udipuri Mahal hurried from her apartments along the curtained purdah corridor towards those of Aurangzeb. A guard parted the curtains for her to enter. Aurangzeb was sitting on a high-backed chair, a paper dangling from the fingers of his left hand, and he had tears in his eyes.

'What is it, my love?'

'My sister Gauharara is dead. A *cossid* brought news.'

'I'm sorry. May she rest in Paradise.' Udipuri went forward and placed an arm around her husband's shoulder. Aurangzeb began to sob, much to her surprise. He had not seen his youngest sister for many years and they had never appeared close – something she'd thought at least partially explained by the fact that Aurangzeb's beloved mother had died giving birth to Gauharara. 'Don't weep. God decides when we leave this life. She was a good woman – pious and active in charitable works. Her place in Paradise is secure, I'm sure of that.'

'So am I. The grief that I feel goes beyond the loss of a sister, strong though that is. She and I were the last survivors of the fourteen children born of the great love between my father and my mother. My grief is, I think, for their loss and that of their other children, some of whom died very young and the rest, well, whose fates you know . . .'

'You should rejoice that your parents had such a great and unique attachment, and you cannot alter what happened after their death.'

'At my age my memory is peopled with the dead. That is not always uncomfortable. But as I've lain awake at times during these months of illness I've often thought of things I wish I'd said or done – or left unsaid and done – within my family, and that has caused me grief. In the small hours I've sometimes wondered whether, if my mother had survived Gauharara's birth, she would have prevented the strife amongst her sons, or was it as inevitable as a brood of young male tigers fighting amongst themselves for supremacy?'

'Brother has often fought brother in your family. "Throne or coffin", didn't you tell me your ancestors used to say on the steppes?'

'But that may not make such struggles right nor justify my part in them. I have recurring nightmares in which my mother weeps as she cradles Dara Shukoh's severed head in her arms, and my father with Jahanara at his side extends his open arms to me through prison bars as he implores

319

my mercy. I wake trembling in mind and body and with a great hollowness at the very core of my being . . .'

'That may be the medicine the *hakims* have given you. I know they have sometimes used opium to make you sleep and it can produce strange dreams.'

'Perhaps. But even so a man's dreams are the product of his brain. These last months I have relived my life more than once. I have never regretted my way of ruling the empire, however harsh some, including my favourite sister Jahanara, may have called my treatment of the infidels in particular. I did what I thought was right for my empire and my faith alike. Let my god be my judge for it. I'm not sure I can say the same of my conduct towards my family . . . yes, I suspected Dara of heresy and my father's fondness of blinding him to his eldest son's failings. But did I have to act as I did? Could I not have reasoned with them? As for Murad and Shah Shuja, they were weak and foolish but they did not need to die. Wasn't I just pretending to be acting for good, moral reasons? In reality wasn't I just hypocritically cloaking my ambition and lust for power, which was pushing me on, with fine sentiments . . . wasn't I just grabbing for my father's throne?'

'Only God can truly read our minds.'

'I fear when He reads mine He will find me wanting. My life in the next world will be one of pain and punishment.'

'Your good deeds will surely outweigh any sin.'

'I can only hope so. While I live I will do all I can to win favour, praying for the repose of my family's souls at their tombs and graves. I will even visit that of Dara Shukoh on the platform of the Emperor Humayun's great tomb in Delhi. But I fear with the skeletal hand of death on my shoulder that may not be enough . . . so I've begun sewing Islamic caps for sale to show my humility. I want no more to be spent on my funeral than is raised from the sale of these caps. I want no great mausoleum built over me, just a simple tomb open to the skies as the first emperor Babur has in Kabul. Also, I've begun to make a copy of our holy book in my own hand to demonstrate further my love for God and His word. But I still can find no ease.'

By now Udipuri Mahal was weeping herself, bereft of any consolation to offer or ideas to distract her husband's troubled mind. Then a thought came to her. 'You spoke of visiting family graves and tombs. And yesterday you mentioned resuming our journey north to strengthen your empire's rule. The north is where your family are buried. Why not turn your mind to the preparations for the renewed journey? It will both serve the worldly purpose of your empire's good and be a spiritual comfort to you as you visit the places where long ago when you were a child you lived together in peace and happiness.'

Aurangzeb gave a wintry smile and his tears ceased. 'Yes. However old and sinful he is, there is always something a man can do, even more so when he is a ruler. I will not despair – despair is a sin. At my council this afternoon I will announce that we will resume our journey north within a week.'

Chapter 22

The Jade Rosary

The hot afternoon sun of late March was beating down on Ahmednagar as Aurangzeb waved aside assistance and walked slowly with the aid of two ivory-handled canes out on to the balcony of his apartments in the city's fort. As he settled himself in a padded velvet chair an attendant quickly opened a green parasol above his head to shield him from the sun. Another placed a glass of iced sherbet by his side while a third discreetly positioned his muslin-covered spittoon within easy reach. Nearly three months ago a severe recurrence of his chest illness had produced a fever which had so debilitated him that he had agreed to Udipuri Mahal's pleas that he should again halt his northern journey to recuperate. Since then, even though with rest he had recovered much of his health, he had not felt strong enough to resume his northern march. Every dusty mile of his previous journey in his palanquin had seemed as exhausting as a hundred would have done on horseback in his youth, each jolt a juddering upset to body and mind, leading to an aching head, aching burning joints and loss of sleep. Such was the effect of extreme old age.

Delhi was still nearly eight hundred miles away and he'd begun to fear he might never see his red sandstone capital again. Others too seemed to think the same. Three weeks previously a *cossid* had ridden in with a letter from his son Azam in his province of Gujarat saying that he'd heard his father was very ill and was riding on the speediest of horses with the smallest of escorts to be at his side. He should arrive this very afternoon, and indeed the reason for Aurangzeb's being on the balcony was to watch for his approach. Yesterday a message had also come from Muazzam in the Deccan saying he was contemplating attending his father's sickbed. Typical of the cautious Muazzam, he said he would be coming more slowly but with more of his men. Both sons clearly had the succession in mind.

So too did Kam Bakhsh and his mother Udipuri Mahal. Only yesterday she had ushered their son into his presence to propound a scheme she said he'd devised to suppress growing discontent in Bengal by opening further ports on the east coast to foreign merchants in return for military assistance against the rebels. The extra trade would also increase revenues, allowing the tax burden on the local people to be relaxed. When Kam Bakhsh had finished his exposition, charmingly if simply expressed, and obviously well rehearsed, his response to his father's questions had been halting. He'd often glanced across at his mother for support. One of Udipuri Mahal's greatest first attractions for Aurangzeb had been her simplicity and lack of interest in and comprehension of political affairs. He'd been able to forget his worldly worries in her beautiful arms. Even now, concerned as he knew she was about her son's prospects, she'd been unable to do much to support Kam Bakhsh as he'd floundered.

Aurangzeb had forborne to mention that he'd rejected a similar approach at the time of the embassy of the Englishman Norris, five years previously, because the merchants were already becoming haughty and disdainful of Moghul power and needed no further encouragement to increase their military forces. Kam Bakhsh and his mother were unconvincingly claiming another's long mouldering scheme as a fresh and inspired invention of their own. Kam Bakhsh showed himself to better advantage when on the battlefield and away from his mother where he'd recently won several successes, albeit small, against rebel bands.

At least Kam Bakhsh and Udipuri Mahal were attempting to impress him and not to usurp him. He was not sure he could say the same about Azam. Since the death of his wife Jani, who had restrained his impetuosity, he had returned to his old rash ways. On one occasion he and his horsemen had ridden into a rebel ambush while undertaking a hasty pursuit of some apparently fleeing Gujarati rebels. Only his personal bravery had saved Azam. And even so he had lost some good men unnecessarily. Muazzam, almost completely taciturn in his father's presence after his release from Gwalior, was harder to fathom. Just possibly he might be the most convincing contender for the throne. But of one thing Aurangzeb was certain. Muazzam would make no overt move while there was even the smallest chance of its going wrong and his father imprisoning him once more, or even executing him.

In any case, Azam would be the first he'd have to deal with, and if he was not mistaken that cloud of dust on the north-western horizon signalled his son's arrival. He must summon up his remaining reserves of strength, both mental and physical, for their meeting.

Two hours later, in one of the Ahmednagar fort's state rooms, Aurangzeb, dressed in his formal court robes and with his ancestor Timur's tiger ring on his hand, sat on a gilded throne with Umar Ali and five other senior members of his bodyguard behind him to receive his son. Azam entered to a fanfare from his father's trumpeters and strode towards the throne. He looked healthy and full of vigour, but the intervening years had taken some toll on his appearance. There were large dark bags under his eyes. His face, like the rest of his body, had grown more fleshy, while his beard was tinged with grey and sparser than he remembered.

'Welcome, my son. Come and embrace me.' With a supreme effort of will Aurangzeb pushed himself to his feet using only the armrests of the throne and not the two canes for support before enfolding his son's stout form in his arms. Releasing him after a few moments, he dropped back on to his throne.

'I am glad to see you, Father, after such a long time, and looking so much better than reports had led me to believe.'

'I intend to live a little while longer yet. I have so many plans to complete.'

'Let me help you fulfil them,' Azam said. 'I'll do anything in my power to assist.'

'Let that be something we talk about in a few days. There is, after all, no hurry. You and your officers deserve to rest and relax and reacquaint yourselves with old friends at court after your journey.'

• ◆ •

'Majesty, I've indeed been able to win the confidence of some of your son's officers, as you requested,' Umar Ali told Aurangzeb as they sat alone in the emperor's private quarters.

'And what did you find out?' Loyalty as well as martial skill and bravery were his reasons for appointing Umar Ali as his chief bodyguard so many years ago. Neither subtlety of mind nor deviousness were necessary or perhaps even desirable in a post so key to the emperor's personal safety. However, he had had nobody else he felt able to trust in his attempts to understand whether more than solicitude for his health lay behind Azam's ride to Ahmednagar.

'Well, Majesty, one officer – a man with some ties to the family of my first wife – told me that Azam has been speaking openly about the succession and the need to be well placed to make a bid for the throne should you die. What's more, before departing from Gujarat he told the senior officers he was leaving behind to be equipped and ready to ride to his support at short notice.'

'Did he indeed? Is there any more?'

'Yes. Another officer – a veteran with whom I served in one of the early Deccan campaigns – confided he'd been offered a promotion and estates by Azam if he helped him succeed to the throne at the expense of his brothers. He claimed not to be the only one approached – many others had been too.'

326

Aurangzeb sighed. 'You've done well, Umar Ali, as always.'

• ◆ •

Aurangzeb allowed ten days to pass after his son's arrival before asking him to appear before his full council. He had tried to prepare himself for the meeting by praying for strength and sleeping as much as he could to conserve his energy, but his cough and the breathlessness that accompanied it were becoming ever more persistent.

'I have called you all to this council meeting today,' he began when everyone was assembled before his throne, 'because I have an important announcement to make. I have been most grateful to my son Azam for the concern he has shown for my welfare by visiting me.'

Azam, standing in front and just to the left of his father, smiled.

'From what I have learned he has done an excellent job as Governor of Gujarat, something of which he and his loyal officials should be truly proud. So good has been their stewardship that I intend to transfer Azam to another post while leaving his trusted officials to carry on their fine work in Gujarat.'

'Another post, Father? What post?'

'The governorship of Malwa – an equally important province and one where there is much to do to improve the revenue collection and suppress corruption and banditry.'

'But Father, I would prefer to return to Gujarat . . .'

'When you first arrived you told me you would do anything in your power to help me fulfil my uncompleted plans – at least I think that was what you said – so please do so now.'

327

'If I must go to Malwa, let me take some of my closest officers with me.'

Aurangzeb turned his eyes on Azam and his son saw in them some of his father's old fire. 'While I still rule they are my officers, not yours, and it is for me, not you, to dispose of them as I think fit. I've told you they are required to maintain your good work in Gujarat. Now prepare yourself to leave for your new province in the next few days.' A burst of coughing choked off the emperor's words for a time but when he recovered he added, 'By leaving when I say you will show yourself as loyal and obedient as you've always been.'

Azam bowed and said nothing, but his expression told Aurangzeb his message had gone home. 'The council is dismissed,' he said.

Back in his room Aurangzeb almost collapsed into the arms of Udipuri Mahal, who helped him to his bed. 'Thanks be to God I've shown them the old tiger can still roar.'

• ◆ •

'Even now Azam's gone, I'm still concerned for our son – is there no more you can do to protect Kam Bakhsh?' Udipuri Mahal asked, Aurangzeb who had recovered only slowly from his show of power at the council meeting the week before.

'I've blunted the ambition of Azam and written in the strongest terms to Muazzam telling him to remain with his forces in the Deccan. What more can you want?' Aurangzeb responded in exasperated tones before adding, 'Kam Bakhsh shows weakness by using you to promote himself to me. When I am gone he will need to show himself to be much stronger.'

'He knows nothing of this, I swear. My request is not for you to give him more power but to send him to some province distant from his brothers with some of your own loyal officers to serve and protect him. My purpose is to get him away from the imperial court and all the intrigue that now swirls around it and which will only redouble in the event of your death – something which I pray is long delayed. I would not be able to bear losing you both to death. I prefer him to leave now for a place of safety.' Udipuri Mahal was sobbing.

If she was prepared to see her son sent from her to some distant province, she must truly be more concerned about his life than his ambitions. Kam Bakhsh had fewer supporters than his elder half-brothers. Perhaps in part that was due to his mother's humble status as well as to his relative youth compared to his brothers, even if he was nearly forty. He also lacked campaign experience. He himself had too often given in to Udipuri Mahal's wish to keep him with her at court.

'Very well. I'll find him a province to rule and send trusted men with him.'

What Aurangzeb did not mention was that the succession had been troubling his own mind for many months. As well as the lowering burden of doubt and guilt about his treatment of his father and his brothers that clouded his mind day and night, he had worried and fretted about how best to stop his own sons from fighting each other for the throne as he and his brothers had . . . how to avoid 'throne or coffin' again. He'd thought long and deep about appointing a single successor before the world but he had insufficient confidence in any of his sons to decide which of them should succeed. He had kept his distance from all his children, determined to have no favourites. He had imprisoned both Muazzam and Kam Bakhsh – one for political treachery and the other for moral weakness. All three had disappointed him at various times in different ways. Besides, Shah Jahan's apparent anointing of Dara Shukoh as his successor had not saved either of them from his own ambitions.

The only solution he'd been able to conceive was one which on reflection might just have swayed him in his youth. He would announce that after his death the empire would be divided between his three sons. It might just prevent bloodshed and it would have benefits in securing closer rule of the empire's constituent parts. The expansions he had achieved might put the task of ruling the whole empire beyond the ability of any of his sons; after all, it had severely taxed his own greater skills. But he feared in his heart that his sons would still fight for the greater prize of an undivided throne.

Nevertheless, once Kam Bakhsh had departed he would write to all three telling them of his decision to split the succession, and after allowing them time to digest the news announce it to his court and people.

•◆•

'It is a year since we halted here at Ahmednagar. It is time I acknowledged the truth that I am likely to die here,' Aurangzeb said to Udipuri Mahal as she wiped a dew of sweat from his brow. Even if his present bout of fever seemed to be nearing its end, it had by no means been the first since they'd been at Ahmednagar and was unlikely to be the last. Although his health had fluctuated throughout the year, as the monsoon followed the intense heat and the cool season the rains, he knew he was

330

growing progressively weaker and the time between bouts of illness shorter. His hacking cough was scarcely ever absent. He was using much of his strength sewing his Islamic caps and transcribing the Holy Book.

'You may well be right,' Udipuri replied, 'but you are comfortable here. The *cossids* bring news quickly of your empire. Why trouble yourself with thoughts of an arduous journey at all?'

'Because I feel I have unfinished family business – a great burden of guilt to assuage which now I will never do. Instead I will die with it weighing me down, condemning me.' His head began to twist from side to side and he began to sweat again. After a few minutes he continued, 'When I feel well enough I read the chronicles of the five previous emperors – all fought with their families, the last three were estranged from their sons, the last two – my father included – fought with them. In my reign, two of my sons fought against me. Our dynasty has beaten foreign enemies and pushed forward its borders but scarcely ever been at peace with itself. Why have we . . . why have I never learned from our history? I believed a lack of religious rectitude was much to blame and tried to constrain my children within the strict boundaries of our faith and to honour and obey me as their father as our creed requires, but to no avail. Near death, I can't have my sons together at my side for fear they will fight over my throne, and it would be for my throne and not for love of me that they came.'

'That would not be true of Kam Bakhsh.'

'I only hope I can believe that. But he lingers just as the other two do on the nearest border of his province, seemingly ready to spring at a moment's notice.'

'He is grateful for your decision to divide the succession, I assure you of that – he merely fears his brothers' intentions.'

'Such pretended fears have often been a cloak for ambition. But what more can I do to save my dynasty? Each day my strength grows less and the weariness of old age further fatigues my brain and body. The power of my mind sometimes fades so much I struggle to remember what happened yesterday, and the events of my youth grow ever more vivid. Despite the comfort you offer I feel alone . . . fearful and alone with my burden of guilt . . .' Aurangzeb began to toss from side to side.

'Calm yourself, my love. Your mind may have faded a little but it remains as acute as most men's. Can you not at least write to advise your sons? Help them from your experience to avoid the perils that you foresee ahead? Guide them on the burdens and duties supreme power brings along with its rewards?'

Aurangzeb sighed. 'I could . . . but what attention would they pay? What attention would I have paid in their position?'

Later, Aurangzeb read through the letters – one to each of his sons – that despite his reservations he'd written that evening, following his discussion with Udipuri Mahal. In each he had insisted that they should abide by his decision to divide the empire and that they should rule well and faithfully, ensuring that their subjects like themselves obeyed the strict tenets of their faith. He said no more to the self-contained Muazzam, but as he'd written to the other two he'd felt a desire to open his heart to them more than he'd ever done before in his life – more than he ever would if they were in his presence.

He had felt a certain release as his fears and regrets tumbled out. He'd cautioned Azam to be statesmanlike and to think before he acted, and in particular to try to see into his enemy's mind – something he remembered cautioning Azam's brother Akbar about so many years before. He'd continued:

I came alone and go as a stranger. The instant which I have passed in power has left me only with sorrow. Life which is so valuable I have squandered. Life is transient. The past is gone and there is no hope for the future. I fear for my salvation. I fear for my punishment. I believe in God's bounty and mercy but I am afraid because of what I have done.

To Kam Bakhsh he had written at greater length, pausing at times to cough and at others to recoup his strength.

Always keep your own counsel. Always choose good advisers who can supplement your own abilities where they are weak but never trust them fully. Remember that there are always traitors in the shadows. Never trust your sons nor treat them in an intimate manner, because if my father had not favoured Dara Shukoh his affairs would not have foundered. Soul of my soul, I am going alone. I grieve for your helplessness. Every sin I have committed, every wrong I have done, I carry the consequences with me. I came into the world with nothing. Now I leave it with this stupendous caravan of sin. Wherever I look I see only God. I have sinned terribly and I do not know what punishment awaits me.

Finally, I commend your mother Udipuri Mahal into

your care. She has been a great comfort to me in my last
years and deserves your most kindly treatment and love.

• ◆ •

The strong breeze whipped little spirals of dust from the dry gardens as his bearers carried Aurangzeb's palanquin back towards his apartments from the mosque. He had been so glad that late February morning to be able to attend Friday prayers. As always, he had found them both calming and uplifting. When his bearers were two or three yards from the entrance to his apartments he called out to them, 'Stop! I will walk the last few steps.'

Two *qorchis* assisted him to stand before handing him his two walking canes. Slowly but resolutely he made his way towards his apartments and went in. After halting for a moment or two to allow his failing eyesight to adjust from the bright sunlight to the dimmer light of his room, he waved away the two *qorchis* and his other attendants. 'Leave me. I intend to rest.'

When they had gone he moved forward towards the bed. As he reached it he felt a sudden tightness in his chest and began to gasp for breath. He was dying, he knew . . . He let go of his sticks and dropped to his knees by the bedside, clutching at the jade rosary always at his side. He would die on a Friday as he had wished and prayed . . . Soon he would know the verdict of his god on his life. For a little while he kept repeating his prayers through his dry lips as his long almost fleshless fingers continued to click through his prayer beads. But soon the beads fell silent . . . the sixth Moghul emperor was dead.

Epilogue

U mar Ali sat on the flat roof of a comfortable house
overlooking the *durbar* square in Delhi. A large
umbrella shielded him from the mid-September sun. His
post as chief of the imperial bodyguard had died with the
Emperor Aurangzeb two and a half years before. He had
immediately returned to Delhi, where as a long-time
widower he had moved into this house with his only
daughter and son-in-law, a *hakim*, and their single child,
a daughter, Rehana, now playing with Ravi, the five-year-
old son of his Hindu neighbour.

Soon after his return from Ahmednagar he had learned
several pieces of news in quick succession – none unexpected
and most sad. The emperor's sons had not been content
to divide the empire. Immediately after his father's death,
Prince Azam had returned to the imperial court at
Ahmednagar and had himself proclaimed emperor. Within
three months Prince Muazzam had defeated and killed
Azam in battle and in turn proclaimed himself emperor

335

as Bahadur Shah. At much the same time Udipuri Mahal had died – it was said of pure grief at the loss of Aurangzeb.

Her son Kam Bakhsh had, however, proved a stronger and more resolute character than many had suspected. Showing himself a skilled commander he had battled with Muazzam and his forces in a two-year campaign. While the half-brothers fought, the empire had begun to fall apart. The Marathas and the martial Sikhs had become even greater powers while the English – 'crafty peddlers' hadn't Aurangzeb once dismissed them as? – had done all they could to profit from the empire's troubles.

Just four months ago now, near Hyderabad, Prince Muazzam – or Emperor Bahadur Shah, as he must learn to call him – had finally defeated Kam Bakhsh, who had died of his battle wounds the next day. 'Throne or coffin', the Emperor Aurangzeb had said of the way Moghul princes competed for the imperial throne. So it had proved again.

In just a few minutes, the new emperor – Aurangzeb's only surviving son – would make his way into the *durbar* square and speak to the people from a dais of which, from his rooftop, Umar Ali had a fine view. Yes, there were the leading horsemen of the emperor's parade already entering the square, green pennants fluttering from their lance tips. Behind came mounted drummers and trumpeters and then more horsemen, tightly grouped around a great imperial elephant bearing an open bejewelled howdah on its back. It looked like Thunderer, but he was surely too old? Muazzam, in fine robes and a turban topped with egret feathers, was seated in the howdah. Behind him stood the man who must be his chief bodyguard, in the place Umar Ali himself had so often occupied for Aurangzeb.

336

Soon, to the strident blare of trumpets, Bahadur Shah was dismounting from his elephant, a little stiff-jointedly. At sixty-five he was only a few years younger than Umar Ali himself. Now he was making his way to the dais. What would he say in his speech? Would the empire prosper again under his rule? What would it all mean for his granddaughter Rehana and her young playmate Ravi?

Historical Note

L ike the previous five books in the Empire of the Moghul series, this is an historical novel. This means that although the story is based on history the characters' words and motivations and the detailed action are fiction. When I put words into a character's mouth they're designed to represent what the character might have thought and said at the time. Sometimes the words are at complete variance with my own 'Utopian' views that all races and creeds should seek to live in peace side by side and respectful of each other's cultures and traditions. This is particularly important to state when dealing with such a controversial character as Aurangzeb, who still raises considerable emotions.

There are a number of sources on Aurangzeb's life. He himself had a chronicle written on his reign, like so many of his predecessors. It was called *Alamgir-nama* and written by Mohammed Kazim. However, Aurangzeb ordered him to cease it after ten years of his reign, forbidding him to write any more because he considered chronicles a form of vanity. Other contemporary chronicles include: Mufazzal Khan's *Tarikh-i-Mufazzali*, spanning from the beginning of the world to the tenth year of Aurangzeb's rule; Rai Bhara Mal's *Lubb al-Tawarikh-i-Hind*, a history of all India's rulers by a courtier of Dara Shukoh's; *Mirat-i-Alam*, thought by some to be the work of Bakhtawar Khan, a eunuch employed by Aurangzeb, but attributed by others to his friend Mohammed Baqa; *Futuhat-i-Alamgiri* by Ishwardas Nagar, a courtier of Aurangzeb's; *Muntakhab al-Lubab*, a record of Timur and his line, concluding shortly after Aurangzeb's death and written in secret by one of Aurangzeb's courtiers, Khafi Khan; *Maasir-i-Alamgiri*, written on the orders of Muazzam after he succeeded his father by a man who had been a scribe at Aurangzeb's court; and *Akham-i-Alamgiri*, an anonymous set of somewhat fanciful stories about Aurangzeb.

A number of letters written or dictated by Aurangzeb in Persian have also survived and been translated. In Aurangzeb's time there were several European travellers in the sub-continent who recorded their impressions of the Moghul Empire. They included Niccolao Manucci whose *Storia do Mogor* is a colourful, gossipy work. Manucci lived in India from 1656 until his death some time around 1717. There were also the Frenchmen François Bernier who wrote *Travels in the Moghul Empire* and Jean-Baptiste Tavernier who wrote *Travels in India*. Sir William Norris, the British envoy to the Moghul Empire at the end of the seventeenth century, left a series of unpublished journals, extracts from which appear in H. Das, *The Norris Embassy to Aurangzeb*.

Among modern historians, in addition to my own

340

researches, I have used extensively the respected Indian historian Abraham Eraly's *The Mughal Throne* as well as Bamber Gascoigne's *The Great Moghuls*, Waldemar Hansen's *The Peacock Throne*, and the *Cambridge History of India*.

As noted above, most characters have their origins in history. However, a few – Jaginder Singh of Amber, Wazim Khan, Umar Ali, Yusuf Khan, Kamran Beg, Rashid Khan and sundry governors and more minor characters – are either composites of people who existed or entirely fictional. So too are Nicholas Ballantyne and Ashok Singh of Amber, only briefly referred to in this book but important in previous volumes of the series.

Aurangzeb was an orthodox Sunni Muslim. His religious policies are, of course, particularly controversial. Some writers contend that Aurangzeb's policies towards the Hindu religion and its temples were driven mainly by political pragmatism and designed primarily to assert political sovereignty. They point out that at other times in his life he made land grants to Hindu temples. His campaigns against the Rajputs – to whom he did not apply many of his measures – seem to have been motivated by his desire to curb their temporal powers more than by religious considerations. It is certainly true (cf. Eraly, p.401) that Aurangzeb employed more Hindu officials than did the famous and tolerant Emperor Akbar. He also exhibited tolerance when reacting to questioning about why he allowed so many members of the Shia Muslim sect to hold office, saying 'What connection have worldly affairs with religion? . . . For you is your religion and for me is mine. Wise men disapprove of the removal from office of able officers.'

On the opposite side of the argument, many other

historians point to discriminatory policies carried out by Aurangzeb. On 12 April 1679 he reimposed the *jizya* – the tax on 'infidels' remitted by the Emperor Akbar. He ordered the demolition of new and recently refurbished Hindu temples, even if by no means all were destroyed. He banned Hindu festivals such as *Holi* and *Diwali* and did not allow – according to Eraly – the use by Hindus of palanquins or Arab horses without permission.

I portray Aurangzeb as sincere in his religious beliefs and tend to follow Abraham Eraly in particular in regard to 'facts' on his religious policies. What is a 'fact' is of course difficult to discern in history, particularly when it comes to evaluating controversial characters – King Richard III of England being a good example. I think it is also worth remembering that in the seventeenth century – the period in which Aurangzeb lived – in Europe the Protestant and Catholic sects of the Christian religion were fighting brutal wars against each other in which those of the other faith were massacred. In England, Oliver Cromwell, 'Protector' of England after the execution of King Charles I, banned some religious festivals, the theatre and many other entertainments like maypole dancing. His iconoclastic followers defaced Catholic statuary. Catholic services were banned and no Catholic could hold office.

Like all the Moghuls, Aurangzeb used the lunar Muslim calendar but I have followed the western Common Era one. Aurangzeb had a long reign and in some cases time scales have been adjusted and compressed, and, of course, many events omitted for narrative purposes. The dates given in this historical note are the actual ones.

Additional Notes

Chapter 1

Shivaji's date of birth is not entirely certain but generally considered to be 6 April 1627 at the fort of Shivneri in the western Ghats. There are several versions of the encounter between Shivaji and Afzal Khan, which is usually said to have happened on 20 November 1659. Another of Shivaji's most famous feats occurred when, after Aurangzeb had sent his uncle Shaista Khan, the brother of Mumtaz Mahal, to suppress him, Shivaji and a small group of his men infiltrated Shaista Khan's camp in Pune and succeeded in penetrating his *haram* and wounding him before escaping. Shivaji's attack on Surat took place in January 1664.

Chapter 2

Aurangzeb was born in November 1618. His father the Emperor Shah Jahan was born in 1592, the son of the Emperor Jahangir and the grandson of the Emperor

343

Akbar. As described in *The Serpent's Tooth* (book five of this series) when Shah Jahan became ill in September 1657, three of his sons – Murad, born in 1624, Shah Shuja, born in 1616, and Aurangzeb – rebelled to prevent their elder brother Dara Shukoh, born in 1615, their father's preferred successor, from taking the throne if Shah Jahan died. Aurangzeb in particular considered Dara Shukoh to be a heretic. The three rebellious brothers acted to some degree in concert – a letter survives from Aurangzeb to Murad outlining how they would split the empire between them. Aurangzeb and Murad defeated Dara at Samugarh, eight miles southeast of Agra, in May 1658. Aurangzeb's forces eventually captured Dara Shukoh and Aurangzeb had him executed in Delhi in August 1659. His small tomb is on the platform of the Emperor Humayun's tomb in Delhi.

Meanwhile Aurangzeb had rid himself of Murad, tricking him into entering his camp and then his tent alone, capturing and subsequently imprisoning him before having him executed. To legitimise the execution he made use of the fact that, in the early stages of his own bid for the throne, Murad had murdered his finance minister. Aurangzeb blandly invited the minister's family to seek justice which, under Muslim law, allowed them to demand either financial compensation or, if they so insisted, a life for a life. While the minister's eldest son refused to seek compensation either financial or physical, the second son, some said bribed, refused money but demanded Murad's death and on 4 December 1661 Murad was executed. Aurangzeb characteristically rewarded the elder brother for 'not enforcing his claim of blood'.

Shah Shuja had been defeated earlier in the war of succession but made several further attempts to intervene. After a series of defeats he fled into the lands of the pirate king of Arakan, east of Bengal, where he disappeared, quite probably murdered. During Shah Shuja's conflict with Aurangzeb, Aurangzeb's own eldest son Mohammed Sultan had briefly joined Shah Shuja. In punishment Aurangzeb confined him in the fortress palace of Gwalior where he died sixteen years later. During the same period Aurangzeb was also responsible for the death of Dara Shukoh's eldest son Suleiman Shukoh, who was forced to drink daily doses of *pousta* – an opium concoction – until he died. Aurangzeb also imprisoned Dara Shukoh's other son, Sipihr, in the fortress of Gwalior.

Ever since the battle of Samugarh, Shah Jahan had been besieged and then imprisoned by Aurangzeb's forces in the Agra fort. Jahanara, his eldest daughter, born in 1614, stayed with him throughout but his two other surviving daughters, Roshanara, born in 1617 and a long-time supporter of Aurangzeb, and Gauharara, deserted him. The mother of all Shah Jahan's children mentioned in this book, Mumtaz Mahal, had died giving birth to Gauharara in June 1631 in Burhanpur. Her death had a profound effect on Shah Jahan who loved her deeply and, I believe, on her children. She of course is buried in the Taj Mahal, the world's greatest monument to love.

Although he had been enthroned in a simple ceremony in July 1658, Auranzgeb's formal and spectacular coronation took place in Delhi on 15 June 1659.

During the first year of Shah Jahan's incarceration, father

and son exchanged letters, full of reproaches on Shah Jahan's side and pious self-justifications on Aurangzeb's. In one letter, however, Aurangzeb cut straight to the point, stating with the deep hurt of a neglected child, 'I was convinced that Your Majesty loved not me.' He also taunted his father with Shah Jahan's own commission of fratricide. Aurangzeb's belief that his father did not love him and his grief at the loss of his mother are, I think, key to his character.

Shah Jahan fell ill for the last time in the Agra fort in January 1666. According to some accounts, realising that he was dying, he asked to be carried to an adjoining balcony from where he could more easily see the Taj Mahal. There, wrapped in soft Kashmiri blankets and with the weeping Jahanara by his side, he died in the early hours of 22 January 1666. Attendants bathed his body in camphor water, wrapped it in pale shrouds and laid it in a sandalwood coffin. The next morning he was taken out head first, as custom demanded, through a newly reopened basement gate down to the riverbank and rowed across the Jumna accompanied by a small party of mourners.

Jahanara had planned 'a grand and honourable funeral' for her father but this was not to be. Aurangzeb had not sanctioned a state funeral. Instead, to the chanting of prayers, the body of the old emperor was quickly and quietly laid beside Mumtaz in the marble crypt of the Taj Mahal. I believe, however, that Shah Jahan had intended to build a separate magnificent tomb for himself, possibly in the Mahtab Bagh, the lovely 'Moonlight Garden', across the Jumna from the Taj.

The peacock throne was seized from Delhi in 1739 by

the Persian Emperor Nadir Shah during his occupation of the city and taken back to Persia where it disappeared, presumably broken up. The peacock throne on which later Persian Shahs sat was constructed in the nineteenth century and was not related to the Moghul peacock throne. Nadir Shah also took with him from the Moghul treasuries the famous Koh-i-Nur diamond. It was extracted from the ground in the mines of Golcunda – the only diamond mines in the world until the discovery of diamonds in South Africa in the late nineteenth century. It was given, it was said, by members of the royal family of Gwalior to the future Emperor Humayun in gratitude for his good treatment of them following the death of the Raja of Gwalior fighting on the losing side at the battle of Panipat when the first emperor, Babur, seized control of north-western India, establishing the Moghul Empire. As described in *Brothers at War* (volume two of this series), Humayun later gave the diamond to the Shah of Persia to encourage him to provide Persian support for his bid to recapture his throne. Eventually the gem came back to Hindustan and became part of Shah Jahan's jewel collection where the French jeweller Tavernier admired it. It was Nadir Shah who gave the gem the name Koh-i-Nur, 'Mountain of Light'. After Nadir Shah's assassination the diamond was taken to Afghanistan by a Persian general who set himself up as a ruler there. One of his descendants Shah Soojah, when he was a fugitive, gave it to Ranjit Singh, the Sikh ruler of the Punjab in the early nineteenth century. Ranjit Singh wore the gem mounted in a bracelet. After the British seized the Punjab, the Governor-General of India sent it to Queen Victoria and it became part of the British Crown Jewels.

The scars still evident to Aurangzeb on Jahanara's face dated from her being badly burned on 4 April 1644 in an incident described by one of Shah Jahan's chroniclers:

. . . the border of her chaste garment brushed against a lamp left burning on the floor in the middle of the hall. As the dresses worn by the ladies of the palace are made of the most delicate fabrics and perfumed with fragrant oils, her garment caught fire and was instantly enveloped in flames. Four of her private attendants were at hand, and they immediately tried to extinguish the fire; yet as it spread itself over their garments as well, their efforts proved unavailing. As it all happened so quickly, before the alarm could be given and water procured, the back and hands and both sides of the body of that mine of excellence were dreadfully burned.

Chapter 3

Timur, (1336–1405), whose ring Aurangzeb is portrayed as wearing, is better known in the west as Tamburlaine, a corruption of 'Timur the Lame'. Christopher Marlowe's play portrays him as 'the scourge of God'. He was a great warrior who conquered much of west and central Asia and sacked Delhi in 1398, taking many of its jewels and craftsmen to beautify his capital city of Samarkand. He was indeed one of the first Moghul Emperor Babur's ancestors. So too was Genghis Khan.

Shivaji arrived in Agra in May 1666. He made his escape at the end of August that year, smuggled out in a basket.

Aurangzeb was so concerned that his courtiers should follow his precepts of simplicity in dress that when one appeared before him in a garment which in the emperor's view was too long and ornate Aurangzeb ordered part of it to be cut off in his presence.

Aurangzeb also discontinued the practice followed by previous Moghul emperors and described in earlier volumes of this series of making a daily morning appearance before his people from the *jharoka* balcony. Such appearances seemed to him to be too close to emperor-worship.

Despite strictures in his religion against the portrayal of human and animal forms, Aurangzeb did allow painting to continue and there are one or two exquisite miniatures believed to be of the emperor himself.

The grip his scheming empress, Nur Jahan, held on Jahangir and how she fed his opium and alcohol habits are described in volume four of this series, *The Tainted Throne*. So too is the story of how Aurangzeb and Dara Shukoh were held hostage for their father Shah Jahan's future good behaviour.

Chapter 4

The wedding of Azam and Jani took place in January 1669. Muazzam was born in October 1643, Azam in June 1653 and Akbar in September 1657.

Aurangzeb is said to have had several wives at different times. The only three who feature in this story in any way are Dilras Banu, Nawab Bai and Udipuri Mahal. Dilras Banu was a Persian princess of the Saffavid dynasty. She was the mother of Princesses Zebunissa and Zubdatunnissa who are characters in this book

349

as well as of Princes Azam and Akbar. She died in October 1657 at the age of thirty-five, a month after giving birth to Akbar, possibly from complications of the birth. Nawab Bai, a Kashmiri princess, was the mother of Mohammed Sultan, imprisoned by his father, and Prince Muazzam. She did not die until the 1690s.

Several versions of Udipuri's origins exist. I have followed the one which suggests she was born in the Caucasus mountains in the ancient kingdom of Georgia which, among its distinctions, claims to have invented wine – the first known production there dating back to around 6000 BCE. Other accounts of Udipuri Mahal's background suggest that she came from Jodhpur or Kashmir. After Dilras Banu's death she was said to have become Aurangzeb's favourite consort.

One of the main buildings Aurangzeb had constructed was the Bibi Ka Maqbara, a mausoleum complex for Dilras Banu, in Aurangabad. It bears some resemblance to the Taj Mahal and Aurangzeb must have had his beloved mother Mumtaz's tomb in mind when approving the architect's plans which were drawn up by Ataullah, the son of Ustad Ahmad Lahori who is usually credited as the principal designer of the Taj Mahal.

Perhaps the most beautiful building Aurangzeb commissioned is the Pearl Mosque – the Moti Masjid – in the Red Fort in Delhi, built around 1660 for Aurangzeb's personal use. Much easier to visit when I was first in India than it is today, it is a true gem.

Aurangzeb's religious measures are described in Eraly's *The Mughal Throne*. Jahanara did protest against them.

Gokla's rising took place in 1669 and he indeed met a

grisly end. The direct participation of Aurangzeb in the battle is fictionalised.

Roshanara's drinking and amorous exploits are described by both Manucci and Bernier who suggest that she was on one occasion caught with lovers who were executed.

Kam Bakhsh was born to Udipuri Mahal in March 1667.

Chapter 5

Roshanara died in September 1671. There is no evidence to support the allegation made by some that Aurangzeb had her poisoned.

The Satnami revolt took place in 1672. The description of the Satnamis' customs and of their sorceress come from historical sources. Ishwardas Nagar wrote more explicitly about them, saying among other things that they were 'extremely filthy, unclean and dirty. They do not distinguish between Hindus and Muslims. They eat dirty pigs and other prohibited foods. If a dog eats from the same dish with them, they feel no distaste or aversion. They do not regard debauchery and adultery as sin.' Aurangzeb did have charms and spells of his own created and sewn on to banners to hearten his men. His direct participation in the battle, including his shooting of the sorceress, is fictionalised.

The marriage of Sipihr Shukoh and Zubdatunnissa took place in 1673.

Chapter 6

Jaswant Singh of Marwar had changed sides more than once during the civil war between Aurangzeb and his brothers, hence Aurangzeb's distrust of him. He died at his headquarters near the Khyber Pass in December

1678. Aurangzeb's actions against Marwar to curb Rajput power, including the saga of the succession, were more extended and complicated than laid out here but the essentials are accurate.

There was an earthquake in Delhi soon after Aurangzeb's reimposition of the *jizya* on 12 April 1679.

Chapter 7
Shivaji's magnificent coronation took place in June 1674 and the details are drawn from accounts of the time.

Chapter 10
Shivaji died at the beginning of April 1680. On his death, his son Sambhaji ordered an inventory of his possessions. It included, apart from jewels, 100,000 pieces of gold-embroidered cloth, 400,000 pieces of silk cloth, 6,800 kilograms of pepper, 2,200 kilograms of ambergris, 4,500 kilograms of gulal – the red powder used in the celebration of Holi – over 45 million kilograms of gunpowder, 31,000 horses, 3,000 camels and 500 elephants.

Chapter 11
Akbar proclaimed himself emperor in January 1681.

Chapter 12
Akbar's campaign against his father was more protracted than presented here but Aurangzeb did indeed employ fake letters to demoralise and disperse Akbar's forces as well as threatening Tahavvur Khan with the destruction of his family if he did not desert Akbar, which he did. Aurangzeb wrote in one of his letters, 'When you have

an enemy to destroy, spare nothing, rather than fail. Neither deception, subterfuges nor false oaths for anything is permissible in open war. Make use of every pretext in the world that you judge capable of bringing you success in your projects.'

Aurangzeb did imprison his daughter the poetess Zebunissa for the rest of her life for supporting her brother Akbar. Zebunissa was said to have been so passionate about collecting books and encouraging scholars that she amassed a library 'the like of which no man has seen'.

Akbar did join forces with Sambhaji in 1681. Durgadas of Marwar helped him flee south.

Although peace was re-established between Marwar and Mewar on the one hand and the Moghul Empire on the other, the relationship remained strained, never again approaching the closeness it had previously enjoyed. Many fewer Rajputs joined the Moghul forces.

Chapter 14

Jahanara died in September 1681 and is buried in a simple tomb, as she had requested, close to the grave of a Sufi saint in Delhi. The following Persian verse – said to have been written by Jahanara herself – is inscribed on the headstone:

Let green grass only conceal my grave,
Grass is the best covering of the grave of the meek.

Chapter 16

The louche behaviour of Adil Hasan and other rulers of Golcunda is described in several historical sources.

Bijapur capitulated in September 1686. Aurangzeb did pay rewards to any brave enough to throw materials, even including corpses, into Bijapur's moat.

Chapter 17

Aurangzeb did imprison Muazzam for his contact with the Golcundi court.

Golcunda fell in September 1687 after an Afghan traitor was bribed to let in a small Moghul force through a small gate. Adil Hasan's insouciance faced with capture is based on fact. With the conquest of Golcunda the Moghul Empire reached its greatest ever extent – 3.2 million square kilometres or 1.25 million square miles. The population was between 100 and 150 million.

Chapter 18/19

Sambhaji's capture with Kavi-Kulesh happened in early 1689, much as described. Their parading through the Deccan, appearance before Aurangzeb, torture and death in late March 1689 are based on historical sources, in particular Khafi Khan. Manucci adds even more gruesome details not used here.

Chapter 20

Sir William Norris did not report to his monarch by letter but the dates given in the 'letter' are accurate, as is the material about his travels, where he visited Aurangzeb, the account of the Marathas, Jats and Sikhs, the release of Muazzam in 1695 and the temporary imprisonment of Kam Bahksh. The description of Aurangzeb passing through the crowd, reading a book and looking neither right nor left, closely follows Norris's own account.

Henry Avery is indeed usually said to be the most successful pirate in history, never being captured. William Kidd was hanged in London in May 1701 at Execution Dock at Wapping and his tarred body exhibited by the side of the River Thames in an iron cage as a warning to others.

When writing his letter Norris would have thought he was addressing King William III of England. He would not have known that the king had died in March 1702, and been replaced on the throne by Queen Anne. Norris – as he had anticipated – died at sea on 10 October 1702, before he reached England.

Chapter 21

Gauharara died in 1706. Akbar died in exile in Persia in 1704. Zebunissa had died in prison in 1702.

Chapter 22

The paragraph of the letter to Azam quoted is from the translation of an actual letter from Aurangzeb to him. Similarly, the first paragraph of the letter to Kam Bakhsh is taken from a real letter from Aurangzeb to his youngest son.

Aurangzeb died on Friday, 20 February 1707, just after morning prayers. He is buried in Khuldabad in a simple grave as he wished. There is no inscription on the red sandstone slab which tops the grave. It is very different from the great tombs in which Humayun, Akbar, Jahangir and Shah Jahan are interred but similar to the first emperor Babur's on a hillside above Kabul in Afghanistan and also to his beloved sister Jahanara's in Delhi.

Epilogue

The account of the deaths of Azam, Kam Bakhsh and
Udipuri Mahal and the accession to the throne of
Muazzam as Bahadur Shah are accurate. Bahadur Shah
ruled for less than five years.

Main Characters

Aurangzeb's family:

Parents:
Mumtaz Mahal
The Emperor Shah Jahan

Brothers:
Dara Shukoh
Shah Shuja
Murad

Sisters:
Jahanara
Roshanara
Gauharara

Wives and Consorts:
Dilras Banu

Nawab Bai
Udipuri Mahal

Sons
Mohammed Sultan}(sons of Nawab Bai)
Muazzam }
Azam} (sons of Dilras Banu)
Akbar}
Kam Bakhsh (son of Udipuri Mahal)

Daughters
Zebunissa} (daughters of Dilras Banu)
Zubdatunnissa}

Nephews
Suleiman} (Dara Shukoh's sons):
Sipihr}

Niece
Jani, Dara Shukoh's daughter

Commanders, Courtiers and Members of the Imperial Household:
Jaswant Singh, Raja of Marwar and general of Moghul forces
Abu Hakim, head of the *ulama*
Wazim Khan, Aurangzeb's spymaster
Umar Ali, commander of Aurangzeb's bodyguard
Kamran Beg, Aurangzeb's chief scout

Aurangzeb's Chief Adversaries:
Shivaji, leader of the Marathas

Sambhaji, Shivaji's son
Kavi-Kulesh, one of Sambhaji's generals
Gokla, leader of the Jats
Adil Hasan, ruler of Golcunda
Sikander, ruler of Bijapur

Other characters:
Raja of Amber
Jaginder Singh, son of the Raja of Amber
Rana of Mewar
Tahavvur Khan, Akbar's friend and confidant
Durgadas, regent of Marwar
Santaji, a young Maratha
Sir William Norris, ambassador from England to the Moghul court
Tegh Bahadur, leader of the Sikhs

Acknowledgements

I would like to express my great gratitude to Charlotte Mendelson, Sherise Hobbs, Emily Kitchin and Amy Perkins at Headline UK and Thomas Abraham, Riti Jagoorie, Anurima Roy, Sohini Bhattacharya and Shabhita Narayan of Hachette India for their help and encouragement throughout the writing of the Moghul series and of course to my agents Bill Hamilton of A. M. Heath in London and Michael Carlisle of Inkwell Management in New York as well as to the staff of Thomas Dunne books for all their work on the American edition.

I would also like to thank the staff of the Archaeological Survey of India for their help and advice and showing me places like the fortress of Burhanpur where so many of the events described happened and the staff of the Bodleian Library in Oxford and the British Library and London Library in London for their assistance.

I am grateful too to Meera and Tanya Dalton of Greaves Travel in London and Mala Tandan of Greaves Travel in India and their staff for all the help they have given in arranging our many recent visits to India.